FIRST ERUPTION

CONQUERORS OF K'TARA

BOOK 2

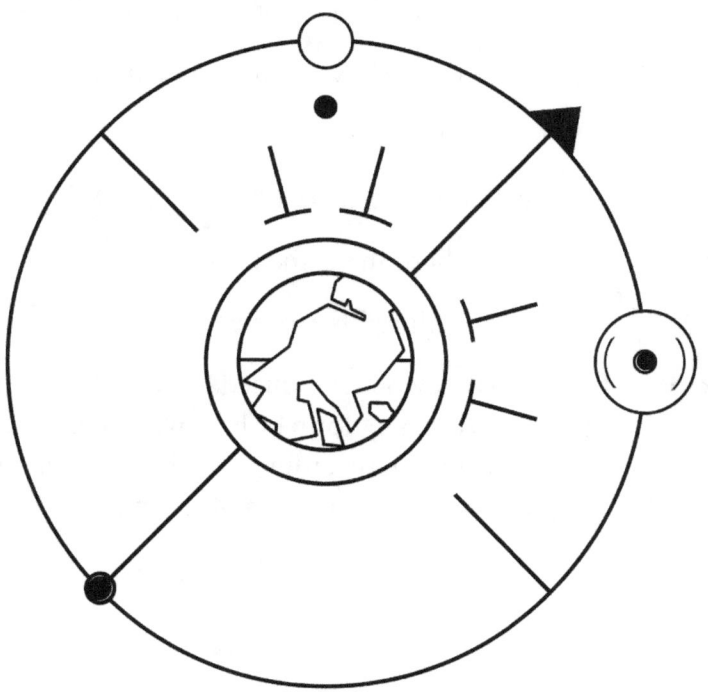

L.A. DI PAOLO

To those who believe.

ACKNOWLEDGEMENTS

My acknowledgments will not be as long for *First Eruption* as they were for *Forebodings*.

To begin, I wish to thank Michele (Mikehleh) Parisi, my illustrator, for working with me to create another series of illustrations as beautiful and striking as the ones he created for *Forebodings*, and doing it with good humor and graciousness despite my repeated requests for changes.

I also wish to convey my deepest gratitude to my good friend and writer, Jim Crichton, from the Philadelphia Science Fiction Society. Indeed, Jim's advice and critique were simply invaluable—they helped me make substantial improvements to the story, as well as to a number of critical scenes. Most importantly, his comments helped me understand the importance of emotion, and I think the story is much better for it. Along with Jim, I must also, again, thank Samantha George, who agreed to proofread the completed manuscript, doing as excellent a job as she had done for *Forebodings*.

Finally, I wish to thank all those—among my friends and family—who encouraged me when I questioned the sanity of this project and was ready to abandon it, as well as those who helped me understand that creation should not be constrained by deadlines—self-imposed or not.

L.A. Di Paolo

Table of Contents

I GNARLERS AND BOLINGAR WINDS

From Hunters, the Hunted

With a hissing voice meant to overcome the blowing winds, Toras said, "Sheffar! These things can walk through the storm, and if we stay here, they'll find us just as they found poor Elmanon back there. We need to move!"

The secundus looked down, unsure. He shook his head. Yes, the vile things had already gotten one of them, sticking the poor Elmanon through and through.

But the man had dared the creatures to come. And they had done just that, crossing the large, empty expanse between the tree line and the rock behind which he had taken cover.

Sheffar could not get over the fact that the creatures had gutted Elmanon right in front of their eyes, and that there had been nothing they could do. Secundus Sheffar, himself, had almost gotten blown away when he tried to cross the glade to help his comrade.

Fortunately for the rest of them, the gnarlers had been focused on poor Elmanon's body, and the squad had taken advantage of it to distance themselves, grabbing onto the low-lying branches of the Old Scraggle bush to reach their current shelter.

However, it appeared they could go no further as there was only barren ground past their current position and trying to cross without solidly rooted plants to hold on to was suicide. Indeed, the Bolingar storm was fierce today, with blustering winds so violent they picked up everything that wasn't firmly anchored by either deep roots or the force of their own weight.

And yet, the commander was right; they had to move on. If they didn't, the gnarlers would get them for sure. The question remained: how *could* they cross? He said as much to Toras when he finally responded.

Laiella, her back on the hard rock of the ledge under which they had found cover, looked at Sheffar with scorn. Her red

1

eyebrows made her grimace even more contemptuous in the dark midday hour. The woman turned to Toras and said, "I agree; we have to move. We can try for that cave over there; I saw the furans make for it earlier, just as the winds picked up. As you've noticed, the creatures seem to be terrified of the furans, so we might be safe over there while we wait for the storm to pass."

Secundus Sheffar said, "And how do you propose to get there without being immediately blown away or having our skulls crushed or bodies struck by a flying stone or branch?"

Laiella replied with a sneer, "My people do this all the time in Bremin, challenging each other during the storms to reach more and more distant shelters. Are you afraid to do what we *strange* people do as a game?"

With angry indignation, the officer said, *"Afraid?!* I am no—"

"Secundus! We will do as the prima suggests. Now how do we do this, Laiella?"

Secundus Sheffar shot a spiteful glare at the prima, then turned away to watch for the gnarlers.

Laiella wasted no time and started giving her instructions to the company, speaking loudly to be sure everyone heard. "Remove any straps or belts from your backs and carry them in your hands if you can; leave them behind if you can't. Keep your entire bodies flat against the ground. And given that none of you are experts, we will have to stay within each other's reach, in case the winds start dragging one of you away and I need to rescue you."

Toras frowned at that, but let it be.

First Barrier Laiella, now *Prima* First Barrier Laiella, dropped down on the ground and got going without further delay, inching out from under the ledge, looking to her left and right. When she was confident there were no gnarlers, she motioned Toras and the others to follow.

Toras was still surprised by how fearless the woman was. Of course, he knew of her reputation in Urbs Lucis. Still, it was

2

something else to see the woman in action, facing situations that scared even his men with calm, cold eyes. Just as the rest of them got going, though, the winds managed to get underneath Laiella and started lifting her. Toras swallowed and called her name, but Laiella simply stopped and forced herself flat on the soil again; her face cool, as it always was. On the other hand, the men's faces had taken on a ghostly aspect—Toras's included. The prince breathed out a sigh of relief when his first officer continued to move with the same confidence.

Laiella motioned the men forward again. Toras, Sheffar, Falor, Yaris, and Hanne began the awkward crawl, doing their best to keep flat.

It was not long before one of the soldiers found himself being dragged away by the winds and yelled for help. It was Yaris, a small-statured middle-aged fellow. But despite his small size, neither the strong Falor nor the fearfully muscular Hanne had been able to grab and hold onto him when they tried to. After making certain the others were safely anchored, Laiella let herself be blown slightly backward toward Yaris, who was hanging on a small rock by the mere force of his tetanic fingers.

When Laiella reached the man, she grabbed onto him, pushed him down, and ordered him to stay flat. The soldier thanked her with inaudible words and followed her back toward the others.

Once more, the company resumed its crawl toward the cave, which was still some ten meters away. Not a moment later, Hanne slipped backward. When Falor tried to grab him by the shoulder he was hit by a broken branch, leaving a huge gash in his arm. The pain caused him to lose his grip on his comrade, and the wind continued to pull Hanne toward the ledge they had come from—where three sneering gnarlers now waited.

An irrational fear took hold of the men who looked at the creatures wide-eyed, except for Toras. The prince let himself be dragged back toward Hanne. When he reached the man, he pushed him down—as Laiella had done with Yaris—and ordered him forward. He then continued toward Falor who was panicking despite his experience and musculature; perhaps, it was because of his injury. Remembering their first encounter with the creatures, three months earlier, when Felor had been killed by one of the creatures, Toras thought to himself: *I am* not *going to lose Falor too.*

Laiella watched all this with a mesmerized look on her green face, while also keeping an eye on Yaris and Sheffar. She watched the gnarlers who were starting to walk toward them. Her mind raced for a solution. *I have* to do *something to help us reach the caves faster. But what?*

Toras had now joined Falor and had dislodged a branch from the man's pants, reducing the winds' purchase. But the prince was having difficulty pulling the weakened Falor behind him. Luckily, Hanne had come back to help him. Still, if they did not all speed up their movements, the gnarlers would be upon them before they ever reached the cave.

Just then, a solution surfaced in Laiella's throbbing mind, and a fraction of a moment later, a crushing weight flattened the men on the ground.

They looked at her, wondering what was happening. They could not hear her words with the blowing winds, but they saw her get on her knees and then on her feet with slow, heavy movements. Toras realized she must be using the Bind because the debris was being diverted away from them all and there was that strange hiss that accompanied some of the Lux Baiulae's Bindings. She motioned with her arms, but they moved bizarrely. No one seemed to understand, until a voice resounded in Toras's mind, urging them to stand and walk.

Though confused and uncertain, the prince sent a quick prayer to the Founders, and pushed himself up. He felt heavy, but he could stand against the winds. He tried to pull Falor up, but the man seemed to weigh a ton, and he yelled at him to stand. Hanne, who had also stood himself up, moved to Falor's other side, and together, the three men went forward. It was a good thing, too, because the gnarlers were only a few meters behind.

Despite the barrage of debris that continued to hit them, and though breathless and bruised and bleeding they were, the guardians forced their legs to run against the unnatural weight until they finally reached the cave.

The furans, huddled in the back of the cave, got up and released excited screeches.

Scorch ran to Toras. No sooner was he by his master than he began to shriek and bob his head back and forth; the gnarlers were approaching.

Toras said, "I know, Scorch, I know. Prima, Secundus, we need a plan, immediately. And everyone, grab your saddles, now!"

While he undid the saddle from his furan's back, Toras became aware of a disturbance by the cave's entrance. He looked and saw Cray, Elmanon's furan. The steed was pacing anxiously.

Yaris, who stood behind Toras, said, "We need to do something about him."

Toras exhaled loudly; this was not the time to deal with a separated furan. He ran over to the animal, determined to send him toward the back at once. But upon reaching Cray, the furan shoved him against the rock. Toras felt himself become angry.

"Cray, we don't have the time for this."

As a matter of fact, the gnarlers were now but a minute away. They grinned at him with ugly, excited snarls.

Toras took a deep breath, calmed himself and carefully put his left hand on Cray's head and his right on the beak.

The furan tried to resist the calming effect, but after a moment that seemed too long, he started to relax. Toras said, "Good, Cray. Elmanon is not here. We will look for Elmanon later. You need to go to the back now," accompanying his words with hand signals.

When a quill bounced off the wall just behind Toras, he lost his patience. He urged the furan to go to the back of the cave. However, Cray did not move and started to become agitated again. Knowing he could not lead the furan against his will,

5

Toras repeated the calming procedure. The furan relaxed more fully this time, and he followed Toras toward the others.

Toras sighed when the steed sat down. He pivoted on his heels, ready to fight, when he heard Sheffar yell, "Commander! They're almost here. We need to get ready. But how are we going to defend ourselves? The cave is just too shallow."

Toras turned toward his prima with a hopeful look on his face.

"I am sorry, Toras, but there is nothing I can do. Bound shields don't help against their quills, and if I generated any Bound weapons, we'd rapidly run out of oxygen, in here."

Sighing with exasperation, the prince said, "All right, in that case, three of us will line up across this side of the column and the other three on the other side. We'll use the saddles to block their quills as best we can. Then, we wait for them to run out of the substance they use to generate the quills." With that, Toras sent the furans to the back, and everyone lined-up with groans and snorts.

The gnarlers appeared at the cave's entrance with thrilled snarls. Their growls quickly changed to shrieks, and they recoiled; they had spied the furans in the back.

But the creatures seemed to have understood that the hated quadrupeds were not going to be thrown at them, and the first organic projectile whizzed past Toras a moment later. His heart skipped a beat, and he turned a worried look toward the back. Cray was staying put with the rest of them, out of the way.

Human groans filled the cavity when an uncountable number of quills planted themselves in the saddles, launched at them by the half dozen creatures in the first row. At the same time, those in the back yelled and danced impatiently to take their turns.

As a seemingly unending barrage of spikes hit the saddles and sometimes crossed the gaps to continue toward the back, the prince wondered why the creatures had not simply laid a siege and waited until he and his companions had starved themselves to death. But the gnarlers were not so intelligent, it seemed. So, they kept launching their projectiles until they had no more to shoot and were forced to enter the cave.

Unfortunately for the attackers, none of their projectiles had hit the mark, though several had come close and had nicked a furan's wing or a soldier's uniform. They penetrated the cave cautiously, warily, their fixed claws at the ready, eyeing the furans who looked ready to pounce on them.

The soldiers moved back, as far as they could go to draw the gnarlers in, and the creatures continued to advance on them. When Toras saw the last of them was inside the grotto, he ordered his soldiers aside and the furans forward.

The steeds launched themselves at the creatures, and the guardians followed them. The risk was still high, particularly in close quarters, but the odds *were* better, especially given the creatures' fear of the furans.

As their attackers began to feel cornered, they became more dangerous, lashing out with their claws in all directions in the hope of repelling the furans. The gnarlers' divided attention caused their undoing and, after a few intense minutes of dodging and thrusting or dodging and biting, all twelve attackers lay on the ground, either with their skulls crushed by the furans' beaks, or with their bodies cut open by the Humans' blades.

Though they could not believe their luck, the company had lived to fight another day, and they had their furans and their commander to thank for it. Now, if only the storm could pass.

Punishment or Ritual

The Black Guard company was forced to endure the foul smell of the dead creatures and the fouler stench of their bodily fluids for another half hour before the storm passed. The men had begun cursing and cussing, but they stopped short when Laiella gave them an angry flash of her stony gray eyes. They spent the rest of the time grumbling and spitting, which the prima had strangely not seemed to mind.

Lord Commander Toras and his company had come to this glen, mid-way between Horn's Pass and the Mountain Lake outpost, earlier that morning, a few hours before the Bolingars. They had traveled here following the receipt of several reports of large numbers of gnarlers attacking nearby villages. The reports had been surprisingly accurate—surprisingly because when unnatural things were concerned, witness accounts often exaggerated the facts—and when the company arrived, they *did* find a large number of the creatures feasting on the remains of some poor bleater-herders.

That had rightly revolted and angered the Black Guard, who made short shrift of the group with the help of their furans. In fact, the soldiers and their steeds had become quite skilled at killing gnarlers in the past three months. That done, the company had taken to the skies to return to Horn's Pass before the Bolingars hit.

However, while flying over a forest within which was nestled a small village, a new wave of the creatures sprung out and moved toward the hamlet. The company was forced to descend and fight on. Luckily for the defenders, when the twin suns approached their apogee, the gnarlers retreated into the woods to continue the fighting there.

The parties exhausted each other in the hot and humid vegetal battleground, until the Bolingars passed and the storm came roaring. At that point, from hunters, the company became the hunted, for neither the Humans nor the furans could withstand the belwohr-toppling winds, or the debris which tore flesh and broke bones. The creatures, however, as incredible and damning as it was, had no trouble at all. The situation had led to Elmanon's death and to the company's desperate escape.

But the fight was over now; the creatures' reinforcements had ceased; and the storm was passing. Toras stood there, by the cave's entrance, stealing glances at his 'Prima First Barrier Laiella Lux Baiula of the Red Sash.' The woman hated it when Toras annoyed her with the long title, which he had simply made up, not knowing how else to address her. Indeed, there had never been a Lux Baiula in the Black Guard—or the Royal Guard—before.

Toras was surprised to find that he liked the woman, despite the fact that she had been forced upon him by his father, High King Octavius I, after multiple costly mistakes earlier that year. Laiella was under orders to remove the prince from command before he made another life-costing mistake.

Toras had resented the woman at first—resented her for merely being there as well as for his loss of Primus Kendor, though she really was not at fault for either thing. He had ridiculed her tactical suggestions even when they were not unsound and had ignored her whenever he got a chance. But Laiella had remained unruffled through it all and had never done anything to embarrass him in front of his men. And though there were still days where he wished her gone, he realized now, spying her from the corner of his eye, that he admired her, respected her—even liked her.

Just now, he heard Falor's voice. Between pained grunts, the man asked the prima a question.

Laiella scrunched her eyebrows, "I used a sonactic Binding to weigh you down and another to keep the debris away. It was a cheat, really, but it was the only way to be sure we all reached the cave before the creatures got us; you're just Alvinorians after all, and men on top of it."

Falor replied with the greatest indignation, "What?! *Just* Alvinorians? And *men* on top of it? I'm sure a man must be better at staying flat on the ground than someone with—Well, you know what I mean."

Falor's comrades started laughing but stopped when the prima made a threatening frown. "No, I do not know what you mean, guardian. In fact, *our* men find their *apparatus* more annoying than we do our breasts. Obviously, you would not have that problem—being Alvinorians."

Falor, as large and imposing a man as he was, turned as red as a leaf and was huffing for a reply when Toras said, "All right! You brought this on yourself, Falor."

9

As he looked toward his commander with a miffed expression and a few aborted sentences, the guardian became aware of something far more compelling than his pride. Covering his eyes against the bright light surrounding Toras's silhouette, he said with some excitement, "Lord Commander, the storm has passed."

The prince turned his head to look outside. His tone was grateful and urgent at the same time, "It has. And I think I just saw something crawl back out of its burrow by the tree line. Grab your things, and let's get out of here. As soon as we've had something to eat, I want to try and figure out what grotto the gnarlers are coming from."

Yaris asked, "Lord Commander, you think they're coming from some underground tunnel?"

Toras nodded. "I was thinking about it while the rest of you were…exchanging barbs."

Laiella looked at the prince with a curious expression.

He continued, confidently, "I remember there are several cave entrances along the foot of the Furan Peaks; they must be coming from one or more of those. I—"

Falor exclaimed, "Lord Commander, that's it! That's where they come from! Do you know that these caves are part of an extended network that spans tens of kilometers? It would explain how they can appear one place one day, and as if by enchantment, reappear in an impossibly distant place the next."

Toras snorted loudly, pulling his head back, half surprised and half pleased with where his thinking had taken them. "That's it, Falor. That *must* be it. We have our mission then."

Just then, Yaris said, "I don't like that, Commander; I don't like caves, and I don't like that the creatures could crop up around us like poison funguys without warning."

Hanne looked annoyed at the man's mispronunciation of the plant name and said, "'Fun*ghee*' Yaris, not 'fun…*guys*.' Plus, poison fungi don't crop up inside caves, and they don't crop up without warning; they always come a fourth into the Rains."

"Yeah, but when do the Rains come, hey? Can you predict that?"

Laiella and the prince looked at each other with bewildered faces. Maybe this was the men's way of dealing with the last few months' stress, but they still had work to do—*soldiering* work to do. So, Toras clapped his hands to bring their attention back to their mission.

Refocus them it did, but the sound also made everyone wince. Maybe it was the cave, the men thought. Laiella must have had some other explanation in mind because she watched Toras with wondering, slit eyes.

Her gaze made Toras somewhat uncomfortable, but he had more pressing things on his mind. He picked up his saddle and walked out, asking Scorch—but ordering the guardians—to follow. Speaking over his shoulder, he added, "Someone take care of Cray, so he doesn't fly off in search of you know who."

Outside the cave, Pickers of all sorts had crawled out of the ground to collect the torn leaves, broken branches, uprooted plants too weak to resist the furious winds, and the few dead flyers caught out in the open during the storm.

Seeing the dead flyers made Toras stop and look at Scorch with what looked like disappointment for a moment. But, although furans were much larger than flyers and were not frequent casualties of the storms, they could still be severely injured as had occurred a couple years back when a foolish soldier thought to go out and train his furan as the storm waned. The winds pulled his furan's wings back like an umbrella until they dislocated, and man and beast came tumbling down to crash on the ground.

"I don't blame you for abandoning us earlier, Scorch. I just wish—aghrr! What could I wish? Your wings may be your weakness, but they're also what made the Alvinorian Guard the most feared army in all Terrae Regis. It's just that the gnarlers are more afraid of you than the gnarlers are afraid of us, and we might not have lost Elmanon if you had been with us."

11

Scorch replied with a resentful look and short complaining screeches before going off to explore the myriad sounds in the woods. Pickers scuttled away when they caught sight of the interloper, but not without dragging their catch into their earthen or wooden abodes, all the while hissing, barking, or growling to keep the furan away.

Toras was on the brink of calling his steed back to excuse himself when a female voice saved him the humiliation. "Lord Commander, how do you propose we search for the source of the gnarlers?"

Toras scratched his head a moment then exclaimed, "I have an old geological map of the region."

Laiella uttered a surprised grunt and said, "Why would you have a geological map?"

The prince raised his shoulders, hoping to avoid answering. But the green-skinned woman did not desist, and he said, "I use it when I take trips with Scorch."

The woman raised mocking brows, and Toras straightened his back and said, "With *this* map, we should be able to find and inspect all the entrances within a fifty-kilometer radius before nightfall."

The prima made no comment this time, and Toras turned away from her to search for his mount. He looked in the direction Scorch had gone and not seeing him, he yelled, "Scorch! Where are you? I need my saddle."

It took Scorch a good twenty to thirty seconds before appearing at the edge of the clearing. However, once there, he stopped for the briefest moment to stare at Toras with his dark, piercing eyes. Toras wondered if he had really upset his furan with his earlier comment. He looked down and to his right, away from Laiella, not wanting to show the growing frustration he felt at being challenged by his steed. He was about to order Scorch over when the furan started forward on his own, and Toras let out a long and silent breath of relief.

Seeing that his master's posture had become more docile and welcoming, Scorch sped up and stopped right in front of

Toras. He then proceeded to tap his master's chest with his beak—which to the Human felt more like a shove—in a sign of reconciliation.

The prince became a little self-conscious just then, with Laiella watching this curious display. He moved to retrieve the map from the saddle, saying quietly, "All right, all right. That's enough, Scorch."

Scorch responded with a final bump and let his master get the map, which Toras unfolded on his haunches.

The prince called Laiella over and began searching for inscriptions that might indicate a cave opening. However, there were no such markings. Annoyed, he started stretching and resetting the map repeatedly. A pinch appeared between his brows, and he called Falor over.

"Yes, Commander?"

"You seem to know something we didn't know about these caves. Would you be able to point the location of their entrances on this map?"

Falor scanned the map quickly and nodded in the affirmative.

"Show us."

While Falor pointed to one general area after another—the map was drawn to a 1:100,000 scale, so not very precise—Toras was distracted by the men's grumblings in the background, grumblings about having lost Elmanon. For sure, the old soldier had not always been a pleasant companion, but he had been a veteran of the Black Guard and losing him was still bothersome. To his men, it meant they were not invincible.

We need to trace our steps back and find his body, so we can bury him and bring back his vest.

Toras shifted his attention back to Falor and asked him to repeat a few things. Once they agreed on the search pattern, Toras told the others they would begin the hunt for the gnarlers' points of entry and exit as soon as they had recovered their companion's body.

The search did not take long, with the now master-less furan leading the way. But it was exhausting; Cray ran the entire way, and Hanne—who had volunteered to take care of him—was forced to call him back several times lest they lose him. When Cray finally found the old soldier's body, he walked to it, slowly, flapping his wings anxiously. Cray stood by the torn body for several long minutes, chirping, squawking, and screeching if anyone tried to approach.

Laiella shook her head and said to Toras, "We are going to have to start leaving our bonded furans behind and riding replacements because we can't have this every time someone dies. And more of us *are* going to die."

Toras pulled his head back as if his prima had said an absurdity. "I am *not* replacing Scorch."

The prima rolled her eyes in desperation. Toras's unwillingness to accept facts was probably the root cause of the king's decision to put her there.

After ten minutes had passed, Toras shook his head and walked to Cray carefully. Cray screeched at him at first, but Toras's soothing words caused the furan to relax and let him approach. Toras put his hands on his head and beak again. After a few calming strokes, the animal's wings dropped, and his tension dissipated. Cray followed the Lord Commander to where the other furans were waiting and was taken by Hanne, who kept him under guard.

The soldiers now busied themselves digging a shallow grave for Elmanon. Meanwhile, Toras removed the dead soldier's vest, trying hard not vomit at the sight of the ripped and empty belly, and handed it to Hanne, who put it in Cray's saddle.

While the furan tapped the saddle and purred soft complaints at it, the men dropped the body into the ground, covered it, and then let Yuuto say the prayer for their dead comrade.

It was around Four Ahs[1] when the squad finally split to begin looking for the Gnarlers' suspected means of movement across the land. Hanne and Falor went with Toras to inspect the entrances to the south of Lianor—the nearby village—while Yaris and Sheffar went with Laiella to the entrances north of the town. The team would meet in the town's tavern at Eight Ahs to brief each other.

It took Toras's team thirty minutes of repeated flight and landings to find the first cave entrance. Toras, the men, and the furans entered the tall cave cautiously, to inspect its interior for signs of gnarlers. Finding nothing, they left to search for the next entrance. Neither this nor the third showed any signs of gnarlers.

When they arrived at the last entrance they had decided to inspect—some six kilometers to the west south west of Lianor—they approached almost without care, certain they would find nothing there either. But as they got closer, the furans reacted with hissing screeches, and Scorch put himself across the way, his hair rising on his back.

Toras's body tensed at once. "What is it, Scorch? You smell the gnarlers?"

Scorch bobbed his head, and Toras raised his hand to halt the men behind. He *tssed* quietly to stop the furans who were walking ahead of the men. Furans did not have large ears to hear, but they did have highly sensitive microhairs on their beaks, which picked up sounds inaudible to Humanoids.

Toras unsheathed his sword and entered the cave with Scorch on his right.

The tunnel leading into the cavern beyond was damp and had a strong, pungent smell. Drops of water fell on the barren ground with unsettling resonance. Toras feared it would get too dark to advance very far, but a flickering twilight seemed to light what must be a large chamber up ahead, and he kept going.

---

[1] Ahs: Hour After Highsun

15

A few moments later, Hanne yelped. Pinned to the wall on the right of the cavern were two dead gnarlers. They were being held there by quills somewhat thicker than the ones the creatures shot at them. Their bellies had been emptied of their organs, and remnants of the latter lay charred in an improvised firepit still burning by a large stalagmite. The creatures' heads had been fixed to glare in the direction of the cavern's entrance.

Hanne asked, "Is this punishment or religious ritual?"

Falor said, "I think the one on the left is the one that attacked me. In fact, I'm sure of it. It had a wide head and a hook on its left arm, just like this one. I stabbed it right in the eye, and it groaned like I've never heard anything groan before; it was a little bit unsettling. I'm sure this is the one."

Hanne said, "Yeah, and I recognize the other thing. It's the one *I* killed. I was so enraged with it, I slashed its leg, and then sliced it from the shoulder down to the navel and spat on it. I think it angered one of its companions."

Toras shook his head, "This *is* probably some kind of ritual meant to warn us of what's coming. It's not good. This means we *have* to find them first."

Hanne said, "How are we going to do that? The three of us and our furans certainly can't go after the creatures in these caves; who knows what we'll find."

"I agree. We'll discuss our options with the rest when we get back to town." The Lord Commander then nodded to himself, as if he had made a decision, and left with his team to rejoin the others in the village of Lianor.

PERMANERE USQUE AD FINEM

II NEW ASSIGNMENTS

The Minder

"Do not presume to know how this makes me feel, Mitsuko. I know you are here to help, and you *have* helped in a couple of situations already. But your mere presence still unsettles my guests and worries them."

Mitsuko Lux Baiula, the Purple Sash assigned to protect the king from potential Temptatori, said, "I apologize if I—"

"Not *if*, Mitsuko."

The Lux Baiula—an immigrant from the far-away continent of Beltania—but who grew up in Dgiba at the mouth of the Jalahrani River on the western coast of Alvinoria—continued in nearly perfect Alvinorian, slurring only the letter 'r'.

"I apologize for my presumption, my King. If I understand you correctly, you wish me to be less obvious, and discuss my concerns about any particular guest in private."

"Yes. Your presence will still worry them, but at least, they will not leave here believing the Sisterhood is controlling me."

"I understand, Sire. I will...do as you request."

"Thank you, Mitsuko. Now, what happened in the throne room? Were you purposefully stoking Lady Moradina's ire? I've known her for a long time, and she has always been a respectful, self-controlled person. But the woman I saw in there seemed to be out of her mind, and she kept looking your way with half-hidden threatening glares. Were you doing something to her through the Bind?"

Unruffled and calm, Mitsuko Lux Baiula said, "I am sorry, Sire. I was not doing anything *to* her, but I *was* probing her brain's signals, as you have authorized me to do. I believe the Lady Moradina has been...affected."

Still unused to the Purple Sash's indirect ways—unusual ways for a member of the Order of the Light—Octavius groaned, "What do you mean, Lux Baiula?"

"I mean...affected by a Temptator."

"*What?* Because of her reaction to your probing?"

"Actually, yes, Sire."

The Purple Sash's reply unsettled Octavius, and it caused him to feel embarrassed. But instead of calming himself, he became even more agitated. He said with an uncharacteristically aggressive tone, "So, you believe her reaction was unusual? But you must know that Lady Moradina has two Lux Baiulae in her service. It is therefore highly likely that she was taught by them to recognize when someone is probing her. It seems to me that *that* is what happened, and that it angered her when you continued probing her even after she became aware of it."

Mitsuko Lux Baiula's brows pinched as she wondered for a very short moment whether the king too was under some external influence. But she knew better, and quickly let go of that thought as she replied to the king's accusation.

"It was something else, Sire, that angered her—two somethings, in fact." That drew a squint from the king, but she ignored it. "For one, it is almost as if an external monitoring thought had been placed in her mind to alert someone when her brain gets probed."

Mitsuko Lux Baiula waited to see the king's reaction. When he motioned for her to continue, she did.

"Secondly, well—please be aware, Sire, that this is only supposition on my part—I sensed an unexpectedly intense firing in the Lady Moradina's cingular cortex, which is an area of the brain associated with lies; as well as intense firing in the prefrontal cortex—a region associated with truth. It was as if both regions were fighting each other for control. The Lady Moradina may be aware that something is controlling her and might have wanted to expose it. That external probe, and this fight between her and our presumed Temptator—"

"*Your* presumed Temptator."

"And this fight between her and *my* presumed Temptator could have caused the mad reaction we witnessed."

Octavius paced the length of his office furiously, hands behind his back, snorting and shaking his head every so often.

20

Then he stopped, relaxed his shoulders and sighed when he heard the chants of the Voces Creatoris.

The capital's choir had been called the *Creator's Voices* because, somehow, the chants had the ability to soothe when a citizen needed calming, to excite when one needed rousing, or to stimulate when one needed inspiration. The choir sang from morning till night, all year long six days a fourth, with singers alternating throughout the day. Their voices were carried across the city by the Bindings of retired Lux Baiulae.

Now, a long and calming diminuendo finished dousing the king's ire and left only logical thought in his mind. He turned to his minder and said, "If it is as you say, then it is the first case of—how do you call it? Turning?"

Mitsuko nodded.

"The first case of turning among the patricians that we know of. But a case nevertheless, and the first of how many to come?" Octavius was about to tighten his fists, but he heard the music again and relaxed. "We should confirm your finding about Lady Moradina. But what do we do if you are right about her?"

With her lips turned down, Mitsuko said, "Unfortunately, the Sisterhood has not yet developed the means to undo the Temptatori's damage, nor have we developed a formal protocol to confirm the presence of…a beacon in a person's mind. Without this, we cannot take any action."

Octavius sensed his logic get prickled. "You said you sensed that thing yourself in Moradina's mind. So, why can't the Sisterhood use the same technique to search for these…beacons?"

"Well, I am not sure I know how I sensed it, myself. But I will let the Yellows probe me at the first opportunity."

Octavius made a grunt then knit his brows curiously and repeated the word 'beacon' to himself; it reminded him of something. His eyes shifted from left to right as his mind dug for the memory. They opened widely when he remembered.

21

Suddenly aware of Mitsuko's watchful regard, he looked up and asked, "How will you confirm if Lady Moradina has been affected?"

"I will ask my Sisters in Urbs Lucis to assist me in this. We will need to do it carefully, working through the two Lux Baiulae in her service, which means that we must first ascertain that *they* are unaffected. We can use them to try to obtain the confirmation we need. If there is something in her brain controlling or monitoring her, having Lorina and Silla Lux Baiulae examine her should prevent the probing from rousing any suspicions."

"All right, please inform Urbs Lucis of it. But remind Krystiana that she is *not* to take any action against any vassal of mine without first consulting me, especially against Moradina."

The king's minder grunted her understanding, vexed by the king's presumption about the Magna Mater. She then exited the king's offices and left him to mull over the day's troublesome events.

And Octavius's mulling was restless to say the least. Indeed, and despite the Voces Creatoris, who now sang a chant about trust and growth, Octavius started pacing again, stopping every so often, and then pacing again. As he remembered the word 'beacon,' his steps slowed. He had heard it from Aithen. It was something the Locari had implanted in him to help them relearn the Alvinorian language. He wondered if the word Mitsuko had used was related to the Locari's Binding or if her use of it was just a coincidence.

His feet started wearing down the hardwood floor again as he considered the other thing which troubled him now: the fact that Moradina was the Lady of the City of Antar, outside of which he had his retreat, and where he would soon be holding a ball. He shivered when he wondered whether the woman's Lux Baiulae could also be under the influence of the Temptatori. Urbs Lucis had—as far as he knew—not captured any of them yet, and it appeared that their Transferred Memories had not provided any clue as to how to identify Noctiferus's servants. *Not good, frightening, in fact.*

A Tavern in Lianor

Prima Laiella was speaking in a hushed voice to ward against indiscrete ears. She did have a Sound Shield up but, given that she was not skilled in this particular Binding, their voices—especially if loud—could still get through. The gnarler hunting party had reunited in Lianor, and they were now discussing their discoveries and next steps over a tallbrew and a small meal in the village's tavern.

"I still would not recommend entering the caves ourselves, even with torches or portable Living Lamps. I would not be able to safely use the Bind in there, and none of us has cave combat experience."

Sheffar looked at the prima with a nod, but others wondered if the fierce Barrier had lost her earlier courage.

Laiella noticed and added, "I am not afraid to die, but I *am* afraid to lead a senseless suicide mission. At best, we would kill a few gnarlers before they get us; at worst, we kill none of them, and they slaughter us all."

Toras said, "All right, Prima, then what do you propose?"

"I recommend calling on Marena Lux Baiula. She is a Yellow Sash with training in Beast Reading. We can send Trackers in the caves, and she will be able to see what they see. If they find the gnarlers, we will know it too, as well as know the creatures' location and how to get there. And if Marena can manage to record all the animals' sensory input, as she apparently can do, we will also have a map of the tunnels explored by them. Once we know that, we *will* have an advantage—a chance to succeed—and I will be more than happy to lead an attack on the foul things with other Red Sashes to lead each team."

Falor and Yaris exclaimed together, "She can do that? Not just read their minds but see what they see?"

"Perceive what they see, hear, smell, touch, feel. Yes."

Yaris blurted a 'Huh,' then asked, "But why did you say, 'with other Red Sashes to lead each team'?"

Laiella sighed. "Because there needs to be someone with each team that can be connected with Marena, who will be connected with the animals."

Yaris frowned at that, as did the other soldiers.

But Toras saw the sense in Laiella's proposal. "We can work out the details when they get here. Laiella, please call Marena Lux Baiula and ask her to join us here illico presto[2]. I assume you can call her through the Bind?"

Laiella said, "I can. But I would also recommend we wait for her at the Mountain Lake outpost, Lord Commander. These villagers—stoked as they are by the clerics of the Church of Aiala who seem to have installed themselves in the region permanently—do not appear too happy to see me here. They will be even less so if they see Marena arrive with a guard of Red Sashes."

Toras was surprised by her comment, then hissed with anger, forcing Laiella to try and strengthen the Sound Shield. Already, the heads of a few patrons had turned their way. She motioned for the prince to soften his voice, but that only angered him more.

"I am their prince, and you, my officer! And your Sisters would be here at my request. The villagers don't have a *right* to object—to any of it."

"That may be so, Lord Commander, but unless someone changes the clerics' minds, these villagers will continue to distrust us Lux Baiulae. And *we*—all of us here, I mean—are soldiers; we are not equipped to deal with the clerics."

"I know! I know. But these are my father's lands, and they benefit from them only because of his goodwill. The outpost is too small for our force to assemble there, so it will be here. I will speak with the village leader and the clerics personally, to be certain they don't interfere with what we're here to do, which is to protect *them*!"

---

[2] Illico presto: at once.

Toras stood and surprised Laiella, but not his soldiers, by suddenly changing the topic. "Here's what we'll do then: we will continue monitoring the area for gnarler activity while we wait for Marena Lux Baiula and defend against them if we see any. But! We *need* to be better prepared in case the fighting lasts through the Bolingars again. That means that we need to identify safe zones to retreat to before we engage with any groups of them."

Toras walked to his saddle, resting on a saddle arm near the tavern's entrance, and pulled out his map. When he got back to the others, he gave them the plan and instructed them to identify all the safe places.

The men nodded, and Toras added, "Once Marena Lux Baiula gets here and we know where the creatures dwell, we will assault them with a force to exterminate them. That means more men." Turning to Laiella, he said, "Prima, after you've contacted your Sister, I want you to get in touch with Horn's Pass and have them send reinforcements."

Laiella acknowledged the prince's instructions with an unreadable expression.

The Manu Dextra

Sitting in her office at Urbs Lucis, the Magna Mater's Manu Dextra[3] looked troubled as she watched the suns through the patio doors. Cross-legged, chin in hand, and her elbow on the lacquered table, she was thinking about…too many things.

The past three months had challenged everyone in Urbs Lucis as they prepared for Zebula's planned invasion and engaged the Serpent across the kingdom, all while attempting to grow their ranks and cross-train Sisters in the generation of Nebulae. And given the uncertainty everyone felt despite—and sometimes because of—their old memories, as well as because of the fact that—as Manu Dextra—Elyana's role was to advise,

---

[3] Manu Dextra: Right Hand.

she was constantly being sought for guidance on solving this or that problem.

Unfortunately for her, her responsibilities did not end there. They included the more 'minor' issues such as figuring out what to do with three of the five girls who had returned from Furan City's Purification Fields with seemingly no better understanding of the principles guiding the Sisterhood. Moradien, in particular, kept defying her instructors and had given Elyana a difficult time earlier that day. On the other hand, Lisandeka and Morla appeared fearful of Moradien and did as she commanded. Only Carrain and Lopenia had apparently learned their lesson during the three months they spent purifying the capital city's outflows, and they now stayed away from the others.

Elyana picked up the pointed hollow sitting on the table, dipped it, and started scribbling in her notebook. She let her hand move about freely, up and down and left and right, and then drew some curves, this way and that, not really paying attention. A few minutes later, she pulled her head back with a quiet snort; she had drawn a face.

Why did I draw this? The other part of herself answered: *Maybe it's because you miss him, his company, his quiet ways—his brooding nature even—his smile, and your conversations with him.* To which the first part of herself said: *Perhaps I should visit the capital. It has been a while.*

Elyana sighed loudly, then stood, walked toward her balcony, and leaned against the door frame. Her eyes were drawn toward the Red Sun. It was now beginning to set, just behind its Blue counterpart which was already half hidden at the sky's edge. The nights had started getting colder, as winter approached, but the days were still warm, and the temperature, at this hour, was still pleasant.

There is nothing I can do about my official responsibilities for the foreseeable future, but I can definitely do away with the headaches the girls are causing me. All I need to do is get through to Moradien. There is something about her that does not

26

make sense; she is the daughter of a respected landholder, and although she has always questioned things, she was never defiant. What happened *to cause her to become so rebellious, so uncaring about her future in the Order—or in society?*

Aloud, she exclaimed, "Could it be that we erred when we tested her?"

In answer to her question, she snorted, raised her shoulders, and bobbed her head.

"Founders!"

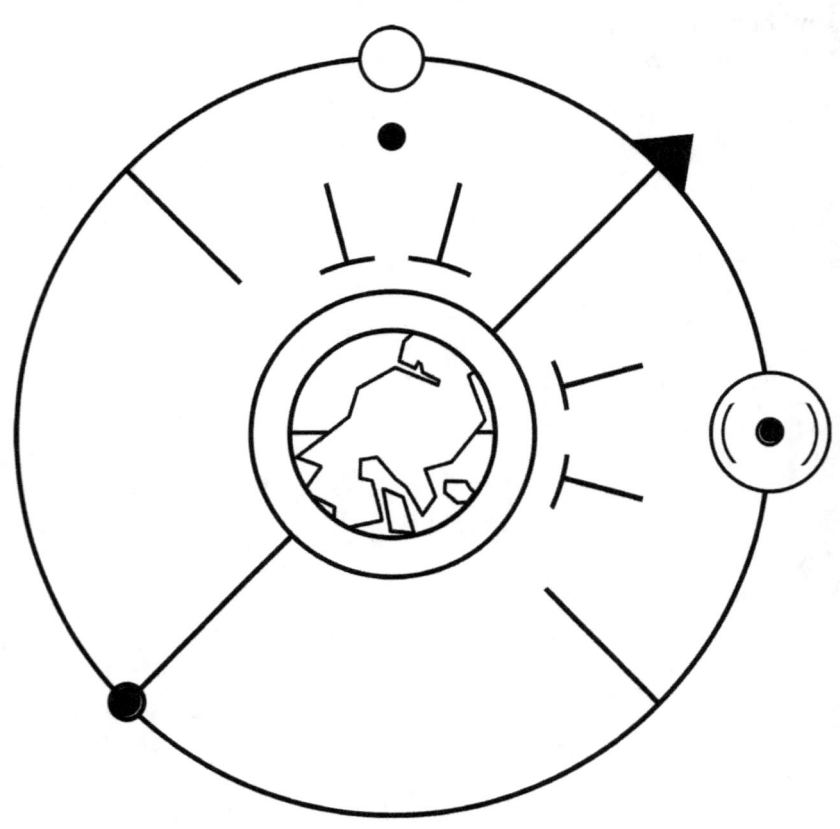

III FEAR AND HATE

Ooldrina

"**O**oldrina, you are not letting yourself connect. To do this, you need to literally open your mind to the Bind."

Biting her lips, the dark-haired girl with the nut-milk skin of her people said, "I am sorry, Lux Baiula, but this thing scares me. When I open, I feel malevolent presence. This thing, it gives me evil thoughts."

"*'This thing?'*"

After a month of having worked with the girl, Clara Lux Baiula was still having trouble understanding her at times. Luckily, the other one, Raaviana, had more facility in Alvinorian and was also learning to control her Binding skills much more easily. *Perhaps Master Methrim can help Ooldrina get past whatever is holding her back. But I would rather not have to call on him. He makes me feel things I shouldn't be feeling.*

Ooldrina replied, "This thing—I mean…opening to the Bind."

Clara shook her head in frustration, paced a moment, then invited the girl to follow her with a patient smile.

The Yellow Sash took the Zebulonian onto the balcony, a large area shaped like a half-moon, with plants covering the walls, and nothing in the center except for a Lacora Leaf cushion. The air was cool, but still pleasant.

Clara Lux Baiula motioned toward the cushion.

When Ooldrina sat herself, the plant reacted with a little bounce and then adjusted itself to support her until she sat straight and balanced.

"I know this feeling, Ooldrina, but it is often imagined. On the other hand, if you had been harmed by uninvited vibrations, I would understand your hesitation. Has this happened to you?"

The girl looked down, biting her lips, and shrugged her shoulders hesitantly, her pale skin absorbing Alba's purple light to create a strange effect.

The girl's reaction confirmed her suspicion, and Clara said, "It goes. Let's slow down then. I will enter the Bind with you."

Ooldrina gave a tentative nod—an upward nod—which Clara had come to understand was the Zebulonian equivalent to 'if it must be' or 'whatever.'

"As with any other sense, the Sensing skill requires input, which means you need to open your mind to the Bind. But you do need to be ready to shield it the moment there is danger. It's just like keeping your eyes and ears open to see and hear what there *is* to see and hear, but letting your reflexes close your eyes if a shard should fly toward them or consciously blocking your ears if a dangerously loud sound should erupt. As you progress, you will also learn how to shield your mind even while it is open to the Bind, though this does dull the perception a bit."

The wide-faced girl gave another upward nod, which she accompanied with raised, rounded eyebrows and audible inhalation. "But Bilena wants send me to Zebulonia next month. I don't have time for to learn."

"*She* wants *to* send me…and *I* don't have the time *to* learn."

"Yes, Lux Baiula, ap—I apologize."

Clara gave a troubled sigh. There was much the Sisterhood did not know about Zebulonian physiology and how they accessed the Bind, and she feared that their methods might very well harm the girl. But they needed her ready for this mission to Zebulonia. If only they had found them when they were younger. *They say necessity is the mother of progress, but it is also the mother of evil.*

"Ooldrina, listen to me. I will not let you be hurt by wrong-headed demands to rush your training, and *I* will not hurt you. Do you trust me?"

Though Clara's straight nose, unwrinkled face, and deep, honest gaze elicited trust, the woman's tone was sometimes quite curt. It took the Zebulonian refugee a moment before she said, "I believe you."

Clara cocked an eye. Did the girl intentionally use the word 'believe' instead of 'trust'? Or was belief what Zebulonians called trust? Clara did not inquire.

"All right. Once you join me in the Bind, we will create a mind-tie between us; this will allow me to sense, see, and hear what you receive from the Bind. We will then practice mind-shielding. If, at any point, I should sense that you are receiving harmful vibrations, I will block them for you if you can't do it yourself. If it happens, stay calm and pay attention; you will sense how I do it. With practice, you will eventually be able to replicate the method."

"Eventually?"

"Eventually. It means 'soon, at some point in the future.'"

Ooldrina stretched her lips in response, in the way she and Raaviana seemed to do when they understood something.

"Do you remember how to establish a mind-tie?"

The girl gave the strange upward nod, but it was accompanied by wide-open eyes, a louder inhalation, and a twitching of her fingers.

I suppose this means 'yes'. "I promise to be gentle, Ooldrina, though it will still be somewhat painful."

The girl responded with unusual confidence. "I am okay ready, Clara Lux Baiula."

With a playful scowl, Clara said, "You will need to spend more time learning proper Alvinorian. But for now, close your eyes and descend into a trance. As you do, listen for your heartbeat."

Ooldrina gave a quizzical look. "*My* heartbeat?"

"Yes. Normally, you would listen for mine. But I actually want you to listen for your own heartbeat. This will allow you to focus more quickly, and once you hear yours, you will more easily find mine. If you do not, I will find you instead."

"You do not wish to make the mind-tie now?"

"No, we can establish it from within the Bind."

Ooldrina stretched her lips again, and began.

31

It had taken Ooldrina slightly longer than it should have before she heard her own beating muscle and—having found it—perceived Clara's, entered the Bind, and appeared next to her. But she had done it, and she had done it faster than during the previous attempts where the girl had started by listening for Clara's heart.

The place Clara conjured was a dark location with a foreboding scenery; she hoped it would trigger the girl's fears while she opened her mind to the vibrations in the Bind; she hoped putting the girl face-to-face with her fears would teach her to ignore those irrational sensations and shield her mind only when real threats presented.

"Your entry was a little slow, Ooldrina. It is essential you continue practicing until you can enter the Bind at will, in case of danger and you need to communicate with someone urgently. But this was still better," Clara said to the girl, whose shifting eyes caused her form's entire face to stretch one way and then another.

Ooldrina gave Clara a weak, pathetic smile. Clara sighed and said, *"All right. Let us link."*

The next moment an undulating rope of pale blue light came forth from the Lux Baiula's form and reached toward Ooldrina's form with controlled intensity.

When Ooldrina saw the rope, her form froze as did her body in the room, and she almost exited the Bind. Ooldrina's tension caused the rope to lash her more intensely than Clara had intended, and she yelped. It also caused her to forget to latch onto the rope, and Clara had to do it over.

"You must stay calm, Ooldrina."

Ooldrina's form was still too tense, and she squealed again, but she caught the rope this time, and Clara gave her a moment to relax.

When Clara saw Ooldrina's form relax, she said, *"Now, send a similar lash back toward me."*

The girl's dark eyes told Clara that her lash was going to be a vengefully fierce one.

"I am not concerned about the strength of your rope, Ooldrina. What I wish is simply for you to control your Bindings. If you intentionally send a whipping lash back, I will accept it. But if I see that your lash is uncontrolled, I will not be pleased, regardless of how fierce or tame it is. Now, respond!"

The girl's form expanded and contracted. A moment later, a violent lash rushed toward the Lux Baiula, who growled in response to the blow.

The Yellow Sash thought: *Calm yourself, Clara; you asked for it.*

Though the connection was not yet complete, thoughts and sensations began seeping through the link, and Clara perceived resentment and fear.

"*That was* not *controlled, Ooldrina.*"

"*I am sorry, Lux Baiula. But you...startle me when you say to respond.*"

"*That is not an excuse. A Lux Baiula must remain calm—always. When I send my next lash, watch it come, but let the fear wash over you, and if I have to shout for you to respond again, let* that *wash over you also.*"

It took another several lashes before the connection was complete. However, each of the girl's responses had been more and more controlled until the last one came to Clara as a tight blue rope of light.

Clara inhaled a calming breath, "*I can sense your fear, Ooldrina. This is what we must work on now. What do you sense from me?*"

With a defeated tone, the girl replied, "*Calm.*"

"*Good. Feel it, and let it penetrate you and still your thoughts. It will help when you open your mind.*"

As soon as the girl heard the words 'open your mind', her pulse sped up frantically, and her form zapped and buzzed. Clara—ever-patient—repeated her instructions several more times and let Ooldrina feel and absorb her calm vibrations. When Ooldrina's own form was finally still and stable, as solid as it could be in the Bind, a mask of deep disappointment marred her face.

"Do not be embarrassed, Ooldrina. It normally takes months to tame one's reactions and years to master them. What you have done in a month is not to be mocked."

The girl looked up a moment, thankful but still not convinced.

"Now, show me how you shield your mind."

And the girl proceeded to do so, veiling her mind so quickly that it surprised Clara. But the block was weak, and the Lux Baiula pierced through it to tell the girl, *"That is fast, but you do it with poor precision; probably the result of your ever-present fear and lack of training before you ventured into the Bind. I believe you can do it better. I want you to open your mind again, and this time, I will send you a rapid succession of vibrations; some will be good and others bad—but don't worry, they won't be real. I want you to shield your mind when you sense the bad ones and leave it unshielded otherwise."*

The girl's form took on a worried look. But in the space of a moment, she gave an agreeing nod; after all, she had come to trust the Lux Baiula and most of the others, too, since her arrival in the awe-inspiring City of the Light, with its eternally flaming spheres; its spires and walls of blue ardamantis; its libraries and laboratories.

It took Ooldrina quite a while to achieve the goal Clara Lux Baiula had set for her, but she did not experience the passing; indeed, to see time pass in the Bind, one needed to either feel the exhaustion of one's body or periodically dip back into the physical world. However, Clara did feel the passage of the minutes and the hours, and she wondered whether this was all in vain. But eventually, Ooldrina succeeded in keeping her mind open and shutting it only when necessary.

"By the sweet milk of Aila, you've done it, Ooldrina."

The girl formed smile, not strong, but a real smile, nevertheless.

34

"You may rest for a few minutes. I will then release the shield I placed over us, and you will open your mind to the Bind."

Ooldrina's form did not waver or show any tension this time, but neither did she stretch her lips in agreement. Instead, she tipped her head forward.

Hopefully, that means she is ready now.

When she released the shield and vibrations started seeping into Ooldrina's mind, Clara took care to process them in her own mind without returning them to the girl, or risk creating a dangerous ever-amplifying feedback loop. It was, in fact, because of her ability to control what others received from her, even when connected via mind-tie, that she had been asked to train the Zebulonians.

Clara received feelings of agitation and worry, waiting just below the surface of the perceptible in her student's mind. She sent soothing thoughts to Ooldrina, and the girl's pulse quieted a bit. *How was the Sisterhood able to train anyone before the discovery of the mind-tie?*

Presently, the Lux Baiula felt Ooldrina's pulse accelerate again. The girl started to open a small patch of bright, vibrant space in the dark gloominess that surrounded them. Clara sent, *"Ooldrina! Why are you trying to take us elsewhere?"*

"I am sorry, Lux Baiula, but this frightens me, and my thoughts just imagine a clear sky."

Clara nodded. *"Please, let go of that thought."*

The girl took a moment to do as her trainer demanded, doing it with a begrudging acquiescence.

"Take seven deep breaths and then resume the exercise. But this time, I want you to tell me everything you sense, as you sense them; it might help you process your fears better."

With downcast resignation, the girl did as instructed. Her pulse slowed again, and she began telling Clara all the things she perceived: random emotions—fright, anger, sadness, joy, happiness, anger, frustration, anger, pleasure, uncertainty, and countless other emotions. As the words passed to Clara,

35

Ooldrina's emotions grew from feelings of confusion, to anxiety, and finally anguish.

Clara gave a muted sigh and sent more soothing vibrations to the girl. What else could she expect? What else could *anyone* expect?! Proper training, to ensure a woman could enter the Bind safely, took years. But things were as they were, and the girls had to be readied for a mission not even a Lux Baiula would undertake.

Clara had initially resisted Larca's request, and she had mentioned her concerns to Bilena. But the Praefecta philosophas told her to continue to do as ordered. That had frustrated Clara, and near the end of their meeting, she blurted out that these careless decisions had begun at the same time as the arrival of Lusk Methrim. But the head of the Yellow Sashate *was* one driven by data, and the available, verified data said that Lusk was a trustworthy person.

Just now, Clara sensed an overpowering fear take the girl. Clara sent a question—she had not sensed any danger herself— but the girl panicked and did not reply. Clara shielded Ooldrina's mind and got them out of the Bind.

Hate

Lusk tried hard to hide his growing panic. Clara Lux Baiula, one of the Yellow Sashes working with Praefectae Saara and Bilena to try and infiltrate Zebulonia, had come to request his assistance with one of the two Zebulonian girls they had brought back from a border town a month ago. The girls were *Alterintrant* Zebulonians and, therefore, daughters of the loathed Janarae. Lusk had to contain his screams and rage when the Lux Baiula came to make her request. Why had they not told him the girls were Alterintrants?

As powerful as he was in the Bind, and as confident as he had become since his arrival in Alvinoria, he still hated the Janarae and their progeny. He had wanted to refuse, ask why they would ever consider bringing Alterintrant Zebulonian females to Urbs Lucis. Still, he had a mission to accomplish for the Dark One, and it required him to be in Urbs Lucis—and to be in Urbs Lucis, he had to be agreeable. So, after much pacing and kicking in his chambers, he accepted his fate. That was when an idea sprouted in his mind: *Perhaps*, he thought, *I can use this opportunity to finally make them pay*. But these were only girls, and refugees on top of it. Could he truly hold them responsible for what the Janarae had done to him?

Lusk prepared to open the door to the room located in the Schola Luciana—the Lucian School. He paused, took a deep breath, exhaled, knocked—and after hearing a muffled voice inviting him in, pushed open the door and entered.

Clara Lux Baiula stood with the girl in the center of the chamber. The woman turned around and said, "Master Methrim! Thank you for coming. This is Ooldrina. Ooldrina, that is Lusk Methrim—the Zebulonian you have been told about. He will ensure you master the current Zebulonian language as well as help you learn the ways of Zebula's Court."

Lusk felt a sudden nauseating sensation course through him. Ooldrina…the name meant 'daughter of Ool', but it could also be 'daughter of Oolviana,' his birthmother's name. The thought unsettled him. Why should the girl have this name? But he was being foolish: if she were Oolviana's creatic daughter, she would not be an Alterintrant because Oolviana, herself, wasn't one. And yet, the setting of her eyes.

No! Illic nolite ire[4].

"Master Methrim, are you unwell?"

Lusk took a moment to clear his mind. "I am sorry, Lux Baiula." Then, with a tone contrasting with his feelings, he added, "Please accept my apologies, Ooldrina. I…acknowledge you."

The girl's expression changed for a brief moment. She might not know much, but she recognized the greeting for a false one. She wondered if the man mistrusted her because of what

---

[4] No! Do not go there.

she was. Her mother had told her how men were treated in Zebulonia, that they were all slaves. In fact, her own birthbrother had been taken away by the Janarae to become one of their slaves. Her mother's only consolation was that her son was serving the queen herself. But this man was too confident, too self-possessed; he did not hold himself like one who had been a slave. Compared to the men from Razeb—the village in the Mountains of the Sagr where she came from, where a large number of escapees from Zebulonia lived—he was too refined, too proud. So why did he mistrust her? And what was that familiar outline of his face? Was it just the fact that he was a Zebulonian, like her?

Lusk noticed the questioning in the girl's expression, and he forced himself to ask, "You seem to be wondering about me." Lusk was *not* going to acknowledge her with her name.

"Yes, Elak[5] Methrim, I never met a Zebulonian male like you; you are different. But I know you dislike me the same."

Clara looked from one to the other with surprise. She said to the girl, "Ooldrina, Master Methrim has no reason to dislike you. Why do you think he does?"

The girl shrugged her shoulders, not wanting to reply, but Clara insisted.

"His greeting—it was not honest, Lux Baiula."

Clara blinked and sighed. She appeared to be weighing her response to the girl's statement. With a short burst of air from her nostrils and a determined stretch of her lips, she said, "Master Methrim, would you reassure Ooldrina?"

Lusk hesitated a moment. *Why do I hesitate? I am the one always in control. I am a Temptator—the best.* Lusk's hands twitched behind his back. *But who cares how I should or should not be? I do not wish to train this girl!*

Noticing the Lux Baiula's growing concern, he replied, "I suppose that my former life and experiences with Zebulonian

---

[5] Elak: Zebulonian word for "male." Zebulonians addressed males by their gender noun.

38

females make me a little reticent to engage with them, Lux Baiula. It is possible she senses that in me."

The girl said, "I know how men were treated in Zebulonia, Elak Methrim. But my mother teached me that it is wrong."

Lusk's alter ego thought: *If she truly believes that what the Janarae do to men is wrong, why does she address you this way?*

Lusk replied to himself that he did not know and closed his eyes to keep from losing control.

Clara, who was becoming more and more uncomfortable with the awkward situation, tried to change the topic by correcting Ooldrina. She said, "My mother *taught* me, Ooldrina."

The girl flushed and stepped back. Clara scratched her throat. "Master Methrim, I have known Ooldrina for a month. I have worked with her daily—hours at a time—and I have never heard her speak of men in denigrating tones. I believe that *she* does not believe as the others from your country do."

"Her address says otherwise, Lux Baiula." Then, turning to the girl with daggers in his eyes, Lusk asked, "Are men in Razeb no longer *shutsha*, then?"

The girl started with resentment and did not reply. Clara asked what 'shutsha' meant.

With a forced smile, Lusk replied, "'*Shutsha*' is a Zebulonian epithet for males. But the word includes the biological form as well as the status of slave, or an expendable thing meant only to serve and be replaced when no longer useful or desired; all males are *shutsha* in Zebulonia."

Clara sighed and looked toward the girl for her reply. But Ooldrina turned away.

"That is why I am…hesitant to help the girl, Lux Baiula."

"Master Methrim, Ooldrina. We have a task to accomplish here, and it is essential we do it. If we do not, Ooldrina and her friend will fail, and who knows what Zebula or the Janarae will do to them. Can we not put aside hesitation and diffidence? Can we not think of the greater needs?"

39

After a tense moment during which Lusk and Ooldrina considered each other, with the girl shuffling with a sense of guilt and Lusk tightening and relaxing his jaw several times, the two finally indicated their consent, one with the Zebulonian upward nod, and the other using the Alvinorian downward gesture.

The Lux Baiula thanked the Originator. The Zebulonian silently cursed himself, wondering why he hadn't simply tried to stoke the girl's distrust.

Presently, Clara said, "Thank you. Thank you both." Then, with a surprisingly silken tone for a Lux Baiula, she turned to Lusk. "Master Methrim, I am aware you were only supposed to perfect Ooldrina's mastery of the Zebulonian language and to educate her in the ways of Zebula's Court. Nonetheless, I would appreciate your help with something else too."

At that, a quiet growl rose within Lusk, but he too had his mission, and he said, "I am here to serve, Lux Baiula."

Containing her relief, given that the meeting might still be derailed by additional, unexpected reactions, Clara replied, "Thank you. I have had difficulty teaching Ooldrina how to shield her mind from negative influences, while keeping it open to the Bind to sense what is there. I...also seem to sense things *after* she does, despite having our minds tied—a thing which puzzles me greatly. I was thinking that, perhaps, Zebulonians shield their minds differently than we do, and that you might be able to help her, if male and female Alterintrants of your race access the Bind in the same manner."

Lusk felt a pit grow in his stomach and a revolting sensation squeeze his chest. He was *not* going to teach a Zebulonian Alterintrant female how to protect herself. He didn't care that she or her birthfamily had escaped Zebulonia, and that they treated males *better* than females in the southern kingdom did.

And yet, he knew he had no choice but to go along with the charade, so that he might carry on with his mission. As he thought about it more, he remembered that the girl was still untrained which meant that he had nothing to fear from her; the

40

pit in his stomach dissolved and his lungs resumed their natural movement.

Suddenly, a victorious thought crossed his mind, and he snorted, reviving the girl's distrust and the Lux Baiula's concerns. Realizing that he needed to explain his snort lest their tenuous agreement shatter, Lusk said, "I am sorry, Lux Baiula, Ooldrina. I was just thinking about the irony of the situation. But to answer your question, Lux Baiula, Zebulonians *do* access the Bind differently from Alvinorians. We can also perceive certain vibrations much earlier than you can."

Lusk watched Clara's mouth twist with concern. He continued, without remarking on the woman's reaction. "It is the same as with music; we can all hear it, but some of us are more sensitive to certain tonalities and notes, which means that we may hear a song that contains them in its first lines earlier than other people would."

Clara bobbed her head, though she was still troubled by Lusk's statement. "Then, you can help."

Lusk tipped his head affirmatively.

Ooldrina could not hold her confusion anymore, and asked, "How? You are an—?"

Lusk responded with a patient grin. "Janarae, like the queen herself, produce mostly female progeny. But, once in a while, they choose to create a male; I am one of them."

"You are son of a Janara?!"

This time, Lusk acknowledged the veracity of the girl's statement with the Zebulonian upward nod.

Ooldrina looked shocked and taken aback by her compatriot's affirmative use of the gesture. There was a tremor in her voice when she replied, "I...never know male Alterintrant."

"I am one of a very few."

Ooldrina did not ask any more questions. After a few moments during which the Lux Baiula considered the possible outcome of this agreement with a softer face than was usual for a Bearer of the Light, and during which Lusk waited patiently

41

for instructions to be given, the girl placed her right hand above her left, close to her body, and tipped her head.

Clara turned to Lusk with a question on her face. Lusk's expression said the girl was ready.

Clara said, "Thank you, Ooldrina. Let us begin then. Master Methrim, do you know how to establish a mind-tie?"

Lusk indicated he did and did not show the apprehension he felt at the thought of having to share his mind with the girl.

"Ooldrina, please sit on the carpet and prepare to enter the Bind again, opening your mind to what may come, but setting the wards I've taught you against harmful intrusions." The girl still showed some hesitation, but before Clara could reproach her, she sat and readied herself. Clara continued. "Thank you. Master Methrim and I will each establish a Mind-Tie with you, so we may protect you. But he will be the one guiding you, while I will observe in the hope of learning how your mind—"

Lusk put up his hands, interrupting the Yellow Sash, with an unusually intense gaze. "Actually, Lux Baiula, I would prefer to be there alone with her."

Clara pulled her head back in surprise, but then blinked—as if in response to some unseen force—and said, "I have full confidence in your capabilities, Master Methrim. And I can still observe the changes in her metabolism for any dangerous increases in stress." Pointing a finger up, she added for Ooldrina, "Remember, listen for your own heart first, then for Master Methrim's."

And with that, the two Zebulonians prepared to enter the Bind.

Lusk seated himself across from Ooldrina, whereas Clara placed herself to their side but closer to the girl. When all were ready, Lusk closed his eyes. Behind the cover of his eyelids and the blankness of his meditating face, he did his best to dampen the hate he felt for the girl and the desire to kill her right then and there as he entered the Bind to meet her.

However, if one had looked at him and had seen the tiny motions of his lips and hands, one would have understood that his mind was afire with contradictory impulses. Some of those impulses caused Ooldrina to flinch several times. Lusk feared Clara might notice and stop him, but the Lux Baiula knew the linking procedure to be a difficult and complex one—even among the best of them—so she made no note of Ooldrina's winces or of Lusk' continual twitches.

Within the Bind, a firestorm brewed, and it was only through sheer force of will that Lusk did not lash out at the girl. Connecting with a Zebulonian female was perhaps the worst thing he had ever had to do—even worse than the vilest thing he had done to those who had been put upon his path. What he did to his victims revolted him, but this—being forced to connect his thoughts with one whose kind had treated him as no more than an object all his life—sickened him. How he wished he could make this girl suffer for all of it. But the Lux Baiula was watching, and she would know if he directed dangerous Bindings at his compatriot.

Or would she? Though he had been forced to teach the Sisters some of his Bindings, he still had not revealed everything. But he could not harm the girl—the Umbra had told him that the battle between the two nations needed to be even and difficult on both sides, which meant allowing the Alvinorians to gain a measure of leverage against the Zebulonians. Perhaps he could not harm her, but he could still tempt her and defile her mind with her complete cooperation.

After four minutes of painful interaction between the two Roamers, Clara started to wonder whether Master Methrim was having difficulty establishing the link. She was about to ask out loud when the Zebulonians relaxed their shoulders and synchronized their heartbeats—the sign that they had established a connection.

Hidden from Clara, whom—for some reason that evaded him—he had not tried to tempt, Lusk now reverted to the inveigler in him, to the tempter of women and men alike; he became Noctiferus's greatest Temptator.

The transformation in Lusk's mind showed in the form he chose for himself in the Bind. Having completed his metamorphosis, he turned his energies to luring the girl.

Ooldrina's form took a step back when she saw his confident, beguiling figure. Her reaction was not caused by fear, but by her response to Lusk's appearance, which lit a fire in her body she did not know existed.

When Ooldrina eventually recovered her still-too-red self-discipline, she asked in broken Zebulonian, *"You—why did you chose this form, Elak Methrim?"*

Lusk knew he had hooked the girl, and he shielded his emotions from her lest she discover them, so intense they were.

Necessity

With contained revulsion on his face, Octavius sent, *"We can continue to protect ourselves the way we have always done it, Elyana—using intelligence and courage."*

Toras stood across from his father in the Bind, while his body sat cross-legged in the newly arranged Contemplation Room at Horn's Pass—a change that had troubled him at first and then made him curious. He said, *"Father, if you had not used your powers on the plains three months back, I would be dead!"*

The coming war had changed many things in the past few months, one of which was the need for the king to communicate promptly with anyone when important or urgent matters were concerned. To assist the high king, the Sisterhood had agreed to bring Unsensing members of his court into the Bind, at pre-arranged times. Lina Lux Baiula, a Yellow Sash recently assigned to Horn's Pass, had brought Toras in it. Elyana, Octavius, Aithen, Mitsuko, and Darya—the latter having recently arrived in Furan City in preparation for a ball her husband was planning—joined the meeting from a

Contemplation Room at Domus Lucis, the Sisterhood's embassy in Furan City. Octavius projected his memory of the Grand Audience Hall to give the Unsensing attendees—and himself too—some grounding in reality.

Octavius's form rubbed its forehead. *"I simply do not like the use of Binding powers. And the thought that our entire family would be known as Alterintrants—if I allowed this—makes my blood boil."*

Darya, who presented herself dressed in a modest but beautiful gown styled after those worn by Kynarian priestesses when they went about private business on the streets of Kynaria, sent, *"Octavius, I am a Sensor, myself; everyone knows it and none of your vassals have ever voiced an objection to it. Why would they object to your sons developing skills?"*

The king replied to his wife's question with a gentler tone than he had used in his replies to the others. *"That is because you have spent most of your time in Kynaria, my Love, and so they have ignored your abilities. But do not doubt that would change if you relocated here."*

The comment seemed to trouble the queen-consort, which bothered the king. However, this was not the place to address his wife's feelings and he let things be.

Elyana sent, *"Sire, this is the way things must be. Your sons need better protection against the Alterintrants, who will become a greater component of the battle when we meet Zebula's Janarae. The risk is too great now to let principles, which were useful in a time of relative peace, guide our decisions as we go forward."*

Octavius's form vibrated intensely. The things he was hearing—this entire conversation—was pushing him to the limits of his tolerance.

Elyana paused to give the king a chance to process her statements, then continued. *"And, as you must know Sire, the use of the Bind is not, in and of itself, a bad thing. It can be used, and has been used, to create wondrous things as well as to make better decisions, and I am certain the princes will show the*

45

required respect for the powers they will develop." Looking intently at Octavius, she finished, *"As we all do."*

The king spent several minutes pacing the virtual hall, looking for things to grab as his mind wrestled with a new truth. Suddenly, his desk appeared before him, and he panicked. He realized he had transported himself into a representation of his offices, where he liked to pace to consider difficult matters, and the others were no longer with him. He received a thoughtcall from Mitsuko, who had become alarmed. Listening for his minder's thoughtvoice, he pulled himself back into the representation of the Grand Audience Hall to the great relief of the others.

Embarrassed by his mistake, the king said, *"I am sorry; in my pacing and searching for things to hold on to, I inadvertently moved myself to my offices."* The remark, which was an innocuous statement of fact, enabled the king's mind to evaluate the proposals at hand with an objective eye. After straightening his back, he asked, *"What do you propose they should learn, Elyana?"*

The king's words drew sighs of relief from Darya as well as from the princes, whose faces and eyes also showed an anxious excitement. The Lux Baiulae's reactions—if one could read them—were more varied, ranging from an expression of satisfaction on Elyana, slight concern on Lina, and curiosity on Mitsuko.

Elyana said to everyone, *"Before any training begins, the princes must be examined to know the extent of their potential. And so long as they have the atomic constitution and the microbial flora for it, they should be taught both defensive as well as...offensive skills...Sire."*

A heavy weight settled on the king just then, but he did not object to the proposal and said, *"Let it be so, then."*

IV ATTACK ON THE GNARLERS

The presence of thirty-three members of the Black Guard and five Lux Baiulae, just outside Lianor, had roused everyone in the normally quiet and peaceful hamlet, though the recent gnarler attacks as well as the arrival of the clerics of Aiala had already disrupted their lives. The guardians were now lining up to hear their orders from Prima Laiella.

The woman looked fierce as she prepared to speak, as fierce as did all Bremin Islanders. But the fact that she was a Lux Baiula on top of it intimidated most men. She intoned, "Soldiers, the creatures we will engage in the caves are unlike anything the majority of you have fought before. But you've been trained to defend against them as well as to kill them. Just remember what you learned, let your body do what it knows it needs to do, and stay with your units because if you get routed in there, it is likely you will stay there. Each unit will be led by a Lux Baiula because we won't be able to use lamps or torches in there, given that the gnarlers—who have perfect night vision—would spot us from farther away. But my Sisters and I will be able to guide us in the darkness.

Men shifted uncomfortably, troubled but also confounded. One asked, "Apologies, Prima. But even if you guide us, how's that going to help us defend or attack if we can't see anything?"

Men grunted to second their comrade's question and concern.

"We will light the lamps as soon as it becomes necessary."

The soldier nodded, though uneasily.

Laiella paused, then pointed to her Sisters. "One of my Red Sash colleagues will join each of three units; the fourth will follow me. Also, only one furan will accompany each unit, or it will be chaos in there, otherwise."

A few of the veterans regarded each other worriedly at the thought of having to face the gnarlers without all the furans.

The prima continued, "Marena Lux Baiula will send her lincots—"

A soldier interrupted the officer to ask what they were going to do with lincots.

Laiella bored through the soldier's eyes with a hard stare. The man took a step back, which was aborted by the presence of another guardian behind him. The man shoved him forward with an insult.

"As I started saying, Marena Lux Baiula will connect with the lincots and use them as trackers. She will send them inside in advance of us so she may know the gnarlers' movements moment by moment. She will communicate the information to each unit's leader. So long as the little trackers don't get impaled by those monsters, we should have no trouble finding them— and avoiding being surprised by them. Our swords and perhaps our bows—but mostly our skills—are what we will need to accomplish our mission today, which is to kill every last one of the vile creatures living in this cave system."

A soldier asked nervously, knowing he might draw the officer's ire with the question, "I'm sorry Prima, but why don't we just force them to come out? Won't we stand a better chance that way?"

Laiella's impatience at the continued questions started to show as her pale green face became darker. Surrounded by her bright red hair, her expression looked dangerous now. "As I've already explained, *Rucius*, out here in the open they have the advantage. Our best chance resides in trapping them in the main cavern where they apparently like to congregate."

The man nodded, forcing himself to look at their captain despite feeling utterly embarrassed. Laiella seemed to take pleasure in the reaction and stared at him until he tugged, uselessly, at the bottom edge of his body armor, realized the silliness of the movement and finally returned to stand at attention.

One of the older guardians asked with a tentative voice, "Prima…will we need to crawl in there, or will we be able to walk upright? I am not worried about my nimbleness as much as about having the space to wield our weapons."

Laiella decided to let Marena answer the question and turned to her for the response.

The Yellow Sash cleared her throat, "From what I could perceive through the lincots' eyes—remember that they are much smaller, so their sense of distance is different from ours, though I did correct for the difference as best I could—most tunnels are high and wide enough for two Humans to stand in side-by-side. The caves do seem to descend steeply in some places, and to narrow in others, but again, most of the network should be easily navigable."

The soldier's acknowledgment hid an underlying itch to ridicule the Yellow Sash for her overly complicated explanation, which the prima picked up. She, too, thought the reply could have been more direct, but she still needed to put the soldier in his place. "You will be able to stand most of the way, Domar. And where you won't be able to, you shouldn't have to bend too far to shorten yourself."

The soldier blushed and clenched his fist on his sword while the others laughed.

"You brought it onto yourself, soldier."

Hanne teased, "Yeah, but it's not as bad as what Falor got in that cave on First Day, so count yourself lucky, Domar!"

Laiella turned to the prince with a reproachful look, as if to remind him these men were his men, and he replied with a careless shrug. Those who had been present that day, and those who had heard about Laiella's remark to Falor regarding Alvinorian men, laughed again. Domar accepted the joke as any good soldier did.

But it was time to return to the business at hand. The prima said, "Now, does anyone have any more questions?"

When all replied with a resounding 'no', she turned to the Lord Commander and asked if he had anything to add.

Toras replied sarcastically, "No. You've covered it all."

Laiella rolled her eyes then ordered Marena Lux Baiula to call her Sisters over to establish a mind-tie. This would be necessary to allow the Yellow Sash to share what she sensed with them, and to allow them to share with each other.

The soldiers prepared to witness the supernatural ritual, some with fascination, others with fear, and others yet with pure incomprehension. One of the soldiers was upbraided when he whispered to his neighbors that he had heard that this 'ritual' was really unnecessary for the women to use their powers, and that they performed it simply to frighten the Unsensing.

As soon as the Sisters formed the circle around Marena, the Yellow Sash uttered the prescribed, "Sorores, nostris mentibus nunc nos ligare."[6]

The next moment, her hair stretched out in all directions while her Sisters' hair stretched toward her. Ribbons of blue light connected the women via their hair—a strange sight really, but also wondrous—and the ribbons zapped and crackled for an entire minute, during which—if one looked attentively—one could see signs of pain tightening the women's lips or creasing their eyelids. When the connection was established the women's hair dropped with a strangely slow, soft motion. The Sisters opened their eyes, nodded to each other, and went to take their assigned commands.

The men stood mesmerized until their Secundi snapped them out of their daze with a bark.

Meanwhile, just outside the village, a number of its inhabitants had watched the ritual in the company of two clerics. From that distance, they had not seen the faces of the women at the center of the circle, but they did recognize the color of their robes, and they did see and hear the flashing, whipping ribbons. Inaudible curses had echoed among them, encouraged by the clerics. Only a few had kept quiet—refusing to join in the superstitious nonsense. Now, they continued watching the movements and doings of the strange force with rapt attention.

---

[6] Sisters, let us now bind our minds.

Having confirmed that all units were ready, Laiella nodded to her Yellow Sister, turned to Toras to seek his consent, and the company took off to fly toward an entrance some five kilometers away.

As the furanteams gained altitude, Marena Lux Baiula eyed the villagers and clerics warily. She did have a few guardians with her, and she knew no one would try to threaten a Lux Baiula, but she needed to concentrate to guide the guardians into the tunnels. Hopefully, they'd stay away and be content to grumble.

When the last of the assault company had disappeared above the clouds, the Yellow Sash walked to her tent, sat on the floor, and entered the Bind. Once inside the ethereal space, she proceeded to connect herself to the lincots she had used to map the cave system and track the gnarlers the day before. The map was not complete, but it was nearly so, she was sure. And she was fairly certain that the lincots had found the cavern where the gnarlers congregated. That is where she needed to take the assault unit today.

Connecting to the small creatures was not a difficult process, but to connect to an animal's mind—and maintain the connection—you needed to either see it, hear it, or otherwise be able to individuate it from among all other animals in an area. That is why Marena had brought along a dozen of the little octopedals, which were endemic to Upper Alvinor and not present in the east, and therefore easily distinguishable from other animals present in the tunnels.

After a minute spent searching for their vibrations, Marena had established the link with the twelve creatures. The flood of sensory feeds dizzied her a moment, but no more. Indeed, after months of intense training in Kynaria, Marena had learned to dull the assault, which would surely overwhelm another Lux Baiula. She had also developed the skills to enable and disable the feeds of individual animals at will. However, this posed a problem of its own in that the enabling of different feeds— sequentially rather than simultaneously—meant that the perspective could change unexpectedly with highly confusing effect when the Trackers skittered in different directions.

Presently, Marena saw through one of the caged lincots that the company had landed, and that a form that looked like Sheffar—the creatures' vision was different from a Human's and not as easily interpretable—was waving a gnarler's claw in front of them to train them on the smell. The Tracker whose sensory feeds she was letting through reacted with furious firing in its olfactory centers, which Marena's brain translated into a sickening, nauseating impression.

As she recovered, she saw a hand opening the cage, and eleven lincots rushing out ahead of the one whose feeds she was perceiving. Not a moment later, all entered the caves and started hunting for their targets. Marena was flooded by the eagerness of all twelve animals. The sweeping wave was made worse by the myriad scents her seer was picking up; it seemed the gnarlers had brought back prey for a feast.

I'm sorry little, one. As much as I like you, I can't stay linked with you this way. It's too much.

And Marena released most of the little Tracker's feeds, except for the olfactory and auditory ones which she began obtaining, one by one, from the other lincots too.

As soon as the various feeds had taken a semblance of order in her brain and she began processing them, Marena contacted the Red Sashes.

"Sisters, no gnarlers have been spotted yet by the Trackers. If they come across any of them in the tunnels, I will let you know. But, hopefully, the majority of the horde will be in the main cavern, and you won't need to worry about getting stuck by gnarlers roaming the side tunnels."

The Red Sashes sent a nod back and led their respective units into the caves with palpable trepidation spreading among the blind men, while Marena returned her attention to the Trackers.

Just then, one of the little octopedals hissed and screamed. An intense, fetid odor accompanied the animal's dying shrieks as it was skewered by a gnarler. Marena did not feel the pain, and she was glad, but the poor lincot's cries had been enough to shake her; she shut off her link with the animal.

Her training in Beast Reading had never involved processing the emotions and sensory outputs of animals in pain given that it was conducted in controlled environments and the Kynarian priestesses did not purposefully harm any of their experimental subjects. She wondered, with a fleeting thought, whether her training was going to prove inadequate. She grunted and hoped no more of the lincots would be caught this way, although she did dampen the feeds a little in case another one should be killed. At least—she thought—it wasn't her little seer.

The Yellow Sash sent a thoughtcall to her colleagues. *"Sisters, a lincot was just speared by a gnarler. I am sending you the location."*

After about ten minutes, two lincots—from two different tunnels—arrived at the large cavern where the gnarlers had been congregated the day before. The signals she received from one of the lincots were unclear, and she could not tell how many creatures there were, though its olfactory senses were overwhelmed. The other lincot's visual signals were sharper, and she clearly saw the horde; it was large, very large. Marena gulped. The Yellow Sash also received auditory signals from three other Trackers. These had found gnarlers traveling secondary tunnels, probably coming back from a failed hunt, if Marena interpreted the grumbles she received from the lincots correctly.

Without delay, the woman sent a message to her four colleagues to let them know of the presence of the horde in the central cavern, and to warn Lira Lux Baiula of the gnarlers up ahead from her.

In the northern -most tunnel, the prince reviewed the orders to dispel his men's nervousness at being in the pitch-black tunnel. His whispered words sounded like the Serpent's hiss at times, which rather added to the soldiers' discomfort.

"Remember, we attack only when Xena gives the signal, which will be when all units have arrived at the main cavern. That goes for you too, Scorch. You attack only when I say you attack." Though Toras could not see the furan, he knew from the sound he made that the furan did not like the order. "Remember, too, to step back rapidly if you disembowel one of them because the substance in their guts will entrap you otherwise. And fight in pairs and keep your backs to each other, because there will definitely be creatures attacking you from behind if you're fighting alone."

The men grunted their understanding, though two did so with a curse, and they continued to follow—single file, hand on shoulder—with Xena leading the way in the dark passageways. Scorch stayed beside his master as much as he could. All of them looked forward to finding some light, and to confronting the enemy.

In another tunnel, Lira Lux Baiula advanced with her team. All stepped gingerly on the uneven ground, lest they trip and fall, except for Runner—Sheffar's furan—who had no trouble at all with the ground, though he was frustrated by the constant tightening of the walls. His complaints sounded like the angry chirps of a Flyer trying to keep other males away from its nest, and more often than once, Sheffar was forced to shush him.

While paying attention to what she sensed around her which might indicate danger, as well as remaining alert to urgent messages Marena or her other Sisters might send, Lira could hear the men doing their best to memorize the changes in slope as well as each turn of the tunnels in case the worst happened and they needed to get out on their own. She promised herself not to let it happen.

After a few more turns and a surprising ascent following what must have been a hundred meters of continuous descent, Lira stopped. She was followed, in sequence, by Secundus Sheffar and the six men behind him, one after the other.

This last part of the caves being wider, the furan was walking a couple of steps away from Sheffar and did not feel him stop. He reacted when he no longer heard his master's footsteps and Sheffar quieted him once more.

Lira whispered, "Secundus, there are three creatures in a side tunnel just ahead and to our left. I propose we advance until just before the passage. We'll leave four men on this side of it, and the rest of us will cross to the other side."

Sheffar replied similarly, "Won't they spot us the moment we cross?"

"I will light the lamps just as we do. That will blind us momentarily, but it should blind them longer."

Sheffar grumbled. "All right—if you say so. Men, let's do as the Lux Baiula suggests. Francis, Domar and Yaris, you'll stay with me on this side—you too Runner, stay with me. Zeb, Larus, and Mirko, you will follow Lira Lux Baiula to position yourselves on the other side of the passage. If the creatures are still in the side tunnel by the time we recover our sight, we'll launch arrows at them. If they're too close for arrows, remember your training and get ready for close combat."

As the unit resumed its strange hand-to-shoulder advance, the high-pitched screech of a dying lincot reached their ears. A few hands inadvertently squeezed the shoulders they held a little tighter.

Marena sent an urgent thoughtcall to Lira, saying, *"Lira, the lincot tracking the gnarlers near you just got speared by them. I will not be able to guide you anymore, but just before the lincot was killed, it showed me the creatures were still a dozen or so meters from the tunnel you're in."*

"Can you send another one to take its place?"

"I am sorry; I am not able to control them yet."

The Red Sash sent a sigh to her colleague then urged the men to follow with an almost inaudible 'come on'. A dozen paces later, she stopped and said, "This is it, Secundus. The three of you crossing with me, get your swords ready; we probably won't get to use the bows."

Shocked growls came from the side tunnel, just a few paces from the soldiers, when a sudden, blinding light lit the caves. Lira urged on the three soldiers following her.

A moment later, her sight returned, and she saw the gnarlers just two longsword lengths away. They were rubbing their eyes, and their hisses appeared confused and angry. Lira wanted to attack, but none of the six men had recovered their eyesight yet.

She hissed, "Come on men, come on!"

After a seemingly interminable recovery, they acknowledged their readiness with hand signals. Lira made a signal of her own, asking them to remain silent, and then scraped the cave floor with her glaive. That drew the gnarlers' attention who—though still blind—drew a dozen random shafts. *Good. Hopefully, they'll continue and run out before their sight returns.*

Sheffar, standing across from Lira on the other side of the passage, looked at her urgently. His motions indicated he wanted to attack now, before they lost their advantage. Lira shook her head and motioned with her glaive on the ground. Sheffar understood and started scraping the ground too. The gnarlers launched a new volley of quills, but these too hit the sidewalls and roof more often than they reached the soldiers.

Lira was trying to determine whether the creatures were close to regaining their sight when one of them looked her straight in the eye and growled furiously. The gnarler, who seemed to be leading the small crew, waved his hooked arm and sped forward.

Sheffar whispered, "Men, Runner, ready yourselves!" He did not name the Lux Baiula; he wasn't sure whether he could command her, but she acknowledged his order anyway.

In the time it took for the men's hearts to pound three furious beats, the gnarlers appeared in the main tunnel. Sheffar lunged forward, uttering a growl so frightening the gnarlers jumped, and his men attacked.

But the monsters' leader recomposed itself surprisingly quickly, and it turned and parried Sheffar's thrust with a swift movement of his right arm. Without pause, it thrust forward with its left arm, which would have hooked Sheffar if Runner had not jumped on the creature and snapped the hook. The beast cried but quickly regrew its member.

The other two gnarlers—one a hulking beast, and the other a more limber one—were launching quills at their opponents despite the close quarters. Lira Lux Baiula used her small shield to block the massive creature's projectile then jumped on it with all the skill a Lux Baiula's motor control gives her.

The Black Guard soldiers surrounded the nimbler gnarler and attacked it from all sides, shameless. But they were surprised and shocked when the creature launched several shafts at them in quick succession. Two men were hit. Lira Lux Baiula, who was fighting behind them, was pierced by a stray quill.

The woman groaned; the poisoned projectile had pierced her thigh, but somehow, she continued fighting. The two soldiers, however, quickly fell to the ground, spasming.

The pack leader, who had been unable to fully regrow its hook continued to fight despite its handicap. The monster flicked its red tongue at the secundus and his furan and fought on, relentlessly, as if it was defending something. But what might it be protecting? The question came and went in Sheffar's mind, leaving no trace. The monster launched several more quills at Sheffar and Runner, the former parrying desperately and the latter jumping from side to side to avoid being struck by the organic projectiles.

Sheffar was growing desperate for an idea. His brain latched onto the only one that came. He signaled his furan to move back and quiet down for a moment. Runner obeyed, though with several starts and stops as he crept backward and waited for his next cue.

The secundus continued to harass the gnarler, and the latter soon forgot about the furan.

The creature redoubled its efforts against the Human, cornering him repeatedly, swiping its malformed arm at him, and continuing to shoot quills, though at a much-reduced frequency.

The last barb scratched Sheffar's neck, and the man shook from the fear that the quill might have poisoned him. He yelled, enraged. He was furious and wanted only to kill the damned thing. He attacked and slammed his shield into the gnarler.

The creature hooked the shield, and Sheffar pulled with all his strength to unbalance the thing, which tried to get him with its other arm. The secundus saw the opportunity he had been waiting for and yelled his furan's name.

Just as the gnarler was about to launch a quill from the side, Runner jumped on it and plunged his beak into its fat neck and broke it. The gnarler thrashed violently but finally collapsed, sending tremors through the ground, which turned off the Living Lamp. Everything went dark again, and the soldiers panicked. The two surviving gnarlers—who knew they now had the advantage—hissed a malevolent laugh before going completely silent.

Sheffar, Lira, and the four standing men groaned. One asked with a shaking voice, "Lux Baiula, can you turn the Lamp back on?"

"I'm sorry. I won't be able to for another two minutes."

The soldier whispered, "Then what do we do now?"

The sounds of a quill hitting the man and the ensuing dying groan pierced the darkness. Lira ordered the men to flatten themselves onto the walls, cover their bodies with their small shields, and swipe with their blades in case another quill came.

But Lira did not make any movement. Instead, she tried to contact Marena, hoping the woman had another one of the Trackers nearby. But there were none, and Lira decided to remain in a trance and open her senses to everything and anything she might feel. She sensed electrical discharges; they were caused by one of the soldiers shuffling his feet. Another soldier's heartbeat reached her and told her he was on the verge of some brash action. A split second's moral debate ended with her forcing herself into the man's mind to quiet him. She then sensed the faint, but definite movement of air displaced by an object thrust toward her. She moved her shield to parry, but it was too late. The quill penetrated her belly from the side with a tearing sound.

Lira groaned with shuddering finality and the gnarler hissed victoriously. But its laughing shriek had given Runner a target. The furan attacked and plunged his beak into the creature's spine.

Her back halfway up a sidewall, Lira tried to enter the Bind to slow the poison's spread. But she no longer had the energy to do so. Hoping that one of her Sisters would find her and take her memories before the entirety of her lifetime and of her experiences vanished, Lira used her last breath to *whisper* the message she should have sent to them. Her brain shut-off as she realized her mistake.

The pained groan emitted by Runner's victim alerted the last of its congeners. The monster turned from the soldiers it had been about to stab and launched its remaining quills at Runner. The furan, luckily, flashed his wings open and caught the projectiles before they penetrated his body. But the quills' venom still spread from his membranous organs, and a debilitating pain took him. Seeing the furan weakened, the gnarler dashed for it.

Sheffar heard the creature's predatory growl and his furan's subsequent cries for help. The soldier could not see anything, except for very faint shadows. He called to Runner, but the furan was in no condition to reply, obviously fighting for his life. So, the secundus put his left hand forward and—with his sword in his right—followed the sounds.

The officer felt his pulse quicken as his brain tried to parse the data it received to decide whether to stop, step back, parry or strike. But after stumbling on a stone, his hand landed on the naked, lumpy skin of the gnarler's back. Sheffar gasped, and in the moment it took him to decide to strike, the creature turned around and knocked him down. The air escaped from his lungs as he landed on a sharp rock and cried out.

61

The gnarler was going for the kill with a vicious, tired snarl when Runner—whose side and wings were bleeding profusely—found the strength to stand up and plunge his beak into the creature's fleshy arm. The gnarler cried and tried to free its arm, but the furan bit down harder and broke the limb.

At that moment, light reappeared unexpectedly and blinded everyone again. It did not take Sheffar long to regain his sight, this time, and as soon as it happened, he put his blade through the gnarler's back and finished it. The creature gave one final scream and slumped to the ground, dead, while Sheffar and Runner dropped, exhausted. Sheffar gave one quick look around; Yaris, Mirko, and Larus still lived. Yaris looked at him with wild, angry eyes. The man had said he hated caves and their blackness. Fortunately for him, one could at least stand up straight in these tunnels.

What would the man have done if they had had to crawl?

By one of the large cavern's entrances, Toras and his team waited eagerly, nervously. They held back the nausea caused by the smell of cooked meat as they imagined its origin.

Toras whispered to Xena, "Have you received confirmation that all teams are in place?"

Xena gave the Lord Commander a grim look. She told him that there would only be three teams because Lira and Sheffar's unit did not make it, and that they must hurry so that one of them could reach Lira before her memories were gone.

Toras swallowed and hardened his traits before replying. "Then it'll be three teams assaulting the things! But Xena—our mission's in front of us. If we can get to your Sister, we will. But your focus must be here."

The Lux Baiula gave the prince a look that would have killed another man. But she knew he was right, and she relaxed her shoulders as much as a Red Sash on the battlefield might ever do, meaning not enough to notice.

Toras continued, oblivious to the woman's sentiments. "How many do you think there are? Thirty, forty, fifty?"

Xena sighed. "I count some forty in front of us. Laiella and Ulva counted another sixty or so between the two of them, beyond those columns. I would say about a hundred."

"That's a four to one advantage. Well, no matter; we'll kill as many as we can with the first volley, and then use the stalagmites and stalactites to our advantage until they exhaust their quills."

Xena frowned, doubtful of Toras's plan. "I do not think they are so stupid as to exhaust their quills like that; they will advance on us."

"Not if they see the furans."

"You intend on having the furans expose themselves?!"

"Not exactly. Will you be able to use your Bindings now?"

Xena tipped her head affirmatively. "There should be enough oxygen in here."

"Can you create some kind of shield for the furans that will block the quills?"

"Hmm, I do not think so. The shields only repel metal-containing objects."

"Damn."

"But, perhaps we can distort the air in front of them. That should at least slow the creatures' projectiles and give the furans time to avoid them."

"Are you sure?"

Xena nodded affirmatively.

"Okay, then let's do that." Toras turned to Scorch and said, "Scorch, do you understand what I want? It's dangerous, but the Lux Baiulae will protect you."

Scorch bobbed his head uncertainly and chirped to ask for more precise instructions.

"I just need all of you to show yourselves. When we attack or when the gnarlers attack, you all can attack, too. And remain calm when you see the quills. Be alert and move to avoid the quills."

Scorch bobbed his head more firmly this time.

"Okay. Xena, please ask Laiella and Ulva to get their teams ready. We'll enter when you give the signal."

Xena grunted with an expression that said she had something else in mind.

"What is it?

"I suggest we create a diversion."

"I was just going to suggest that. Can you create a sound, or do something to turn the creatures toward the far wall?"

"I can do better; I can launch a small firewhorl into their mass."

"No, that will cause them to turn in our direction, and I don't want them to see us until we're all in position. Please do as I ask, Lux Baiula."

The Red Sash gave the prince a hard, icy look, but still she held her tongue and acquiesced. She understood it would not do to question the Lord Commander's order in front of his men. So, she sent the message to her Sisters and then prepared to create a disturbance on the far wall.

As Toras got his men ready, Xena interrupted him with a scratch of her throat. "I am sorry, Lord Commander, but First Barrier Laiella disagrees with your plan."

"What?!"

"She says it would be better to cull their numbers before going in…with a few volleys of firewhorls."

"I've already said no to you, why would I say yes to her?"

Xena looked shocked, as if the prince had just uttered the stupidest question.

"Please let Laiella know that I am in command, and that I disagree with her, as I did with you. Clearly, she doesn't think my plan foolish or she would have said that instead of suggesting a *better* one."

Xena nodded. Obviously, the prince knew his prima's ways. She sent Toras's reply to Laiella.

"Well, what did she say?"

"She will do as you command."

"Finally. Now, the diversion."

A moment later, a loud, repeating noise rattled the gnarlers and caused them to turn in its direction. As the sound continued, some dropped the food they were holding and stood nervously, unsure whether to approach the wall to inspect it or flee.

"Let's move," Toras said, and Xena repeated the command to her Sisters.

As they went in, Toras looked toward the other two teams. He motioned them to position themselves behind the large stalagmites.

Toras felt his pulse quicken at the thought of the impending battle; they had never fought, let alone attacked, such a massive horde. All they had done to date was to fight small parties of the creatures. This was something else entirely, and he hoped he had not just brought them here to die. As he continued to advance, he wondered if this was the gnarler's home. And if not, where was their home—if they had one? And why, then, were they gathered here?

Xena's voice interrupted the prince's thoughts. "Commander, we are all in position. And the noise *is* keeping the creatures' attention on the wall; they must be dumber than we thought."

But one hulking gnarler with a reddish color to his blubbery skin looked in their direction to contradict Xena. The creature's flesh looked strangely gelatinous. If not for the gnarler's enormity and the large lumps, which indicated the presence of a massive musculature, everyone would have dismissed it with a laugh. An angry roar rose from it just now, causing its companions to turn away from the wall and toward the other side. When they noticed the Humans and furans, they shrieked.

Toras said grimly, "Well, I was hoping to hit them first, but it is what it is. Let's hope none will surprise us from behind."

With a roar of his own, Toras ordered the attack. The furans positioned themselves in front of each team, doing so cautiously; they were courageous and ferocious animals, but they were not foolish; they did not suffer from the death-wishes Humanoids often fell prey to. The three Lux Baiulae quickly generated

Bindings to—hopefully—protect the furans, and arrows and firebolts started seeking flesh. Chaos erupted.

The corpulent gnarler, who must be the creatures' leader, growled and quills started flying toward the invaders. But it did not order its congeners to assault them; it seemed the furans were keeping them back, for now.

Toras looked at Scorch and the other two furans with clammy hands, praying to the Black Skies that the Lux Baiulae's Bindings would work. He gave a relieved sigh and smiled a grateful smile toward Xena when he saw the furans easily sidestep the quills.

The gnarlers reacted with confusion, and though their leader now prodded them, they dared not advance. Many fell—mostly the thinner ones—from the arrows and firebolts that landed on them with full strength.

Xena gave a sidelong glance at Toras. "Your tactic is working, except not as many are falling as should."

Toras nodded with a worried look, then started launching arrows too, aiming for the leader. But the creature could not have cared less for itself, though it seemed to be angry and frightened for its congeners. It motioned urgently with its short arms and made yelping sounds, as if pleading a group of them to hide. Toras and Xena looked at each other, confused, unable to understand what was happening.

Unexpectedly, Xena's face was drained of its blood; she had gotten a thoughtcall from Laiella, who was telling her that she had just sensed a vibration coming from one of the defending gnarlers near her.

She asked the prima: *"What do you mean, you received a vibration from it?"*

"It was a...a thought. It felt like a thought. A soothing, pleading one. And it sent the image of a lactating female. They are not all combatants."

"What???"

Ulva, who had been listening to the thought exchanges but had remained silent all this time, clarified Laiella's statement.

"Xena, I think they carry them in the folds of their skin. I just saw one wiggle as its mother moved to avoid our arrows. And there are others, a little bigger, hiding underneath them."

"Then what do we do?"

The prima sent, *"We need to let them go, Xena. Tell the Lord Commander. Now."*

Xena recovered some color as she prepared to transmit the message and turned toward the agitated prince. "Laiella says there are lactating females and little ones among the creatures in front of them." With a tone that left no room for debate, she added, "We need to let them go."

Toras stood frozen for a moment, but a quill forced him to loosen up enough to crouch and hide behind a stalagmite. He shook his head and fought against rising rage. "These creatures are dangerous, Lux Baiula. They're man-eaters! What do you propose we do? Retreat? Raise a flag to give them safe passage out of here before we resume the fight against their males?"

Xena returned a hard glare at the prince. "Laiella, Ulva, and I are in agreement; we cannot target them. We need to find a way out for them."

Toras was about to scream. They *disagreed*? He growled instead, then said, "Are these young ones and the females fighting too?"

Xena shook her head.

If not for the situation, Toras would have put the women under arrest, but he had no choice now. His reply came as a hissing mutter. "All right. There's a tunnel on the back wall. Order everyone to leave the path leading to it safe. If the females and their offspring escape that way, we won't pursue. But if the creatures use the tactic to surprise us from behind, we will kill them *all*."

The Red Sash seemed to be relieved as she nodded and sent the order to her Sisters and then shouted it for the squad's men to hear.

After a fleeting thought about the reasons he mistrusted the Sisterhood passed through his mind, Toras returned to the fighting.

A few moments later, short versions of the gnarlers, accompanied by larger ones with swollen lactation pouches on their sides, made their way toward the exit on the back wall. The females shot hateful glares at the Humans, though one seemed to be looking in Laiella's direction with a thankful expression. Toras gulped when he thought he heard the leader sigh with relief just before growling something at its soldiers and they renewed their attack with even greater fury.

Ten minutes into the fighting, a scream came from the prince's left. The first man had fallen—someone in Laiella's unit. But the prima was not paying attention and kept launching firebolts at the gnarlers in between the quill volleys.

Toras yelled, "Prima, one of your men is down!"

Laiella shouted back, "He is a soldier; he knows death."

Toras turned to launch another arrow at the gnarlers then ordered Laiella to see to the man. The Red Sash gave an annoyed growl and called her furan back while she checked on her soldier. The other six guardians in her unit turned glaring looks at her. While Laiella saw to Corian, shouts of alarm rose from the others; the furan's retreat had encouraged a dozen gnarlers to advance on them.

Laiella ordered another guardian, Ruvius, to see to the injured soldier. She then returned to her fighting position and re-created the Binding in front of her furan, Root, before sending him back to stop the gnarlers' advance.

The creatures stepped back, at once, when they saw the furan reappear. Their leader hollered something in their yelping, unintelligible tongue to urge them forward. When they still hesitated, it rushed ahead of them, toppling any who stood in its way, obviously frustrated by its congeners' fearfulness and the unending battle.

Laiella commanded her men to fire at the giant at will, while she launched one firebolt after another at it. Everyone, and most

68

of all Laiella, looked on with shock as the beast continued to march toward her team's position, heedless of the several arrows stuck in its blubber and unaffected by the Bound projectiles which had slowed even the Serpent.

Root screeched at the thing and then made short, vibrating calls to his mates. Scorch responded with similar attack calls, and he turned toward Toras with pleading eyes, requesting permission to attack. Toras took a deep breath, nodded, and ordered Laiella as well Ulva to make way for the furans. Not a moment later, Scorch, Root, and Bold launched themselves at the gnarlers.

Toras and Laiella looked at each other and decided that it was time to get into the fray as well. They had brought down about a third of the creatures. With the odds slightly better, the order was given; soldiers advanced against the snarling enemy— the red shoots challenging each other, the more seasoned guardians focusing their minds and hoping to come out of the engagement alive, and the three Lux Baiulae focusing their minds and sending probing signals to various parts of their bodies to assure their readiness. The one common hope they all had was that the creatures had nearly run out of quills.

Unfortunately for them, many still did have quills to shoot, but they seemed to be weaker, no longer piercing the plated armor. Despite this, the shafts did scratch or penetrate unprotected parts, and three guardians fell in the first few minutes of the melee.

Bold, Secundus Yuuto's furan, was killed when it pounced on the leader and it snapped his neck with sickening noise. The other two furans froze, troubled, if only for a moment, understanding the need to be careful lest they, too, meet their end.

Toras was sweeping his longsword with furious motions, and when the blade connected with its target, claws and bones broke from the pure strength of the impact. But he was beginning to feel the exhaustion and slowed a bit, to focus his energies better. Every so often, he accompanied his attacks with an unusually mighty bellow, which seemed to shake his opponents. Stranger still, the growls shook *him* on the inside. By the third time this happened, the distraction almost cost him his life as one curiously short gnarler aimed its spike at his belly. Toras decided to ignore the unusual feelings to strike and parry with more controlled motions.

As for the Red Sashes, they used motion as a killing art, carrying their attacks with amazing precision, stepping and spinning and ducking and striking with remarkable efficiency and effect. And yet, their energy reserves were dwindling, and the Lux Baiulae had to ask each other for cover while each retrieved a few sweet-salt cubes from their pockets and ingested them. The substance sustained them for another little while, but their movements were now slower.

The Black Guardians, though not halflings like the prince, or killing machines like the red sashed Sisters, had begun the fighting with the skill, courage, and prowess they were known for. They too had succeeded in thinning the gnarlers' ranks, but fatigue was beginning to show in their slower strikes and blocks and in the greater number of near misses they were experiencing.

Three of the six red shoots—all of them rookies from the past spring's recruitment efforts—had discovered that their bravado meant nothing to the gnarlers who preferred to fight as pairs even when facing a single opponent. That being so, all three men were now calling for help. One was saved in extremis by Secundus Yuuto, but the other two were cut through and through by their laughing attackers before any help arrived.

The gnarlers' chief, having removed one furan, now made its way toward the remaining ones, knocking down several men while doing so. As it approached Root, four of the giant's companions, taking courage, attacked Scorch.

The colossus took the final steps toward Root with snarls that spoke of its intentions more than any words might have done. It seemed to know that the furans were keeping its fighters from fully engaging the Humans, and it wanted them out of the way.

Root attacked the beast with the temerity common to his predatory kind, advancing more often than retreating, and using his agility to wound his opponent while keeping himself out of reach.

Sadly for him, his biting and clawing managed only to cut through blubber and did nothing to stop the gnarler's fury. Soon enough, Root felt his muscles cramp. The leviathan—seeing an opening—reached for his neck. The furan pushed his claws deep into the creature's flesh, and still he could not free himself.

The giant was slowly crushing the air out of him.

Realizing that he could not escape, Root tried to call for help, but no sound could exit his clenched throat. So, he made one last effort, beating his hindwings against his forewings for as long as possible before losing consciousness.

Scorch had just killed his opponents when he heard the rustling of Root's wings. Bloody and wearied as he was, he rose on his hind legs to look toward his companion. When he spied the other furan's limp body, a raging bellow escaped him, and he sprang forward. Soldiers who heard him got out of his way, but not the gnarlers. Scorch toppled them like toys.

In an instant, the furan was upon the hulk. He enveloped it with his wings and plunged his beak into its fat, blubbery neck.

Toras, who had just slashed the throat of the last gnarler that attacked him, took a moment to breathe and assess the situation. He saw that though they had killed a good number of their opponents, their own numbers had also dwindled, and he understood then that unless they ended the battle quickly, they might not make it out alive. Even Laiella—the fierce First Barrier of the Lucian Guard—was struggling against four gnarlers who had decided to band against her. He knew she needed help and was about to go when he heard Scorch's cry— a cry he could recognize amid a thousand others.

His heart sank when he saw Root on the floor and the colossus on top of Scorch, pulling his wings as if to rip them from his body. Toras ran his bloody hands through his hair in desperation as he tried to decide whom to help when an unexpected voice returned hope to him.

"Lord Commander, Lord Commander!"

"Sheffar! Sheffar, my good man! Quick, Scorch and Laiella need help."

Without hesitation, Secundus Sheffar sent Runner toward Scorch while he and his men ran to assist Laiella.

Toras took a deep breath and returned to the fight with a roar to urge all the others to end the battle. With the echoing cries of his soldiers pushing him forth, the prince threw himself at his next target with deadly force, a force that came from that place where the last embers burn, waiting only to light afire what remains of the structure.

It took another five, interminable minutes for the battle to end, with the three furans cooperating to finally bring down the creatures' leader. And the moment it gave its final, raspy grunt, the dozen or so now leaderless gnarlers scattered like cacklers, their eyes having strangely turned from red to gray.

The company now sat, slumped against a wall as far away from the fighting scene as they were able to find. As their state of alarm diminished, signals from their other senses—particularly their sense of smell—resurfaced. One of the younger soldiers retched when his nostrils were invaded by the nauseating stench of the dead gnarlers. That odd greenish cruor that was the creatures' lifeblood pooled around the bodies along with the substance from which they made their organic projectiles. The soldier's vomit caused another of the surviving youths to empty his stomach as well.

Laiella sat by the prince, shaking her head. Her mind was troubled by two things: Lira's demise and the female gnarler who had contacted her.

Lira's death, without the transfer of her memories, was deeply felt; it was a loss not only of the person, but also of the interactions she had created and sustained within the Sisterhood, and of all the memories and experiences she had accumulated and carried. As these thoughts went through Laiella' mind, she glanced at Ulva and Xena and sighed. *At least*, she thought, *the twins are safe.* She then shivered imagining what would have happened if it had been one of them to die in the same condition as Lira.

As for the female gnarler, Laiella was certain the creature had sent her a thought—to warn her that some of them carried children. Thinking of the fact that she and the others had been ready to kill them all truly unsettled her. The gnarlers were sentient creatures. *But they murder and eat your people!* A growl escaped Laiella.

"Prima. Are you okay?"

"I am fine, Lord Commander."

Toras nodded but wasn't so sure his officer was fine when he saw her pulverize the short stalagmite she had her hand on. Still, he let her be; she was probably frustrated by the same things occupying his mind: the loss of so many men and of one of her Sisters.

If there was one thing Toras hated, it was the loss of men. He hated it not because of the unfairness—they were soldiers after all and knew the risks—but because those who joined the Black Guard swore an oath of celibacy and relinquished all familial ties. This helped them focus during battle, but it also meant that the ties among the soldiers were strong and often over-compensated for what they lacked. Because of it, losses were felt very deeply. That was why he had yelled at Laiella when she would not see to her injured soldier. Toras would need to give these men some time to recover once they got back to Horn's Pass.

The furans, too, needed to grieve. In fact, Scorch, Root, and Runner were already assembled around Bold's body to mourn him. The brown-faced Runner, who had mated with Bold a year ago when Bold had been in his female phase, was most affected by the death, and he led the mourning ritual with a low, long vibrato while covering Bold's body with his outstretched wings. Scorch and Root followed him, placing their forewings on top of Runner's. The three of them would be upset when the men stopped them to return to camp. Indeed, their mourning ritual usually lasted through the night. But although the Black Guard had won the battle, this cave was not a safe place to stay, and they would need to go soon.

Watching the furans reminded the prince of the gnarler's chief, and he surprised himself and everyone else when a laugh escaped him. Indeed, he found himself disappointed because he would have liked to face the beast. But alas. *Maybe it's better this way,* he thought, *seeing that it took three furans and a dozen arrows to kill it. Still, it would have been nice to test my skills against a true colossus.*

Toras was shaken out of his puerile thoughts when Laiella scratched her throat.

"What is it, Prima?"

"Marena said she needs to study the leader so we can prepare against its type in case we have to fight any more like it. It means we need to take its body back."

"What?! You can't be serious."

"I am. That creature was very nearly impervious to whatever we launched at it. If there are more like it, we need to know how to fight them. We can only do that by studying this one."

"Does she know how much that thing weighs? And how much effort it's going to take to drag it out of here and through the tunnels? We might have to chop it up!"

Laiella responded with a glare.

"All right. Let me speak to the secundi."

Toras approached the officers with a look that said he was about to ask them to do something they wouldn't want to do. Their expressions turned sour before he even spoke. "Sheffar, Yuuto, after you're done preparing our dead for carrying, use a couple of belts to tie to the leader's hands so we can drag it back."

The secundi shot incredulous looks at their commander, but he set his jaw and pointed toward the Lux Baiulae. The secundi cursed but nodded and went to do as ordered.

Toras watched the men get to their tasks, their motions and expressions and verbalizations displaying their sorrow in varied ways. Meanwhile, Yuuto, a Pargahni, whistled a mournful song as he cleaned the dead before they were enveloped by the others in the carrying sheets.

Toras should have felt somber too, especially hearing Yuuto's tune, but instead he felt…joy. He said to Laiella, "Do you realize something?"

The woman looked at him with raised brows, waiting for him to continue.

"We've won our first real engagement against the gnarlers. It has cost us some, for sure, but now we know that we *can* fight them."

Laiella's reply was not as prompt and pleased as Toras had expected, but he did not insist for a more joyous response; she had lost someone, too, after all, and it seemed this loss troubled her more than the loss of their comrades troubled his guardians. They would remember their fallen companions even if they did not carry their memories. Something for him to keep in mind.

V TORMENTS AND IRRITATIONS

While it Swirls

Sitting in his dayroom and staring at the glass of merotto[7] he had been sipping for the past twenty minutes, Lusk made an accounting of his mission to date. Presently, his thoughts were on Ooldrina, whom he had decided not to turn. He would simply penetrate and abuse her mind while teaching her the things the Sisterhood expected her to know for her mission to Zebulonia.

The girl had continued to resist him, but each time with less conviction, and that had encouraged him, given him a sense of power over this Janara's spawn.

The rational part of his mind balked at that. Wasn't he also Janara's spawn? *No!* Lusk quashed the question and returned to Ooldrina.

This morning, she had almost welcomed his advances in the Bind. Soon, he would be able to bed her in some place of his imagining. Where would it be? At the top of the Mountains of the Sagr? In the chambers he had had in the queen's palace? Or perhaps on a beach?

Are you sure you wish to do that? Don't you remember sensing—

No! Oolviana's daughter would not be an Alterintrant. This one is the daughter of a Janara. You know it.

I do not know it.

Lusk's mind paused its internal dialogue for a moment, then a suggestion came: *You could simply ask her who she is.*

No, I will not ever willingly put myself in another female's power again.

Fine, the question will remain then.

What is not in question is my progress with the Lux Baiulae.

---

[7] Merotto: an alcoholic drink made from the fruit of the Merotto—a Kynarian tree.

Really? You have turned a few apprentices, yes. But as for the Sisters, you have merely been able to keep them stupefied.

Except a Yellow and a Purple—both are now Converts. Noctiferus and the Umbra will be pleased with that.

He would be more pleased if you had also turned the sweet Elyana. But it seems that every so often she suspects you again. Perhaps it is time to try different methods with her.

No! I do not wish to. And I do not need *to turn everyone; just a sufficient number to weaken the Founder's enemies.*

Lusk took the last sip of merotto in his glass then went to pour himself another glass of the alcohol from the bottle standing on the Wine Warmer on the windowsill. The Warmer was an elegant piece of stone, with a depression on the window-facing side to hold the bottle in position while the curved window's glass concentrated the suns' rays into the liquid.

After returning to his divan and letting himself plump into it, he thought of another girl he had considered turning: Raaviana. But though he had considered it, he had decided against it because she, too, was the daughter of a Janara, and abusing her would mean intimate proximity which he did not wish to force upon himself—Ooldrina was enough. And yet, he hated the chirpy green-eyed girl as much as he did Ooldrina.

As he thought about it more, he realized that Ooldrina was indeed enough; Raaviana would suffer the consequences of his vengeance once she and her irritating dark-eyed friend got to Zebulonia. His plan having crystallized, Lusk nodded to himself, relieved.

He now swirled his merotto, which climbed over the sides of his crystal glass with a curiously lustful motion, and his mind drifted to Luvius Arco. He had met the young patrician earlier that fourth when the young man arrived in Urbs Lucis on business for his wealthy merchant father. *There* was a young man whom he would not only tempt but also turn to make him one of them—a Temptator. Luvius had the makings of it, except for being too boastful. Temptatori needed to be discrete, circumspect, self-effacing, and non-threatening. Lusk would need to help the young man rein-in his pride.

And Luvius would be easy to turn for he liked to climb the ladders fast and did so with all the charm his looks and position gave him. In fact, the boy believed that these things alone should be sufficient to gain him any available opportunity—or for opportunities to be created for him if none existed. So, Lusk was going to do just that: create an irresistible opportunity for Luvius. First, though, he needed to gain the patrician's confidence, and he knew just how to do it. *A fourth's work is all I will need.*

Something inside of the Healer-turned-Temptator snapped when he realized the truth of his plans for the boy. The thought revived a deeply buried loathing, and the anger caused him to crack the glass's lip. He stood with frustrated motions and went to the wallchute to drop the cup in it.

Turning from the wall, he froze in place. A violent spasm shook him then. He yelled and fell to his knees. It was as if a torrent raged through him and scoured his organs in a violent revolt against the alcohol he had imbibed. Many Alterintrants were intolerant of wine; it had something to do with their microbial flora, which responded to alcohol with a release of toxins as they processed it. Lusk knew of this weakness, of course, but the constant turmoil in his mind often led him to indulge in things he should not.

The Zebulonian slumped onto his side and did not wake for several hours while his liver neutralized the toxins.

When the Master's Wings Calls

A few kilometers from Kartak, mid-way up the Furan Peaks, the Serpent descended from the sky, a sky lit by the dark red light of the descending Red Sun and the remaining rays of its blue twin, which already kissed the horizon. And it came down describing wide, sweeping spirals as if to study the Human who waited on the ground.

There was a woman of the sort he liked: a predator, like him, though he wondered whether he might not enjoy the taste of her more. But this one was not for the Alis Domini to devour.

The Serpent's landing caused a nauseating whirl of scents to rise from the decaying matter that accumulated on this terrain in the fall. Indeed, the myriad creatures that came to mate here in nonus[8], died here to give rise to an explosion of decomposers—both vegetal and animal. These died in their turn and were themselves decomposed by the omnipresent microbes of K'Tara to eventually return as rich organic matter to the plains at the foot of mountains, taken there by the Great Torrent River to give rise to new life at the start of spring. But this coming spring—thought the Serpent—it was not life which would awaken, but death.

Once he settled on his haunches, the Serpent said, "Adveni.[9]"

The ruddy, muscular woman replied with a forced smile, "Quid cupis, Alis Domini?[10]"

The Serpent responded with the self-important voice that vexed the Leate. "There are two Luxori in the kingdom who must be brought before the Umbra. You will find them."

The woman frowned. "Luxori?"

"Alterintrant males."

"I know what the term means, Alis Domini. But I was not aware there still existed any—aside from a boy who's a member of the *Sisterhood*, no less."

The Serpent seemed to be caught off guard by the Leate's statement. His eyes became slits as he considered the information. Having come to a conclusion, he shook his head and said, "That boy, whomever he is, is of no concern to us. Our Master knows there exist two others who could pose a threat to our plans. That is why you must find them."

---

[8] Nonus: The ninth month of the Alvinorian calendar.
[9] I have arrived.
[10] What do you desire, Alis Domini?

The woman nodded to herself and said, "Do you have their description?"

"No one knows who they are. But one of them is in the north. He may, in fact, be the subject of your second mission."

The Kartaki straightened, curious to hear the Serpent's suspicions and what this second mission was about.

"I felt what I believed to be the vibrations of a Luxor surrounding the high king when I attacked the Alvinorian capital, this summer. As it happens, our Master wishes the man to be removed—unless he is one of the Luxori, in which case, you will bring him to me, alive."

The woman blinked, snorted, and blinked again.

Noctiferus's Wings said, "You should not be surprised, Leate. Our Master finds the king's lack of faith dangerous; it puts at risk the coming of the Day of Union."

The Leate said, "Yes, I suppose it does. Especially if he is an Alterintrant male, though no one has ever observed him using the Bind in any way. Still, I will need to send the best, just in case. I think I have just the crew for this mission." After a short pause, she continued, "Getting into the palace will be very difficult."

"Hopefully, Lusk Methrim has been able to turn a few guardians to ease your entrance. But if not, I expect your assassins to get in and accomplish their task notwithstanding the complications."

The Leate, or Leader of the Assassins and Temptatori, indicated her understanding with a firm nod.

The Serpent continued. "Make certain that your people are absolutely loyal, in case one or more of them should be captured."

The Leate responded with steadfast confidence that if any one of her people were captured, they would immediately remove themselves.

"As for the other Alterintrant male, he is rarely visible in the Bind. However, when he does appear, his vibrations seem to indicate he is somewhere in the south, near the Shadow Woods.

81

Make use of whatever contacts you have, but you must find him too."

The woman did not reply immediately. Her eyes moved left-to-right as she thought of the Serpent's request. Finally, she said, "The south is a large area. But if this Alterintrant is hidden in a shielded zone, then perhaps I have a way to find him."

The Serpent cocked his leathery brow with curiosity.

"I have recently turned a dissatisfied Kynarian priestess who now lives among us; she can read the minds of...beasts."

The Leate's hesitation on the word 'beast' incensed the Serpent. But, given that he did not wish to project any insecurity—there *was* no such sentiment in him—he did not remark on her pitch and simply shouted, "And how is this important?"

"If the shield that hides this Alterintrant is what I think it is, it will hide all vibrations in that area, including those emanating from the animals living there. The Kynarian can scan the south to look for 'dead zones.'"

The Serpent's expression, as much as it could change, went from one of irritation to one of embarrassed surprise and back to its usual, haughty appearance.

"I see why you were chosen for this role, Leate. Deliver, and you will know our Master's gratitude."

The woman indicated her understanding with a half bow, which pleased the Serpent who responded with a satisfied rumble.

The Serpent continued, "Onto another topic, then. How are your ranks growing?"

"At a steady pace, though not as fast as what our Master may expect. I suppose the placid life we've had under our *oh so great* Octavius has sapped our people of their ambitions. But the dozen women we turned a few fourths ago are on their way to becoming decent Temptatorae. In fact, I have just sent them out to begin working a few choice targets."

"*Decent* Temptatorae...It is a pity your male counterparts have become so rare."

The Temptatorae's leader's face darkened suddenly. Why would this *serpent* insult her kind this way? She hissed her response. "You should know that a good Temptatora can more easily turn another person than a man can. And in fact, a woman can turn a man—and sometimes another woman too—without even *being* a Temptatora."

The Alis Domini replied with a dismissive whip of his tail, "Yes, I know about Human females. But we digress. I need you to increase their training as well as increase your recruiting efforts. You should know, also, that Master Methrim is otherwise engaged and will not be able to help you here."

The Leate snorted and raised her shoulders scornfully. "Why did I ever think he might be of any help? He has been trapped in either Urbs Lucis or Furan City ever since this summer." Then, looking at the Serpent, she added, "When I find these two Luxori, perhaps I can turn *them* to our cause; make Temptatori of them, and if not, at least convert them."

"Perhaps, but I believe our Master has other projects for them."

The woman nodded.

Raising her head to look at the descending suns, the woman now asked, "Didn't you tell me those *things* are supposed to join us at some point?"

"I am calling them now, as a matter of fact."

And as if by magic, from between the trees, there appeared one very large creature and seven smaller ones, walking and watching with nervous motions, as if afraid of what might lurk in the clearing.

The Serpent pulled back his nostrils in disgust. The assassin asked why there were so many of them, to which the Alis Domini replied that it was because the creatures did not know that he could kill them with just his thoughts no matter the number.

Presently, the Serpent grunted toward the approaching gnarlers and waited for their greeting. The leader—one of the most corpulent gnarlers he had ever seen—made a strange crouching bow toward the Serpent, while it gave the Human a hateful glare.

Without looking at her, the Serpent told the Leate that he was going to switch to thoughtspeech to communicate with them, and that he would speak aloud anything of importance to her. The woman responded with a complaint because though she was an Alterintrant, thoughtspeech was not one of her skills. But she had no choice; the Alis Domini always did as it wished—except when the Umbra got involved.

The Serpent refocused on the blubbery creature in front of him and sent the image of a company of Humans resisting and then attacking the gnarlers.

The gnarler's leader replied with a hissing grunt, followed by another hateful scowl shot at the Human. The Leate looked at the Serpent, hoping for an explanation, but none came.

"Our Master this one serves. The Leate she is."

The gnarlers turned weighing gazes at the Human.

The Serpent continued, *"But, with a thousand hammers, the others you must begin to strike. In their settlements you must strike them."*

Crushing Boulder, the leader, sent his reply with the image of a thousand Indwellers amassing to strike at the Humans, *"My people I will muster. For the desecration of my kind they will pay, and their bodies we will leave to rot."*

The Serpent sent a nod followed by the image of himself watching them crush the high king's people.

Crushing Boulder noted his understanding with a yelp.

"Yours, the woods will be when this land you have emptied. But the settlements, to the Leate and her people you must leave."

The plump and muscular gnarler gave an assenting nod. He then turned his fat head to gaze at the assassin with pondering, red eyes. Switching to verbal communication, he said with almost comical difficulty, "Why...neeed they live? Aall...Afterkinds they are. To us, K'Tara belongs."

The Leate's hand moved to her dagger as she yelled, "What?! What is this beast saying?"

The Serpent raised his head on his long neck with such a swift, startling motion, that the Human and the gnarlers stood down at once.

"There is no need to challenge each other. We all serve the same master and his will I have told you."

Turning to Crushing Boulder, the Serpent said, "The Kartaki, alone they *must* be left. In this disobey me, and upon you all the rokons of the north will descend."

All seven gnarlers responded with yelps and pulled back in a sign of submission. The leader clicked his tongue, confirmed his understanding of the Master's wishes, and left as he had come, followed by his awkward retinue.

After the gnarlers had been swallowed by the woods, the Serpent pivoted toward the Leate and said, "I recommend you tell your people to stay away from them."

And with that, the Master's Wings stretched his toothed neck forward and launched himself into air, causing a whirl of sickening scents to rise from the ground.

When all were gone, the Leate swallowed hard and wondered about the Serpent's deal with the gnarlers. He had told her in no uncertain terms that she and her people would still have a place in the new world that was to come.

Hopefully, he is telling the truth because I will find a way to have his hide if not.

With that, the woman turned around and returned to her small villa on the northern edge of Kartak to begin making plans for the hunt and the assassination.

Blooming

Tania Lux Baiula tested Aithen two days after the king had agreed to have his sons learn to use the Bind and found that he did have the atomic constitution of a strong Sensor. His microbial flora, on the other hand, was quite weak. That had upset the prince who asked if anything could be done to enhance it. Tania had explained to him that there was indeed a way; that he could become a superb Sensor if he underwent some *treatments* to modify his microbial assemblage.

The prince had asked what the treatments involved, and the Lux Baiula hesitated in replying. When he insisted, she replied that transfection was not the issue, but that the secondary effects could be—unwelcome. She explained to the prince that the mixture of colonies of a strong Sensor gave the skin a certain texture and odor, which could be perceived as offensive by those unused to it.

Aithen had replied, "But I have never smelled anything unpleasant on…any of you. And as for the texture of the skin—who would touch me anyway? No one can—"

Strangely embarrassed for a Lux Baiula, Tania had added in her comical Yerlayan accent, "Excepte for a woman you mighte court, my Prince. And the commoners and even your soldiers, they do atte times speak disparagingly of us when out of earshotte—and sometimes even within earshotte."

Aithen had not said anything for a while. He wasn't certain he should reveal to Tania what his matrimonial plans were. Though, in all truth, his plans were of no consequence given that the Selection Council might refuse his request to marry Elyana. And then what? If he were forced to marry an Unsensing woman and she couldn't bear to touch him, what would he do then? An involuntary growl had escaped the prince. But he explained to Tania that he didn't give a damn about what ignorants might think, and that if all it took to enhance his Sensing abilities was to change his microbial flora, then he would undergo the procedure.

Tania had agreed and finally explained that there was, however, nothing the Sisterhood could do about his Binding skills, which would remain weak even with the best of training because he simply did not have the proper constitution for that. That had seriously disappointed the prince, for what good would even *superb* Sensing skills be to him, who needed to battle enemies? But after Tania had explained all the things he could learn to do even with just his Sensing skills, he had grunted a small smile and asked that Tania schedule the transfection procedure and begin his training.

So, Tania had done just that. She had performed the first of nine treatments the day before and had chosen this day to start the prince's education in the Sensing arts.

Presently, Aithen was listening to Tania describe to him an exercise where he would need to enter a trance and open his mind to external flows. Aithen had stopped opening his mind in this way a few years back, following a night during which—after coming back to his chambers drunk, somehow deciding to meditate a bit to relieve his nausea and headache, and then falling into a light slumber—he had felt demons walking and jumping on his body, pushing, and tugging at his blanket all the rest of the night. That had scared him more than anything he had ever experience before, and he had decided then and there never to open his mind to external influences again.

When he hesitated to do as instructed and was forced to explain to the medic why he was refusing to proceed with the exercise, she said, "Such things do happen when one has an altered mental state. That is why we prohibit the consumption of alcohol. You shouldde probably refrain from drinking from now on—unless you do so in moderation, of course."

Aithen wondered if Tania meant that some malevolent person or demon had indeed attacked him or whether she meant that he had imagined the entire experience. He asked her as much.

Tania did not answer him. Nevertheless, she assured him that so long as he was in control of both his body and his mind, the dangers he might face in the Bind would be no worse—in terms of terminal consequence—than those he faced in the physical world. And just as he had learned to protect himself from physical harms, he could learn to protect himself from the dangers of the Bind.

When Aithen motioned his agreement, Tania said, "All right, then. Elyana has already taught you how to enter the Bind through meditation, but that process is slow and not useful when you suddenly find yourself in a dangerous situation. So, for this exercise, I want you to practice entering it at will."

After a series of silent questions and recalls and answers and confirmations that flashed through his mind, Aithen nodded confidently. Tania pinched her brows inquisitively.

Aithen explained, "I have observed Elyana entering the Bind in situations where she is fully awake. Each time, she brings her thumb and index together, as if to scratch her thumb. So, it must be some sort of association mechanism."

Tania replied, "Indeed. You are very perceptive, my Prince. Here is what I want you to do, then. I want you to pick a gesture you will not mind using in public when others might be watching you; something not so obvious that it would tell Alterintrants what you are doing. Once you have it, start practicing entering the Bind while making that gesture, counting down from ten, and repeating the sequence, each time reducing the count down by one. When you reach the last sequence, you should enter the Bind simply using the gesture."

Aithen dipped his head resolutely and proceeded with the exercise. He entered and left the Bind, again and again, each time grabbing his right thumb with his index and middle fingers, and each time, he was able to enter the Bind at the end of the countdown. But the process was starting to wear on the prince. By the time he completed his thirteenth attempt, he decided to try and enter the Bind without counting down anymore.

Tania's face scrunched up, but she let him be—and he failed. The prince tightened his jaw and resumed the countdown at six. And although he felt he might be able to enter a trance without counting down anymore after completing the count down from 'three', he decided to finish the entire sequence. When he counted down from two, he successfully entered the Bind, exited it, and reentered it a moment later without any more counting. A large smile painted his face when he came out of trance the last time.

"You are a quick learner, my Prince. But it does not surprise me; I have known you for a long time, and I know you are a skilled learner—as is your brother, Toras. One thing makes me curious, though." When the prince nodded for her to ask her question, she said, "I see you grab your thumb as people might do when nervous. Is that why you do it?"

The prince replied with a proud frown. "I think it might be a good way to confuse potential adversaries—if they think I am nervous."

Tania showed her surprise with a soft snort.

The White Sash continued, "Well, let's move on. Given your atomic constitution and your microbial flora, one of the best skills you could learn to effectively protect yourself against assassins or against enemies in the dark is Corae Sentiens."

"Presence Sensing…to sense people approaching. Isn't that simply the result of having a highly sensitive hearing? My cousin Aria has that ability, and it is quite annoying—to her as well as to others."

"I suppose you could call that 'Presence Sensing,' but what I am talking about involves your microbial flora. Your meditative abilities should allow you to feel the minute impulses generated by your microbes in response to another person's flora. A strong Sensor can feel a person several meters away."

The prince pulled his head back in surprise.

"If you are willing, my Prince, that is what I will teach you to do."

Aithen nodded but wished to understand how the ability worked. Tania—knowing the prince—gave him a detailed biological and physical explanation for the power. This done, Aithen indicated his readiness with a thankful expression, and Tania proceeded with the lesson.

They spent half a day practicing Corae Sentiens. At the end of it, Aithen was mentally exhausted, but he was hopeful and excited for the first time in a long time. Aithen had therefore accepted the rigors of the lessons, and these had continued for several more days.

The prince progressed rapidly—faster than most women, in fact—though he was only learning a laughingly small portion of what a Sister learned, and he only truly stumbled when Dana Lux Baiula began teaching him the principles of some offensive skills; it surprised, frustrated, and embarrassed the prince that—although he was an athletic man and a soldier—he was having such difficulty learning Bound offensive skills.

***

In Horn's Pass, Toras was being trained by Laiella and Na'Riina Lux Baiulae. The latter had just arrived from Urbs Lucis.

Na'Riina was not a pleasant woman, nor a comely one. In fact, she was quite unattractive and looked more like a man than a woman with her square face and short hair. Still, she knew combat and was almost as fearless as the prince was, and he had come to respect her despite his earlier reservations.

Laiella had questioned the decision to train the prince, what with his fiery temperament. But he had accepted her advice—when she had insisted, to prevent him from making an unforgivable mistake—which meant that she had not yet had to take the ultimate measures against him. And in truth, the Prima hoped she would not ever have to, because even though she would have the resolve to do it, she knew a good portion of his men would never forgive her for it.

Aside from the fact that he had resigned himself to her 'advisory' role, there was something else which, in the end, had made the prima consent to training him: the memory of the physical effect his shouts had had in the caves, when fighting the gnarlers. It appeared the prince was developing Binding powers unbeknownst to him; the Sisterhood therefore had no choice *but* to train him. Laiella had told the Manu Dextra as much, who had informed the Magna Mater and then sent Na'Riina.

Toras was now shouting curses at everything and nothing in particular, shouting and cursing because he was unable to enter the Bind, which required him to enter a meditative state.

Na'Riina glanced at her Sister with an expression that spoke of her opinion of the prince's lack of self-control. Laiella shrugged, and the block-faced woman tried to ignore the young man's rants while she racked her brain for a solution. After a couple of minutes of head-scratching and frustrated huffs, Na'Riina remembered something: Kelysia had recently discovered that intuition could be used to learn things transmitted through the Bind. She snorted happily while she hypothesized that intuition, coupled with Sensing, could perhaps be used to develop Binding skills. She explained her idea to the young Lord Commander and his prima.

Laiella was not convinced, but she connected with Toras, which had been a complicated affair in-and-of-itself, and then began calling various Bindings, hoping that if the prince could feel them, he might learn to replicate them.

And the prince was, in fact, able to sense most of his prima's Bindings. However, he was having difficulty repeating many of the vitactic[11] powers. His frustrated remark, when he finally succeeded in causing a *worm* to twitch, surprised Na'Riina. Again, Laiella just shrugged and gestured with her hands to tell her that the prince had *very high* standards for himself.

On the other hand, he seemed to be exceptionally skilled with sonactic[12] Bindings. Indeed, the prince seemed capable of mimicking almost any sound he heard and of modulating them rather precisely, too. The prince was definitely enjoying the sonactic exercises, and he progressed quickly, until he was able to push a sizeable stone off a table. When that happened, he was ecstatic, almost childlike in his exuberance.

Na'Riina expression showed her surprise—and pleasure—at finding her hypothesis was correct about using someone's Sensing abilities to learn various Bindings. She said, "That was most impressive, Lord Commander."

---

[11] Vitactic powers required the use of microbes to carry out an effect; they were also enabled by one's microbial flora.

[12] Sonactic powers involved the use of sound projection to act on objects.

Toras looked toward Laiella who gave a simple, acknowledging nod, her lips barely stretched—her usual response when she was pleased with anything. But the woman was not surprised. The prince did have an uncanny ability to mimic sounds, which he often used to make his men laugh when they were tense.

The dark-haired Red Sash continued, "Now, let us do it again."

But Toras asked a question. "Lux Baiula, how is it that I can't mimic Laiella's other Bindings, like the…how did you call them…the vitactic ones?"

"The fact that you cannot mimic vitactic Bindings is nothing unexpected; we all have different talents. But your natural sensing abilities, combined with your vocal skills, do allow you to mimic sonactic Bindings quite easily. I heard you learned the martial arts in the same manner."

"Yeah, it is. I only needed to look at my father's guardians to know how to make the motions as expertly as them—better even."

The boasting was annoying, but the woman did not look at her Sister this time; she knew by now that Laiella would simply shrug her shoulders again.

"Well, whether you are learning through osmosis or not, chatting is not going to teach you anything. So, let's continue."

Toras frowned indignantly, then straightened himself and said he was ready.

The prince and the Lux Baiula practiced this way for another hour. Laiella showed him how to generate sounds that turned into powerful punches when projected with the Bind. Toras easily learned to replicate these other Bindings. By the end of the hour, he succeeded in toppling over a table, impressing the Lux Baiulae, but also giving them a new worry, which they kept to themselves.

With a tired sigh, Na'Riina said, "Very well, you will continue to do this with First Barrier Laiella until you master the skill, Lord Commander. When you are ready, we will teach you to control your muscles for maximum defensive and offensive effect."

Instead of responding with the expression of agreement or understanding the Lux Baiula had expected from him, Toras exclaimed, "I can't believe Father never allowed me to learn this before. I could have been so much farther ahead and been able to easily k—"

When a clear frown of disapproval twisted the women's lips, Toras checked himself and said, "I know. I know. The reason to learn martial arts is not so we may kill, but so we may defend ourselves and others."

Laiella nodded her simple nod, but she was clearly relieved.

Na'Riina added, "And killing should only happen by lack of alternative. It is also important to remember, my Prince, that the defensive Bindings, which you will learn next, do not protect against all projectiles. They especially do not help if one is caught unaware. To the contrary of what many believe, our powers do not make us impervious to injury or death. But they can help prevent injurious actions from being carried out against us in the first place. The longest-lived among us are those who are always alert and, when once alerted to a threat, respond with only as much force as necessary—if necessary."

Na'Riina waited for the prince's acknowledgement, but when she saw his eyes shift and his lips turn down as if considering the truth of what she said, she asked, "You disagree?"

"I understand the limits of your powers, as you describe them, but I know for a fact that it's impossible to be on constant alert and live long; a body needs rest once in a while."

The Lux Baiulae regarded each other with surprise. Na'Riina said, "Well, I exaggerated, of course. But I suppose you know what I meant."

The prince did not reply and instead stared at the Lux Baiula, expressionless. Na'Riina launched her fist forward.

In Kynaria

A rotund but frustrated voice screamed, frightening the school gardens' treeflyers, "*Aghrr*! This is so confusing. I have no idea where these lincots are going. I really don't understand why each priestess can't just follow and lead one lincot at a time."

"I know, Carasina. But how else would you manage a situation where we need many more creatures than there are priests or priestesses?"

"I would just link to the leader, and guide that one."

Aria replied, "That might work to charge an enemy, when all the lincots are following the leader, but it would not work to scout, or defend when the lincots must spread out."

"I suppose you're right."

"I am. If you're going to use visual signals, you need to learn to shift more quickly between each creature, so you don't miss too much. But what I do, is I learn the magnetic layout of a place, so even if I'm not following a particular animal, I can know fairly well where it is when I do open my senses to it again."

"You can do that?!"

"Yes, and I think I can even use this technique to follow *any* animal."

"What do you mean—any animal?"

"I mean that somehow, the magnetic vibrations combine with an animal's own vibrations to create something very specific and actually very easy to recognize and follow. This happens even if it's an animal I've never linked to before, or if it's one of a hundred other similar creatures in an area."

Carasina's eyes went wide, followed by her eyebrows.

"I've been practicing in Priest Yuri' geology class for two months now, and I think I've got it pinned."

Carasina said, "I thought we weren't allowed to try to expand our skills beyond what has already been studied and approved."

Aria replied indignantly, "How can they prevent me from following my senses where they take me? How are we expected to just tell ourselves 'No, I won't sense that'?"

"Well, there are reasons, Aria. Some can harm us physically, while others can harm us mentally. To do something without being guided, without being taught its properties, its benefits and risks is dangerous."

Aria shrugged dismissively.

"So, do you mean you would open yourself to any vibration, even illicit ones, just because you can feel them?"

Aria gave an exasperated sigh, "Cari, you're exaggerating now. You know I wouldn't. Anyway, do you want my help with the lincots or not?"

"No. I'll just ask Magistera Annan for some private lessons. I don't mind getting into trouble with you for silly things, but not for this, and not now that we are on track for Passage."

"Fine."

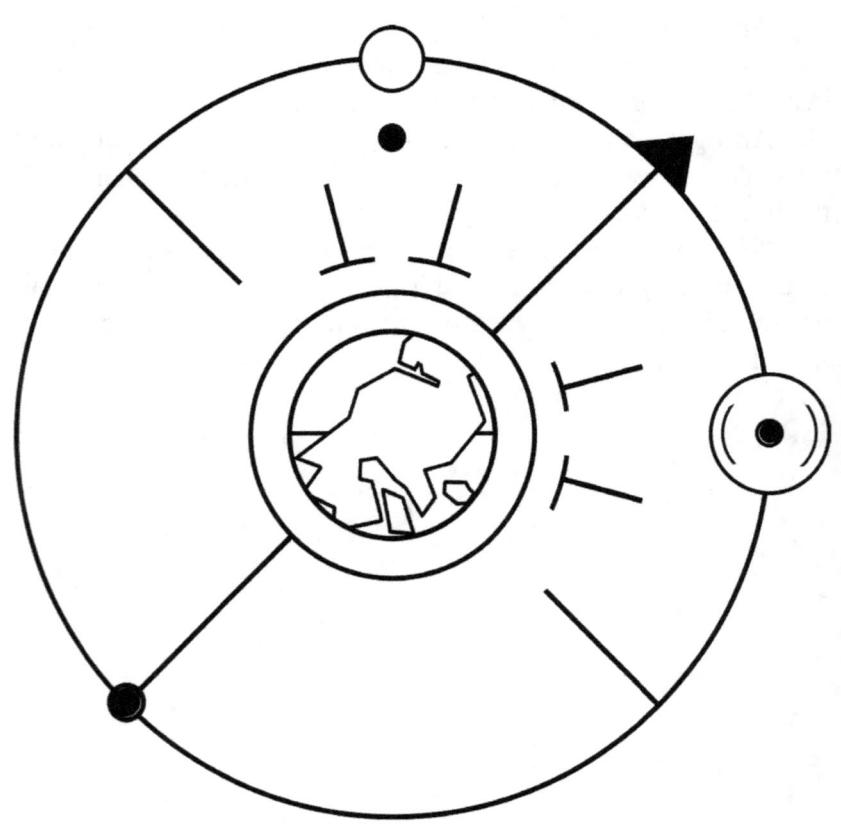

VI DEEDS

From the window of the bedroom in an imagined house, the house where he had spent the first six years of his life being raised by Oolviana, Lusk watched the spaceless void beyond as he tried to forget what he had done earlier that day. But the void was suddenly replaced by a dark, endless precipice staring at him. It moved toward the window, ever expanding until it blackened the space inside the room as the memory of his deeds flared up. He clenched his teeth and fists to the point of chipping the former and blanching the latter.

That morning, Lusk had finally lulled Ooldrina into trusting him completely, despite her earlier resistance. He had taken her, not to turn her to Noctiferus's service, but only to take revenge on her for what Zebulonian powered women had done to him and for then being forced to help—help!—two of their offspring.

Every moment spent in the Bind with Ooldrina had been torture because to help her get over her fears of the ethereal space, he had had to share his mind with her.

But now, though she had learned the things Clara had asked him to teach her—opening herself to the vibrations in the Bind and shielding herself only when necessary—she had also learned a much greater fear: the fear of Lusk Methrim; one who would no longer be the slave of any Janara. And yet, his exultation had been bitter-sweet because his actions had cost him *oh so much.*

Lusk could not stop retching as he remembered Ooldrina's screams and horror when he had defiled her mind—and through her mind, her body, which did not make a difference between physical reality and the imaginary. He could not stop gagging nor remembering.

Memories of her imploring cries kept flashing in his mind, while his conscious-self tried to submerge them—drown them all. But his best attempts were no better than the laughable resistance a child might put to blocking the shouts of an angry parent. Not knowing what else to do, Lusk conjured the darkest void to sink himself into and separated himself from all emotions.

It was not long before his efforts failed again and the memories of his actions resurfaced, bringing with them a pain that became ever greater and more intolerable with each new episode.

Every so often, the irrational—or perhaps the rational—part of him became alarmed and asked whether a Lux Baiula might discover what he had done to Ooldrina. Hopefully not. At least, Ooldrina would not tell; she was in his power, completely. And while the knowledge of what he had done would continue to torment her, he had seen to it that the trauma wouldn't cause her to waste away.

Vomit reached into Lusk's mouth again as he remembered the sense of utter and complete separation from reality plastered in Ooldrina's eyes after he was done with her and walked away, leaving her alone in the middle of the collapsing structure he had imagined. Her face had been blank, blank except for the soundless tears that flowed down her pale skin. Ooldrina had been taught by her mother to trust and respect males, but Lusk had made a liar of the one and destroyed all trust in the others.

He tried once more to reach for the soothing blackness of the void, but a precipice appeared instead. His form shook, and then all was gone. His mind found respite in dreamless torpor.

PERMANERÉ USQUE AD FINEM

The arrival of patricians from near and far, of high-ranking officials from Urbs Lucis and Kynaria, and finally of the royal family and the high king's court—most arriving on voranback and a few atop magnificent furans—had provided Antar's populace with quite a spectacle that morning of the Fifth Day of the second In-Between Fourth of the month of Decimus of the Imperial Year Eighteen Hundred.

When Gaius and Octavius had initially planned to hold the Royal Ball in Praeghe, their advisors had thought them crazy, what with the unrest in the kingdom, and the Serpent and the gnarlers bringing chaos to all corners of the kingdom. Holding a ball in Praeghe would have been either a sign of utter foolishness or of arrogance. But the former had not been seen in a month, and the latter had remained close to the foot of the northern mountain ranges. So, after carefully considering the pros and the cons of holding a ball at all, the king had decided that the need for it was greater than the current danger, requesting only that the reception be held at his summer palace, which stood on his lands just outside of Antar, away from any source of danger.

Gaius had agreed, invitations had been sent, and preparations had been made for what would be the most talked-about Royal Ball in a decade, not only because of Lord Gaius's involvement but also because of the circumstances under which it was being held.

Prime guests of this to-be-remembered ball included the members of the king's court, the First Senator, the Magna Mater, the Praefecta consuasores and the Manu Dextra; Lords and Ladies from across the kingdom, the representatives of the kingdoms of Jarah and Pargah, and finally Juur no'Duur, the king of Yerlah himself.

As was Gaius's habit, a section of the grounds had also been prepared to allow commoners and lower patricians to enjoy themselves at the ball. These had received and accepted the invitation either with excitement or with timidity. Indeed, although they were used to having the king nearby when he came for his yearly retreats, they had not been invited to a ball since Ori's birth.

In the palace's inner courtyard, sitting or standing under the permanent golden canopy which was emblazoned with the family's crest on one side and painted with frescoes of the major events of the kingdom on the other sides, people greeted each other or conversed and enjoyed the food, the gardens, and the music, while waiting for the king and the queen-consort to appear.

The only thing to put a momentary frown on the royal guests' faces was the presence of five Lux Baiulae of the Red Sash—five Barriers, the deadliest of the Sisterhood—standing guard before the doors of the king's palace. Everyone knew that Urbs Lucis had sent Red Sashes to help protect the high king after the Serpent's attack on the capital, but seeing them here, among them, with their stern and deadly looks despite the joyful music, did give people pause and made some properly uncomfortable.

Standing by a fountain in the shape of the two-headed furan of their blazon, High Prince Aithen was speaking with his uncle Claudius about his cousin Aria's progress at Kynaria's School of the Church. The prince wore a bright green coat with a row of buttons on either side of his midline and black suede pants, while the old Claudius had a black tunic and green pants on with a green paludamentum—or cloak—that encircled half his shoulders.

Aithen had started to ask a question when something on the other side of the grounds caught his eye and arrested the words in his mouth. With atypical urgency, he asked, "I am sorry, Uncle. May we continue later?"

Claudius raised a curious eyebrow and looked around before replying, not wishing to be left alone. When he saw his royal brother nearby, he nodded a yes to his nephew and went to see the king.

Aithen left at once, with slightly more hurry than was proper, but he really couldn't help it, now.

As he walked in Elyana's direction, he didn't know whether he wished her to see him approach or not. After a few steps, he decided that she shouldn't see him until he was close, so that he need not be embarrassed by his reaction to a smile the woman might give him while passing people on his way to her.

Aithen had only seen Elyana twice in the past three months since her reassignment to Urbs Lucis to take on the newly created post of Right Hand to the Magna Mater. The last time had been during a formal visit she had made to the capital. He had been aching to spend some time with her and had both fantasized about—as well as dreaded—this moment. Now, here she was, and Aithen was nearly running toward her while at the same time fearing the reunion.

I need *to find a way to get her alone.*

His heart stopped when Elyana, who had just picked some fruit from a bountiful table, lifted her head to look in his direction. And she stretched her lips. *Oh,* no one else except for her colleagues would have known that was a smile, but *he* knew, and it sent his heart skittering as he continued to approach.

Dressed in a black uniform adorned with a pattern of stylized flying furans all over and the insignia of the fortress at Horn's Pass on his right shoulder, Prince Toras was enjoying a glass of sabara wine with High Captain Harlion.

He said to the officer, who was looking in the high prince's direction, "Is something happening between Aithen and Elyana?"

"Ah! You noticed? I do believe your brother is besotted by her and that, were it not for her reassignment to Urbs Lucis, he would have begun courting her months ago…which would not have pleased everyone. But it looks like *someones* will get a chance to be displeased today."

Toras raised his eyebrows curiously then frowned, which Harlion understood to mean that the prince himself was one of those who would be displeased.

Harlion shrugged and continued. "In any case, it is highly unlikely that he will get very far, since Lux Baiulae are basically vowed to celibacy." With a wink, he added, "Though I have known of Sisters who have taken advantage of passing opportunities—if you know what I mean."

"Huh. I didn't know you to have such a crude sense of humor, Captain."

Harlion swirled the wine in his cup, then said, "I hope your brother knows what he is doing because he is likely to have his heart torn to shreds."

"Well, Aithen's not the most emotional person, so I suspect he'll be okay if he gets refused, though he might get broody for a while. But I'm not sure how I would feel if she accepted his advances; I know the ages don't matter because Lux Baiulae age differently, but Elyana is practically family!"

"There's that too," replied Harlion, just as a stirring throat song, with a crescendo that spoke of strength and life and hope, came to life to rouse the royal guests to attention.

The song, and the knowledge of what would follow, stopped all conversations, trivial and important ones alike, and people moved as promptly as they could to their assigned tables without undermining the nobility or self-possession they wished to project.

Aithen, Toras, and the young Ori met at the royal table. Ori smiled at his brothers and waited next to them with a grin that spoke of incredible excitement. Because important events such as this one only occurred every five years, this was only the second he had experienced as a fully sentient person since his accidental birth thirteen years earlier.

The plebeians and lower patricians pressed each other along the low bush wall that surrounded the inner gardens to watch the royal couple's arrival. Members of the Royal Guard, commanded by Primus Julian, the leader of the Praetorian Guard[13], lined the perimeter to ensure no one tried to sneak in.

Once all the noble guests and royal family were at their posts, a Royal Howler standing hip-high in its deep green and red leathery plumage cried its call to invite the high king and queen-consort into the gardens.

High King Octavius and Lady Darya made their entrance with all the regality their subjects had come to expect during the past sixty-seven years. The king walked with a reserved yet proud smile, and the royal consort with an equally reserved though warmer smile on her still beautiful visage. The two walked with interlaced fingers that told each other of the long years spent apart though they continued to long for one another. Octavius also welcomed Darya's gentle calming squeezes, for he had never much enjoyed being the center of attention, except when speaking or when, as a youth, he had competed in the yearly games.

The king and queen-consort embraced their guests with a sweeping gaze as they entered the canopy, but when their eyes fell on their three sons standing side-by-side, their hearts were lifted and a genuine smile brightened their faces.

As they made their way to their table, the couple stopped at each of the First Rank tables to thank the honored guests. Among them were King Juur no'Duur of Yerlah and his spouse who bent forward from the hips; the Magna Mater, Elyana Lux Baiula, and Praefecta Ramela who nodded respectfully; First Senator Leo who tipped his head with more assurance than he felt; the king's brothers, Lords Claudius and Gaius, who clasped hands with the king; the members of his court, including High Captain Harlion, Lord Warbender, Lord Kaffin, Irania Lux Baiula, and Mitsuko Lux Baiula, who gave firm, confident nods; Lady Moradina who gave the royal couple the warmest smile despite the unpleasant memory of the king's last encounter with her; and finally Ylana Dar'Muntake, who looked royal herself, and who welcomed the

---

[13] Praetorian Guard: The high king's personal guard.

king and the queen-consort—her compatriot—with a bow and pressed hands. The king welcomed her too, although seeing Dar'Muntake and Krystiana in the same place reminded him of a grudge he had developed against the two women two months back. Indeed, it seemed to him that somehow, the two had conspired to have a young man assigned to him as a personal attendant, a young man who was related to both of them: to Krystiana through his membership in the Sisterhood—as strange as that was—and to Dar'Muntake through their blood relation.

Oh well, his services are not unwelcome, and he seems loyal regardless of the means by which he got appointed to me. I suppose I should not hold it against them, lest I jeopardize what we have to do here.

Having resolved his internal debate, Octavius finally took himself and his wife to the royal table where the two–and especially Darya–were greeted with warm embraces by their eldest sons, and loud and joyous exclamations by their youngest.

Octavius and Darya moved toward their seats, as did their sons, with Aithen on the king's right, Toras and then Ori on their mother's left. Harlion and Mitsuko Lux Baiula also seated themselves at the royal table, taking the last seats to Aithen's right. Once all were settled, the king made his address.

"My dear guests, thank you all for accepting our invitation to this unexpected ball. I know many questioned its timing. But given that things have been better for a couple of months, and that both Urbs Lucis and my frumentarii have confirmed a decline in the threats, I decided to hold this event so that we might come together to hear each other as well as hear the music that binds us and helps maintain the fraternity among us…a fraternity we cannot do without if we are to overcome what is already here and what is yet to come." And Octavius turned his piercing gaze toward Ylana Maryn Dar'Muntake, Supreme Priestess of the Order of Kynaria and effective leader of the island nation.

Many glanced furtively in her direction, with either awe or unease. Indeed, Kynarians rarely visited Alvinoria and remained an essentially unknown quantity to most people despite the centuries-old blood ties between the two countries.

"You should know also that we have recently decimated a large horde of the creatures that have plagued the towns and villages along the foot of the Colossi's Peaks and Furan Peaks during the past few months. My son, Prince Toras, Lord Commander of the Black Guard, assaulted a horde of a hundred gnarlers at the end of the first fourth, and he, his soldiers, and the Lux Baiulae crushed the creatures with minimal losses."

The audience clapped hands on legs joyously to congratulate the prince.

Toras stood in response but promptly sat back down to let his father finish, though not before acknowledging Aithen's nod which somehow gave him more pride than the applauds of the king's subjects.

Octavius continued. "His company has also brought back one of the creatures and the Sisterhood," the high king recognized Krystiana with a smile, "has put its best minds to studying its biology so as to identify the means to defeat them, as well as to better protect ourselves against them."

"I know that a number of you have seen your holdings and your people suffer from the Serpent's and the gnarlers' attacks. However, the damage would have been much worse were it not for the agreements you reached with my eldest and heir, High Prince Aithen, during the meetings presided by him last Sextus, and for this, I am deeply grateful to him. The success of his meetings with you bodes well for the future of the Crown."

Octavius smiled in Aithen's direction, and the audience— except for Lord Arotek and his neighbors who glared, and for a few in Juur no'Duur's camp who looked annoyed by the thought of having to acknowledge their vassalage—the audience clapped hands on legs once more and with renewed vigor.

Octavius continued, "Just as I feel pride in my sons, you should take pride in your own people, because my armies and Urbs Lucis's forces alone would be unable to protect all your lands without their involvement. So, tonight, we celebrate to remind ourselves that although the worst is yet to come, we have what we need—as a people—to overcome what obstacles we may find in our way. And as further demonstration of my belief in our strength, we will hold the Cross-Alvinorian Race this year, as we always do."

The crowd erupted in cheers and clappings that lasted for quite a while. They might have continued longer if the king had not clapped his hands to speak.

"Dear guests, please sit and let the music and the food reaffirm our bonds."

On cue, the Voces Creatoris began a new chant, this time a Kynarian one, which they would follow with those of other cultures, in sequence. The Kynarian chant was a light, joyous one, evocative of the chirpers endemic to the island. People responded with smiles and lively steps or handshakes as they started milling again or walking toward the royal table to see the king and his consort. The princes and the high captain stood and went to mingle, as was their duty, though Toras did not have a mind for political socializing and Aithen had other thoughts occupying him today.

In preparation for the king's interactions with his guests, Mitsuko Lux Baiula approached and placed herself just behind and to the right of Octavius. One of the first to visit the royal table was Lady Moradina. Octavius received her with a certain sense of anxiety—anxiety dulled somewhat by the soothing music—not knowing whether she was still a friend and an ally, or whether she had become a foe. Urbs Lucis had investigated the landholder's potential turning but had been unable to confirm anything. Her two Lux Baiulae had been probed and found to be devoid of any outside influence, but Lady Moradina continued to behave erratically. Her personal physician, Lorina Lux Baiula, had not identified any medical reason for that behavior. Neither did her advisor, Silla Lux Baiula, find any evidence for the concerning mental responses that Mitsuko had been mentally slapped with earlier in the month. The only finding of possible concern to Silla was what looked like ghost images of intense firing in the same cerebral regions Mitsuko had probed. So, interactions with Moradina must remain guarded—for now.

Moradina Solis bowed before the king—avoiding Mitsuko Lux Baiula's gaze—and said, "My King, my Lady, it is a pleasure to have you back in Antar."

Darya thanked the woman with slightly less warmth than usual. Mitsuko limited herself to studying the woman with her normal senses, in case a probe should trigger an unpleasant reaction. She had agreed with the king that she would cough twice before probing anyone if she suspected anything. If the examination revealed something of concern, she would interrupt the conversation with three additional coughs, no more, no less.

Mitsuko's silence indicated to the king that all seemed safe, and he said, "Lady Moradina, if this were Antar, you would not be its landlady."

"Yes, yes. I know your domain is not within the municipal limits of Antar, Sire. But the same waters bathe both territories, do they not?"

"Of course, Lady Moradina. And they are always the most magnificent and welcoming here." Octavius paused a moment, considering something, then said, "How have things been since you visited the capital?"

Suspicious lines appeared on the lady's brow, but they were quickly replaced by a large smile. Using the king's name—which irritated his wife—she said with a trebling laughter, "Octavius, Antar has been fortunate to not have suffered any attacks by either that flying reptile or those vile creatures from the mountains." In a lower, conspiratorial voice, she added, "But there *are* certain persistent rumors that do worry me."

"Rumors?"

"Indeed. That Zebula has spies in the kingdom...perhaps even—."

Octavius had expected small talk from the woman, but this?! He searched for a proper reply to end the conversation there, but Darya cut the woman off in his stead. She said, "Spies are nothing unusual, Lady Moradina; they are to be expected ahead of a war…in our kitchens as well as in our barracks."

The Lady Moradina closed her lips tight and did not make a reply, though she very much appeared to want to do so.

Turning to his wife first and then to Moradina, Octavius added, "Indeed, my Love. And though they may preoccupy you, Moradina, it is best to leave such topics for more appropriate venues. On the other hand, …"

Behind the king, Mitsuko covered her mouth to cough—twice.

The king stiffened but chose to ignore the warning and finished what he had been about to say, "…it *would* please me if you came back later to tell me how the refection of Antar's library is proceeding, Lady Moradina; that is a topic which is not only more appropriate for an occasion such as this, but also dear to me."

Lady Moradina pulled herself straighter, understanding her dismissal, and said, "Yes, of course, my King."

Then, turning to Darya, she added in a tone too sweet to feel real, "My Lady, I hope you enjoy the ferments I had my cook bring in. They are among the finest in the kingdom, as you know."

Darya responded as pleasantly as she could. "Indeed, I am well aware of their reputation, and I am certain we will enjoy them."

Octavius thanked Lady Moradina, and the woman left. He then tipped his head slightly backward and whispered, "Mitsuko! You coughed!"

"I did, Sire. I sensed the conflict in you as you prepared to invite the Lady Moradina back."

"So, am I not to debate questions with myself, or weigh decisions any longer before I make them?"

Darya preempted the Lux Baiula, saying, "Octavius, I noticed the hesitation too, and Mitsuko Lux Baiula acted only as is her duty."

"I thought she could tell the difference between normal and abnormal reactions. This is going to grate on me regardless of the soothing or joyful music."

Darya spied what looked like guilt or shame underneath the Purple Sash's stolid mask. That surprised and troubled her, and she decided to intervene before matters worsened and the day was ruined. "Octavius, dear. This is not the first time in your long reign that you have had to deal with threats to your life, and each time you had to contend with restrictions to your movements or interactions. You accepted them before, when the threat was lesser, and your protection is as important now—if not more so—as it was back then."

"*Ughrr*, all right. But let us get up and meet our guests at their tables rather than have them all pass by here—I need to move."

And so, Rackeli, the king's majordomo, asked everyone in line to return to their tables. A few were annoyed by the procedure because it indicated that a less formal encounter between them and the king would ensue. Nevertheless, they obeyed and went back to their seats, hoping the majordomo would, at the very least, retain their priorities.

The king, his queen-consort, and his minder stood and visited the tables indicated by Rackeli, and then a few others of their own choosing.

Across the canopy, Aithen—who had not been able to find Elyana—and his cousin watched the crowd while they talked. Ulvius asked, "You're watching your parents?"

"Yes, I haven't seen them together in a while, but it's as if they had never separated."

The neatly-dressed Ulvius, son of Lord Gaius and the foremost mining lord of Alvinoria, said, "Or perhaps it's as if they *had* separated and longed to be back together…being with someone every day is often worse than being without them for a while."

"Perhaps. But I do not think I could stand the distance, myself."

With a downcast voice contrasting with his appearance, Ulvius replied, "Well, I know one thing time definitely doesn't fix."

"You are thinking about your brother?"

Ulvius nodded. "Yes. It's still hard to adjust to it, even after three months—especially for Father."

Aithen gave his cousin a sympathetic smile. "Loris was a good person; we all miss him."

Not a military man or one who supported the idea of constant military readiness, Ulvius responded with a sourly, "How many more are we going to have to miss, cousin?"

"I don't know…a large number. But Ulvius, let's not speak of death, please. What do you say we get a drink?"

"Nah, I think I'll go see Aria. She'll be returning to Kynaria soon, so I should take advantage of this time to catch up with our dearest cousin."

"Do you know if she still feels the pain of having lost her fiancée?" Aithen asked.

The prince's cousin signed in the affirmative and said, "She does. But not as much as I would have expected, truthfully. Larad had really loved her, and he was hoping to marry her next year, after her Passage."

"Well, her studies do require all her focus. Perhaps she will mourn later."

Ulvius replied doubtfully then added, "You should speak with her too. Maybe you can drag some tears from her; you know how much she cares for you."

"I'll try to find her later," Aithen replied with a groan.

With that, Ulvius left, promising to let Aria know.

I hope Aria doesn't still have those feelings for me; she's no longer a child or foolish adolescent, after all. And it would really annoy me if she chose to make things awkward between Elyana and me tonight.

112

Thinking of Elyana made him wish to see her just then. As if responding to his wishes, a number of people standing on the ball floor, conversing and drinking, pulled apart and let the purple-sashed woman appear between them, at the other end of the canopy. She was talking with King Juur no'Duur. Aithen felt an urgent need to go to her and take her from the king who seemed to be staring at her with a predator's expression. The sense of urgency was increased by the music which—though it was meant to awaken joyful feelings—was brewing fiery passions in Aithen. Unable to contain his yearning for the woman any longer, the prince decided to go to her and interrupt her conversation with the Yerlayan king.

Elyana's cream-colored dress fit her life a soft, tight glove on a beautiful hand. The deep purple cape surrounding her shoulders, and the same-colored sash around her waist, gave her a most irresistible look despite being a Lux Baiula.

While listening to the Yerlayan king ramble about his land's beauty, Elyana noticed Aithen's approach out of the corner of her eye, and something bolted in her, despite her composed outward appearance.

When Aithen arrived by the two interlocutors, he gave a short nod toward Elyana and immediately turned to Juur no'Duur with a broader smile than he felt like giving. "King no'Duur, it is a pleasure to see you. Our last encounter was a short one, and I hope that before this day is finished, we will have the opportunity to talk about the beauty of your land, which I have not visited in a long time. But I would speak with Elyana Lux Baiula now, if you will."

The king understood that his conversation with the Lux Baiula was at an end, whether he was finished or not. Juur no'Duur gave a crooked smile, then replied, "Of course. You are the Crown Prince, and I but a humble vassal of the high king, your father."

With that, the man gave Elyana a mildly frustrated smile, saluted the prince, and left.

Aithen snorted quietly before the woman's name escaped his throat with a little more warmth than he felt comfortable expressing in public.

The Lux Baiula replied with an intentionally formal tone. "High Prince."

"Wha—I swear if anyone brings me down, it will be you."

"I would not choose to do that, Aithen."

A smile accompanied Aithen's snort this time, and he asked, "Would you walk with me?"

"I would."

Aithen became momentarily tense, wondering whether he should offer her his arm. Would it be appropriate? Would she accept it even if it were?

As it happened, Elyana did not take his arm but came within a hand's distance of him, and the prince started on the path that crossed the gardens. As they neared the first bushes, the pair marveled at flyers singing with the music. They also stopped to watch small and colorful, leathery buzzers whizzing from flower to flower and adding to the wondrous sights of the fragrant vegetation. The prince and his companion walked like this for a while—Aithen preferring to ask questions and then listening to Elyana's responses, which the woman was happy to give. When she spoke, Aithen captured her words with rapt attention, noticing the details of her facial expressions and the gestures she made to mark one point or another.

When Aithen seemed to be done with his questions, Elyana decided to ask a few of her own. But Aithen kept minimizing the importance of his answers.

It is true he has always been somewhat reserved, introverted. I suppose I should not expect him to open up just because of—because of our—

Well! It appears I, too, am having difficulty admitting my interest in this thing between us. Perhaps I should ask less personal questions.

"So, how is the furanry coming along? I heard that you might have just completed the training of the last fifty furanteams?"

Aithen replied to this question with much more pleasure, comfort, and confidence. "As a matter of fact, the last fifty teams have been released for active duty. It has not been easy, though. We did not have enough males to mount three thousand riders, and not enough time to capture more from the Peaks. So, we've been forced to use as steeds those in their female phase too."

Elyana opened her eyes wide. "That is very risky."

"It is, but what else can we do? I just hope the herbs your Yellow Sisters provided will keep them from getting pregnant until the war is over."

"Yes, though if this war lasts as long as the Dark Battle, some are sure to get pregnant."

"Well, then, let us hope this war is short. But it's not just that; the recruits have had very little time to learn to communicate with their furans. Most of them are still at the *pull and kick* stage; it takes months of continuous training to reach the *tap and tug* stage, and years to reach the point where they can communicate through barely perceptible pressures and position changes. This worries me more than our mounts becoming pregnant because if our soldiers have to fight with them when we're in battle, they will surely die."

"Hm, yes. Hopefully, they still have some time to perfect the bond."

"I hope so too. Regardless, I *am* looking forward to the display Harlion has planned for the announcement at the fair next fourth. I get a little overwhelmed, just thinking of it, despite my misgivings about the furanteams' inadequate training. I also wish we were able to show the entire force. But Father wishes to keep it—"

Aithen stopped as if his mind had suddenly gone blank. Elyana turned a worried eye to him and called his name, but he did not respond. She decided to probe him through the Bind, and when she latched onto his vibration, she became aware of some unusual firing in his brain. Just then, Aithen snapped out of his daze.

He looked at Elyana with guilty discomfort. She questioned him with her eyes—intensely so—until he finally said, "I'm sorry, Elyana. There is something I should have—I've wanted to—Ugh, something I should have informed you about a while ago, now. But there was just never a good time for it. And now, here we are, trying to enjoy a stroll and—"

"Aithen! Stop blabbering. What is this thing you should have told me? What just happened?"

Aithen did not hesitate anymore but searched for the right words to ease the impact of his news. "I...I have a...sorry. You know that I enjoy going to the Royal Bay, yes? Well, for the past eleven years, I have been meeting there with the most wondrous of creatures, creatures so wondrous I thought they must not be from K'Tara, but apparently, they are, and *we* are not."

"Huh?"

Elyana stood there stupefied, for the first time in a long time. She didn't know what to think or say. Then a Transferred Memory surfaced and provided a potential answer: *The Locari. They disappeared but were not extinguished.* She wanted to ask how he met them and why he had kept them secret for so long. So long! Instead, she asked, "But what does that have to do with what happened to you just now?"

Aithen looked around uncomfortably before noticing Arotek and his wife coming their way. The couple noticed them as well, and Arotek stopped to consider, as if unsure whether he should let the prince have the privacy he had a right to. Aithen knew the man would end up taking himself and his wife in another direction. Still, he preferred to move into a more secluded area anyway, so he invited Elyana to follow him, and they walked to a bench sitting underneath one of the Bok trees in the villa's gardens. This Bok tree, as many others on the king's properties, had been treated with resonant minerals so as to prevent the transmission of sound. Once there, Aithen gave one final glance toward Arotek, saw he and his wife had taken the path back toward the palace, and motioned Elyana to sit.

"When I met with them in Sextus, their leader told me that they must relearn our language, to help us with what is coming. He said one of them—a Locar in its female form—would connect with me so that we might communicate regularly to help her learn our language. We've been communicating this way almost daily since then."

Elyana's eyes widened from disbelief, but she was too stunned to say anything. Aithen looked down a moment, then continued, "When I froze earlier, it was because of the Locara; she contacted me. Every time she contacts me, I paralyze for a minute. But we're only supposed to meet at pre-arranged times, when I'm on my own." Aithen added apologetically, "I *forgot* to let her know today would not be a good day to connect. Anyway, she won't contact me again. Not today, at least."

Elyana stood from the bench and started pacing from one edge of the tree's umbrella to the other. A myriad thoughts and emotions lit her mind afire. How could Aithen have been communicating—through the Bind, no less—with a Locara for months without anyone noticing? Without him telling her? And how had he maintained secret his meetings with them for over *ten years?!* And how did the Locara communicate with him? The prince wasn't an Alterintrant, even if he had the atomic predisposition. Finally, she stopped herself and faced the prince.

"Aithen, I do not know where to begin! Do you realize that if anyone else learns of this—including the king—they will be just as bewildered, and will fear what secrets that creature may have heard while connected to you, or worse, fear that you've become a traitor?"

Aithen almost shouted his reply. "A traitor?!"

Elyana looked around to check for signs anyone had heard despite the Bok's sound-dampening effect. "Yes, a traitor. For having kept your connection with the creature secret. Has she ever been connected while you had conversations with others, when discussing *Crown* matters?"

Aithen swallowed then took a deep breath as he put his hands up. "She has not been connected with me—Sorry, she has never *remained* connected with me during meetings. But you are right. I need to disclose this fact and disclose it carefully. As I said earlier, I have wanted to inform *you* of it for a while already. Now you know, and I would appreciate your advice regarding the manner in which I should inform everyone else."

After swallowing some more, the prince continued, "I will tell my father tonight; he must know too, and it will be tonight. He will know how to handle things with the nobles if they must be told too."

Elyana said with a sigh, "All right. Now, tell me how this Locara connects with you."

"She placed some type of *beacon* in my mind."

"A beacon?"

"That is the word that seemed to match her thought the best. Ah, yes, they speak by sending thoughts, images—not words. It took me a long time to learn their language, and unless I visit with them frequently, I easily forget the language. In any case, the Locara placed something in my mind, which allows her to communicate with me anytime she wishes."

Elyana's eyes widened in surprise. "No one can *place* anything in another's brain, unless it is done via surgery, although one could, metaphorically, place a thought in someone else's mind."

"Well, regardless of how it is done, she enabled me to receive her thoughtcalls without the need for me to be listening. From what you've told me of the way Lux Baiulae use the Bind to communicate, the Locaran way seems far more advanced."

Elyana snorted several times, and her expressions changed from troubled to concerned to puzzled to curious and finally to excited as she took in the meaning of what the Locari seemed to be capable of. "Aithen, this is all still shocking, and yet I cannot help but be excited about what we could learn from you, from them."

Aithen narrowed his eyes as he wondered what Elyana meant by 'What we could learn from you, from them.' The expression sounded too much like what is said of a test subject in an experiment.

But Elyana's mind was now totally transfixed by the possibilities. She was properly excited as she said, "What you described is something we have been trying to achieve for ages. But I wouldn't call it a beacon; it sounds more like a…monitor."

She bit her lips while her eyes shifted from left to right as her mind continued to race to make sense of the possibilities this *device* opened up for the Sisterhood.

"Aithen, this may constitute the single most important advancement for my Order, *if* it is a skill that can be learned. Would you agree to have Elia or Tania probe your brain, to look for this thing the Locara placed in your mind?"

Aithen's eyes opened wide, and he pulled his head back as he said, "Ugh, no. I do not think so, Elyana. And I think I would need the Locari's permission before letting anyone look at what they put in me."

Elyana brushed her face and said in quick sentences, "Of course. I understand. Well, then you must let me join you on your next encounter with them; so I can meet them and question them directly; ask if I may be allowed to learn this Binding technique."

The importance of the Locari's technique to Elyana and to the Sisterhood was clear to Aithen. He replied cautiously that he would ask the Locara about it the next time they connected. However, he wasn't certain she knew what meeting with the Locari involved. He explained it to Elyana in case she hadn't realized yet where the meetings occurred.

"Underwater?!"

Aithen tipped his head.

After a moment, Elyana nodded to herself. A Transferred Memory originating from Birra Lux Baiula told her that the Locari may indeed be living in the sea, given that they were an amphibious species.

Elyana thanked Aithen and then asked to continue their walk through the gardens to allow her mind to think about other things lest she remain too excited to do anything else or converse with anyone else about anything else the entire night. Aithen was happy to oblige her, and he was surprised when Elyana placed herself within a finger's distance from him, her hand brushing his own, every so often, as they found more mundane things to speak of.

He thought her behavior strange. Surely, she must feel some resentment or diffidence in the face of this secret he had kept from her for so long. But then he remembered who Elyana was: the most rational woman—the most rational person—he knew, aside perhaps from his father. This fact brought back a sad memory, one which still upset many people: the memory of her decision—without any consultation—to refuse the Serpent's demands when it held Juliana Lux Baiula in its claws, causing it to kill the woman. Elyana had done that despite her friendship with Juliana, despite all consequences to herself. She was like that, able to compartmentalize thoughts and emotions at will. Many viewed her as a cold, uncaring woman because of it. Toras was one of them, and he would surely wonder how he could fall for the woman. Still, shouldn't she be somewhat upset with him? Aithen was startled out of his thoughts when Elyana spoke his name.

"Aithen. You were elsewhere for a moment."

Urgently, he replied, "I'm sorry. I was not with—"

"I know. I could tell from the look on your face, the way you then looked away from me, and the motions of your hands, what thoughts were going through your mind."

Aithen looked alarmed and Elyana added, "Being able to read body language is a skill all Purple Sashes must have; how else could we properly advise the people we serve?"

"Yes, I suppose. And you are not upset by…the thoughts you think were going through my mind?"

Elyana replied with a doleful smile. "Aithen, if you knew the storm raging in *my* mind presently, you'd understand how

120

important it is that I be able to lock away anything I chose, whenever I need to do so. And I need to do it now. And as for the thoughts that I know were going through your mind…why would I be upset? I'm the one who said no to the Serpent."

Aithen exhaled loudly, stunned or perhaps more amazed by the woman. After a moment, he said, "Elyana, I need to tell you something I learned the last time I was with the Locari. They said…they said that…there are traitors in Urbs Lucis."

Elyana stopped in her tracks and froze, her face taking on a dreadful appearance. Aithen had never seen her so frightened. He could feel her heart pumping erratically, and her stomach lurching. Forcing words out, she said, "Traitors? *Traitors*? Why did you not tell me right away?! Why—"

"I…I just never found the opportunity; I learned of it the day before the Serpent attacked Furan City. And then you were re-assigned to Urbs Lucis, and each time I thought to tell Irania, the memory of it simply…vanished. I don't know why. I just couldn't keep the threat in my mind—until tonight. When Current connected with me, this time, I was able to keep it my grasp, for some reason, and tell you about it."

Elyana looked struck and disconcerted.

Several minutes—interminable minutes—passed before Elyana said another word. With her chest lifting against the weight of the revelation, her fingers tapping her right leg and a voice that had lost all its earlier excitement, she said, "Did they say who these traitors are?"

Aithen shook his head.

"Anything else that may help us root them out?"

The prince shook his head again, embarrassed by his ignorance.

"Thank you. I do not know what to do with this information, just yet. I need to consider it before I say anything."

"You will not tell Krystiana?"

"No."

"Why not? You must. You cannot keep this secret, Elyana."

"I will tell her tomorrow. But it is even more urgent I be allowed to meet with them, so I may ask them about these traitors. Please ask them if I can come with you the next time you go—hopefully very soon."

Aithen nodded cautiously. "I am sorry, Elyana. Really. I was hoping to enjoy this moment with you, and now I've ruined it all."

"Aithen, if it is as you say and you could not remember it until now, then you had no choice. But I do wish to enjoy this evening too." Elyana paused and turned her head up to look Aithen straight in the eyes. "What I mean is: I wish to enjoy a moment with you. Can you put all this talk of traitors aside and walk with me and converse about...trivial things?"

Aithen felt his mind swirl from the sudden change of tone. *How does she do it, to quarantine unpleasant thoughts so easily?* Aithen surprised himself when he did the same and said, "I believe we still have ten or fifteen minutes before we need to return to the courtyard."

Elyana gave the prince a welcoming smile, and Aithen presented his arm and said, "Would you?"

When Elyana wrapped her arm around his, Aithen struggled to contain the flood of emotions. But he let them flow over and away from him and started to walk.

The two walked this way, actually chatting about the most trivial—but fascinating—things that crossed their minds until Kildare came to call them back to the festivities.

The prince's squire, unsurprisingly, blushed at seeing his master and the Lux Baiula so enlaced. Then he remembered the time Aithen had asked him to let Elyana into his bedchamber while he was getting dressed and grunted before turning and starting toward the courtyard, looking back once in a while to make sure the prince and the Lux Baiula were following.

Toras had spent most of the morning and early afternoon with members of the Royal Guard or with his cousins, sometimes tailed by Ori. Every so often, he also stopped to speak

122

with one or both of his parents given that he did not see them much—if at all—at Horn's Pass. Presently, he was walking back toward Harlion, after visiting with Darya, when he passed by Aithen, who was standing alone by a food table and kept glancing toward a group that included Elyana, their cousins, and Juur no'Duur. He noticed his brother's irritation and agitation and stopped to ask him what was happening. Seeing that Aithen did not wish to answer, he said, "Well, whatever it is that has you in such a state, you look strange standing there by yourself. You should come play with us." Toras pointed his head toward Harlion and a few guardians who were taking turns at a game of Stacking—the only enjoyment they were allowed.

Aithen considered Toras's suggestion for a moment, and finally decided to accept the invitation, hoping that it would help him forget about Elyana for a while. The Stacking game was not a difficult one, but it did require a person's concentration as they aimed an arrow fitted with a leather head at a pile of flat stones stacked from largest to smallest. The goal was to topple the stones one at a time. Each stone was worth one point, and the bottom one—being the heaviest—was worth an additional three.

As it happened, the game did take Aithen's mind off Elyana for an hour. The match had been challenging, but it had also been enjoyable, especially when his cousin Ulvius decided to join. Indeed, Ulvius had apparently decided to stop mourning his brother and kept looking at Aithen with such a large, sincere smile that Aithen was forced to forget his own, silly, irritations.

In a noisy corner of the gardens, Elyana and Irania now walked with Fausta Lux Baiula. The latter had been acting as Lord Arotek's advisor for two months now, and because the king was anxious to know what she had to report on his vassal's activities, Octavius's former and current advisors questioned their Sister under the splashing sounds of the Winged Sprayer. The fountain had been so named because it had in its center a sculpture representing one of the only K'Taran creatures to remain active during the Bolingars, a large reptilian known as the Winged Sprayer. The animals sprayed jets of water onto themselves and their congeners to protect against the deadly suns as they flew in search of those who succumbed to the suns' rays because of their stupidity or misfortune.

Fausta, were it not for the purple-stiped white sash which cinched her robe could have passed for a Yerlayan courtesan. Indeed, her dress was jarringly revealing for a Lux Baiula, which meant that it showed her cleavage, and it was sown with rather immodest fibers, which molded her hips and body more than was appropriate for a Lux Baiula. As for her demeanor, it was as seductive as her dress.

Elyana knew that despite her appearances, which she had adopted during her time as advisor to king Juur no'Duur, Fausta was not a frivolous woman but a sharp, smart and highly intelligent person, in addition to being a first-rate medic and an excellent political advisor.

Watching her, the Manu Dextra thought: *Sometimes, I wouldn't mind dressing like her.*

Replying to Irania's last question with the unctuous tone she had had from even before her time at no'Duur's court, Fausta said, "The man is an idiot, Sister, and he will betray the king if he sees the chance to do so. It is no secret that Arotek never loved Octavius, but his wife's constant maligning of the royal family is surely turning him against the king. In fact, were it not for his wife, in the present situation, he might very well be a supporter, even if only for his own selfish benefit. And the woman cares almost as little for *us*." Elyana and Irania gave Fausta an aggrieved look. Fausta added, "My appearance has nothing to do with it; believe me. Lady Aroteka has her own court, and her attendants are more scandalously dressed than the pleasure workers you find in some lands." Fausta saw their disbelief and added, "Her public attitude is all a façade."

Irania said, "I have never liked those two; now I have even more reason to dislike them. What is your assessment of the risk they represent, Fausta?"

"There is a large contingent of their neighbors who are disgruntled with things in the kingdom and who are pushing Arotek to make a claim for secession of their territory; I am fairly certain his wife is behind it."

Irania shook her head with real concern. Elyana asked, "What we need to know, Fausta, is what you can do to prevent the worse from happening. Do you have a plan? Does Lady Aroteka trust you enough—outwardly at least—to let you do what you must to cripple their efforts?"

With a tone that left no doubt as to the solidity of her plans, Fausta replied, "I do; it is already in motion, in fact. And Lady Aroteka will not be a problem."

Irania's and Elyana's nods showed their gratefulness. And they showed—to one who could read their unreadable faces—that they understood what Fausta had left unsaid.

The women moved to more mundane topics and enjoyed the scents and sights of the Royal Gardens as they made their way back toward the central canopy.

In the middle of the afternoon, everyone watched as Octavius and Darya walked away from the courtyard, followed by the princes, the high captain, the Supreme Priestess, and the Magna Mater and her Manu Dextra. The king and queen-consort took the impromptu council toward a large greenhouse surrounded by Bok trees. Master Rackeli waited there to let them in. Attendants brought in some refreshments and departed promptly, leaving only the majordomo to see to the king's and his guests' comfort for the duration of the conference.

Octavius watched, strolling around the greenhouse, as everyone sat down in the center of the structure, which had a wide patio set with comfortable Green Lacora Leaf chairs—a rarity, as most plants in Alvinoria had red or reddish leaves. Octavius was glad that the Magna Mater had invited Elyana to attend the meeting. But he noticed a furtive glance between Elyana and Irania. The glance was followed by what looked like Irania's anxious smile and Elyana's inaudible sigh—if he

125

interpreted the expansion and contraction of her chest correctly; it seemed Irania felt guilty for holding the office, whereas it appeared that Elyana had not yet made peace with her reassignment, though her position was one of great honor. As Manu Dextra to the Magna Mater, Elyana was now, in fact, the second most powerful woman in Alvinoria—or third, if he counted Darya ahead of Elyana. But his wife spent so little time in the kingdom that her true influence was much diminished. Fortunately, Darya did not appear to mind the fact and was now content to act as a liaison between Kynaria and Alvinoria, as well as to see to their niece's education, which appeared to be a greater challenge than any political objective could present.

When all were seated, Octavius began, "Given that this is the first opportunity we have all had to meet in person since the Serpent's attacks on Horn's Pass and then on the capital itself, a few months ago, it is important that we take some time to discuss the situation, even if only to confirm our alliance and reaffirm our commitment to each other." All acknowledged the king's aims, though some did do so less fervently than others. Octavius continued, "We have confirmed by now that the one behind all this—the Serpent, the gnarlers, the Temptatori, even Zebula's imminent invasion—is Noctiferus himself."

A few of the attendees shifted on their seats, causing the quiet clicking sounds that the Lacora plants made when rearranging their leaves to maintain contact with the sitter. Whether his guests stirred because they believed or because they disagreed with him, or simply because of his use of the name, Octavius did not know, but he could guess.

"None of us fought the first battle against him, five hundred and eighty years ago. But we are fortunate that there are women in the Sisterhood with memories from individuals who *did* face him, and Krystiana is having those women write down the memories so that we may use them to better protect ourselves."

Heads turned toward the Magna Mater, who gave a confirmatory nod. Indeed, she had instructed her Sisters with Transferred Memories of the Dark Battle to begin writing them

126

down, but those memories were not necessarily accessible at will, and the volume of them meant that it would take the women a long time to recall and transcribe them all.

The king continued, "We are also fortunate for the cross-training that has occurred between Kynarian priestesses and Lux Baiulae—though it is limited—because it has brought us our first victory. Indeed, Marena Lux Baiula was able to safely map the caves where a horde of gnarlers was quartered and to then guide my son, his men and the other Lux Baiulae as they moved in to attack and bring back this first victory."

Octavius and Toras exchanged proud smiles just then.

"This would not have been possible without the cross-training Marena received." Octavius tipped his head in Ylana's direction to thank her. But the woman did not respond with the encouraging smile he had expected. *Hmm, there is something brewing in her mind.*

The high captain clapped his hands lightly to request permission to speak. The king motioned for him to ask his question.

Harlion embraced the three leaders with his gaze to ask, "Is it possible for the Kynarians to train more Lux Baiulae in Beast Reading? Or for the two Orders to cross-train *all* their members?"

Ylana, looking dramatic with the yellow of her dress contrasting with the brown of her skin and the orange of her irises, responded, "Unfortunately not, Captain. These skills take time to develop, time which we do not have; it took Marena seven years. And, as unpleasant as it is to say, my people do not have the atomic constitution to use the Bind as Lux Baiulae do. Therefore, cross-training the adepts of our respective orders—as you suggest—is not feasible."

Krystiana nodded to confirm the Supreme Priestess's statement.

Octavius said, "That is why our alliance is most vital to our survival. None of us can face our enemies on their own, but with our combined forces and capabilities, we *can* protect our peoples and lands, and sooner or later, defeat the enemy." Almost as a thought to himself, Octavius added, "At least, the Rokothians have remained quiet all this time, and we can hope that it stays that way." Snorts and swallows followed, but no one said anything, although Toras pinched his face questioningly.

Octavius invited him to speak up.

"What about the lands of Mo'Tarkoth, Beltania, and Unumia? Is there any danger any of them will get involved?"

Octavius blinked, pleasantly surprised. *Sometimes, I underestimate him.* He turned his gaze to Harlion, to give him the opportunity to reply.

"We do not have people in Beltania, Lord Commander; it is too far anyway for us to receive timely news from that remote continent, and the Sisterhood is unable to send its agents there. And though the king's minder was born there, she grew up here and retains no valid connections with the land. But my frumentarii have not reported anything of concern to date, not within Alvinoria nor on the waters surrounding Aquinos. So, it may be that none of them will be implicated in this new war."

Toras said, "So, there's a risk, even if it's small, that another nation might become involved and threaten us."

"Yes, but small, as you say."

Octavius continued, "I believe we do need to find a way to monitor the Beltanians, but the danger we face already is a sufficient menace in and of itself. As I was saying, then," Octavius embraced everyone with a sweep of his eyes, "it is vital that we remain united and fiercely so until this is done and over, despite the unavoidable disagreements which will arise. Only through this continued commitment to each other will anyone of us agree to put their people's lives at risk for another one when the assistance—or sacrifice—is requested."

Heads bobbed, most firmly, one tentatively.

Octavius's lips tightened in displeasure. "Do you disagree, Supreme Priestess?"

The woman did not respond right away. She glanced at Darya intently, paced, and then stopped before turning back to

Octavius. "Our land has not been threatened by anyone or anything, and to directly and publicly engage ourselves in your war would bring the Nethers upon us just as surely as they are upon you now. And we are currently in no position to defend ourselves against such enemies."

Faces took on a rainbow of colors and aspects at hearing the disloyal words. Harlion's face showed disgust, the princes' faces bewilderment, while the Lux Baiulae's faces remained mostly unreadable, but hard, as did Darya's.

The princes and captain shot up and started demanding that the Supreme Priestess explain herself. Octavius stilled them all with his hand. He motioned his sons and captain back to their seats, and when the princes refused, he gave them such a glare that they relented lest he kick them out. Octavius relaxed his own muscles and stilled his emotions—Ylana's statement was a betrayal of their centuries-old covenant, but he resisted the impulse to mention the blood ties between the two nations, and instead decided to appeal to her logic.

He crossed his hands and said, "Ylana, you are aware of the threat made against Kynaria by the Serpent and its accomplice." Ylana nodded reluctantly, knowing where Octavius was going with this. "Therefore, it is only logical to assume that an attack on your land *will* come, even if it has not yet occurred."

Toras tried to suppress a growl at hearing his father's words. Why did it matter if Kynaria was threatened or not? The two nations were solemnly bound to support each other. The mixed bloodline of House Coriolis was strictly maintained with the approval of any royal marriage by a Selection Council composed of both Alvinorian and Kynarian nobles and clerics to ensure the two nations' continued alliance! So, why did it matter who was attacked and who not? Aithen noticed his brother's mounting anger and made a veiled hand gesture to exhort him to patience.

Ylana said, "As you say, Octavius, it has not yet. But we rooted out a spy of theirs last month, which means that the Dark One may now be aware of our weakness, and I conclude from this that he may choose to let us be because of it."

Darya glared at her for her cowardice and for calling the king by his name again, and in *this* venue.

Octavius shook his head in her direction then turned to Ylana, thinking: *I can't understand what is happening here. Ylana is a sensible, rational leader. And yet, where is the logic in her statement? No matter, I must continue to try. But...but this spy...the furanry...I can see Harlion and Aithen are thinking the same thing.*

"Supreme Priestess, was that spy you uncovered aware of the three thousand furanteams training in your land?"

Ylana took a few moments to consult her memory, and when she replied, her voice had a troubling crack in it, "I do not believe so, Octavius. The training camp is in the north desert; no one lives there. And the spy was not a member of the inner circle, which is where we discuss matters of state."

Aithen asked, "Did you question the spy? And who was it? A man, a woman? from where?!"

Octavius gave a warning sign to his son to calm him.

Ylana gave a nervous smiled. "It was one of us, a priestess who had traveled to Alvinoria in Quintus and returned in Nonus. And yes, we questioned her but did not learn anything. She seems to have lost her mind."

Octavius looked at Krystiana as he continued, "Ylana, if she is still alive, I strongly recommend you send her to Urbs Lucis so she may be further questioned there."

The Supreme Priestess laughed. "What? That is not possible Octavius. I would not send her to you, much less to Urbs Lucis with whom we have no accord."

The greenhouse became suddenly very agitated with both indignation and disbelief, and chaos erupted. When Octavius was finally restored some calm, he did not say what he felt like saying: that the woman was opposing their every request. Instead, he said, "Supreme Priestess, you must realize that it is essential we learn what this spy learned and communicated, if she communicated anything." Octavius paused then added, "This is a matter of security."

Many long minutes of tense waiting ensued while Ylana considered the king's request. In the end, she opened her hands and asked Darya to respond in her stead.

The Lady Darya of Laranir stowed away her personal feelings and motives and spoke as Kynaria's Interlocutor was expected to speak. "Sire, as has been the case for centuries now, no one may invade the privacy of our citizens, regardless of the reason. But, if a Lux Baiula travels to Kynaria, she may assist in the questioning of the spy."

Noticing a gesture from Ylana, Darya added, "It would also be preferable that it be Marena Lux Baiula who is already acquainted with our ways and laws."

Octavius closed his eyes to hide his relief after initially listening to his wife with very apparent apprehension, wondering how she was going to split her loyalty. Relieved to have gotten at least this if not what really mattered yet, he thanked Darya, then Ylana, and finally turned to Krystiana.

Without a moment's hesitation, the Magna Mater said, "It cannot be Marena. She is needed to fight the gnarlers. But we will send a Purple Sash back with you."

Octavius groaned.

Ylana said, "A Purple Sash?"

"Purple Sashes are highly skilled in reading people, whether using the Bind or not."

This time, Ylana stood and shouted, "I will *not* allow any Lux Baiula to enter the mind of one of our citizens!"

Seeing her leader's error, Darya intervened, "Supreme Priestess, I do not believe the Magna Mater suggested that a Purple Sash enter the mind of our prisoner." Darya sought Krystiana' confirmation and the woman responded affirmatively.

"Indeed, our Purple Sashes can read a person's motivations and state of mind simply by studying their body language."

There ensued a long silence during which Ylana mended her wounded pride, while others sighed, or shuffled on their seats, or patted dust off their clothes to calm themselves.

Octavius took this opportunity to glance at Harlion and Aithen with silent gestures to let them know that they would discuss their response to protect their training camp in Kynaria later, regardless of the investigation's outcome. The three of them had agreed, two months ago, to establish two secret camps to train the furanteams. One had been set-up in Kynaria and the other on the Unnamed island, off the east coast of Alvinoria. The Coriolan Ten Thousand *would* be re-established, but their existence would remain a secret until the last possible moment.

When Ylana sat herself again and addressed Krystiana, everyone froze. But they welcomed the release—as one welcomed the Red Sun after a long, frigid night—when Ylana told the Magna Mater that she would accept the assistance of a Purple Sash.

Octavius said, "Thank you, Supreme Priestess. I also give you my assurance that no one will violate the rights of your citizens." Ylana blinked to signify her willingness to trust him. Octavius continued with a remarkably calm voice though his statements were not the kind to be said quietly or serenely. "Now—and forgive me for insisting, Supreme Priestess—but your earlier argument about your apparent weakness, it will not protect you, and you well know that someone bent on conquest does not leave any land untouched. You know too that even if Noctiferus does not send his hordes to murder Kynarians, your nation will nevertheless be annexed by Zebula, whom I suspect to be under his influence. Your freedom will be removed, and your way of life will be irremediably transformed unless you resist him and his pawns with us."

Ylana's face turned a dark color again, and Darya clutched her hands together nervously.

"Is that what you wish for your people?"

The tall woman, who did not seem to be able to sit still, stood again and paced a while longer before pausing, her body facing away from the king.

"Ylana."

It seemed the king's plea, or his earlier argument, had an effect because the Supreme Priestess's features softened as she swiveled on her heels and said, "You are probably right—at least about Zebula—Octavius."

The king breathed a sigh of relief. He said, "I *am* right about Zebula. It is only logical, whether or not Noctiferus is behind her."

He noticed Krystiana's stirring at his last suggestion. Of course, he believed Noctiferus was behind it all, but it was unnecessary to push Ylana on this point. He tried to appease the Magna Mater with a thin smile.

Ylana replied sarcastically, "Yes, yes, I know about your love of logic, Octavius. Still, you are *probably* right, and I am not denying our alliance. But Kynaria has been at peace for a long time, and we do not have warriors to mobilize whether it be to defend or attack."

Ylana paused.

Octavius shot a disbelieving glance at his wife; why hadn't she kept him informed of this if it was true?

"Nonetheless, I might be willing to provide some support, in addition to continuing to provide land and food for your training camp—if it remains secret."

Octavius exhaled, relieved that the woman was not turning her back on them, but he was not completely satisfied. Indeed, what the Kynarian leader suggested had its own risks. He was going to say so when his eldest jumped in, drawing an exasperated sigh from his mother.

Aithen said, "Supreme Priestess, we understand your reluctance to openly engage in this war, but if you do not and the Alvinorian plebe and patriciate *believe* that Kynaria refused to lend its support, you will be hated by all. When that happens, suspicion will fall on our House, too, for being *halflings*."

Harlion gave a firm supportive nod and added, "And the religious fanatics of the Church of Aiala will be certain to take advantage of such circumstances."

Ylana obviously resented the reproachful comments and tightened her jaw lest she lash out in front of the high king. She turned searching eyes at Octavius, to gage his thoughts on the matter. She saw him arms crossed, tapping his thumb on his shoulder, his face twitching as if having some internal debate. Unable to wait for his response any longer, she started saying his name when he spoke up.

He was looking straight at her but speaking to the others. "Please give the Supreme Priestess and me a few minutes."

Everyone rose more or less reluctantly. Darya stood to go too and gave her husband an entreating gaze. Only Mitsuko remained seated. She had been quiet since the beginning of the conference, and now, she looked at Octavius with objecting eyes.

"You too, Mitsuko."

When she hesitated, he insisted, and she walked out, following the others, her face a mask of heated stone. One could tell from the tightness of it that she disagreed vehemently.

Aithen sat himself on a lonely bench outside the greenhouse. The others sat or stood a few meters from him, asking Darya why the Supreme Priestess might have taken such a position and whether it was true that Kynaria no longer had any military force of consequence.

He turned to glance at the king and his interlocutor, hoping to catch their body language. He cursed when Rackeli walked to the greenhouse's wall and touched the root of the shading plant. A moment later, the entire side of the greenhouse darkened as pigments moved from the roots and stems to the leaves which covered the surface.

All Aithen could see now was the king pacing, stopping, facing Ylana every so often, and pacing again. But he could not see either leader's face. Octavius did seem to have his arms crossed. *He's probably afraid he'll make a fist or make threatening gestures if he uncrosses his arms.* Presently, Aithen watched the king's majordomo come to call Krystiana. The

Magna Mater excused herself and followed Rackeli back into the greenhouse. Aithen noticed a shadow of questions pass over Elyana's pinched brow. She was probably upset she had not been asked to join, but then, the king and Supreme Priestess were also without their advisors.

Aithen continued to observe what he could. He tried to decipher from the interlocutors' behavior what was going on. But without seeing their expressions, there was little he could tell given that even the king's pacing had stopped.

Just then, a voice startled the high prince. It was Elyana. She had come to sit by him, not too close, but close enough for him to feel her skin's warmth.

She asked, "Are you wondering what they are saying?"

Aithen gave a glum smile. "Yes, and I am also a little irritated for having been dismissed."

"As we all are, especially Mitsuko. She was actually considering entering the Bind to—"

Aithen whispered, "To *spy* on them?!"

"She would not have spied on them. She would just have probed their emotions. But she only mused about it."

"Can you tell what they might be saying?"

"With the shaded wall, it is not so easy."

Elyana narrowed her eyes as if to better see and focused on the three rulers.

Every time her lips twitched, Aithen wanted to ask if she had detected something.

After a couple of minutes, Elyana turned her head slightly in Aithen's direction while keeping her eyes on the greenhouse and said, "I think Ylana has made a demand or suggested something Krystiana is having difficulty accepting."

"How can you tell?"

"She is too rigid. She was moving a little earlier, but not anymore."

Aithen sighed. "Why didn't we know about the Kynarian military situation, if what Ylana said is true? I just don't understand it; after all, well…"

He glanced toward his mother, guiltily.

Elyana understood from his use of the contractions that the situation really troubled him. "I think we have all been complacent these last years. The Sisterhood is still deficient in Red Sashes, the furanry was just rebuilt, and the Kynarian military is apparently much diminished. I know you think your mother should have known about the Kynarian situation, but she does not have a seat on the government of Kynaria; she is only a link between the king and the Supreme Priestess, not—"

"Not between Kynaria and Alvinoria. I have always disagreed with that arrangement. My mother should have full diplomatic authority. But still, she should have known *something!*"

"I would not blame your mother, Aithen. In fact, I am certain she is feeling embarrassingly mortified by all this, and I am sure she would be grateful to anyone who would remove her from the *interrogation,* over there."

Aithen made a guilty frown and nodded. He thanked Elyana, then walked toward the others. From the way his mother moved her laced fingers, he could see that she was indeed extremely uncomfortable. He cleared his throat and interrupted his mother's questioners with a pretense to want to speak with her. From the way she closed her eyes when she looked at him, he could tell she was grateful; grateful to be taken away from the questioning horde among whom was his brother. But Toras had never been one to know how to diffuse an unpleasant situation, and he often made things worse. Aithen wondered for a moment how Toras could be so loved by his men, despite his faults.

With his mother holding his arm and thanking him quietly but fondly, Aithen took them toward Elyana. As they walked, Aithen apologized for getting upset with the Supreme Priestess, and Darya did her best not to admonish him for it. He knew that if she had not been the Interlocutor, she would have supported Octavius directly and frankly. But her hands were truly tied, tied by a role she hated, for more than one reason. And he wondered

136

how the first Supreme Priestess thought the conflict of interest inherent to the Interlocutor's role could be acceptable.

When Aithen and Darya arrived by Elyana, the latter pointed toward the greenhouse with her head and said, "Whatever it is, it is done."

Indeed, the three leaders seemed to have come to some agreement because the king bobbed his head, followed by Krystiana and then Ylana. It was good, but it was also worrisome because the king and Magna Mater had nodded first, which meant that they had agreed to compromise and to let the Supreme Priestess dictate the terms of the agreement.

The prince and queen-consort eyed each other anxiously. Their questions, and everyone else's, would be answered shortly. Presently, Master Rackeli opened the door to the greenhouse and called everyone back in.

Sitting at a table in the crowded outer gardens, Kildare listened with suspicion to another young man in his late teens to whom he had been introduced by Rovere, Kil's cousin whose family lived in Antar. Rovere and his parents should have been on the other side, but their family was part of the lower patriciate. These were members of noble families that were too large for their own good, so large that—except for the eldest or the most intellectually or esthetically fortunate among them—they were forced to labor or to conduct commerce like commoners, despite their names. The situation obviously created much resentment toward the more fortunate members of the family, as was Kil. But his cousin had never resented him for his luck.

Luvius, Rovere's friend, was dressed in a pristine white shirt, which was opened exceedingly low on his chest, and well-waxed brown leather trousers and shoes. To Kildare, he looked like the son of a wealthy family, but with too much time on his hands and no life goals.

137

The young man said, "Your cousin told me you might be able to help me get an apprenticeship in the high prince's stables."

Kil blinked. What was his cousin thinking? He glanced at him, annoyed. Rovere just shrugged his shoulders. He turned back to the other and said, "I am sorry. But what would you do in a stables? Do you have any skills with furans or vorans? Have you ever cleaned a stall?"

Luvius smiled. "Of course not. But I wasn't thinking of apprenticing as a stall mucker. Rather, as a stables manager. I do have good skills in accounting, and I love furans. Vorans, I don't mind, but they're too...pretty. I prefer the fierceness of the furans."

Kil blinked again, and his brows narrowed with shocked surprise. The fop thought vorans were too *pretty*? "I...I do not know. Maybe. But the high prince does not just hire anyone."

Luvius looked thoroughly disappointed. Rovere was going to intercede for him, but Luvius stopped him. Then, with a very different diction than he had used before, and with a smile that made Kil excessively uncomfortable, he said, "It is okay, Rovere. You cousin is right to not trust me yet; he just needs to know me a little better." Looking with discomforting intensity at Kil, he asked, "Do you drink, Kil?"

Kil gave a hesitant yes, and Luvius called a waiter over while straightening his position and refastening the two lower buttons on his shirt.

When the waiter placed the drinks in front of Luvius, the young man pushed one toward Kil and the second toward Rovere. Luvius's sudden change in posture, the tying of the two buttons and offer of a drink, and the manner in which he had done it all only agitated Kil more. He felt an unexpected heat warm his blood. He hurried to down his drink, then found a reason to excuse himself and left with an urgent step to think over what had just happened.

VIII THE DANCING AND THE RESULTS

It was with great excitement that the Royal Ball was finally and officially opened that evening. Those who had come with a spouse took out magenta sashes and wrapped their wrists with them to identify themselves as married. Those who had come with a fiancé put on red and blue wrist sashes to indicate they were engaged but not wholly committed yet. The rest danced as they were.

After the meeting earlier that afternoon, moods had been generally depressed, but the hopeful music—always present and always heard, even if only subconsciously—had lifted most everyone's spirits. By now, even the high prince wished only to dance.

Toras, who sat next to him, said, "I'm going to go and ask Aria to dance. What about you? Don't your feet feel like spinning and stepping to the song? Don't you feel like dancing with *someone*?"

Yes. Aithen's belly fluttered as he thought about who he wished to dance with. He was tapping his feet, not to the music's rhythm, but to the rhythm of his nervous thoughts.

Toras said, "Brother, I think I would go for her, if I were you. I've watched you all day long, and I know you're smitten with her."

Aithen's eyes went wide, but Toras ignored his reaction. "I think you should ask her to dance."

"It's not so easy."

"You mean because of mother and father, or because of everyone else?"

"Both"

"Well, as for our parents, if they knew who *I've* set my eyes on, I'm sure they'd think your interest in Elyana Lux Baiula acceptable by comparison."

With an incredulous tone, Aithen asked, "You met someone, in Horn's Pass? And what about your oath of celibacy?"

"I'm not talking about it now. Anyway, as for the rest, it doesn't matter what they think; you're the high prince, heir to the throne." Then, with a motion of the head and a mischievous grin, he said, "See you on the ball floor."

Aithen wanted to curse at his brother, but Toras was right. How much longer was he going to hesitate and restrain himself? How much longer was he going to growl and moan and sigh, start and then stop himself again, and hold himself back?

Well, this is it! Like Toras said, I'm a prince, the high prince! I have the right to woo and desire any woman, whether she be princess or commoner or—or Lux Baiula!

And Aithen crossed the ballroom with a determination he had only ever felt in battle. But instead of his heart pumping to ready him for action, and his senses honing themselves to prepare him to wield the sword or the arrow, his heart now pumped only to dampen his palms and flush his body with jittery tension, while his senses sharpened themselves only to search for anyone who might sneer at the sight of him inviting a Lux Baiula to dance. *And what if she refuses?*

When his eyes crossed hers, his stomach lurched, and his step paused for the briefest moment. Elyana had seen him approach. She seemed to understand his intentions because she looked around in a seriously un-Lux Baiula manner, as if anxious about what was about to occur. Aithen almost stopped himself when he saw Krystiana next to her, but someone came to take the woman to another table. That left Mitsuko and Irania Lux Baiulae sitting at the Sisters' table, but they did not appear as threatening as the Magna Mater had, and Aithen resumed his approach.

Aithen looked at Elyana's colleagues with a blank face, then turned and asked a little too abruptly, "Elyana, would you dance?"

Elyana looked at her colleagues out of the corner of her eyes, and—not seeing any hand movements—replied, "I would, my Prince."

With that, she stood, took Aithen's arm and followed him to the middle of the dancing lines.

The room grew quiet, as if a Lux Baiula had blanketed everyone and everything with a Sound Barrier. Even the notes of the fiddle and accompanying instruments seemed to have been suspended in mid-air. Octavius, who was conversing with Darya when the unexpected pause in the chatter and laughter and stepping happened, turned his head in the direction pointed by everyone else, and sighed.

Darya was about to ask her husband what was bothering him when her own eyes fell upon her son and his partner, and she groaned.

The prince and his partner were now both aware of the gasps they were causing.

Darya hissed, "Did you know about this?"

"I have suspected it for several months, and I intended to speak to him about it, but it escaped my mind amidst everything else. I should have done it earlier. Now, the discussion will be harder."

"Indeed."

"We will both speak with him *after the ball*. It would be inappropriate to intervene now."

Octavius paused, then added, "But we do need to do something to rescue them."

Darya agreed, though she was not looking forward to confronting Aithen about his amorous intentions. Octavius took his magenta wrist sash from his pocket and laced it around Darya's wrist, who placed her own ribbon on his wrist. Of course, everyone knew they were married, and there was no danger anyone would attempt to court one or the other accidentally. But the wrist sashes were a tradition, and the king and queen-consort knew the importance of maintaining customs. The two walked onto the ball floor and moved to place

141

themselves in the center of the parallel lines—Octavius next to Aithen, and Darya next to Elyana.

Other couples, either not wanting to insult the king or believing that the king was accepting his son's selection for a partner, took position.

However, people still looked at the high prince and Lux Baiula askance, some with hidden scornful sneers and others with curiosity; only a very few looking with honest glee. Some of the former found the idea of physical contact with a Lux Baiula unappealing because of the strange thickness and appearance of their skin, especially in the very powerful Alterintrants, which Elyana was; others among them found the idea of a relationship between their prince and a Lux Baiula improper. As for the latter, it was possible they were merely happy to see that the Coriolan line would not end with Octavius, although Gaius looked at his royal brother with honest, joyous surprise.

When Octavius bowed to Darya, a new song erupted from the throats, and music burst from the instruments, like fireflowers from a pyrotechnician's implements, though the music and song were not meant to chase evil spirits away but only to bring joy and delight.

The dance was known as Dance of the Flowers. It was an allegorical dance brought to Alvinoria by the Yeltcheki some two hundred years earlier. Since then, it had spread across the land like a virus due to its beautiful form and alignment with the reserved traditions of Alvinorians.

The story was that of a soldier returning from war, and who asks his lover to forgive him for his long absence with a flower brought back from the faraway land that kept him away. The dance called for wide, expressive motions, steps, and spins; the male partner implored and motioned toward the accursed land that kept him away. The female pushed and pulled, dancing between refusal and desire. The dance finished with a thrilling twist, symbolizing the acceptance of the flower by the woman.

Toras and Aria caused a little ruckus as they arrived and moved themselves closer to Aithen and Elyana. Aithen's stomach clenched a moment when he crossed eyes with Aria. His cousin smiled, but her expression was more reserved than was typical for her, and Aithen knew she must be feeling some disappointment at seeing him with Elyana. He forced himself to smile in her direction, wondering why the girl should ever have thought of him as a potential partner. Marriage between cousins among the nobility was not rare, but it was not something Aithen had ever considered. But as he recalled the time he had kissed Aria, when he had been fifteen and she ten, he sighed and hoped she would move on, because he was somewhere else already.

Toras noticed the exchange between the two and was about to grunt in his brother's direction, but he changed his mind when he looked at Elyana and saw how *she* looked at his brother. The two had obviously fallen for each other. So, when the song called for another twirl, he moved himself around Aria with such lively steps that she was forced to pay attention to him lest they step on each other's feet. When his eyes crossed Aithen's, Aithen gave him a thankful nod.

Elyana looked at Aithen curiously when he swung his arm out next to her to initiate another twirl. But Aithen simply shook his head dismissively and continued with the move.

Although partners never touched during any part of the dance, Aithen now felt an overwhelming, indescribable sensation assault his body as he and Elyana circled each other. His hands, perhaps a centimeter from Elyana's body, felt the warmth, the electricity, the attraction of it more powerfully than he had ever experienced it when he had actually touched a woman. Elyana's intense gaze only added to the thrill.

Elyana almost lost a step when she noticed the Magna Mater glancing in her direction. But with the evening come, and the Living Lamps dimmed for the dance, she couldn't see the look on Krystiana's face; she hoped it was not disapproval. When Aithen had come to request a dance with her, Elyana had agreed without hesitation, spurred only by a desire to finally give in to her interest in the prince. Per various unspoken conventions, she should not have; she should have consulted the Magna Mater on the matter before engaging publicly in something that might spell trouble for the Sisterhood and the Crown. But why should a woman her age request permission to court a man? *Well, it is what it is.*

Elyana returned her attention to Aithen just as the music ended, and men and women bowed to each other in thanks for the dance. Many couples separated and chose new partners for the next song.

It was expected that the high prince would also choose a new partner, but he didn't, and people frowned—especially those who had brought their daughters with the hope of introducing them to him—as did Darya and Octavius. Aithen saw the frowns—all of them—despite the dimmed lights. But he didn't care. This song was not one he would want to dance to with anyone else. In fact, he did not think he'd want to dance with another woman, period.

To be forced to pretend to enjoy it? To smile at them and make small talk when my thoughts are occupied only with her?

So, he ignored the looks of disapproval and engaged with Elyana in the next dance, which—tough it was a quieter ballet where the dancing partners moved around each other with more subdued motions—allowed hands and bodies to brush each other lightly.

It did not take Aithen long to feel the thrill procured by the touching of the hands. He loved the warmth and the smoothness of Elyana's fingers. The two twirled around each other, and the more they did, the greater the space around them became.

Along one side of the ball floor, an unpleasant conversation was beginning. Sitting there were Arotek and his wife, separated from Krystiana and two other Lux Baiulae by two chairs. Krystiana had come to sit there after her dance with Lord Claudius. Without turning her head in the Magna Mater's direction, Lady Aroteka said, "This is scandalous."

Krystiana gritted her teeth and replied without naming her neighbor first. "There is nothing that prohibits it, and the high prince and Elyana Lux Baiula are two of the most respected persons I know. They are also young and cannot be blamed for wanting to enjoy a dance."

At that, Ursa Aroteka, her face as ugly as that of the mythological creature she was deservedly named after, grunted and turned toward her husband to continue to unleash her venomous words. When Arotek showed his agreement with snorts and head shakes, Ursa raised her tone to be heard by the others sitting nearby.

Mitsuko and Irania Lux Baiulae looked at Krystiana with concern and irritation. How could that most detestable woman speak so carelessly of one of them?

Krystiana thought: *Why didn't Elyana tell me of this before? It cannot be something new. It must have happened when she was still in Octavius's court.*

When Aroteka made another rude comment, Krystiana sighed, knowing that she was going to have to do something about the woman, which meant speaking directly *to* her and thus "honoring" her with her name. She projected her voice so Arotek did not hear, "Lady Ursa, I believe we are all here at the high king's pleasure, and it is wise, as you know, for his guests to remain civil toward each other. But if the king's ire does not frighten you, know that I hold it from reliable sources that you are quite the temptress, and not at all faithful to your husband. I urge you to be careful and not to disparage others as you are wont to do."

Ursa flashed murderous daggers in the Magna Mater's direction—a hazardous thing to do given Krystiana's power and position in the kingdom. But her scowl was quickly replaced by a blink of surprise and a befuddled look.

Mitsuko called the Magna Mater's attention, then sent an urgent thoughtcall to her, *"Mater, did you use Confusion on the woman?"*

"I did. Only mildly. She will be fine, Mitsuko."

"But—"

"Mitsuko! Let it be. I will have Fausta probe her later, to be sure." Krystiana pointed her chin toward Elyana and sent, *"For now, I must think on what to do about her."*

"Yes, it is unusual, but not unheard of, Mater. And her interest in him is not necessarily surprising."

Krystiana turned to Mitsuko with raised brows.

"The prince does have physical and mental qualities that would make him a fit prospect for one as intelligent and beautiful as Elyana."

Krystiana pulled her lip up and her brows down in a frown. *"That is not the point, Mitsuko. This relationship could jeopardize our Order's independence. It was careless and foolish of her to declare her interest in the high prince so...publicly."*

"I suppose it was so, Mater. But if I may..." Mitsuko waited to receive permission from the Magna Mater before continuing. *"I do not believe it will put the Sisterhood at risk."*

"How not?"

"I am sorry, Mater. I do not mean to contradict you. But you know Elyana; nothing will deter her from her duty or the principles and laws she lives by—our principles and our laws. This means that if the day came when she needed to make a decision that would go against the prince's or the Crown's wishes, she would make it without regard to personal consequences. Such an event—if it were to become known— would demonstrate our fierce independence more than our celibacy, which is often interpreted in ways not very flattering to us."

Krystiana blinked, reflected for a moment. *"Huh. Thank you, Mitsuko. I do not think anyone ever presented the situation quite that way to me before. But you should know that appearances also matter, and that they may be as damaging as deeds."*

Mitsuko replied, *"I wish that concept did not exist."*

"It exists because human brains, like those of many other animals, make assumptions about things so that we need not do all the work of learning and verifying each and every time another situation presents itself to us."

"Well, perhaps we should."

Krystiana sent a grunt of annoyance through the Bind.

Sitting at the royal table, Toras listened as Aria complained to him and Ulvius about her frustration with life in Kynaria.

"I know how important completing my studies is. But there are things happening here now, and it seems silly to be studying while Alvinoria is being attacked by gnarlers and Serpents and—"

Toras corrected his cousin a little too stiffly, saying, "There's only one Serpent, Aria. And what would you do here, anyway?"

"I could help fight these creatures; enter their minds to track them, like Marena Lux Baiula does for your Guard."

Toras raised shook his head.

Ulvius said, "It is probably better this way, Aria."

"This way, how?"

"I mean, you finishing your studies, so you can be a master Beast Reader before thinking of engaging in a war. War brings death, nothing else."

Ulvius gave Toras a mildly accusatory look, laced with pain, and Toras could not help responding with an offended tone. "Ulvius, your brother didn't die at my hands, nor did he die because I sent him to face the Serpent. He died, as did many others, while defending against it."

Aria said, "He's right, Ulvius. Your accusation isn't fair. Yes, war brings death but it's to defend our people against an enemy with whom *political* negotiations are not an option, especially in this case."

Ulvius felt the sting of his cousin's words, but he sighed and said, "I suppose you're right, Aria. But I still wish it didn't exist, even though the need for metal to forge weapons is filling my coffers."

Toras and Aria gave their cousin a befuddled look.

Ulvius asked, "And when will your father declare the war, anyway?"

"I don't know. Why?"

"Because the shippers are also charging a fortune, and it would be better if all debt and accumulation of debt were cancelled already."

"I suppose he's waiting for proof that Zebula will attack."

Ulvius nodded then said, "Anyway, where are your brothers, Aria? Why don't they ever join us?"

"They hate politics more than you hate war, I guess."

Ulvius gave his cousin a disapproving look. "It still would have been nice of them to join us here. It's probably going to be a while before there's another opportunity."

A little annoyed by her cousin's rotten mood, Aria replied, "I don't know what to tell you, Ulvius. They've always been this way. But let's change the topic, can we? What I'd like to know is what Toras thinks of Aithen courting Elyana."

"Well, it's weird. But, if he wishes to do more than chat and laugh with her, he'll have to make his case in front of the Selection Council, and I don't think they'll approve."

Ulvius asked, "What if he ignored them?"

Toras snorted several times before replying. "It wouldn't go well for him, nor for Father who'd be forced to do something he probably wouldn't want to consider."

"You mean, he—"

Aria gave a long sigh, watched the high prince and Lux Baiula a while longer then said, "Well, regardless of anyone's opinion about it, Aithen and Elyana do look good together. Don't they?"

On the ball floor, Aithen and Elyana continued to dance as though they were the only ones there. They no longer thought, but only enjoyed the touching of flesh—even if only that of their hands—and the thrill they felt as they pulled away and then pulled toward each other again, always staying at arm's length, as was required. When the song finally neared its end, Aithen found it difficult to slow down; he wanted to keep moving, moving with Elyana. But the slowing reawakened his senses to the rest of the dancers, to the king and queen, to the realization of what he had done. The cautious, restrained part of him fought with the one he had not known until tonight. When the last note vanished, Aithen smiled at Elyana with a deeply felt but controlled smile. He locked eyes with her for a very brief moment and then walked her back to her table, his eyes darting around the canopy in search of the disapprovals he was sure to find.

After the prince had thanked Elyana for the dance, which she returned with the conventional reply but with eyes that gave her thanks a more profound meaning, and he had moved away, he was accosted not so subtly by both Ori and Toras.

Ori said, "Aithen! I've never seen you dance like that with a woman before. And it's Elyana you danced with!"

"I think our eldest brother's in love."

Aithen stopped and looked back at Toras with narrow slits.

Ori looked shocked. "In love…with Elyana? I mean, she's beautiful, but—"

Aithen interrupted the young prince. "Ori, please…stop."

Toras jumped in and said, "Aithen is in love, but he doesn't know if it's right or how to deal with the fact, and with everyone knowing who's engorging his—"

Aithen shot the deadliest glare at his brother, his jaw tight and shaking. Toras stopped himself, but raised his hands to add, "Relax brother. I thought it was strange, and still think it is, but you two are obviously besotted with each other, and as Aria told Ulvius and I earlier, you look good together."

"'Told Ulvius and *me*.'"

"What? Whatever, Aithen. I just thought I'd let you know I'm okay with it, though I don't see how it can lead to what you're hoping for."

Ori, not understanding what Toras was alluding to, asked, "What do you mean? Why can't it lead to where Aithen is hoping for? What is he hoping for?"

Toras shrugged his shoulders. "He knows."

"It is just that there are rules, Ori. But I am going to take a walk now because I do not feel like being stopped or questioned by Mother or Father. And please do not follow me, Ori."

Aithen strolled a while. It took him a few spans of the gardens' paths to relax, clenching and unclenching his fists, before he succeeded; he would have liked to beat some sense of propriety into Toras. But once he had forgotten about that, his mind slowly returned to what burned inside him: the memory of Elyana's touch, and of the shivers it had sent through his skin—through his entire body. His brother was right: he *wanted* her. But his reason kept reclaiming its place and pushing aside his emotions with warnings about breaking convention and ignoring the wisdom of centuries.

The inner battle continued for a while inside him until he reached the gardens' outer edges, and his eyes fell on the plebeians and minor nobles of the area who were enjoying themselves without the need to guard themselves all the time. He sighed and wondered what his life would be like if he were one of them.

I would not have known Elyana, for one. But if society were not structured as it is, I might have met her anyway. Yeah, but would she have liked you then? You are what you are because of the way you were raised; because you live in this society.

"Aghrr! It's no use." And Aithen felt himself envy the commoners' freedom.

A voice startled him just then, "Aithen?"

"Elyana! What are you doing here?"

"Can't a woman take a walk in the Royal Gardens?"

His surprise was still audible when he replied, "Of course." He then looked at the Guardians posted along the edge, wondering what rumors *they* would start. Hopefully, none; they were his men, after all.

Suddenly, Aithen said, "I would like to show you the pond. Have you seen it? It is always amazing during the Second In-Between Fourth, when the Red Sun lingers behind its brother."

"I have not."

Aithen gave Elyana his arm, and the two went.

***

After the Royal Ball was ended, and all the guests had left or retired to the guest rooms, Octavius and Darya enjoyed some quiet in their chambers. Just now, Octavius closed the glass door to the balcony. A fierce rainstorm was on its way, perhaps to wash away the drinks that had been spilled on the plebeian side of the Royal Gardens. His majordomo had been shocked by the mess; fluid and food crumbs lay everywhere, and he had told the king as much.

Octavius, dressed in his black sleeping robe, walked toward his wife sitting comfortably on the Lacora Leaf divan. Darya raised her hand toward him to invite him to sit. The king would have plumped down if he could have, but Lacora Leaf seats had a tendency to rebound if one pushed on them too hard, so he sat himself down carefully, with a groan.

Darya pulled her legs up onto the divan and took Octavius's hands in hers and rubbed them gently. She said, "I do not remember you being so tired before."

With an unusually croaky voice, Octavius said, "I am getting old, Darya, and change at this age is as rapid as it is in the beginning years, except that it is toward degradation."

"You do not look it."

"No, but I certainly feel it."

The conversation paused a moment, and Octavius said, "But you, my dear, you have been less jovial than I remember you to have been just six months ago. Is it because of the worry I caused you a few months back? Or because of troubles in Kynaria?"

Darya looked at the king with mildly accusatory eyes. "I frankly do not know why I have been so depressed lately. But I do know that I no longer find joy in entering the Bind."

Octavius watched his wife with pensive, worried eyes. He brushed his chin a while then tapped it and raised his finger.

Darya regarded him curiously.

"When is the last time you lay on a microbial mat or had a microbial bath?"

Darya laughed, "You think that rejuvenating my flora is the answer?"

Octavius tipped his head. "Why not?"

"Well, it has been nearly a year, and the granules I drink, though they help maintain the flora, certainly cannot restore lost species; a visit to the thermal at Urbs Lucis might help..."

When Darya paused, as if to reconsider her statement, Octavius said, "Then you should go. On your way back to Kynaria. You should stop in Urbs Lucis."

Darya sighed and added, "I could go, Octavius. But in truth, though the bath may restore my flora, it will not restore my smile. What I truly want now...is to remain here, by your side, and no longer have to return to Kynaria—at least not for extended periods anymore."

Octavius's expression changed suddenly. He felt guilty; he felt stupid. He leaned forward, took his wife's chin, and kissed her. He kissed her warmly, passionately, guiltily.

"I would enjoy that very much too, but now may not be the best time to pass the throne to our son, which is nece—"

"I know, I know. I can't move my residence here until there is a new queen-consort to take my place in Kynaria." Darya sighed again, then shook her head and said, "Speaking of Aithen, when will we sit with him to discuss his relationship with...Elyana?"

"In the morning, before he leaves to return to the capital."

"What are your thoughts on it?"

"You know what they are, Darya."

"Yes, I suppose I do. I wish we could have prevented this rather than need to stop it, though I don't know why I should want to stop it; I could whip the gods for these contradictions they force upon us."

Octavius smiled, "Yes, well, I don't think the gods have anything to do with it; it's our laws and customs, even if they don't always make sense. And as for myself, I…I am not certain she is the best companion for him; not after her decision when—"

"I know. I know, Octavius. You don't need to say it. But I am sure that if you look at the events of that day rationally, you'll find she did the right thing."

Octavius took his wife's hands and squeezed them with a fierce passion. Darya leaned her head on his chest and the two listened to the rain, thinking, sighing occasionally and caressing each other in response; they did not need to ask what the sigh had been for. They had been married for sixty-seven years, and despite their long separations, they loved and knew each other as few others did.

***

In one of the guest rooms, two Lux Baiulae now sat on sturdy but supple and luxurious Lacora Leaf chairs, made even more luxurious by their green color.

Elyana had not sat much, though. During the preceding fifteen interminable minutes, she had heard Krystiana—her friend and Magna Mater—tell her how disappointed she was. Disappointed! If Elyana had been a redshoot, she would have broken down and run away. Only twice before in her life had anyone made her feel so humiliated. The first time had been when she was beaten by a young recruit at the yearly power games, and the second time when an examiner told her she would not be elevated to Full Sisterhood that year. But no one had ever told her she had disappointed them, disappointed them because of her lack of judgment.

After a long series of snorts and grumbles while looking toward the window to recover her self-possession before she said anything, Elyana finally replied with as much temper as she could muster, though her voice still did quiver ever so slightly.

"Frankly, and with all due respect, Krystiana, I do not know why I should need to justify myself to anyone. I am, after all, not a youngling, not a naïve *fool* who will throw herself in a man's arms without any concern for anything else."

Krystiana said, "You are right, Elyana, and if you had set your eyes on anyone else outside the Royal family, I would not have concerned myself with it. But because it *is* the high prince you have fallen for, I am obliged to intervene. If I do not, the Light's Assembly will, despite my or Ramela's assurances that your romance would not damage our reputation."

Elyana sat in silence, chewing her words. She knew that Krystiana, being her friend, was trying to help her prevent things from getting worse for her.

Krystiana continued, "Ramela is also concerned, though she is a level-headed, rational woman and has always been one of your staunchest supporters. She is concerned that with the troubles we are facing, your relationship with the high prince will make all your advice and all your decisions suspect. She is concerned that it will give ammunition to a certain Junior who is intent on defying our customs."

Elyana's face, already dark with anger, darkened even more at hearing the girl's name again. Between clenched teeth, she said, "That girl should be sent back to her mother!"

"Indeed, she should, but we don't kick-out Juniors. And if we can't bring Moradien back in line, we may be forced to Unbind her. But we digress. What will you do about the high prince?"

The Magna Mater's question dizzied Elyana: 'What will you do about the high prince?' As if he were some troublesome howler or furan that must be locked away or put down. She took a moment to assemble her thoughts, then shrugged.

"I do not know Mater. I believe I have fallen for the prince, despite myself, despite conventions, and despite all rational warnings. But, there are no laws against this, and…" In a rare moment of self-doubt and vulnerability, Elyana hesitated before saying, "…it would mean a lot if you would continue to trust in me, as you have always done. I have never failed you or the Sisterhood, and my relationship with the prince will not change that. And whatever I resolve to do, I promise you that I will not allow it to damage the Sisterhood, the Purple Sashate, or anyone's reputation."

Krystiana looked at Elyana with an expression that went from uncertain to confident, a confidence reinforced by their history and the deep trust she had indeed developed for the younger woman. And she trembled for the prince; Elyana would do nothing to damage the Crown's reputation—she knew that—but she also knew that Elyana would not put the prince's emotional or physical needs ahead of any political imperative—assuming the Selection Council allowed an eventual marriage.

Elyana felt all the tension in her body dissipate, almost to the point of causing her to wobble, when Krystiana nodded. She put her hand on a chair, trying to do so as inconspicuously as possible and steadied herself. She then thanked her friend and Magna Mater and left to return to her apartments.

PERMANERÉ USQUE AD FINEM

IX IRRITATIONS, ADMONITIONS, AND PLANS

In the Dining Room

The morning following the ball, the radiant suns—with the Blue Sun slightly ahead of the Red as the Second In-Between Fourth neared its end—warmed the air with a purplish color made slightly gray by the fog which rose from the ground as the previous night's rain evaporated.

Octavius, Darya, and Aithen were breaking fast with a light meal. The air inside the king's private dining room was starting to feel heavy to Aithen as his father's words slowed, and his voice became tighter, indicating the approach of an unpleasant topic. A thought diminished Aithen's mounting anxiety for a very brief moment: *For all his self-control, he isn't very good at hiding his unease just now.* The thought evaporated when Aithen heard his name.

"Aithen, your mother and I wish to speak to you about a matter that is perhaps—no, surely—personal to you, but very important to us because it is important to the maintenance of a strong kingdom."

Aithen felt his jaw tighten. He had an idea what his father wanted to talk about.

I hate it when he says he wishes to speak to me, rather than with me; it never means anything good. Is he going to let me say anything, or is he just going to tell me how it is, as he usually does? Well, this time, I am not going to simply accept his judgment; I can't.

Octavius watched his son's reactions. Seeing him tense but willing to listen, he continued, "I had already noticed upon my return from Spiritii, this summer, that your interactions with Elyana had changed; they were different...more...well, warmer. So, I promised myself to understand what was going on. But with the Serpent's and the gnarlers' attacks increasing in frequency as they did, and with Elyana going back to Urbs Lucis, I never got to the chance. Yesterday, however, both your mother

157

and I," Octavius looked to his side to ensure Darya was with him in this, "were presented with the undeniable fact of your amorous relationship with Elyana given that you made no attempt to hide it. And it got people—many people—talking."

Indignation stiffened the prince's entire body. But he still made no reply except for letting through a few angry sounds.

If he says that he cares what those idiots think, I'm going to explode.

"Aside from the difference in age, which may or may not be an issue, and apart from the fact that she saw you being swaddled," Aithen jaw muscles tightened visibly now, and his face took on a dangerous look, so Octavius pressed on with the more important facts, "there is the issue that she is a member of the Sisterhood—an organization which is feared as much as it is revered, and it was understood a long time ago that to maintain the trust and goodwill of the people, amorous relations between the members of the House and the members of the Sisterhood should …not be permitted."

Octavius and Darya observed Aithen's changing expressions apprehensively. Not that they believed he might walk away from them or curse at them, as Toras had often done in similar situations, but they did not enjoy hurting him this way, and they hoped he would…simply understand, given his status as heir to the throne.

Aithen's reply came with cutting sharpness. "Father, I *know* what people think; I *saw* their looks last night. But they also know Elyana, and they know *me*. They respect her, and they know she won't try to influence me to advantage the Sisterhood. They also respect me and know that I will not be influenced by her or the Sisterhood, nor someday—if I am lucky enough to receive the crown—use the Order to subjugate them into compliance. You saw how I handled the Senate and the Landholders when you went missing this summer."

Octavius and Darya frowned at that, and Darya wanted to interject, but Aithen continued.

"And I know what the conventions are, but they're not a prohibition or a law! So, it must mean that there can be exceptions, and that our forefathers and the Sisters of old simply didn't wish to list them all and left things at that—conventions. Well, this is one such exception to the conventions! I...love Elyana. She's the only woman who has ever made me feel this way, the only one who's ever gotten me to open up and make me smile, and—" Aithen cut himself short there, not knowing what else he might say, if he continued.

Octavius looked toward Darya, head shaking and shoulders slumping. She looked back and motioned him to be patient with a gentle smile of encouragement. He made a small nod and let Darya speak now.

"Aithen, it is obvious you love her; it was plain in the way you danced with her, in the way your eyes lingered on her each time she left your side despite your attempts at appearing aloof, as well as in the way you spoke of her just now." Darya watched her son blush and continued before he felt embarrassed by her piercing gaze, "And if it were only about the *conventions*, I would say 'go ahead, and be with her', but it is not only about that. Your father has his reasons to be concerned, as do I. Do you truly realize that her fealty is to the Order and will always be? Her ability to be with you may be even more limited than mine has been to be with your father. In fact, it *will* be."

Darya paused a moment, considering whether she should say what she had in mind to add about their age difference, but Octavius interrupted her.

"And because your feelings for Elyana are clouding your logic, your relationship could endanger you as well as everyone else around you."

"*What?* My feelings, clouding my logic? How—"

Octavius lowered his head combatively and said with a cold, hard voice, "Yes, your logic. It is already clouded. You say that the landholders and senators respect you, and that they know you would not be influenced by the Sisterhood if you had an amorous relationship with one of them. But you are young, and you have not yet carried an intimate relationship in public; you should know, therefore, that the elders and landholders *cannot* know whether you would or would not be influenced by such a relationship. Moreover, although your feelings for Elyana were not known by them when you spoke to the Senate and to the Union Council, and although you did not bring Elyana to your meetings with them—a fact that several remarked on as a positive thing—there *were* those who suspected that she must have done something to you, to give you the strength and courage to speak to them the way you did."

Aithen could no longer contain his indignation and exclaimed, "What? Father, this is nonsense. You cannot believe what you are saying!"

"There are a few senators and landholders who thought that she might have used the Bind to give you courage and make you say the things you said. In particular, Senator Sur'Elando and his followers believe that you must have been under the influence of the Sisterhood when you berated him during your speech to the Senate and followed that insult with words that left everyone confused—the way Lux Baiulae are known to do."

Aithen was seething. How could those ignorants think that of him? How could they think him so incapable as to need a shadower to blow words in his ears? He was High Prince and High Lord Commander of the Royal Guard! And they dared suggest that he was incapable of speaking with authority, incapable of putting idiots in their place? And his father thought his logic was clouded? *His* logic? "Father, you really can't—"

"Aithen, these are exactly the types of situations that the conventions—as you call them—are meant to avoid, especially in a time of unrest and danger. Moreover, you know very well that your union to Elyana would need to be approved by the Selection Council, and I know already that they will not."

Darya shot an incredulous look at her husband—he hadn't said anything about this to her before.

An exasperated groan rose from Aithen and his fists clenched to the point of blanching. He shook his head and pressed his lips until they were almost white. He asked with a challenging tone, "Father, do you disapprove of my courting her, aside from the risks it poses and from the Selection Council's position about it? Do *you* think she influenced me when I spoke with the Senate and Union Council?"

Octavius reflected on his answer for a moment. What should he say? That he, Octavius, had no valid objection? As king, his personal feelings could not be the basis of a decision that could affect the kingdom. But he loved his son, and he knew him to be a rational man.

"No, Aithen. Rules and political considerations aside, I do not disapprove of your relationship with Elyana, even if it *does* make me uncomfortable seeing you together in that manner. And I know that your statements to the two bodies and your reactions to Sur'Elando were entirely your own. But I do believe this relationship can lead to trouble, and I do not see how we can convince the Selection Council to make an exception for you. So, I urge you to consider things with a detached mind in the next few days."

Octavius paused then added, "You know that if the Council should deny your petition and you continue to pursue Elyana, the throne will—" Darya stopped Octavius before he uttered the terrible words he had been about to say.

But Aithen heard them anyway, and the thought of them hit him like a punch in the kidneys. *Toras? Toras be king? And Ori is too young. But it doesn't matter whether they could or could not. I am the eldest and the throne should be mine. How can he make this threat to me?!*

Aithen stood up and scuffed the tiles for a while. He did not know what to say; he felt trapped. He wanted to scream, to curse at his parents and the whole world.

The king and queen-consort simply followed him with pained, troubled, and frustrated looks. They continued following him with their eyes and regarding each other until they saw him stop in the middle of the room.

A sudden realization had hit Aithen. *He's right about the throne. But he didn't tell you to stop courting Elyana. Which means he's just—*

Cautiously hopeful, Aithen said, "You are not going to stop me?"

Darya looked at her husband with incredulous eyes. Of course, she too wanted her son to have the woman he loved, but how could he be happy with her? And what about the risk to the throne? However, Octavius cared for his son too much, and he would not force anything upon him that would hurt him. The queen consort thought: *Oooh! How is it that even after a hundred years of life, one cannot put reason ahead of love?*

Octavius placed a soothing, quieting hand on Darya's arm, then answered Aithen's question, "No. I am not. You are a good man, Aithen. You are a rational, even-minded person, and I trust your choices. But, as I said, you must think all this over seriously because the repercussions could be severe—for you as well as for me, though I would probably recover more easily than you would."

Still stupefied, Aithen started to respond, "Thank you, Father. I—" He took a long-held breath before continuing, "I was not expecting this. You know I would not do anything to endanger your rule. I will think things over—I promise. And I will give you and mother my decision in a few days along with my thoughts about mitigating any untoward effect if I should decide to continue...courting Elyana." Aithen paused, wanting to add something to address his father's other concern, but he felt a knot in his stomach as he formed the words. He took another deep breath then said, "I want you to know, too, that if I should decide to make things official with her and the Selection Council should reject my petition, I would neither oppose nor resent my loss of privilege."

A mixture of feelings washed over the king's and queen-consort's figures. Octavius showed the battle in him with the twitches on his face, a battle he knew the father in him must win, and the king lose.

Darya kept her own struggle in check, but knowing her husband, she took his hand and squeezed it the way she always did to sustain him in moments of uncertainty and difficulty.

The trick worked, and Octavius nodded to himself and then to his son and said, "I will expect your decision in a fourth, Aithen."

Aithen replied with thankful eyes. He then excused himself, a little more abruptly than he had intended, and left to prepare for his departure.

In Urbs Lucis

In one of the student bedrooms in Urbs Lucis, a strong-willed red-haired girl spoke. "The two of you know very well that the Order of Light will never change; not until a new generation takes over. And I will not wait decades for that to happen."

Morla, a stiff girl with curly, black-hair said, "You're right, and I will not let my freedom be repressed for decades or let anyone treat me like some lowly commoner either; like a muck-scooper! Moradien and I are daughters of nobles, and we definitely don't deserve to be treated that way—not that it would be okay to treat *you* that way either, Lis. But if you have a right to rise from your station, *we* certainly shouldn't have been forced down to that level!"

Lisandeka gritted her teeth. She did not like to be reminded of her very humble origins. She said, "I am not a muck-scooper either, Morla."

"Of course not, Lis. Anyway, what do you suggest we do, Moradien?"

"I say we help Master Methrim because he's the only one who can actually help *us*."

Morla asked, "Help him do what? And how would he help us?"

Moradien took a deep, impatient breath. "We need to help him help us, help him change the minds of those who are keeping us in the middle ages."

Lisandeka wrung her hands nervously, then said, "How are *we* supposed to do that?"

Moradien shook her head as if befuddled by her friend's stupidity. "Our role is to bring more girls to our side, all the novices and juniors, if we can. When there is a sufficient number, Lusk will take care of the rest."

Lisandeka and Morla gave each other worried looks then turned to their leader with questioning gazes.

"What? It surprises you that I call him by his first name?"

Morla replied defensively, "It's just very…telling. That's all."

"Well, perhaps if the two of you were more confident, he would reward you with his first name too. Anyway, we need to bring the other girls to join our demands for a renewal of leadership. And we need to begin with those two bleaters, Carrain and Lopenia." Pointing at Lisandeka and then at Morla, she said, "You need to bring Carrain back, and *you* need to bring Lopenia."

Lisandeka asked, "What makes you think Carrain will listen to me?"

"Because you're from a peasant family too. You need to convince her that joining our cause will be good for her."

Lisandeka picked at her nails nervously without responding. Then, she made to answer, but changed her mind again.

"What, you can't do it?!"

"It's…it's just that she really hates me."

"You need to find a way to get through to her, Lissy. And if you can't, Master Methrim will show you how."

Lis shook her head a few times then threw her hands up resignedly. "Fine."

"Better." Then, turning to Morla she asked, "And you? Will you be able to do your part?"

Morla replied she would. The girls separated to get to their classes.

In the Guest Rooms and at the Stables

Around Eight After Highnight, Elyana had gone to the stables to see Aithen off, for she knew the prince had urgent things to take care of in the capital and was departing that morning. Their farewells had been outright uneasy and made heavy by the humiliating lectures each of them had been subjected to because of their courtship. Elyana could tell, from Aithen's behavior, that he must have been dressed-down by the king and queen-consort, but she did not inquire about it. Instead, Aithen had asked *her* why she was so distant...and she had lied to him. It appeared each of them was making the decision on their own. Was it pride or foolishness that kept them from discussing the matter? And was one cause better than the other?

Aithen did tell Elyana something that brightened her outlook a bit. He told her that he had contacted Current and asked her if it would be possible for Elyana to meet them. Apparently, the Locara had been suspicious but had, nevertheless, discussed it with her leader then and there. The latter had agreed to a meeting four days hence. This had put a smile of hope on Elyana's lips as Aithen departed atop Xyre, though the feeling quickly turned to worry. Indeed, she realized that her hope had nothing to do with Aithen, but everything to do with her role as a member of the Sisterhood who needed to know what those creatures knew.

The Purple Sash spent the rest of the day walking the Royal Gardens, socializing very little, and working. After dining with the Royal family and other guests who had also remained to enjoy the king's property and the company in a quieter setting, Elyana accompanied Krystiana to her apartments, having signified to her that she had some crucial information to share. The walk had not been the most pleasant given that Elyana had not yet forgotten the shame caused her by her friend's remarks, and she could not make small talk.

When they finally got to the Magna Mater's chambers, Elyana told her some of what the prince had shared with her during the ball, that he had contact with...beings that can communicate instantly across vast distances by placing some kind of monitor in the brains of those connected.

This revelation shocked Krystiana. She asked how the prince had come to be involved with things of the Bind, and why Elyana had called these Alterintrants 'beings.' Unfortunately, Elyana had had no answer for the Magna Mater.

Despite the lack of detail, Krystiana recognized the importance of the revelation, if it should prove to be true—which it must be if the prince was, in fact, already having such communications with the so-called beings. She told Elyana to come back in an hour so that they might discuss the matter further with Bilena and Saara.

The four women were now connected through the Bind, and Bilena was pacing with equal excitement and frustration following Elyana's revelation.

"Elyana, you do realize that this could change everything for us. We would no longer need to be in each other's presence to connect via mind-links or mind-ties, and we would no longer need to rely on appointments to meet in the Bind or to send repeated, and often fruitless, connection requests when the other person is not listening. We would be free and able to communicate with each other whenever we needed to, and we would be much more effective at informing each other of attacks across the kingdom and dispatching units of the Royal Guard and Sisterhood to defend against the rokon and the gnarlers."

"I do, Bilena. The high prince has contacted them to request a meeting, but—"

The old Saara said, with a much smoother voice than in the physical world, *"But? They won't meet with us?"*

"Indeed, not."

Bilena asked, *"Is it because they distrust us?"*

Elyana hesitated. She did not really know that the Locari distrusted the Sisterhood, but they seemed to believe there were traitors in Urbs Lucis so perhaps they *would* not want to meet with any of them. What answer could she give without being then forced to disclose what they had revealed to Aithen regarding the possible presence of traitors in Urbs Lucis before she had had a chance to investigate the matter? Her mind made a strange detour then, and she thought: *And how would we all meet, if they agreed to meet? Certainly not underwater.*

Finally, Elyana sent, *"I do not yet know what their reservations or restrictions are. But I am to travel with Aithen to go and meet with the creatures four days hence."*

Bilena asked, *"Do you know where the meeting will be?"*

Elyana remained quiet, looking away, not wishing to lie, and not wishing to say she wouldn't tell them.

Seeing Elyana's strong hesitation, Krystiana came to her rescue. *"Bilena, Elyana knows what she is doing, and she is doing what any member of the Purple Sash would do when planning a meeting with an unwilling or distrusting party. Elyana will brief us upon her return next fourth and let us know how things stand."*

"Of course, Mater."

Satisfied, Krystiana asked her Manu Dextra, *"Do you leave tomorrow, then?"*

Elyana replied, *"I do."*

"Very well. And you have my thanks, Elyana; I know bringing this to us wasn't easy...given the situation in which you obtained the information."

Elyana stiffened at that and said, *"My duty is to the Order first and always, Mater."*

Bilena and Saara's forms turned suspicious eyes to the other two women. The Magna Mater noticed their reaction and responded with an anodyne comment to divert the praefectae's attention from her previous remark.

167

Elyana now excused herself and exited the Bind to get ready for her departure the next morning.

When she woke, Elyana quickly prepared herself and went to the stables to give her instructions to the two guardians who would accompany her to Furan City. She then walked back to her guest rooms to have some of the food that a servant had brought in when she woke, and to wait for the guardians to come fetch her. Elyana felt a small shiver as she reached the small palace's courtyard, for it was now autumn, and the air cooled quickly each time the suns hid, even if only for a moment. A Lux Baiula could prevent herself from feeling the cold by expending some of her energy, but why would she do that? As she approached the guest house, located in the east wing, Elyana was surprised by a sudden, momentary darkening of the young day as a dense cumulus cloud passed in front of the two suns, the Blue Sun slightly ahead of its larger, but milder, reddish twin. This, somehow, elicited unsettling thoughts in her, and Elyana shook her head to dispel them. But they wouldn't go. She wondered whether she had let herself be fooled by sentiments which should have disappeared decades ago, and she groaned as she remembered reaffirming her duty to the Order above and before anyone or anything else that previous night.

Those glum thoughts entrapped her mind so completely that she climbed the steps, entered the apartments, and sat herself on the balcony without even realizing it. She put her face in her hands, and several small growls left her throat.

The suns reappeared, just then, warming everything again and causing a treeflyer to sing in response. Somehow, that made Elyana smile, and the smile reminded her of Aithen. The thought of him, of seeing him again and spending time with him alone— Aithen had told her that he always went alone to the bay where he met the Locari—that possibility stirred her deeply. She felt a powerful need to be with him, ask him all the questions that trotted in her mind, hear him share his thoughts on the mysteries of nature and life that fascinated them both, and talk about the future that would be once the war was over.

Just as she completed this thought, another intruded into Elyana's consciousness, originating from her mind's rational part. This one erased her smile as easily as a gust of wind carries away the colorful buzzers sapping a flower's sweet nectar.

We are just chemical machines, in the end, aren't we? What else could we be if the moment the suns shine, our mood improves, even if nothing else has changed? And nothing has changed, as I have yet to decide what to do 'about Aithen'.

X WHAT SISTERS, SOLDIERS, AND GODS DO

Carriers

The coop in Urbs Lucis was a loud place during the day, full of the carriers' rumbling squawks. And it was also a place few ever visited, perhaps because of the smell—which Emissa Lux Baiula found on the contrary quite pleasant—or more likely because they feared that one of the flyers would land on them. But despite people's dislike of the flyers, these were still an essential important means of communication throughout Terrae Regis, and the source of much enjoyment for their caretakers, especially on racing days. For Emissa, the carriers were also a source of solace. Indeed, for a Lux Baiula, she was not a strong Alterintrant, and she had always felt like an outcast because of it.

Today was the last day of training in preparation for the next race, set for the Eight of Undecimus. With the careful motions she always used to grab and hold the animals, Emissa was assembling her racers into a transport cage.

Presently, she held Blue in her hand. Blue was one of her favorites, because—in the male form—it was an agile and muscular flyer, but also because she had raised it by hand after losing its parents in a race the previous year. Now, Blue was in its male phase—most carriers started in the male phase and switched after their first clutch, which they had with older animals in their female phase to learn caretaking from them—and it was superb.

"Hmm, I know that if anyone can win me this race, it's you. But I also hate to think of the risks I'll be forcin' upon you; the Cross Alvinorian race is not an easy one."

The carrier watched her with keen eyes, but who knew if it understood her. Perhaps, a Kynarian cleric would know. *I wish I'd gone to Kynaria to learn their use of the Bind, as Marena did.* Emissa sighed and then checked the flyer's wings. The lamellae were full, slick, and without rips. *Good.* Next, she

171

checked Blue's throat by gently prying open the beak. Its throat looked clear and flashed a beautiful pink. *Good here too.* Finally, she checked its ring. Rings were put on a few days after a carrier's birth, when the toes' bones were still flexible enough to allow the ring to be pushed over the feet. Once on, the loops never came off, but they had been known to break. Because Emissa did not want her flyers to be lost without a means for their finders to contact her, she always verified the rings' integrity. The one on Blue's foot was still there, solid, and legible. She nodded to herself, caressed the flyer tenderly, and said, "All good, Blue. In you go."

As she closed the door to the cage, a chirpy voice surprised her.

"Emissa, dear! Wherever are you taking your flyers?"

The carrier master turned around to see who it was. *Oh, it's her. Haven't seen her in a while. Wonder what she's doing here.*

Laranis was a middle-aged Yellow Sash, nearing a hundred, with skin so tight to the bone one wondered how she could be a Lux Baiula. But what the other Sisters disliked most about her was her constant attempts at engaging them in her psychological experiments. *Hopefully, that's not the reason for her visit today,* thought Emissa.

"I am takin' them to Kilt on the Argon. This will be their last training flight before the Cross-Alvinorian Race next fourth."

"Ah! You must be excited."

After a brief hesitation, Emissa replied, "Yes."

"Hum, that doesn't sound overly enthusiastic. It is more of an anxious reply."

"Yes…of course it is, Laranis. The Cross-Alvinorian Race is the second most challengin' race, almost as demandin' as the Terrae Regian race."

"Oh?"

"The Terrae Regian race is longer but mostly over water. This one is shorter, but they have to cross the mountains, which means they have to fly much higher, where there is less oxygen."

"Well, that shouldn't be too difficult a thing to do since the body can easily be trained, whereas the mind, that is another thing."

Emissa turned to get the last racers and rolled her eyes. *There she goes.*

"I have been wondering lately whether continuously putting another—even an animal—in danger affects the mind of the doer."

Without looking back, Emissa clenched her teeth and narrowed her eyes to murderous slits. *If she's insinuatin' that I'm such a one as to put my animals in continuous danger without regard for their health, I'm going to push her off the roof.*

The woman must have noticed the tension in the gracefully plump Yellow Sash's jaw, and added, "Not that I think you carelessly endanger your animals, dear, on the contrary. I'm thinking to compare carrier masters when they send their flyers off on a mission, with guardians when they ride their furans or vorans into battle, to test the hypothesis that sending an animal into danger maintains a greater sense of responsibility for their survival than when riding one into battle."

Having grabbed the last racer, Emissa stood and turned toward her colleague, surprised by the idea. "That is a very intriguing hypothesis, Laranis."

The Yellow Sash broke into a grateful smile. "I must say that I like it. But did you know that new techniques may be developed soon that would allow us to no longer need carriers?"

"Whatever do you mean?"

"I have heard that—" Laranis lowered her voice as if embarrassed to be spreading a possible rumor, "that High Prince Aithen has the secret of it."

"What?"

Laranis replied defensively, "That is what I've heard. He is not an Alterintrant, but somehow, he has the secret of instant communication between any two people, and he told Elyana in Antar, this fourth." Laranis paused again on Elyana's name.

Everyone had heard about her behavior at the Royal Ball. "He is in contact with some tribe that can communicate that way."

Emissa stood there, contorting her face. How could this woman be a Truth Seeker with such indiscriminate beliefs? "Are you sure you heard right, Laranis? Because the learning of the Binding Sciences is somethin' quite frowned upon in House Coriolis. Moreover, the prince is a military commander, not a scholar."

Laranis shrugged her shoulders, then said, "Well, the king did authorize the Sisterhood to start teaching his sons Binding skills, recently."

Emissa opened her eyes wide.

Without any malice, Laranis said, "If you came down once in a while, Emissa, you'd be able to hear things first-hand."

The statement stung Emissa, however factual it might have been.

A light wind saved the plump woman from having to explain her preference for isolation. The breeze blew the coop's pungent smells toward them, nauseating Laranis. At once, the woman made an excuse about needing to return to her experiments, bid Emissa good day, and left.

The carrier master waved a thankful goodbye to the mind philosopher, grabbed her cage, and hurried to the stables where a coach waited to take the racers to their point of departure.

Responsibilities

A haughty, self-important voice said, "I am sorry, Captain, but you have no right to detain any of my clerics, regardless of what you think they did."

Harlion ground his teeth, almost to the point of breaking one.

"I do not *think* they did something, Galadrin," the First Cleric narrowed his eyes warningly, "because I *saw* them with my own eyes, as clearly as I see you now. They were inciting the civilians of the Forging District to disobedience, and I *can* detain them for that."

"Captain, I do not doubt you saw people get unruly when my clerics spoke to them of peace and the truth, which the Church cannot be held responsible for. Or are you claiming that we are not each responsible for our own actions, for our own self-worthiness?"

"*Aghrr*, release his priests!"

While his men fetched the jailed clerics, Harlion turned an icy stare at Galadrin and said, "You cannot continue to hide behind your priestly cloak, First Cleric. I know what you are doing, and you know I know, and sooner or later, I *will* stop you."

The leader of the Church of Aiala waved a dismissive hand. "My responsibilities are to the souls and bodies of our people, and so long as the Founders command it, I will continue to discharge them as required."

Harlion knew the priest was goading him, but he could not resist the desire to show the man how illogical he was. "And how does discouraging the king's subjects from doing what must be done to prepare for the coming battles ensure their safety?"

"Helping them understand that peace is better than war will help preserve their bodies."

"War is coming regardless, and they will soon be at the receiving end not only of the Serpent's claws, but also of Zebula's spears and who knows what else, Cleric; your preaching will not protect their bodies for the Day of Union."

"The Founders will take the bodies of the dead as well as those of the living, High Captain, so long as they use them to follow the Word. Or did you not learn the Scriptures?"

Harlion was seething inside. The Scriptures. The man spoke of the heresies of the Second Scriptures as if they were *The Scriptures*. How could anyone believe that the Founders desired the bodies of rebels and anarchists? How could anyone believe, at all? Harlion was about to give the cleric another warning when the noise of men walking up from the jails interrupted him.

Galadrin turned toward his priests. The men looked furious but were otherwise quiet as they approached him. Galadrin said, "I will not debate the matters of the Church with you, Captain. You are a man of war; I, a man of peace. But you *are* welcome to attend my prayers to gain a better understanding of what it is we are truly defending. I know that you are a believer, underneath all that angry opposition."

Harlion looked a little troubled just then and lost some of his countenance. No one had ever before remarked on his spirituality, nor had he ever spoken with anyone about his changing views. But spirituality was not religiosity.

Secundus Krptus observed his captain from the corner of his eyes, wondering whether that might be true. It would be nice if Harlion were becoming more religious, because it would make it easier for him to tell the captain that he would soon be joining one of the religious orders.

The high captain said, "First Cleric, what I may or may not believe is none of your concern. What is, is seeing to it that your priests do not continue to incite discontent toward the Crown. If I should find them doing so again, I can and will bring the case before the senate—or before the king himself."

Galadrin's lips split into a cynical smile as he motioned his priests toward the door and followed them out. Meanwhile, Harlion wrestled with his conflicted emotions, which colored Krptus's face with concern.

A Replica

With an arm on the table in the *Officers' Lounge*, Laiella said to Toras, "You do have an interesting way about you, Lord Commander, and I can see how—if you lived in the city rather than in a fortress such as this, and you were not sworn to celibacy—you might have a dozen dreamy-eyed girls all hanging on your sleeves for attention."

Sheffar, who sat next to the prince, said, "I'm sure he would have a hundred girls hanging off him. A hundred girls in his chambers too."

Trying to contain himself in front of the Lux Baiula, Toras said, "First of all, *Sheffar*, I am not a fish to take a hundred females, even if I had a chance to. But when I accepted this command, I made an oath—as we all have, and you know why we make it."

"Yes, yes, but it doesn't hurt to fantasize."

Laiella ignored Sheffar's response and said to Toras, "What I would like to know is how you can remain true to something you are forced to do."

"Lux Baiulae are celibate too, aren't they?"

"Most are, but not because of an oath; more because we choose to be, and because, well, by convention."

Sheffar yelled, "*Convention!?*"

Laiella glared down the officer, "Conventions keep order as much as laws and oaths." She watched for any reply then continued, "Anyway, what is truly frowned upon is developing emotional ties to a man, but not the occasional scuffle."

Toras asked with an amused snort, "Scuffle?"

"*Yes*, scuffle. At least, that is what we, Breminese, call it. The sudden flare of emotions, rushing blood, hypersensitivity—it's very pleasant and without risk since there is no copulation."

The secundus yelled. "No–?"

The prima said, "Are you going to continue interjecting like a child, Sheffar?"

Toras decided to intervene, to avoid his secundus being irreparably humiliated, and said, "The secundus is just very expressive, Prima; I'm sure you've realized that by now. Anyway, we *should* move on to more serious things."

Laiella grunted in agreement, but only after shooting another scornful glare at the secundus.

Toras asked, "How are the preparations for our next attack on the gnarlers? And has anyone in the Sisterhood located the Serpent yet?"

Secundus Sheffar cleared his throat a few times then said, "Everything's ready, Commander, except for the lincots. The new litter should have been here already, but they apparently got sick. Marena Lux Baiula said she should be able to come with them next First Day."

"All right, and what about the Serpent, Prima?"

"No one has sensed it for the past two months. Some think it simply left, returned to wherever it is that it came from."

"You believe that?"

Laiella said with obvious contempt at the idea, "No, I don't. When an enemy simply disappears, it often means they are gathering forces for a bigger surprise. And since it hasn't yet attacked southern Alvinoria or the towns and villages to the west of the mountain ranges, I am sure it will return."

Toras said, "My thoughts exactly."

Sheffar exclaimed, "But how do we prepare if we have no idea what the Serpent may be coming back with?"

The prima gave a suffering sigh and said, "I do not know about preparing against things we haven't faced yet, except for mental exercises to steel nerves and physical training to keep fit and limber. And we can continue to hone our skills defending against the gnarlers and attacking. I just wish there were a way to practice combatting the Serpent."

Toras shouted with a finger pointed at Laiella, "Exactly! That's what I've been secretly working on for the past few fourths."

Sheffar and Laiella both gave the same questioning look.

"Yes, secretly. As Sheffar knows, one of the issues we had, when we faced the Serpent, was soldiers freezing when it came down on them and letting themselves be snatched by it. So, I had our carpenter create a mock Serpent, same size, same weight—as close as we could estimate it anyway—to practice against."

The secundus and prima both blinked. Laiella said, "I was wondering why the men were so jittery this morning, all of them looking toward the woodshop as if they thought a belwohr was going to come out of it. Was Master Neros testing his replica?"

Toras grinned mischievously. "Yes, he was. I think you'll like watching the exercises today. In fact, the first guardians will be put through them in…seventeen minutes."

Sheffar yelled, "Seventeen minutes?"

"Yes. Prima, you're coming with me. Secundus, please get confirmation about the lincots. We need them for our next attack on the new horde of gnarlers."

Laiella frowned suspiciously. She did not say anything but wondered what crazy thing Toras had planned.

As they descended the fortress's main steps, the prince took a moment to soak in the keep's new aspect. Several towers and long sections of the parapet had been destroyed by the Serpent, when it attacked four months earlier. That had truly frightened and troubled the fortress's inhabitants because the structure was supposed to be impregnable, eternal; it had been built by Lucian masons and reinforced with the Bind. But the Serpent had wrecked it.

Urbs Lucis had sent its masons and a few Yellow Sashes to help rebuild, but who knew if today's Alterintrants were as powerful as those of days long gone who had erected the original stronghold. Whatever the case might be, the fort had been rebuilt, and not just rebuilt but also strengthened—according to the matronly yellow-sashed chief engineer, at least. Indeed, the Yellow Sashate had learned following the battles of Horn's Pass and Furan City that Bound Shields *could* repel the Serpent. So, the masons had been instructed to lace the outer surface of the walls with a special magnetic mineral, which the Lux Baiulae had then activated to create a permanent shield, saying that it *should*—though it sounded more like a *might*—repel the Serpent when it attacked next, because there *would* be a next time.

Still, it warmed Toras to see the fortress repaired, including his own quarters located on the imposing structure's second floor. It had withstood the test of time for nearly five hundred years now; surely it must stand strong another five hundred.

Can it maybe stand another thousand or ten thousand years? It would be nice if it did. Though the Order's geologists say that the peaks are continuing to rise quite quickly and that this rising will *destroy the fortress well before another thousand years have passed, Bind-strengthened or not.*

That thought saddened the prince, but a new smile crept onto his face when Master Neros's apprentices opened the large doors to the woodshop—an enormous barn really—and the master carpenter came out walking backward, giving directions to eight guardians and as many furans who were respectively pushing and pulling the Serpent's replica out into the courtyard with encouraging shouts and pained groans.

The thing was equally awesome and frightening. The replica was held in the air between the arms of a gigantic swing. The contraption, in and of itself, was nothing surprising for a master carpenter. What was truly incredible was the replica's remarkable likeness: Master Neros had built the frame out of heavy wood and covered the surface entirely with leather. He had even sculpted the head and face with such exquisite precision that the apparatus—except for its lifelessness—could have passed for the Serpent itself.

Oohs and *aahs* rose from across the compound, though a few soldiers stood rigidly, watching with tight jaws and clenched fists—despite recognizing the silliness of their reaction—as the replica was taken outside the fortress's gates. Huffing and puffing, the men and their four-legged helpers positioned the construction thirty meters from a large pond between the fortress and the village of Horn's Pass.

Laiella said, "That is truly impressive, Commander. Did you instruct Master Neros to do it this way?"

"I did. I wanted the training to be as real as possible. I had him not only replicate the likeness, with claws and everything, but also the estimated weight of the creature so that it will swing down swiftly when it's released from its starting position. He also added some gears to cause it to move sideways as it descends; I want the soldiers to fear for their lives when they see it come down."

Laiella opened her eyes wide. They *would* be afraid. She, herself, felt her skin crawl away as she surveyed the thing with her eyes. She asked what the exercise would involve.

"You'll hear—as soon as the men are assembled. And once we're done with this exercise, we'll train them in the air against Lina Lux Baiula's projection."

This time Laiella pulled her head back. What could Lina have prepared that she did not know of?

Toras saw her question and said, "Lina told me a few fourths ago that she is skilled in creating *projections* of objects of almost any size. That gave me an idea, and when I asked her if she could do it, she said 'Yes, I can,' and she's been preparing herself for it since then."

"I still would like to know what you got one of my Sisters to do without my knowing, Commander."

Toras gave a mischievous smile, "She will recreate the Serpent to simulate aerial combat. The danger to our guardians will be less real than the danger this replica represents, but she said she could make it singe them if they touch it. I've seen some demonstrations, and it's burnin' amazing."

Laiella raised a brow and said, "Commander, you should have informed me of this."

"I'm sorry, Prima, but you *have* been very busy these past fourths. Anyway, I'm sure you would have approved."

Laiella was not appeased. Instead of keeping a stony face this time, she let her irritation show plainly. Toras was the fortress's commander, but that did not give him direct authority over Sisters in his company, except during military engagements.

A frustrated hiss began making its way through the commander's throat when the resonating sound of the tabellarii beating the muster call put an end to it.

The men gathered a few meters back from the Serpent's replica, between it and the pond. Toras walked toward them and positioned himself right underneath the colossal construction. Men whispered with incredulity or challenges; if the thing were to get unlatched just now, the Commander would be killed before he could turn and realize it was coming down.

In the distance, villagers could be seen coming out, pointing, and chattering with visible agitation.

When Toras explained the training's goal and how it would proceed, some men swallowed hard, shifting their feet and doing their best not to appear nervous. Weren't they members of the bravest guard in Alvinoria? But, despite their innate temerity and the intense and continual training they were subjected to in order to ensure they became immune to fright, many still suffered from the sequelae of the attack on the fortress four months earlier, and they felt their stomachs tie-up as they watched the replica hanging there above them. Seeing their comrades grin and hearing their stomping feet did not reassure them.

After the first squad took position at the point of intersection with the replica's trajectory, Lord Commander Toras said, "Shielders, protect! Remember that your shields' handholds have been modified to break-off the moment the Serpent latches onto them, so I expect you to keep holding them to protect the archers until the very last moment."

"Archers! Your duty is to pierce that thing with as many arrows as you can and keep shooting until you see the thing's pupils."

"Of course, I expect all of you to stoop when it is time to do so, if you don't want to end up in the infirmary."

When he was done, Toras did not order them to get ready— he wanted them to be surprised for maximum effect. The soldiers watched him with frowns on their tense faces as he closed his eyes, counted, and listened for the latch which Master Neros was now unfastening from some distance, out of sight.

The sound of the air suddenly displaced by the gigantic facsimile and the screech of arms against frame startled everyone, even the bravest. A few stepped back despite themselves; others simply froze. But, responding to their onlooking comrades' desperate injunctions and following the example of the more seasoned soldiers among them, all the men raised their shields, and arrows started flying. When the replica detached from the frame and kept flying over the soldiers' heads to land in the large pond with a tremendous blast, a roar of awed screams and curses rose. The entire thing lasted only sixteen seconds, but it had frazzled some soldiers and thrilled the others. A corpse would have awakened if it had lain there underneath the gigantic, swinging contraption.

Two guardians lay unconscious and bleeding on the ground. The Guard's medic apprentice ran to them at once. The rest looked at each other, cursing and cussing, and doing their best to calm their hearts while laughing. The onlookers shook their heads, dreading their turn in front of the thing or, conversely, looking forward to it.

Laiella looked at Toras with horrified eyes, still under the shock of what she had just witnessed. She kept her voice low, but it was icy. She said, "Commander, for what purpose did you just possibly lose two men? Is this *foolish* exercise absolutely necessary?"

"It's not foolish, and it's more than necessary. Men were lost both here and in Furan City when the beast snatched them from the parapets to hurl them onto the ground or swallow them whole. That happened because they *froze*, or because they didn't let go of their shields when the Serpent's claws grabbed them. They need to learn to face the creature in full control of their minds *and* of their bodies, and this," Toras motioned toward the contraption, "is the best way—the *only* good way—I know to do it."

Laiella did not object anymore, not in front of the men. And the prince was right about the need to steel the men's nerves. But she would have taken some time to prepare them for the exercise. Toras's way had placed them at risk of serious injury if not death. She would speak with him about this later, but for now, she gave a begrudging grunt and said, "Why aren't we practicing with them?"

"Did I freeze when the Serpent came at me? Would you freeze?"

"No, but that is not the point. I would prefer no one get killed during training, and if we do the exercise with them, we can talk them through it, to be sure no one freezes and that they stoop, as you said, only at the last moment."

Toras looked back, annoyed, but Laiella insisted, and he relented. Just then, a cry came from Master Neros to get out of the way so that the replica might be pulled back into position, and Toras called the men to himself.

"Soldiers, that fear that still grips many of you in the face of the real thing is even affecting you when confronted by its lifeless likeness. So, we'll continue with these exercises, rotating squads until each and every single one of you has let go of the fear. And I hope that we won't need to send too many to the infirmary in the meantime." Toras eyed Laiella, then added, "To be sure, the prima and I will take turns practicing with you. Now, the next troop. Assemble!"

Commander and officer spent the remainder of the day—breaking only for a reparative lunch—showing the men how and when to stoop to keep themselves safe, and encouraging them to remain at their posts in front of the descending replica.

The training had been grueling, for everyone and especially for Toras and Laiella since—with a guard of a thousand, and troops of fifty—that had meant ten turns each, and Toras's sixth turn almost cost him his shoulder. After that, he was forced to call the stoops a few seconds earlier than he had before. But by the end of practice, Toras was confident his men were readier than before.

The suns were now starting to set. The Blue Sun was slightly ahead of its Red twin as the current In-Between Fourth was ending, and the First Bolingar Fourth was approaching, a fourth during which the Blue Sun would precede the Red by almost an hour. The men were waiting to be served a highly welcome meal, sitting in the field surrounding the pond. Indeed, the prince had requested that the cooks set the meal out here, thinking that it would finish desensitizing the soldiers to the

Serpent if they were forced to eat underneath its replica, which was hanging high above them, looming, dark, and—with the setting suns— seeming even more alive than it had earlier in the day.

Most soldiers did start ignoring it after turning their heads to look at it a few times. But there were those who continued to repress shivers as they gave it furtive glances. The contraption reminded them too much of the real thing, which had taken their comrades' lives and had come very close to taking theirs as well. It was possible these few would never dispel the fear completely.

But they would have another chance to face their fears tonight, because another exercise was presently being set up for them. Indeed, the prince had agreed with Lina Lux Baiula to conduct the training with the projection at dusk, since that is when the Serpent preferred to attack.

Just now, the bugler sounded the horn and everyone, except for the two injured soldiers who were at the infirmary, stood with anxious anticipation of the next crazy exercise their commander had conceived of.

Machinations on Earth

In her still exquisitely and precisely modulated voice, the bi-millennial Alia, Empress of Earth and its Colonies, and Savior of Humankind, said to her interlocutor, "I received a note, this morning, informing me of several communications the Threat Detection Unit has picked up in recent months. These communications refer to something called," Alia paused for effect, "the Morphosis Plan. Have you heard of any such plan within our governments?"

Genghis did not respond right away; he waited perhaps a half-second while looking at his Minister of Science from the corner of his eyes. But that might have been too long already. With a voice slightly less perfect than Alia's, but nevertheless finely controlled, he said, "Hmm, 'Morphosis Plan'. It strikes me as familiar. I believe I heard about it on Gunick, when inspecting the troops there."

"You have? And what is it that you recall about it? What *is* this plan?"

Presently Genghis cursed the reactions of his still partly biological body. How had the name the plan gotten out? How?! The general stopped the self-questioning; he was used to Alia's insinuations and knew, after the twenty-three centuries spent at her side—if one ignored the three hundred years of banishment he spent on Enceladus after his first attempt at conquering the very same planet he was targeting again—that he needed to respond at once lest she see beneath his synthetic surface.

"I believe it has to do with some scientists there discovering—or on the verge of discovering, in any case—a new terraforming technology." Genghis turned toward his minister and pinched his brows in the way he often did when he was about to ask an unplanned question to alert the man. When he saw the man pull his lower jaw forward, he said, "Thabo, do you recall our visit with Gunick's Land Ordinator last month? What did he say about this plan?"

Thabo felt his heart clench. He had feared such a leak for so long. He scratched his throat a few times to think through his response. Since Gunick did indeed have a project to explore new ways to terraform small planets—albeit known by another name—he felt comfortable enough to support the general's lie, but his reply would need to be such as to then divert the empress's attention from their plan. Still, the need to lie caused him visible stress, which he hoped Alia would ascribe to his usual uneasiness in her presence. After clearing his throat one last time, he said, "Empress, the plan is indeed intended to investigate new terraforming technologies…but it is in its very early days, and the name of the project is not yet settled. In fact, it has been known by at least five different names, al—"

"That is unimportant, Minister." Addressing herself to her general again, Alia said, "But why haven't I heard of this before? Why does it appear to be so secretive that it has not made its way into my daily briefing feeds, and why aren't there any official communications about it?"

Genghis felt his body tense, but he told himself to relax, and his face regained its usual business-like expression. Just now, however, he found himself wishing that he had indeed transferred his brain into a fully synthetic body—as Alia had urged him to do time and again, though her preference was for him to transfer his mind into a positronic brain—so that he need not fear being betrayed by his twitching muscles. He said, "Empress, you know how the Gunickans are; they are a highly insecure, small planet on the outer rim of the galaxy, and I am certain they wish simply to be sure of their science before they make any official announcements."

"It may be so, and they have been secretive about silly things in the past. But do try to obtain more information about this plan and be ready to brief me tomorrow. I, myself, want to be sure that this new technology—if and when it is developed— does not get disseminated without my consent. I do not care what they do in the outer rim, but I *would* care if their technology were to be used to alter planets closer to us and in which I *do* have an interest."

By now, Genghis knew how to stay out of rabbit holes and to think on his feet. He said, "I will look into it, Empress, and bring you everything there is to know about their technology. But as Thabo has indicated, it is in its very early days, which means years away from being deployed—if it should prove to ever be successful."

Alia acknowledged her general's assessment and walked out to her balcony. She often did that during unpleasant conversations, perhaps to admire New Rome, the empire's capital, which was located on the highest peak of the Eurasian continent, and in which she was still able to find beauty despite the desolation of the rest of the planet. A sort of laugh escaped hear throat as she reminded herself of the fact that many— including Genghis—wondered whether she could feel anything at all.

Watching the empress, Genghis thought: *I will need to speak with Thabo as soon as we are done here. The leak must be in his department, and the leaker* must *be found and removed.*

Wishing to continue admiring the view—one which had not become dull for its familiarity—and not wishing to yell her question, Alia sent it to Genghis and Thabo electronically.

Genghis cringed because, if her 'natural' voice was beautiful and perfect, what he heard when she used her mindchip to communicate was not very pleasant at all.

She sent, *"General, Minister, how are you going to quash the revolt on Kepler?"*

Genghis turned to Thabo and asked him to explain how the revolt was going to be crushed. This was the question they had come to discuss, and they had therefore prepared at length for it.

The minister of science cleared his throat even more nervously this time, for somehow, the topic felt even closer to their true aims than the name of their plan being picked up by the TDU.

Genghis was losing patience with his minister and expected that Alia would voice her own impatience very soon. He turned to look at her and noticed her tapping her index finger on the railing. *That is very strange. I've never seen her display her emotions physically.*

When he heard Thabo scratch his throat again, he sent him an electronic whip.

This time, the empress sent a loud "Well?" through the speaker in the office.

Thabo replied via the brainchip, *"My apologies, Empress, I...I am not feeling well today."*

Alia sent, *"I wonder whether Minister Thabo is still fit to perform his duties, General. I wonder too, why you need him to send for you."*

"Empress, I assure you Thabo still has his utility. I can certainly provide you certain updates myself, but they would be generalities. The minister, on the other hand, can give you the details you prefer."

Alia sent a sigh, which the brainchip replicated as a quiet screech, then sent, *"If you had transferred your mind to a positronic brain, you would be able to carry all the details in it."* The empress listened for a response, which she knew she would not get. Genghis was probably biting his tongue, she thought. She sent, *"Anyway, go on Minister. Or do you wish to abuse my patience?"*

Thabo shook and sighed silently, then proceeded to inform the Savior of Humankind—one he believed to be their goddess and to whom he owed only the truth—of their preparations to arrest the revolt on Kepler, omitting anything related to their true mission. Up until some months ago, this would have been impossible for him to do, but Genghis *had* almost convinced him that Alia's reign was ending, just as the earlier gods of Earth had had their times of greatness and then made way for new ones to carry Humanity through its next stages. But what new god would replace her if it must happen? Genghis had had no reply for this question, except to say that the Universe would provide one, and Thabo's scientific mind struggled to see the signs of a new divinity emerging.

Still, Genghis might be right about Alia, and if so—if her decline was affecting her mind in ways that would cause her to do harm to Humanity—then they had no choice but to keep their plans from her. But shouldn't a goddess know all? Perhaps the very fact that she could not see what they were hiding was proof of her decline. The thought gave him some measure of reassurance, just as much as it distressed him.

Thabo described in the greatest detail the new weapon they would be using to subdue Kepler's insurgents, its effect, its reach, and its limitations. The empress was glad to know the weapon would cause limited injury when aimed at healthy individuals. Her comment made the small man question his tentative belief that perhaps the empress was becoming unfit to continue to see to the good of Humanity, and he glanced toward the general with eyes wondering if they were not wrong about her. But Genghis did not notice his movement, and Alia thanked Thabo then turned to her general for the strategic details.

The general provided information on the mission's commanders, the vessels, the number of troops, and the planned disposition of ships and troops around the rebel planet. The empress did not seem to like his answers and asked why fifty thousand soldiers were needed for this mission. Genghis gave a curious frown; Alia knew how many soldiers were required for ground assaults. Why was she asking this? His pause caused her to ask again, and—after a loud enough grumble—he explained the situation on Kepler, reminding Alia that she had demanded that no weapons of mass effect be used. He added that the new device developed by the ministry of science, which Thabo had described, would require a ground assault, which meant large numbers of troops.

Alia listened to it all very carefully, every so often asking Genghis to confirm one thing or another, nodding to herself, then instructing him to continue.

It was all very curious to the general, who observed her carefully from his position in the office and he ached to be done with the meeting. Genghis had seen her standing there on the balcony more times than he could count, her perfect silhouette outlined by the capital's blue, green, and red lights which twinkled in the distance, thinking thoughts that only she could grasp. But despite her far-reaching sight, she had misjudged one thing: Human nature. And her blind spot had cost him, as well as everyone else who lived on or around that god-forsaken planet, dearly indeed.

Finally, Alia asked when they would depart and how long the mission would take.

Genghis replied that departure should occur in a month and that the entire mission—if successful—would require approximately six Earth months, not including the travel to and from Kepler.

Alia gave one final look to the sprawling capital, nodded to herself, came back in, and went to her seat. She did not need to sit, but she had realized a long time ago that with most Humans—and Thabo was one of them—doing such things as un-transformed Humans did made them more comfortable around her.

Genghis and Thabo waited patiently for the empress to either dismiss them or launch onto another topic. Just now, she tapped her finger again. Genghis and Thabo looked at each other tensely.

Using her voice now that she was near them and did not need to have a confidential conversation—though Genghis was probably not going to enjoy it—Alia said, "Minister, what is the state of the conversion research? Have your scientists been able to replicate the procedure that was used to transfer my mind? And have they been able to reproduce in full the sensory experience of organic bodies?"

Genghis's facial expression contorted itself in a furious rictus. How *dare* Alia discuss this topic with others without informing him?

The empress noticed and said, "Genghis, I am concerned that what we have created will soon unravel itself unless this is done. I am aware of your sentiments about it, but this procedure is necessary for the empire's continued survival."

Alia watched for hints of consent, opposition, or uncertainty. Believing she had noticed signs of the latter, she added, "I know what you desire, Genghis, and I would not force the conversion upon you unless the technology were such that you would have the experience you have been yearning for."

She knows what I desire? She has no idea what I want! I wish to end *my life; finish it as a real Human; not continue to live for a thousand years more to enjoy the pleasures of the flesh!* Genghis tried to restrain himself, but his voice was tight when he started to object.

Alia raised a hand to stop him.

Switching to private mind-to-mind communication, Alia said, *"Whether you realize it or not, Genghis, I am concerned with your happiness, and I know that remaining in this state much longer could very well lead you to make the same mistake you made so long ago now, when you tried to take that planet. I do not want you to go down that path again. Not now. Not with the growing tensions and discontent across the empire."*

It took all of Genghis's self-control to not admit the truth to the empress. He was glad she had used mind-to-mind speech, because had she spoken her suspicions aloud, Thabo *would have* revealed everything.

But, though the minister of science *had heard* only silence for the past minute, he could tell from the general's reaction that their mental exchange had not been any more pleasant than the spoken ones.

Reverting to oral speech again, Alia said, "Those are the reasons for my question to the minister, General."

Genghis understood that unless he wished to take on Alia, here and now, he had no choice but to go along with the charade as Thabo began to explain the status of the science. Indeed, he was not a betting man, and he was not certain he would be the victor if he confronted Alia.

It was a good thing for Genghis that his teeth were made of zirconium, or he would surely have cracked his incisors listening to Thabo nervously extol the conversion technology's advancements to the empress.

After ten unbearable minutes, with Alia asking for more details and Thabo providing them with ever greater discomfort, Genghis detached himself from the discussion and turned his thoughts to the Kepler mission, from where he would then take his troops to his intended destination—Fate willing.

A Projection

Toras yelled, "All right, this next exercise is for the furanriders only; the rest of you can relax and watch." The majority relaxed while the two hundred who rode furans responded with annoyed grimaces. "You will be facing the enemy in the air, which means that both you and your mounts will have a chance to temper your nerves this time."

Men shouted back questions about the wooden replica's flying capabilities.

Toras turned around to look for Lina just as she approached him. He swiveled back toward the men and said, "Lina Lux Baiula will generate a semblance of the Serpent so that you may practice air combat against it. I will let her explain what you should expect."

Lina Lux Baiula projected her voice to give her explanations. However, she was not as skilled at it as Elia or Elyana were, and men in the back complained about not being able to hear. So, she stopped tried again, but her attempt resulted only in a strangely distorted voice. She grumbled and decided to do it the normal way: by shouting.

She said, "I will use a sonactic Binding to form the image of the Serpent. This will move just like the creature does and be just as large. You and your furans will think it quite real." Men looked at each other, most doubtful, others in anticipation. "If you touch the form, it may burn and cut you—a little—but no more."

Some faces scrunched up. One man asked another, "How would she know how the Serpent fights? She's never even faced it."

If her voice projection was weak, her hearing was at least as good as any other man's, and Lina said, "I have faced it, guardian; in Lord Commander Toras's mind. He allowed me to look, and I saw what he saw when the Serpent attacked the fortress. I will therefore be able to replicate its movements and its image quite accurately."

Some men looked impressed, while others made some puerile comments about what else the Sister might have seen in their Commander's mind. That got them icy stares from both the prince and the Lux Baiula.

A young soldier asked if they should tell their furans that the Serpent would be a fake one.

Toras replied, "I don't think it matters, whether we tell them or not; it won't change their reactions. They already like to chase after imaginary prey or defend against imagined foe."

A veteran said, "In any case, Bartus, I doubt your furan would understand if you told him." That got a laugh from the others.

After he called the men back to attention, Toras sent them to fetch their mounts and ready themselves. As they did, he called Laiella over and explained his plans for the practice. Laiella had no objections this time.

Meanwhile, Lina Lux Baiula began imagining the Serpent, an unnatural hiss starting to rise from her throat. As her Binding increased in intensity, the shredded black and brown silk she had had dumped on the ground before her began assembling itself into the shape of the creature, surrounding her and hiding her from everyone else. The onlooking soldiers gaped and made comments about being glad they weren't the ones who would be facing this *thing*, while those walking back with their furans gasped and were jerked by their furans who reacted with alarm.

A moment later, the semblance started climbing, accompanied by the same unnatural hiss, its wings flapping awkwardly as the wind caused the shreds of silk to separate. Lina strengthened her Binding and tightened the mass. Its motions now blew wind over the ground, and the deep swooshing sound brought chills to the men and caused the furans to back away.

Toras looked toward Laiella, who shook her head skeptically. He said, "This might be scarier than the real thing."

A few soldiers were heard warning others that the Lux Baiula had perhaps used her magic to summon the Serpent itself.

The civilians, who had been alerted of the exercise and told not to panic when they saw *a* Serpent appear over the fortress, watched from their newly built homes, swearing and hoping that the prince was not unleashing something else at them.

Shocked gasps rose from every corner of Horn's Pass at the sight of the apparition, while a fear-laden cacophony grew from the panicked bleaters and cacklers and other animals in the reddish dusk. As for the prince, he rubbed his hands in excited anticipation and shot a mischievous grin at his prima.

Laiella's expression was one of pleased surprise. The prince might be impulsive, but he did have an extraordinary ability to think beyond the ordinary. She turned from Toras to her Sister and watched the woman with a measure of admiration.

After making the projection perform a few test dives and turns, Lina signaled her readiness to begin the exercises. Laiella clapped her hands and ordered the first forty furanteams, commanded by their secundi, to take position in the air.

The prince watched with excitement, anticipation, and visible trepidation. He said, leaning his head toward Laiella, "I'd really like to be there myself!"

When the furanteams had taken position, placing themselves some one hundred meters to the west of the vision, Secundus Yuuto yelled from above, and Laiella gave Lina the order to commence.

At first, many riders, who were trying to control their mounts' movements and did not know how to react to the projection, prevented their furans from moving at all. When the projection hit them, all felt the burn and cuts, and they cursed. The pain drew them into the reality of the exercise, and they readied themselves for the next pass.

Just now, Lina sent the serpent down with a spiraling motion and the secundi ordered their men to spread; teams moved up and down and left and right, and those that moved too slowly got singed and cut again.

This time, Lina took her projection as far as she could manage it, to give the men a moment to strategize, and then sent it back down as fast as she could. The secundi tried to anticipate the projection's movement and ordered their men one direction or another before it hit them. But again, many were burned when Lina caused her serpent to change suddenly direction. This continued for a few more minutes, and each time the Serpent's semblance passed the teams, a quarter of them got sliced and scorched. Toras and Laiella shook their heads in disappointment. At that rate, after four passes, all would be dead if they were facing the real Serpent.

It was not until after the ninth attempt that a secundus—more sensitive to his furan—had an idea. He called the other officers to himself during the pause and told them his plan. Toras looked at Laiella curiously when the men seemed to disagree more forcefully than they usually did.

After what sounded like a few more curses—Toras could not tell from the distance—the teams repositioned themselves, Secundus Yuuto waved, and Lina relaunched her projection.

This time, all the teams avoided being touched by the burning, cutting, flying puppet, and shouts of joy erupted from the air and the ground. Twice more, the furanteams avoided the serpent altogether, even when Lina took the form through an impossible sequence of turns. Toras nodded with satisfaction and curiosity; he would need to ask the men how they had suddenly improved their responses, when they came down. However, it was now time for the teams to attack the vision, and Laiella blew her horn to signal the change.

Lina paused the projection a few hundred meters away from the teams, glad to have a chance to take a few cubes of sweet salts from her pocket. When she received the signal, she attacked again.

It took the teams eleven passes, this time, before they figured things out, and although Toras and Laiella thought they'd never be able to avoid the thing while also attacking it, they did succeed in the end. And when this first group of teams landed, they were received with all manner of commiseration, hoorays, and questions from those going next.

The remaining four groups had a much easier time of it, having learned from Secundus Yuuto that the trick to defending was to give the furans complete control of the responses. To attack, on the other hand, they needed to instruct the furans on their intent and then give them the freedom to adjust their movements by themselves as the Serpent's projection approached and changed direction. Indeed, by doing so, the furans were able to make minor adjustments to their flight while still allowing the soldiers to stab or shoot at the form.

When the first to last group went, Toras and Laiella joined the men atop their own furans, and they practiced the movements not without a few infuriating burns and cuts for themselves and their furans. Scorch flew as furans fly when facing their fiercest competitor, the Sprayer, with dizzying and abrupt direction changes, and reduced responsiveness to anything else, which now included commands from their riders. The third time Toras felt his stomach heave; he pulled hard on Scorch to try and steady him, but that put them right on the Bound simulacre's path on the next pass, and both got severe burns from the encounter. Toras remembered Yuuto's instructions and let go of the reins.

By the time they completed the exercise, both Toras and Laiella were exhausted, what with taking ten troops through the first exercise and then four through the second. Plumped down on his divan and a tall glass of grasswine in his hand, the prince now turned a hopeful look toward his prima. When she returned a pleased gaze at him, he downed the rest of the wine with a single, proud gulp and a large grin on his face.

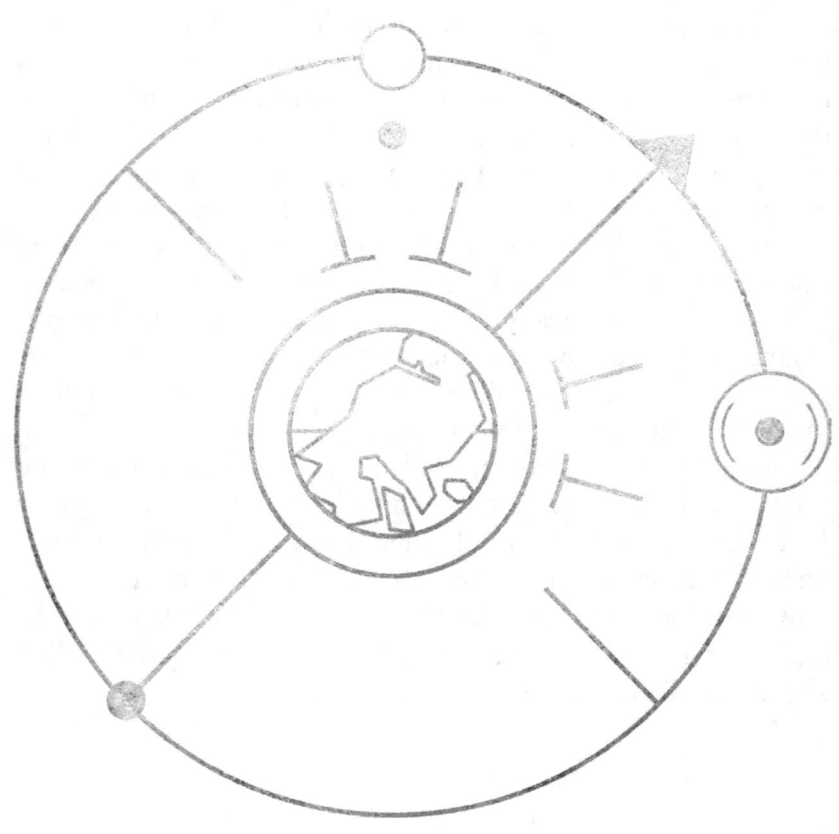

XI FAILURES

First Attempt

A ithen was sitting in his antechamber this quiet evening when melancholic thoughts about his youth crossed his mind. The thoughts stirred a need for something soothing, and he stood to pull the cord next to his Lacora Leaf chair to call Kildare. The boy walked in a moment later and asked what the prince needed.

"Would you bring me a glass of Merotto, Kil?"

"Of course, my Prince. Would you like it warm or cold?"

"Warm. Please bring it to the balcony."

The squire tipped his head and left.

When Aithen opened the sliding door to the balcony, the cool air of autumn enveloped him immediately. It was a pleasant air, laden with the scents of the furtree, which bloomed at this time of year.

He walked to the stone wall surrounding the deck, leaned his elbows on it, and gazed at the sea. At this time of the night—the darkest part of it—the sky was lit with a pale purple light. This light allowed one to see well enough to still play ball, which he and Toras used to do when younger.

Shadows that passed over the corner of his eyes attracted Aithen's attention toward the royal apartments. Curious, he turned his head. His curiosity turned into alarm when several shapes jumped onto the balcony of his father's private quarters.

What is that?

"Guards! The king's bedchamber!!"

Aithen rushed into his rooms, grabbed his sword from the cabinet next to his bed and ran out, bumping against Kil who had heard his scream and was coming to him.

"My Prince, what is happening?"

"Kil! The king and queen-consort are being attacked. Rouse the guard. Quick!"

His heart thumping, Aithen's mind raced to assess the situation. The Red Sashes would be able to stop the attackers, wouldn't they? And his parents—if they were both in the king's chambers—should both be safe there, right?

As he raced toward the south wing, Coris and Piros, Aithen's personal guardians, joined him, asking what was happening. Aithen gave short, angry responses and continued to run. When they reached the main hall between north and south wings, they were met by Harlion, who had been alerted by Kil. Between ragged breaths, Aithen said, "Captain! Send another man with me; place twenty here and send another thirty into the gardens to block the attackers' escape. Quickly!"

Harlion had no time to acknowledge the orders; Aithen was already rushing up the steps to the king's chambers. Shouts and screams rang out, now, and alerted the entire palace. Servants opened doors to peek but stayed in their own quarters; they knew not to get in the way during an attack, even if there had not been one in decades.

Standing in front of the king's apartments, Aithen paused to listen, despite his drumming heart, to try and tell what was happening inside before rushing in. The sounds of things crashing on walls and on the floor came through easily. With a wary look toward his guardians, Aithen opened the outer doors. No one in the office chamber. The entrance to the guard chamber on the right was ajar, showing an empty room. The door to the antechamber on the left was open, and this, too, was empty.

"They are in my father's bedchamber."

Aithen approached with barely contained anxiety, tested the door; it was locked.

"We need to use the secret passage."

The men nodded and followed Aithen. They ran out of the apartments, took a left. Toward the end of the hallway Aithen pressed his hand into a brick, and a door slid aside. They entered.

When Aithen opened the inner door and pulled the curtain in front of it, his heart stopped. A black-garbed attacker held his mother, while two others threatened his father, who was assisted by Julian, and three others were fighting one of the Red Sashes.

Almiar and Jashan were down. Coris, behind him, asked where the other Lux Baiulae were.

Aithen shrugged his shoulders desperately then said, "I'll go and help my mother. Piros, you go three meters to the right and position yourself to assist my father. Coris, and you..."

The man said his name was Boros.

"Coris and Boros, you continue until you reach the end of the wall so you can help Dana Lux Baiula. When you hear me whistle, charge!"

The men acknowledged his instructions, and Aithen started toward the left, staying behind the curtain which the attackers were not watching. His father's image, standing sword-in-hand, with a feral grimace on his face flashed through his mind; it was quickly replaced by that of his mother, with some type of glaive on her throat and horror on her face. Who carried glaives? Only the Barriers, as far as he knew.

With his mother and her assailant now only a meter in front of him, Aithen looked toward the sides to check on his men. When he knew they were in place, he took a calming breath, whistled, and charged.

He was on his mother's captor in a flash, sliding his right arm under the man's own arm to move his glaive away from his mother's neck. The man's muscles tensed-up at once. The prince forced his right arm further out while he plunged his dagger into the man's back.

When her captor fell to the ground, the queen-consort did not turn around immediately, Aithen panicked. He stepped over the now-dead man and grabbed his mother by the shoulders. Still, she did not move. In front of them, chaos had erupted; the assailants were now surrounded by his father, their soldiers, and one Lux Baiula. But the assassins did not appear to be troubled and instead kept attacking. Tables lay broken, and the Lacora Leaf chairs sat limply on their sides.

Aithen looked at the queen-consort with frightened eyes, and when he tried to push her toward the chamber's secret door and she resisted, he screamed, "Mother, are you not well? Can't you move?"

It took Darya another moment to recover control of her muscles, and when she did, she nearly fell limp in Aithen's arms. "Mother!"

"I...I was paralyzed, son. I am well now. Please go help your father."

Aithen breathed a silent sigh of relief and said, "I will, but you need to get out, quickly."

Darya did not give much resistance, though she kept looking toward the king with worried eyes. Aithen urged her on and pushed her out through the secret door, then joined the others.

Down in the gardens, a dozen men hid among the bushes, waiting for the assassins to come down, while Harlion and another dozen searched the palace grounds for lurking men. Irania and Mitsuko Lux Baiulae arrived presently from the palace's first floor, where they had their offices and demanded to know what was happening.

Harlion said, "Assassins entered the king's chambers. I don't know how many, but the Praetorian Guard along with the Barriers, and now also the prince and a few other men, are there."

Irania asked, alarmed, "Why are you here? Why aren't you there to help defend the king and his wife?"

"Because there are already too many in there, and I think there are at least three or four other assassins hiding somewhere on the palace grounds. I suggest you go back in and stay in your offices."

Irania responded with an icy stare made worse by the purplish moonlight.

Harlion relented and said, "But if you prefer to help search the grounds, you are more than welcome."

Irania turned to Mitsuko to ask if she could reach one of their Sisters up there, but the woman shook her head.

Irania said, "Me neither. We really need a better way to connect!" After the frustration passed and knowing they couldn't do anything for those fighting up there, Irania and Mitsuko nodded to the captain, and all of them went to search the grounds.

Stepping to his father's right, Aithen said, "Do you mind some help?"

"Not at all, son. I see no need for politeness here."

Their opponents looked at the two of them wide-eyed. Julian and Piros, who stood to the king's left, welcomed the prince while keeping their eyes on the attackers. Aithen pointed toward Coris and the others and sent Piros to them.

Aithen thought that now that the assassins were slightly outnumbered, they would have chosen to run, but it was not so. The two men facing them were obviously angered by the arrival of reinforcements, but they seemed intent on completing their mission no matter the cost. After nodding to each other, the tall man rushed the king and the prince, while the smaller one attacked Julian.

The man who came against prince and king was not only tall; he was also muscular and excessively agile. The man came to within striking distance of the king in his first move. Aithen felt his heart clench, but when he saw his father parry and then push the man away, he could not help but let a brief sense of admiration and relief surface.

The assassin recovered quickly, however, and he repositioned himself, grinning tauntingly at Octavius and ignoring Aithen. Then he attacked, but instead of aiming at Octavius, he went for Aithen's leg. Aithen swiveled in time to avoid a deep laceration, but he already had his first cut.

The man stepped back and began again, this time taunting both father and son.

Next to them, Julian groaned and fell. Neither paused, and neither gave their opponent a distracted opening. It was not long before the assassin who brought down Julian, a short man with dead green eyes, positioned himself in front of the king.

Father and son took a deep breath each, set themselves, and lunged at their respective opponents.

Behind them, someone else uttered a dying croak. Aithen's mind lost its concentration for the briefest moment; it was brought back sharply into focus when a glaive flashed toward him. Aithen reacted with a well-trained soldier's automatic motions, motions made slightly swifter by the recent training he had received from Tania. But despite his immediate reaction, his distraction had sufficed to give his adversary an opening, and the glaive slashed his right flank. Several, more ferocious exchanges ensued between the two.

It seemed the assassin felt luck was on his side now, and he harassed the prince until Aithen was forced to recede. After a few more harried parries, sidesteps, and slips, Aithen heard his father groan. He stole a glance toward him, as he pushed his opponent back, and saw his father's exhaustion gaining him. He determined then that he had to bring his fight with the giant to an end. He paused with his eyes focused on the man, keeping him away with his arm forward. He started closing his eyes, wishing to use Corae Sentiens, but he wasn't ready to trust in his Sensing skills. Instead, he made his eyes into slits, took a few deep, calming breaths, and with the assurance he had developed over the years training with the best of the Royal Guard, he beckoned the colossus forward. When the man's thigh tensed, Aithen spun and cut the man's head off.

On the other side of the room, Dana moved like a ghost. But her two black-garbed opponents were no ordinary persons either. Dana parried with incredible speed and precision despite the fatigue she must be feeling, and she lunged once in a while when she was fortunate enough to confuse both her opponents by her movements. Her motions were so precise—or were they lucky? —that she dodged her opponents' strikes by only a few centimeters each time. If the fight had been less chaotic, she might have dispatched all the men on her own, but there were too many fighters and the battlefield was so encumbered she was unable to move and strike effectively. Presently, her opponents eyed each other, starting to feel drained by the interminable bout. One, a dark-skinned woman, nodded to the other as if they had just agreed on a new tactic. Dana used the moment to lunge toward the man, who stood on her right, with such precisely timed movements that the other's reaction could not prevent her blade from finding its target. Having done that, she spun and faced the woman.

King and prince were struggling against the man with the dead green eyes. The assassin was exceptionally skilled and kept evading them both and striking from surprising directions, each time moving closer to the king. Just now, the man managed to deflect Octavius's strike and then slide beneath Aithen's sword.

By the time Aithen turned around, the man shot his arm up and struck from above. The blow was ferocious, and Aithen shook. Without wasting time, the green-eyed assassin prepared to repeat the same attack; Aithen readied himself to parry another blow from above, but the killer suddenly lowered his arm and slashed the calf on Aithen's forward leg—the same leg that the giant had cut. Aithen screamed and dropped to the ground.

The man quickly turned toward the king.

Octavius tried to strike the assassin before he completed his turn, but the man pulled himself back at the last moment. Not finding his target, Octavius hit a heavy ardamantis pedestal instead. The force of the contact sent shards of pain through his arm, and he groaned.

Before the king recovered, the assassin approached him and extended his arm toward Octavius. An urgent injunction against letting the man touch him reached the king. But Dana's warning was in vain; the king—always too calculating and not tending to react on impulse—responded too slowly, and the assassin's hand touched him. His muscles became suddenly rigid and unresponsive.

Just when Aithen found the strength to charge again, the man stepped around the king and grabbed him from behind. Octavius took on the same horrified look as Darya had, and Aithen almost lost his senses, screaming and calling for the others' help, suspecting what was going to happen to his father now.

But no one was available to help Aithen, who watched with horror as the assassin placed his glaive on the king's throat with a wild grin accompanying his dead green eyes, which spoke of victory.

Aithen yelled, "Release him!"

The prince's yell finally interrupted the fighting between the guardians, the Lux Baiula, and their opponents, but weapons kept at the ready as they eyed the other end of the chamber to see what was happening there.

The man holding the king replied with a thick southern coastal accent, "R'lease im? Why? So our great king may continue to call the Nethers upon us? Take im is what we'll do, to bring his spirit b'fore the Founder!"

Aithen raced to think while trying to make sense of the mad words. But the man was already pressing his glaive into his father's throat. He looked at Octavius with a fear he did not know he could feel, and it was made worse by the total lack of reaction from his father. In fact, Octavius had closed his eyes.

When the assassin started to thrust his blade fully into the king's throat, the king made a frown as if from some painful, but invisible effort, while Aithen emitted a pleading groan. All gasped when the assassin cried out in pain, an awful rictus pinching his face, and he let go of his glaive, which fell to the ground with a clang louder than the screams. A moment later, the man collapsed. Whether he was dead or merely unconscious, Aithen could not tell.

The guardians and the Lux Baiula did not waste time, and they turned on the other assassins before any escaped. As exhausted as he was, Piros lunged toward one of them with frightening ferocity and plunged his sword right through the man's belly and out his back with a vicious growl, while Second Barrier Dana took the female assassin with her glaive. The last hitman, who was being charged by Boros, jumped onto a marble table and from there over the guardians and made for the balcony from whence he jumped down to the ground. A chase and fighting ensued in the gardens. Dana Lux Baiula made to follow, but there were at least two dozen guardians after the coward, so she dismissed the man with a disgusted *'bah'* and returned to see to the king.

In the king's bedchamber, there reigned a scene of relief and confusion.

Aithen's traits were a mix of gladness and puzzlement, while the men's faces showed relief but also anger and humiliation. However, Dana's mind, though it should be concerned with her fallen Sisters, was occupied with a suspicion; she was going to ask the king a question, but the prince halted her.

"We need to see to the injured and the fallen."

The woman nodded resentfully and not without shooting a look at the king that said, 'I *will* ask my question.'

The accounting was completed within ten minutes. Almiar was dead. The others, Julian, Jashan, and Boros were injured but would live, according to Tania Lux Baiula, who had just arrived. The Sisters had fared the worst in this clash. All three Red Sashes under Dana had died—*incomprehensible*.

Presently, the king saw his son approach with the Second Barrier, who looked intensely troubled. Aithen pulled him over to a corner.

He said, "Father, for a moment I thought this was the end of you. For a moment, you were completely in the man's control and I was sure he was going to slice your throat. But he didn't. What happened?"

Octavius prepared to answer as he had planned to do, but Aithen did not wait for his reply. Instead, he turned toward Dana and said, "Did you use the Bind to bring the man down?"

Dana shook her head, but her eyes stayed fixed on the king, who remained expressionless. When Aithen turned to him with the same question, Octavius felt everything inside of him scream. His son's words felt like an accusation of the worst kind, "Or did *you* do it?"

The king's body stiffened, and a roar rose from the deepest part to quash his son's impudent question. But he held it back and instead gave his son such a furious look as to shrivel a stone. Sadly, the damage was done, and Dana looked at him with an expression demanding the answer to the same question she appeared to have had.

Octavius wondered for a moment whether he could reject his son's question and keep Dana at bay. But he knew that what they suspected was not something the Lux Baiula would accept to let be. Feeling cornered, but not wanting to expose himself in front of the others in the room who did not know of his powers, he stormed off without even a signal and went to his office chamber, expecting that his son and the Lux Baiula would follow; and if they didn't, just as well!

But Dana and Aithen did follow.

When they arrived in his office, Octavius ordered Aithen to shut the door and stood himself straight and solid as a column of thrice-bound ardamantis, discountenanced only by the queen-consort's arrival.

Darya ran to her husband, despite the evident tension in the room.

The king struggled to let himself embrace the queen-consort, given the anger he felt toward his heir. But he *had* been afraid for her and he took her in his arms—if only for a moment—despite the contrary feelings he was feeling.

When Darya released him—or rather, when he finally pulled himself away—Octavius pivoted back toward Aithen, his hands closing and opening several times. He said, "It doesn't matter how I overcame the man. What does is that he is alive, and hopefully, he will be able to give us some answers."

"Father, I'm sorry, but it *does* matter. There was no way for you to overcome the assassin unless—"

Frustrated, Octavius cut-off his son and tried again against all odds to change the discussion's focus. With a threatening edge to his question, he asked, "Why are you asking this, Aithen?"

The prince passed his hand through his hair, unable to answer; it seemed the king's tactic had worked; the queen-consort, on the other hand, seemed to ache to ask what they were talking about, and it appeared she was going to do it when Dana spoke and asked a question in the way that Lux Baiulae did to leave no room for escape.

Dana said, "Sire, did you use the Bind to 'overcome the man' as you say, and if so, what Binding did you use?"

The king shook his head dejectedly; Darya watched him apprehensively; Aithen appeared to be waiting for an answer he did not truly want; Dana was the only one who simply waited for the truth.

Octavius swept both the Lux Baiula and the prince with an angry, glacial stare before saying with a slow staccato, "I entered his mind...by force."

Darya shook her head forlornly while Aithen stood there like a statue—a guilty statue. Octavius looked down, and a small, cynical laugh escaped him.

Suddenly, Aithen became alarmed, and he spun toward the Lux Baiula. It seemed he feared she would denounce him for the crime of mind rape—as Marcus Vrol, Octavius's old captain and friend, had been accused forty years earlier. And Dana was, in fact, resolving herself to some action.

Octavius watched all this as in a dream, or rather, as if in a nightmare. He watched his son stare the Lux Baiula down with such unyielding determination that she eventually stepped back, though her features remained filled with danger. It softened

Octavius a little to see his son try to limit the damage—though only a little.

Aithen now turned toward him with uneasy motions, starting to speak and stopping himself several times; perhaps he wanted to apologize.

"Father, I don't know what to say. It's obvious—given this and what you did when you rescued Toras and his men from the wrigglers a few months back—that your skills are far beyond mere Sensing abilities." Aithen glanced warily at the Lux Baiula before continuing, "It's just that…everyone saw what happened…and I don't know whether to just be happy you're safe or concerned for the possible consequences."

Octavius sighed in the way that one does when one recognizes that the same social constructs they use to control others will now be turned against them. He said, "Laws are what they are, Aithen. They are…imperfect, as I have already said many times before, especially laws written in reaction to a frightening, traumatizing event. But I *will* deal with whatever comes, and I will go to Urbs Lucis to speak with the Magna Mater—*after* we find out who these assassins are—or were, who sent them, and why."

When Darya protested his intents, Octavius raised a hand and said as his gaze fell upon Dana Lux Baiula, "I am High King of House Coriolis and sovereign of Alvinoria. I will *not* submit to the Order, but I will go there with the full immunity of my position to meet with the Magna Mater and discuss the matter with her. In the meantime, what happened here—how it happened—will not be discussed with anyone. This applies to you too, Dana, as you are in my service, and until you are properly discharged from it—if that should be your desire—your duty is to me and me alone."

It appeared the Lux Baiula disagreed with the king's statement for her face hardened to the point of shattering, her chest rose and did not deflate, and her lips stretched taut as she said, "My Sisters and I were sent here to help protect you, Sire, *not* serve you."

A great chill descended upon the royal office now. The chill sent tremors through everything and everyone, even in the other rooms.

Aithen felt his chest tighten, and he gasped; Darya swayed from the shock; both watched with disbelief and fear of what the king might do.

Octavius took a deep breath, crossed his hands, and said with a tone he might have used if were pronouncing someone's banishment, "In that case, Lux Baiula, you are—"

But he did not get to finish his sentence. Dana interrupted him to say, "I am sorry, Sire; I was a fool. Things should be as you say, and I will do as you request."

It took everyone an inordinately long moment to register the Lux Baiula's sudden reversal. Still, the release of the tension around the chamber could be felt like a tangible thing once they did.

Just then, the door to the king's office opened with a swoosh to let Tania in. The woman cleared her throat; her countenance showed great need; her head tipped in the king's direction, but her eyes scoured her Sister.

Octavius shouted, "What is it Lux Baiula?!"

Tania did not flinch under the king's ire, but she replied urgently, saying her Sister's name with an unexpected curious, edge, "Sire, if you don't mind, *Dana* and I must see to our fallen Sisters and perform the Memory Transfer before their knowledge vanishes."

The king hesitated a moment, still discombobulated by Dana's abrupt reversal. Then he noticed the movement of the White Sash's fingers; a surreptitious, angry look passing from her to Dana; and clandestine vibrations flowing between the two women. It seemed—

"Sire, please. May I take Dana?"

After piercing Dana with an intense sidelong and still furious gaze, Octavius said, "Yes…yes, you may."

The head of the king's powered personal guard, Second Barrier Dana Lux Baiula of the Red Sash, left with the most contrite mien the king had ever seen on a Sister, that is, she excused herself with a full bow of the head and a deflated chest.

Octavius watched the two women exit his office and continued following them as Tania closed the door with a glance in his direction, which said she knew what had passed but that his will would be done, and he thought: *I will need to speak with her. But I am glad to know that she may be a true ally.*

Once the door was shut, Octavius's feet screeched on the stone floor as he turned around to look his son straight in the eye. He noticed Darya's anxious expression, but his mind was on his heir now, and it struggled with a desire to beat sense into him despite his late—but ineffective—action in trying to stand down the Lux Baiula.

"Son, what you did out there, the question you asked me…do not *ever* question me again in front of others. I thought I had taught you that a long time ago, but it appears not."

Aithen made no attempt to defend himself. He stood where he was looking dejected and shamed. Seeing him so distraught finished softening Octavius. After all, what was the point of living such a long life if not to learn to forgive, and to forgive even when one was actually hurt by another's action. In the present case, Octavius knew he would walk away fairly unscathed though some annoying restrictions might be forced upon him.

He said, "We should return out there."

With that, Octavius took his wife's hand with an encouraging smile and led her out of the office, looking back once to be certain Aithen followed.

The dead—friend and foe alike, though they were separated by a couple of meters—had been placed in a row on the balcony to be taken to the morgue by a team of furans. Tania and Dana looked troubled and disheartened. It appeared their fallen Sisters' brains had been deprived of oxygen too long already.

Octavius asked, "Dana, do you know what prevented you from using the Bind against the assassins?"

The Second Barrier looked sideways but kept her hand on the forehead of Jira—one of the rare Sisters who had some humor—as she replied, "They shot something at us, coated with a toxic substance; I can still feel the effects of it."

"Have you ever heard of such a weapon used against Sisters?"

"No, I haven't Sire."

"Have you, Tania?"

The White Sash shook her head worriedly.

Octavius heaved a heavy sigh, glanced at both his son and his wife, lowered his head, and walked out of his chambers to go find High Captain Harlion, his beat-up guard next to him but augmented by Piros and Boros.

Dangerous Thoughts

With an unsteady, tenuous form, Lusk said, *"I am sorry, Umbra, but the assassins were unsuccessful."*

Noctiferus's lieutenant on K'Tara replied without any equivocation, *"You mean they* failed *their mission. And do you know* why *they failed?"*

Lusk Methrim forced himself to remain calm, but he still could not face the Umbra with assurance, though he must, for how would he make his report to Noctiferus himself on the morrow, if he couldn't make this one without trembling inside? He tightened the threads of his form and said, *"They found unexpected resistance."*

"That is quite a euphemism, Vaedrin. They failed because they did not find the support they expected. And why did they not find it?"

The threads of Lusk's form threatened to dissolve again as he looked down and said, *"I...I have been unable to turn all those whom I should have turned."* He added defensively, *"It has been more difficult than expected."*

"I have no care for your excuses, Vaedrin, and your failure is very disappointing. It would make me question your abilities

if I did not know them as well as I do. I must therefore question your resolve and fidelity."

Again, attempting to defend himself against the Umbra's accusations, Lusk said, *"It is the Humans; they are simply not as easily stupefied as Zebulonians are, Umbra."*

"Now that is a useful comment. You will need to adjust your methods, Vaedrin, which you are certainly capable of doing."

This time, Lusk let his indignation darken his figure, stiffen it and shake it intensely.

But the Umbra could not care less and he continued, making an unusual pause in the middle of his statement, *"So! Tell me about...the man. How did he survive Rakel's attack?"*

Lusk blinked in surprise and hesitated a moment, uncertain what the Umbra was referring to. 'The man'? Was he still referring to the king?

"I do not wish to repeat myself, Vaedrin."

Lusk had still not gotten used to the Umbra calling him by his birth name, and each time he heard it, his anger flared. But he could not fight Noctiferus's lieutenant, and—hoping that the Umbra was indeed asking about the king—he said, *"I am sorry, Umbra. I was told that Rakel had the king in his grip when he dropped to the ground, limp. When this happened, all the others were killed by the king's guardians, except one who escaped and came to inform me."*

The Umbra's form writhed with contempt. He asked, *"What happened to Rakel?"*

"I believe—"

"I did not ask what you believe!"

Lusk sighed a silent sigh, and said, *"From what I know of the king, I am certain Rakel is being questioned, but I have no doubt he will die before revealing anything."*

"Again, you misunderstand me, Vaedrin. I wish to know what this Binding is that knocked out Rakel."

Lusk's form shook, mimicking the trembling of his body, in his room. He considered his words very carefully this time, then said, *"The only thing we know is that it nullified Rakel's own disabling Binding, after which he dropped to the ground."*

Lusk was going to add 'as I said earlier' but decided against it, probably saving himself a whipping.

An exasperated expression passed over the Umbra's form. He said, *"Who did it come from? Did the king generate the Binding?"*

"It is not known, Umbra. It could have been one of the Lux Baiulae defending him."

"We need to find out if the Binding came from the king. If it did, then he is the second Luxor we are hunting. Our Great Master will be displeased with your failure tomorrow, but perhaps his disappointment will be tempered by the fact we might have found the second Luxor."

Lusk became aware of his body's reaction in his room; a simple swallowing, but a troubling response all the same. What did the Umbra expect? Attacking the king in his own palace was a risky mission, a mission with a low probability of success to begin with! Again, Lusk's form bit its tongue and clenched its jaw. His uneasiness obviously annoyed the Umbra, whose form made a frown.

Lusk found himself having dangerous thoughts, thoughts unsafe in the presence of the Umbra who would surely sense them if they became but a little louder. And yet, Lusk could not help the curious question that popped in his mind just now: he wondered about the Umbra's fitness. Indeed, Noctiferus's lieutenant had made a mistake, referring to a 'man' as if he no longer knew who the king was. And there was that strange pause. Something was most definitely amiss with the Umbra. If these were truly signs of his decline, did they bode well or ill for Lusk? He wondered and dared not hope lest his form give away his treacherous thoughts.

"Umbra, you said the king might be the second Luxor. Does this mean you've located the first?"

"I have. But it is none of your concern."

The Umbra ended their encounter presently, but not before reminding Lusk, with veiled threats, of the importance of his meeting with their master on the morrow. The Healer-turned-Temptator bowed his head resignedly and confirmed, with more assurance than he felt, that he would be ready and would not shame Umbra.

Subjective Senses

A heavy, troubled silence weighed on the two Lux Baiulae examining the bodies of their fallen Sisters. The morgue, located in the basement floor of Domus Lucis, smelled of incense and death.

Tania and her aide had grim looks on their faces; the older woman's wrinkles, though they were less than the wrinkles of a typical ninety-five year-old woman, spoke of her concern for the Sisterhood—an organization she had joined decades earlier with the hopes that she might help do some good in the world, whereas Elia's face, though she was only a third of the White Sash's age, testified to her own frustrations and worries.

The two had been studying their Sisters' organs for signs of a poison or venom that they might recognize for over ten hours now, and they had found nothing. They had also probed the microbial flora on the bodies' external and internal integuments, and still, they found no clues as to what might have paralyzed their Sisters before they were killed. That left very few avenues of investigation, and little time left to do it.

With a hint of exhaustion in her voice, Tania said, "Elia, are you able to probe the bodies to study the blood's chemistry?"

The Yellow Sash groaned. "I am familiar with the elements and molecules we monitor to maintain homeostasis, but I am not so acquainted with the thousands of foreign molecules that may enter the body."

Tania threw her sullied gloves in the sink with a frustrated motion and began pacing the room, looking for ways to get the answer before more of their Sisters fell that way.

The tall, skinny, yet beautiful Elia said, "Tania, you know it does no good to put yourself in such a state. And something tells me that things will probably worsen before they improve."

Tania's exasperation intensified her accent as she replied, "Are you a Yellow or a Purple, Elia, to ma*ke* su*che* silly statemen*tse*? Of course, it will get worse!"

Elia gave the older woman an injured look, and then wondered whether this new threat would reveal to the world that the Lux Baiulae's cold rationality was only a façade. She said, "Tania, my statement was not silly. And you getting all out of sorts really won't help us figure this out. In any case, I think there *is* something we can try."

Elia's statement lit up the older woman's entire face before her lips and eyes turned down apologetically. The rapid change surprised Elia. But then, the Head Medic was a very proud woman, proud not only of herself but of the White Sashate—and very protective of it—and anything that embarrassed it, including her own behavior, was anathema to her. Her contrition was, therefore, real and deeply felt.

When she finally recovered her composure, she said eagerly, "What is your idea, Elia?"

"Well, all of us probe ourselves regularly to ensure our bodies and minds are in good health. When we do, we look for specific signals that are indicative of the proper functioning of our organs. But as we do that—and the more we do it—we also develop a subjective sense of what things should feel like when they are in good health. This subjective sense is not quantifiable, but it can tell us whether there is anything unusual happening…or circulating. I think we can use this sense to probe the bodies of our Sisters."

Tania looked at her colleague doubtfully, her upturned hands accentuating her perplexity. "You mean we just probe for…for what?"

"We probe for the things we usually probe for to know if everything is as it should be while also letting ourselves feel everything else, opening our senses to what is in the background.

217

If something isn't right, we will sense it. If we both sense it, we will know there is something amiss there. If we then narrow our focus on the source of that feeling, we should be able to pinpoint its origin. If it's in an organ, or in the blood, we can then…well, send samples to the lab at Urbs Lucis where they can isolate the poison or venom. And if K'Tara wills it, they will identify it too."

"Hum, so we probe for anything unusual?"

"No, we probe for the usual, *and* we open our senses to anything discordant."

"That will be slower."

"No, it will be faster. You may know that if a furanrider consciously tries to direct every movement of his mount and know their position relative to obstacles as they race toward their target, they will crash. That is because the conscious mind can only handle so much; the complex calculations and identification of the unknown must be left to the unconscious mind."

The Head Medic blinked, surprised by the younger Sister's confidence and remarkable theory. "All right then. Let'sse do itte."

Elia understood from Tania's heavily accented statement that the woman was excited by the experiment, but also anxious to find an answer that would help the Sisterhood defend itself against this new weapon the assassins used to kill three of them.

Elia proceeded to give the White Sash a few instructions before they entered the Bind to probe the bodies, one after the other, for the traces of the compound that had undone them.

What Sisters Shouldn't Do

Bilena, wearing a long white dress threaded with bright yellow weaves for some color, in addition to the yellow sash that marked her as the Head of her Assembly, moved her fingers with an agitation which indicated she had contained her concerns for too long. She first looked toward Saara then turned to Krystiana and said, "Mater, do you truly trust Elyana to keep the Order's needs—the Order's reputation—before anything else? Even when her mind will be overcome by the throes of desire?"

Krystiana frowned and said, "You make it sound as though a Sister has no control over her body or her emotions, Bilena. And you forget that Elyana is a Purple Sash, which she could not have achieved unless she had an absolute command of her actions and reactions. You *know* that."

Bilena recognized the truth of the Magna Mater's words, but to her it was a matter of principle. She tapped her fingers on her left arm, eyeing the Head of the White Sashate for the support she knew the old woman probably wouldn't give, for indeed, Saara had some strange views about what Sisters *could* do and *should not* do. Just the fact that Saara made the first a possibility and the second an admonition and not an interdiction made her suspicious in Bilena's eyes.

Saara scratched her old throat and said in her raspy voice, "I agree with your concerns, Bilena. Elyana's relationship with the high prince does have the potential to harm her *and* the Order."

The Praefecta philosophas narrowed her eyes distrustfully as she waited for her colleague to complete her thoughts.

"But it can also increase her understanding of the world and of herself—and as a Purple Sash, that is certainly a good thing for her as well as for the Sisterhood. True, the relationship might be distracting, but you know Elyana's priorities, and they are to her duty first. And in the end, the Selection Council might end the relationship even if we don't. Still, a Lux Baiula shouldn't have to inhibit her womanhood so completely as to be a castrate."

Bilena shot daggers at the old woman. That was not at all what she had hoped for.

Krystiana stood and walked toward the spheres on her desk. She felt the flame of the blue globe, playing with it. It helped her untangle things when her mind was troubled or when she needed to find the right words to answer a question or meet a challenge.

After a moment during which furious needles passed from the Praefecta philosophas to the Praefecta medicas, Krystiana swiveled on her heels and said, "That will be all for now, Praefectae. I will see you again at prandium."

Saara was not at all surprised by the sudden dismissal. With a hopeful nod toward the Magna Mater and a cocked eye for Bilena, she left.

But Bilena was taken slightly aback by the lack of a decision regarding the matter at hand. She turned hesitantly, wondering whether she should insist for a reply, for a confirmation that Elyana's relationship with the high prince would be ended. But the Magna Mater looked at her with eyes that said, 'You worry too much, Bilena—things will be fine.' So, she gave Krystiana the expected salutation, and left without a word more, though she paced herself so as not to catch up to Saara.

XII FEAR AND PAIN

When the Master Calls

L usk had spent most of the night awake, either in his apartments—in the section of the residential building reserved to visiting foreigners—or pacing the grounds of the Inner Sanctum. That had eventually attracted the unwelcome attention of a pair of the dangerous-looking Barriers, and he was forced to return to his apartments to try and find sleep.

It had taken his brain another half hour to finally disconnect from conscious thought.

When he woke, at Six after Highnight, the Blue Sun was already visible in the chilly sky, and the Red Sun, just behind it, started mixing its golden rays with those of its darker twin. The resulting greenish light gave this second day of the month of Undecimus a rather ominous appearance as it passed through the thick cumulonimbus clouds. Lusk felt a shiver pass through him, but it was not the cold that had caused it.

A little less than an hour, now, before he met with Noctiferus. He went to the basin that stood in the corner of his bedchamber and washed his face with automatic motions. That done, he wiped his face dry, sighed, took his toothbrush and started cleaning his teeth. After a moment, he realized he had forgotten to put the bone paste on the brush. He felt like cursing, or maybe like slamming the toothbrush into the washbasin, grabbing his things and...and...nothing. He completed his morning ritual, then went to sit in the corner of his Contemplation Room, head against the wall. On a typical day, he should have lit the stick of cleansing herbs. But what was the point? He was preparing himself to meet with evil, not to purify himself and meditate to find peace. So, he stayed with his head on the wall for a while, trying not to think about anything.

Alas, the passing minutes did not bring any calm, and with a grunt, he decided to go through the useless ritual. He stood and went to light the cleansing herb stick, which stood atop a white stone pedestal—the only furnishing in the room, aside from the soft carpet and the Living Lamps which gave off a softly glowing red light. He started murmuring an incantation as he took the stick and moved it around his body to cleanse it with the herb's smoke. His mind initially resisted the ritual, but it eventually accepted to let go of all the battling thoughts, and, releasing a long, soothing breath, he moved to the center of the room, and sat on the carpeted floor.

There, he began counting down to enter the Bind. As he counted, he felt his heart start to bolt this way and that as if it were going to leap out of his chest. He paused, took a deep breath and, when his pulse slowed again, resumed his descent into the Bind.

The brightness of the space within the ethereal world blinded him, but he was used to it, and he waited a moment—or what he knew was a moment, though it did not feel like it in here—until the images became more distinct. Just then, he thought of retreating to his saferoom, a space in the Bind he imagined for himself when he needed to think on a problem or process difficult emotions. He would have gone there the night before when he couldn't sleep—if he had not been afraid to find Noctiferus in it. And, in any case, he had to wait to be called by the Umbra for his appointment with their Master, so he stayed where he was, in the middle of the vastness of the Bind.

Lusk did not even bother to imagine anything more pleasant than the omnipresent bright white light, but he was glad when his mind had finally adjusted and he started to notice the myriad colored ribbons which indicated the presence of other Humanoids, most of whom were only there by way of their dreams, and a minority of whom—such as the Lux Baiulae— who had intentionally entered the Bind for one reason or another. The latter, he must be wary of, and he moved himself among the myriad dreamers' pulses where he could wait in greater security while remaining accessible to the Umbra's thoughtcall, whenever it came.

Lusk felt his tension vanish in the midst of the countless dreams, spying on them, watching the million dreamers' wild imaginings, many terrorizing and just as many exciting and thrilling. He wondered if the world would be different if everyone could see other people's dreams. Not even all Roamers had that ability, but he did. Though he had always had difficulty interpreting them and had never bothered to learn their meanings. So, he used his power to merely entertain himself.

"Lusk Methrim."

Lusk's mind jolted at the sound of his name, and his body shook in the Contemplation Room. Though he had heard that voice only once before, he remembered it only too well as a dark, oppressive, and frightening entity. Lusk struggled to contain his accelerating pulse, but he must; it would not serve him to lose his connection with the Bind now.

This time, someone else called him, *"Vaedrin!"*

It was the Umbra summoning him, probably upset that he had not heard him reply to the Founder yet. So, Lusk focused his mind on the Umbra's vibrations—vibrations that had always seemed too perfect and monorythmic. A moment later, he found himself in the middle of an alien landscape, on some sort of dry plateau with dizzying depths between the peaks, which looked ancient with their rounded crests. The sky was dark and speckled with stars he could not recognize, and a moon—just as unrecognizable—lit the place with a harsh white light. This was not Alba, which gave a soft purple glow to brighten the K'Taran sky.

Lusk locked away all his fears; in fact, he locked away all his emotions so that only the logical part remained. He kneeled in front of the Umbra and gave the expected salutation. *"Umbra, I am here at our Master's call."*

With a small growl, the Umbra said, *"Indeed, you are."*

Presently, the Zebulonian heard his name pronounced with the god's power and command, reverberating across the alien landscape.

Lusk called up the response but started to panic when he could not remember it. But he recovered quickly and sent his reply with a dead monotone, *"I am here and await your presence's blessing, Founder."*

A form now resolved itself in front of Lusk. An imposing form, of a man dressed in a dark blue uniform trimmed with gold, a red toga draping his broad shoulders, and boots strapped to the perfect shape of his legs—the exact image of the Founder standing next to Aiala'Rhi, the Originator, in the Rhiian religion.

Lusk could not help looking down when the god set his eyes on him; he felt his heart thump and became alarmed, which caused his form to dissemble momentarily.

The Founder now dismissed the Umbra, who blinked out of the Bind at once, and Lusk panicked again. He did not like the man, but his presence was still something he could anchor himself to—could turn to—if the god should become displeased with his answers.

With a slightly less reverberating but crisper voice than before, Noctiferus said to Lusk, *"Do you know why you are here, Lusk?"* Lusk said yes but did not look up. *"Good. Know that you deserve my gratitude for having accomplished your initial task well. But penetrating our enemy's ranks is not sufficient."* Lusk's form unraveled for the space of the moment between the Founder's last word and the next. *"Tell me this: why do you think we are engaged in this mission? Why do I demand what I demand? And why do you, the Umbra, and the Serpent serve me?"*

Lusk was expecting to be questioned, and he knew one did not exchange pleasantries with a god, but to be put to the test without any warning was still jarring; his mind lurched, then raced for an answer, the answer the god expected. But how could *he* know what a founder might want? Hoping to please the god, he gave his reply in the Ancient Tongue, *"Da veniam, Domine. mentem tuam non scire possum. Servio quod rogatus sum."*[14]

Noctiferus replied in the same manner, *"Et mihi bene servis, Lusk Methrim. Discere tamen debes me homini inscienter servienti, vel conscio non amplius eodem ardore servienti, fidere nequire."*[15]

Upon hearing the Founder's words, Lusk expected *His* wrath to descend upon him for reasons he might never come to know, and he could not prevent his own form from loosening up again and bringing a frown to the god's very solid face though *He* was also here in thoughtform.

But a punishment did not come, and Noctiferus said, *"Do not fear my words, Lusk Methrim; they are not a sign of my discontent. However, I must be certain that you serve with your eyes open because that is the only way your fervor will reach the levels required for the tasks ahead."*

Lusk's form turned questioning eyes to Noctiferus as he sent. *"I...do not understand, Founder."*

"Then understand, *Lusk Methrim."*

Lusk was at once enveloped entirely, from within and from without, by something unknowable and alien to all his senses. Images and thoughts that were not his own entered his mind and showed him and told him things he was neither looking at nor listening for. But the Sendings were too much for him; he could not make sense of the images, and he only heard shreds of what Noctiferus revealed. He heard, *"...bring peace...must perish...the faithful...to our world, among your gods."*

It took some time for Lusk to refocus on the present and hear the Founder again, a time that stretched across promises of

---

[14] I am sorry, Master. Your mind is not something I can know. I serve because it was demanded of me.

[15] And you serve me well, Lusk Methrim. You must learn, however, that a man who serves without knowing, or once knowing does not continue to serve with the same fervor, is not a man I can trust.

inconceivable things. When he *did* refocus, he heard, *"Know that though it may be granted to most to act according to their faith without true knowledge of my wishes, it is only because they do not have your tasks to accomplish, and their failures are thus of little consequence to me though they may be consequential for them. You, on the other hand, have great responsibilities, and your sacrifices must be sustained by true knowledge."*

"Will you continue to serve and execute your tasks diligently and fervently with the full knowledge of our aims, Lusk Methrim?"

Numb as he was, and though he realized he had not heard half of what the Founder said, Lusk bowed his head and extended his upturned hand to the god, saying, *"I will, Founder."*

The air now rumbled around Lusk; it rumbled with the intensity of the roars of a thousand satisfied varagoths who have filled their bellies after their month-long fast. Noctiferus said, *"As a sign of my gratitude, I will now allow you a moment with your…mother. But know that though the experience may or may not be an enjoyable one, it is my reward to you."*

Lusk's form turned incredulous eyes to the Founder. In the physical world, he felt himself swallow, perhaps both from a sense of pure anxiety at the thought of seeing his mother after so long—after what he had become—and a sense of disbelief. The god wouldn't be trying to trick him, would *He*? His doubts fell into the void the moment an image appeared on Noctiferus's right, showing the inside of an unfamiliar shack.

He continued watching, apprehensively, hopefully, the two emotions battling within him. He asked the god when he would see his mother, as a child does at the coach station when they await a parent returning from a long trip and cannot see their face among the multitude.

Noctiferus did not answer. *He* simply motioned toward the image, and soon, a female with skin the color of nutmilk and graying hair finally walked in from the left.

The woman *was* his birthmother, Oolviana Methrim. Lusk gulped again and could not prevent his eyes from forming the tears that flowed at that moment.

He wanted to walk into the vision and touch her, but he was sufficiently aware to know he could not—or could he? Couldn't Noctiferus allow him to speak with her or even touch her? Or was this only a dream the god was feeding to his mind? No, it was real. It must be. It felt real.

He asked the Founder whether he could go to her and speak with her. The god said no.

Lusk snapped his head back toward the vision, not wanting to miss anything, and he continued watching Oolviana, the one person who had loved him truly and taken care of him. He found himself looking up at Noctiferus every so often with a sense of...*gratitude*? The feeling angered him, and he let it go lest it spoil the moment.

Oolviana looked older, much older than he remembered, and she now walked with a limp. Could she have aged so much since he last saw her? Perhaps the Founder had played a trick on him; but he *did* recognize Oolvania—it *was* her. He would know her if the Dark One caged him in a pit for a thousand years; he would never forget his birth mother's face.

Presently, he saw a sorrowful mask on her as she dragged herself toward the table to set it with dishes...for three people. Did she have a new family? When Oolviana went to the old cabinet at the back of the room to retrieve two seatdrapes, Lusk understood but also became confused. The Placing custom required that seatdrapes with the likeness of family members who disappeared before their time be placed on the dining chairs at supper. He understood that Oolviana might be setting a seat for him, but who was the other one for?

He moaned silently when he saw a painting of himself, as a teenager—somewhat chubby and with blondish hair and no red streaks—on the drape Oolviana placed on the chair facing him. He followed her with increasing curiosity and tension as she moved to the chair at the right end of the table where she placed a drape with the likeness of ...a girl.

Lusk did not recall having a sister; Oolviana must have given birth to the girl after he, himself, was taken away by the Janarae at the age of six. Had his birthsister also been taken away, then? Or did she die from some illness? He stared at the girl's picture for a while, trying to recognize himself—in case the girl had the same creatic mother as him—or Oolviana—in case the girl was Oolviana's own creatic daughter. The angle made recognition difficult, but something in the painting's features struck him suddenly cold. He felt wobbly and the Founder asked him if he was unwell.

Lusk's reply was sent with the same tightness his voice would have had in the physical world. He said, *"Founder. Is the girl on the seatdrape...is she my...who is she?"*

Noctiferus answered simply, seemingly without any understanding of the reasons for Lusk's state of shock and fear, *"She is Oolviana's offspring. Her name is Ooldrina."*

Lusk's mind reeled. It took him a moment or an eternity to finally regain command of himself. It happened as the more doubtful part of himself thought: *But of course, her name is Ooldrina. What else would it be if she is indeed Oolviana's offspring. You are being foolish!*

"Lusk Methrim! I can see you are preoccupied with the girl. Know that though she was birthed by your mother, she is not your sister. Do not be troubled by her. As for your mother, she is safe, and she will remain so until our mission is successfully concluded."

Oh, the twisted ways the Dark One had to make one believe they wanted what he forced them to do. Lusk's earlier gratefulness threatened to turn to hate again, and he repressed the feelings lest he reveal them. Yes, Noctiferus had kept his mother safe, but it had cost Lusk his soul, and what was there now, his mother would barely recognize if she ever heard him again. In a way, he was glad he could not communicate with her. *But the girl—* When Lusk tried to scrutinize the figure on the seatdrape again, the vision vanished without warning and was replaced by the blackness of the foreign landscape that surrounded them. Lusk turned pleading eyes to the god who shook his head *No*. Lusk thought: *It is better this way. You do not really want to know the answer to this*—

Noctiferus stopped that thought in its track, said, *"Lusk Methrim, it is time to discuss less pleasant matters such as the failure of the last mission."* The god voiced the next words with such compelling force that all thoughts of his mother and sister vanished as if they had never been, *"Tell me about it."*

When Lusk hesitated to respond despite the request's irresistibility, the Founder added, *"You do not need to fear, Lusk Methrim. The reason for our encounter was not so that I might punish you—you are still too valuable for that—but so that you might know the reasons for your sacrifices, which I have already revealed to you, and to give you your new orders, personally."*

"Now, tell *me of this failure."*

The Dark One's words felt like a fruit press squeezing juice out of a platoya. Lusk took a long breath and answered the question resignedly. When he was done explaining the assassins' failure—his own failure given his part in its planning—Lusk turned his eyes down and awaited the god's verdict.

The Founder seemed to consider Lusk's account for a while, perhaps comparing it against the visions carried to *Him* by the stellar winds—or maybe simply comparing it to whatever the Umbra might have told *Him*. When *He* was done, *He* turned depthless eyes on him and said, *"I know you are a meticulous servant, Lusk, and that because of it your progress is often slow. But this has led to the failure of another one's mission. Learn from this and be equal to the truths I have revealed to you this day."*

After a pause that might have lasted a single moment or ten or a hundred, Noctiferus said, *"Now, I will give you your new assignments."*

231

The things the Founder told Lusk he must do, as part of his new mission, prompted a surge of vomit in his throat. Fortunately, it only happened to his body and not to his form in the Bind.

"Cognovi quanta sacrificia mihi per mei obedientiam facere debeas, Lusk Methrim, sed scito te frustra toleravisse, nam beatitude te matremque tuam expectat." [16]

Noctiferus made a motion, and the dark landscape was replaced by the lushest sceneries Lusk had ever seen. Was the Founder showing him paradise?

Noctiferus continued, *"Hic est domus mea, ubi animae tuae in aeternam vitam procul ab existentiae K'Taran tuae lite recipientur."* [17]

Lusk felt his heart jump at the thought of being reunited with his mother, away from all the evil he had known. But did this paradise the gods described really exist? If it did, shouldn't Noctiferus be content with his life there? Why would he be looking to conquer K'Tara? Lusk's eyes, both on his form in the Bind and on his body in the Contemplation Room, narrowed, betraying his doubts.

"I see you mistrust me, Lusk Methrim. Why is that? Speak."

Lusk wanted to shrink, but he pushed back against his fear, resisting it with all his strength, and said with as much courage as he could muster, *"I do not wish to question you, Founder. Please forgive me. But my mother's body; it is not worthy. Why would you receive her?"*

Noctiferus stared at him with His infinite eyes, as if to weigh him or look inside of him to try and understand how a mere mortal might choose to question *Him* so. With a snort that Lusk felt on his form, but a snort accompanied by the tiniest stretching

---

[16] I understand the sacrifices you must make in your obedience to me, Lusk Methrim, but know that your sufferance will not be in vain, for in fact, bliss is what awaits you and your mother.

[17] This is my abode, and it is where your spirits will be received to live in eternity, away from the strife of your K'Taran existence.

of *His* lips, Noctiferus said, *"One's body may not be a worthy receptacle for a god, but one's spirit may still be worthy of eternity."*

When Lusk's form continued to show signs of doubt, vexed ripples flowed through the Bind and past Lusk. The god demanded to know his final question.

Lusk steeled himself and quietly exhaled in his room before saying, *"Please forgive me, Founder. It is only my ignorance which causes me to appear doubtful. But the body is made unworthy by a neglectful mind, whether intentionally or not. How can you receive my birthmother's spirit, given that she has let her body degrade in that manner?"*

The god's lips stretched into a smile that showed signs of his impatience. *He* said, *"Clementia hoc sinet, Lusk Methrim, clementia pro fide tua, ministerio tuo, sacrificiis omnibus tuis data."* [18]

If the god had designed to solidify Lusk's commitment to their cause with *His* reply, it did not have that effect, and Lusk was forced to shove all his thoughts, emotions, and lingering—or renewed—doubts to the deepest part of himself lest Noctiferus should hear them. But he did wish more than anything else to be with his mother again, and he wasn't sure he would ever be able to escape the god. So, he chose to hold on to the hope that the god had placed in his mind about the possibility of paradise for him and his mother. That done, he nodded his acceptance of his new mission: completing the turning of selected Alterintrants in Urbs Lucis, and then returning to Furan City where he would have to befriend the king's staff to obtain the collaboration of one of them to complete the failed mission. Both of these tasks, he would need to complete by the use of any and all means possible. He knew what that meant, and the thought of what he would need to do flooded his mind with such

---

[18] Clemency will allow it, Lusk Methrim, clemency given in return for your faith, your service, and your continued sacrifices.

self-loathing that his body would have retched in the Contemplation Room if he had not locked away all emotions.

Noctiferus's final words for him covered his mind in a dark, oily foulness that prevented him from uttering even a simple moan.

"Your body is one worthy of union. The tasks you have been given will test you beyond anything you have experienced before. I know that; I have seen it. But now knowing why *you serve, your spirit will find the strength to carry you through your labors. This will make you, Lusk Methrim, worthier still."*

After this, Lusk did not hear Noctiferus call the Umbra back. Lusk did not listen or watch—his mind was blank except for the one thought he continued to repeat to himself: I serve. Mother lives. I serve. Mother lives. I serve. Mother lives...

He did not hear the Umbra tell him their Master had left, and he did not see the Umbra exit. Lusk was left in the middle of nowhere, with the afterglow of that dark, alien world and harsh, white moon. He did not know how long he stayed in the Bind before returning to his body, but he collapsed in the middle of his vomit when he did.

The Captive

In the basement of a large but rundown house on the northwest side of Kartak, a woman and two toughs faced an unusually pale-looking man. The woman had the looks of a lean, burly chap rather than of a female, but with rather bewitching eyes. One of the males was a large, filthy-looking fellow, and sat spitting bits of his dirty nails carelessly on the ground. The other man was a clean, well-proportioned, and sour-looking fellow.

After shivering for the hundredth time, the prisoner asked with a weak groan, "How...did you find me?"

The woman replied with an enticing chuckle, "That's your first question? *How did we find you?* Not, *where are we*? I will tell how we found you: we located your compound thanks to a

234

most kind and skilled Kynarian priestess who joined our…cooperative recently. We were then even luckier to have amongst us someone who's immune to the befuddling vibrations that hide your walls. He led us in. But let me tell you that capturing you was as complicated as I had anticipated; for a centenarian, you can still hold your end of a Binding."

Marcus tried for a cynical snort, but it left his nostrils rather inaudibly. After recovering from yet another incontrollable shiver, he managed to ask the other two questions he had, "What do you want with me? And what did you *do* to me?"

"Nothing except that we need to deliver you to someone who has a peculiar interest in men with Binding skills. As to what we did to you: we simply gave you a nice wash. But don't you worry, you will recover if we suppress the washings."

Marcus groaned and forced a couple of 'what' out of his throat.

"What will make us suppress the washings?" Marcus the Reader bobbed his head, "Your collaboration of course."

This time, Marcus's snort came out loud and clear and was followed a whooping, pained chortle. "I…I won—"

"Ohh, you will. Believe me, you will turn. Do you know the word? *Turn?* If you've ever been tempted by something before you secluded yourself in that compound, well, turning you will free you to follow your desires, to no longer resist them, except that to have them, you will not only *need* to serve our Master, but you will *want* to do so. And I am skilled at turning people like you."

Marcus did not respond, did not try to protest the woman's assertions. He gave one more exhausted, sickly groan and let himself fall back into unconsciousness.

Addressing the clean, angry-faced fellow, the woman said, "Tell Kina to prepare our prisoner's bed, and to make it soft and comfortable. Tell her to prepare a slightly weaker solution of the inhibition soap too; I want to begin his turning tomorrow."

Eenosh turned with a grunt and went to do as ordered but not before giving the Leate a resentful look.

Decision

With the wind whistling outside the Palace of the Light and grey clouds moving above the city-state, six women discussed the planned mission to Zebulonia. They were seated in the Bilena's office.

Larca said, "Bilena, do you believe the girls are ready to go or not? That is all I wish to know."

It irritated Bilena that Larca never spoke directly to Sisters of other Sashates unless to insult them. But she had known the woman for many decades and knew it was useless to make a case of it. With a resigned sigh, Bilena answered, "They are, Larca. Clara can confirm it."

In fact, Clara wasn't so sure the girls were ready. Ooldrina had become very defiant and depressed lately and was actually demanding to be sent on her mission. Clara wasn't certain why, but…but she could never seem to put her finger on the reason. Still, the girls had learned what they needed to know for their mission. So, Clara said, "Indeed Praefecta, they are ready. But I am still doubtful this entire thing is a good idea."

Larca spat. "You're doubtful? What else would you have us do? Send one of us who has no knowledge of their language?!"

Krystiana held back a sigh. Larca's more collaborative attitude, which she had adopted around the time of her being named leader of their war effort, had been a mere interlude, and she was back to her old ways. How Krystiana wished she had been there, thirty years earlier, to prevent the woman's ascension to the leadership of the Red Sashate. But alas. And no matter how hard she looked, Krystiana could not find the reason people kept promoting to roles of leadership individuals who had no business leading anyone. It remained—to her—the greatest mystery of all.

Knowing that she must intervene to prevent the discussion from degrading, Krystiana said, "Larca, you know as well as the rest of us that sending two girls—who are barely old enough to bear child—to spy on our enemy is a *very* risky proposition. But it *is* the only one we have." She looked at Bilena and Clara with a determined posture. "I will not hear any more expressions of doubt about it."

Clara's shoulders dropped resignedly while Bilena's face darkened, which gave Krystiana a new worry. But things were what they were, and when Bilena finally nodded, Krystiana said, "All right. When do we send them?"

Bilena replied, "As soon as the arrangements can be made. By the end of this fourth, they should be returning from Furan City where, as you know, Elyana took them so they might know who they are being asked to put their lives at risk for. They will need to fly on furanback to the border, and then by voran across the Sagr where the high king's contact will meet them. At the beginning of next fourth would be best, for travelling purposes. They should be at the border by the end of it, and in Zeblinia…a few days later."

The Magna Mater and the others nodded.

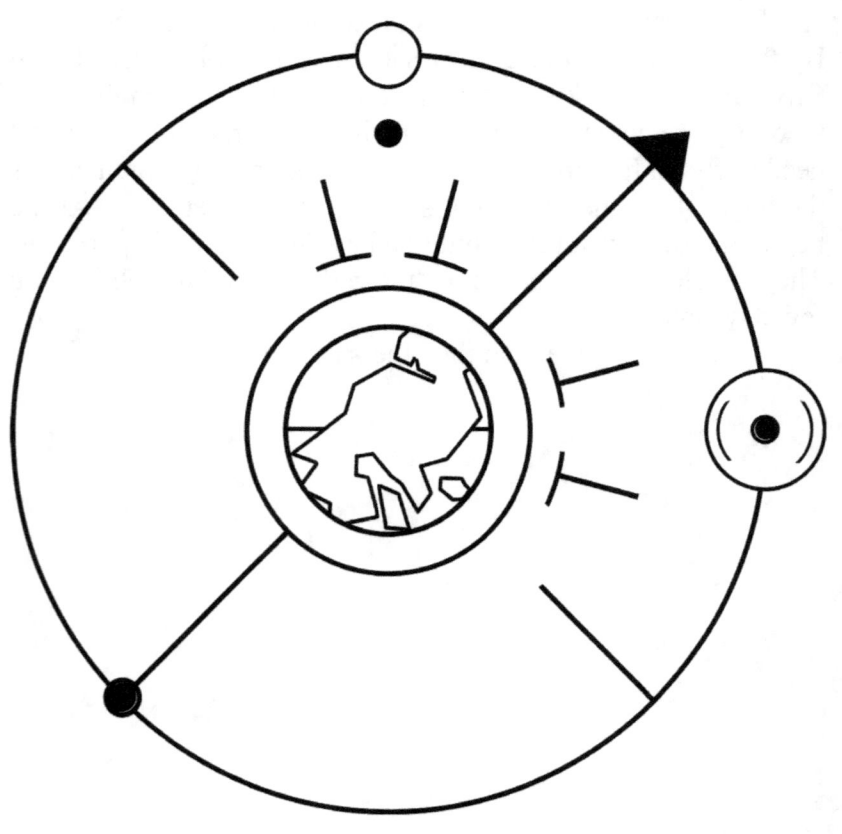

XIII DISCOVERIES AND MEETINGS

On the Way to Urbs Lucis

Getting down from Kaless—a young furan descended from his first mount, Lumos—and acknowledging Sergeant Tamas's greetings, Octavius *aghred* and massaged his back.

The king and his escort had flown for two long days, during which they had also had to contend with the Bolingars, and they had just arrived at the Mountain Lake outpost. They were on their way to Urbs Lucis where the king was to meet with the Magna Mater to "discuss" his never-before-revealed Binding skills with her—skills he had used to incapacitate his would-be assassin.

On this trip, Octavius was accompanied by a personal guard, which now included a new guardian, who was assigned to replace the dead Almiar. The king wasn't sure about the man, but Primus Julian had vouched for him. He was also accompanied by Dana Lux Baiula—the only Sister who had survived the assassination attempt on the king——and four other guardians; this was as much for his protection, as it was to reassure everyone he would not eclipse himself again as he had done months before.

Tamas received the king with his typical jovial demeanor, though with a certain restraint—meaning that he restricted it to verbal joviality, without the shaking of hands and shoulder claps he used with Prince Toras.

"Please see to our furans, sergeant, and have some food prepared at once; I am hungry."

"Certainly, my king."

Dana had watched him questioningly during their first day of flight, but as time passed, her curiosity changed to surprise. Octavius had noticed her gaze; he had even heard her snort at one point, despite the wind. He knew he was the cause of it.

She was watching him again—from the corner of her eyes—as he patted down his uniform. Primus Julian, who was unsaddling his furan next to her, said, "He is a man of his word, Lux Baiula, and he knows where he stands in the grand game. He goes to Urbs Lucis because he promised, but—"

"He also knows there will be no consequence for him."

Julian said, "Well, at least nothing that will undermine his authority."

"It appears House Coriolis is charmed by the Founders."

Julian grunted. "I wouldn't say that to him; he is not a believer. And they have their troubles and difficulties, like anyone else. But the king *is* the most principled man I have ever known, and his sons are not so different from him. I only wish that principles could more often lead to the intended results."

"Yes, I've heard about Prince Toras's decision to go to Galior to defend the village against the Serpent. It was brash…but honorable."

When Julian detected a hint of emotion in the Lux Baiula's reply, he asked, "Do you know anyone in Galior?"

The woman nodded but hardened her face to cut the thread.

Julian grunted and let her be. Principles. The prince *did* do something others might not have, and he did it because of his principles even though it cost him dearly. But Julian was thinking of something else; he was thinking of his twin sister's death. He wished the king had acted on his principles when the Serpent had his sister in its beak, instead of letting others dictate his actions; his sister might still be alive. But of course, he knew things were not that simple. Julian shook the thought out if his mind, excused himself, and left to see to the raising of the tents.

Dana walked to the place where the royal company's belongings had been dropped off to retrieve her arms, gourd, and satchel. The woman noticed the curious looks some of the outpost's men were throwing her way, as she did that. She narrowed her eyes and glared, and they looked away. Having grabbed her things, she went to sit by a tree to enter the Bind and inform her contact in Urbs Lucis about the company's progress. When she sat, the men peaked at her again.

The fact was that Red Sashes, especially Barriers, fascinated them. They looked so fierce yet were exceedingly attractive in their tight-fitting uniforms. But the outposted soldiers had also heard rumors about the king's "Bind-wielding guardians": out of four, only one survived—Dana Lux Baiula—whereas only one of the men who had faced the assassins had been killed. The men probably wondered if the Sisters' reputation was overdone. They wondered, and they eyed her, trying to decide the matter.

Dana could sense the soldiers' curiosity despite her closed eyes, and she spent another moment imagining what was going through their minds: fright, perplexity, awe, perplexity. If they knew how easily she could snap their necks, perhaps they'd stop looking her way, she thought. And yet, why wouldn't they after the feared Lux Baiulae had failed so miserably in their duty? Hopefully, Elia and Tania would find the cause of her Sisters' demise so that they might ready themselves for the next attempt on the king's life. What she did *not* look forward to was Praefecta Larca's questioning once they got to Urbs Lucis. The leader of the Red Sashate detested failure more than anyone else, and she was harsh—frighteningly so—with those who botched their duties. As the leader of the special royal protection unit, Dana was responsible for the actions—or deaths—of those beneath her. Well, things were what they were, and the Red Sash resigned herself to the fact that the Praefecta milites's wrath would be descending on her soon. As unpleasant as that would be, it would be nothing compared to the flogging Dana had decided to submit herself to. In fact, she looked forward to it.

The king spent some time in the company of the others while satiating his hunger. He did not take part in the conversation but answered the few questions Tamas asked. When he swallowed his last bite of ground singer[19], he stood,

---

[19] Ground singer: a meat-tasting, manure-feeding plant that emitted a song-like sound, as the wind blew across its lacunar stem, to attract pollinators.

left instructions with Tamas for their departure in the morning, and bid everyone goodnight, followed by his Praetorian Guard.

Once inside his tent, he sat himself on a small chair, leaned back and thought a while longer about the result he expected from his meeting with the Magna Mater—and her council, if she required it.

The king wasn't too worried since there was nothing the Sisterhood could do about the fact that he was a Binder, nor could they force him to remain in Urbs Lucis to be trained! But the mere fact of having to be interrogated by them and having to answer all the questions they were certain to ask wearied him already. On the other hand, he was worried that they might try to impose restrictions on his use of any more Bindings, and that they might force him to train with Mitsuko or some other Lux Baiula in Furan City. They might also want to test him, and he had already decided that that was something he would categorically refuse. *All this is just an irritation, really, because I can decline anything and everything if I wish it. No, what really worries me is them questioning me about Marcus and any action they might then take against him—which I would not be able to oppose—such as expulsing him from Aquinos. Although, perhaps, with the war...*"

The cry of a night Chirper startled him, and as it continued, thoughts of his wife standing paralyzed with a knife on her throat invaded his mind. This was not the first time their lives had been threatened, but it was the first time—in their long lives—that she had been in actual physical danger. He could see her now, exactly as she had been in his bedchamber, terror in her eyes, and horror in his. He growled.

I should have sent her back to Kynaria. I should have. He snorted cynically. *Such a long life, and yet, how much of it have we really enjoyed—together? And now this war, through which no one will pass unscathed, if we pass through it at all. Will I ever know her as my wife alone and no longer as my queen-consort? Will we both live long enough for Aithen to take—*

242

Octavius stopped the thought before it depressed him further. He swallowed a cup of milk left there for him, lay himself down, and invited sleep to douse his worries.

It took another eight hours on the next day for the king's company to reach its destination—Urbs Lucis. The city-state was grand and magnificent with its white walls and blue crystalline pinnacles. Octavius wondered how much the Order spent on keeping the structures in such a pristine state despite the centuries that had passed since its foundation, nearly six hundred years earlier. He yelled a question to Dana, and she replied that the Order paid unaffiliated Alterintrants who used sonactic Bindings projected at the surfaces to shake off algae, moss, and dust. Octavius made a sound, which told of his surprise, but it was quickly lost in the wind.

He then scanned the fields surrounding the city; from this height, they were simple enchanting, with the red grasses covering every piece of land that was not cultivated, meaning about half the area. The crops, which were now ready for harvest, created a fantastic contrast with their bright yellows and dark greens. When they were close enough to see over the outer walls of the city as well as to catch the sounds of the palace, Octavius was surprised by the commotion, and he yelled another question.

Dana shouted back that more and more commoners were coming from the surrounding regions to seek the Order's help or advice in preparation for the war. Moreover, the Order's recruiting efforts since the attack on Furan City—though not as successful as the Magna Mater wished it—had brought in hundreds of new recruits—thus the increased activity.

Octavius recognized the truth of it when he observed large groups of women in white robes in the shielded paddock at the back of the Inner Sanctum.

Once they landed, he was greeted by Second Barrier Sasha, a square woman with shoulders as broad, and arms as muscled as those of a fisher. The Lux Baiula nodded in welcome and told the king he and his company would be taken to the diplomatic apartments before the meeting with the Magna Mater, so that they might refresh themselves. She then exchanged with Dana the customary salutation between Barriers: the fist was planted fingers up on the belly and then pulled away as if to remove a knife.

Octavius, curious about the trainees, asked, "Has any of the new recruits surprised you with their skills yet?"

Second Barrier Sasha grunted and said, "Not yet. But hopefully one will soon, Sire. We are bringing in a dozen or so women every fourth, but most are adequate at best."

A dozen or so every fourth. Not a lot. Octavius nodded and let the woman take them to the residences.

Hopes

Walking with Raaviana on her right, Elyana on her left, and the high prince to the left of Elyana, Ooldrina listened with half an ear. A guard of eight men surrounded them, not to protect her and Raaviana, but to protect the prince, in case there should be any more attempts against members of the royal family.

The prince had been a little tense when he first joined them. But despite the fact that the Manu Dextra had already told her and Raaviana about the assassination attempt on his father, and told them that the prince might therefore not be his usual self, Ooldrina had decided to react toward him with diffidence. Her reticence was increased when she wondered why the prince would join them on a walk through the city when her people were preparing to invade Alvinoria.

Striding along the vast and busy main road of the capital, Ooldrina noticed some Furanites glancing at them suspiciously, and she could not keep her jaw from tightening. Was it because of their nut-milk colored skin, red-streaked black hair, and broad face? Or was it simply because they were Zebulonian? And were they focusing their stares on her because they somehow knew that she was soil—? She stopped herself from completing that thought and tried to not grind her teeth. But the Manu Dextra noticed and frowned in her direction.

The prince began telling her and Raaviana about the freedoms that all men and women of Alvinoria enjoyed since the writing of the Coriolan Carta. Raaviana listened with awe and hope. Perhaps she dreamed of becoming Alvinorian. But all Ooldrina could think of was to get away.

When the prince was finished, she wondered whether he would try and explain to them why they should be happy to have been found by the Lux Baiulae to help defend against the people of their native country. But the prince did not do that. Instead, he asked her and her friend if they had studied the Coriolan Carta.

Raaviana jumped in to tell him that she did study it a little and that the Carta's writer must have been truly wise, to which the prince replied that he had been no different than anybody else, except that he had decided to put on paper the truths which every Human already held and to enforce those truths by making them the source of the laws of the kingdom.

Ooldrina blinked in surprise and felt her diffidence disappear for a moment. The fact that the prince would *not* try to take credit for what his ancestor had done or even *name* him— Elyana Lux Baiula had told them that the Carta's author was the prince's great-great-great grandfather, King Lucius the First— was unlike anything she had ever experienced. Perhaps the prince *was* a goo—No. She didn't care.

As they passed a street sweeper, the prince took advantage of the occasion and started to talk about the systems which kept the city clean and healthy, and Ooldrina returned to her own thoughts.

Presently, Raaviana asked in nearly perfect Alvinorian, "We heard from some Juniors in Urbs Lucis that when an apprentice here breaks the rules of the Sisterhood, you use them to clean the outflows of the city. Is that true?"

The prince cocked an eye in surprise. Elyana was going to reply but he raised his hand and answered Raaviana's question himself, "It is correct that the outflows are sanitized, partly with the use of the Bind, and that sometimes Juniors are sent to the Purification Fields as a punishment. But the punishment is given by their superiors, not by the Crown and not by anyone outside the Order. Most of the cleaning is actually done mechanically and with the use of extremophilic microbes. The controllers—the women assigned to oversee the operation of the fields—are Sensing women of low ability who ask to be trained to do the work because it pays well. They monitor the microbial colonies and make adjustments, which I do not understand, to enhance or restore them when overwhelmed due to storms or by the excess of refuse that comes during festivities. And their aides—sometimes Sisters in training who are sent there by their superiors as a punishment—do help sterilize the outflows."

Ooldrina exchanged a few lip twitches and frowns with Raaviana; perhaps those Juniors—Moradien and her followers—were right to be angry with the Order's hierarchy.

The prince spent the next fifteen minutes answering Raaviana's questions about education, healthcare, and religion in the kingdom. Ooldrina asked none. This seemed to concern the Manu Dextra, who looked at her with searching eyes. But Ooldrina averted her.

Having answered all the questions Raaviana had, the high prince asked *them* a few questions in return, which Raaviana answered with delight. Every so often, the prince looked at her with questioning, hopeful, but not insistent eyes. After the fifth or sixth time he tried to elicit some response from her, he turned to her with a disturbing expression; it was the expression that her mother used when she knew that Ooldrina was troubled by something and wished her to know she was there for her. *Why would this man look at me this way?! He's just a young royal full of himself, barely old enough to have kids of his own.*

As these questions and thoughts rushed through Ooldrina's mind, the quartet arrived at the central market. The place was packed, and though the plebeians kept a respectable distance from them, and the patricians a smaller one, everyone was much closer to them, close enough to properly make Ooldrina's and Raaviana's features.

All turned to bow to the prince and nod to the Lux Baiula. But many, too many, tried to hide their displeasure at the sight of the two girls. Now, Ooldrina was certain the Furanites hated them. And the fact that they donned robes that marked them as apprentices of the Order of the Light made no difference.

A group of people at a booth some five meters from them even started pointing fingers and covering their mouths to make who knew what mean remarks about her and Raaviana. Ooldrina wanted to lash out at them, but her green-eyed friend just shrugged her shoulders and gestured to calm her.

When Ooldrina turned to look at the prince with an angry, hurt and resentful expression, he did not notice because he was already staring down his compatriots. The group stepped back with mortified faces, and they made profuse apologies that drew the shoppers' attention to them. Everyone was put on notice against showing any disrespect toward the high prince's guests, be they Zebulonians.

The prince now looked at her and her friend with a soothing smile, and Ooldrina froze, then blinked and swallowed. The prince seemed to not have noticed Ooldrina's discomfort and was still smiling when he spun toward the merchant whose booth they were standing by and asked him for some fruit he called platoyas.

After speaking some deprecating words intended for the ears of the insolent group at the nearby booth, the shopkeeper gave them all the sincerest welcome Ooldrina had ever heard from a male. He then ordered the boy behind him to pick the best platoyas for his honorable guests while he asked the prince about the girls.

A moment later, the teenager—who had come around the bench—cleared his throat and handed each a plump yellow, fragrant fruit as he bowed deeply to each.

Ooldrina felt discombobulated and just stood there with the fruit in her hand while Elyana Lux Baiula and Raaviana moved to take a bite each.

Noticing her hesitation, the prince prodded her with a gesture and then savored the fruit, himself.

As much as she promised herself not to be impressed by the fruit no matter how good it was, Ooldrina could not help a sound of enjoyment from escaping her.

The prince heard her, and he said aloud, louder than was necessary really, as if to be heard by everyone in the area, "I am glad you like it. It is one of my favorite fruits too. And I must say that—seeing the expression on both your faces, and having heard facts about Razeb and the Mountains of the Sagr which I had had never heard before—I find myself hoping that more of your people will *choose* to come here so we can learn from you as much as you can learn from us. I know the war will limit our ability to do so in the near future, but as soon as it is over, I will discuss the idea with the king and with Magister Setarcos to establish a program to do just that."

Ooldrina and her friend exchanged confused, but hopeful, looks. This man was not their prince, or his father their king. But if all northern rulers were like him, they might well choose to become Alvinorians.

They turned to Elyana. The woman smiled, then waved them on and took the group to a large shop up the street, one of the largest, which also boasted the most mouth-watering spread in the market.

The man who welcomed them immediately stopped everything he was doing, asking a young man who looked to be his son to continue taking care of the customer he had been serving. When he was done telling the prince and Lux Baiula how pleased he was to see them both, he embraced Ooldrina and Raaviana with his eyes. He said, "My Lady Elyana, the Founders burn me if I am mistaken, but I will swear these two beautiful young apprentices are Zebulonian."

"Indeed, they are, Master Brak; they are Ooldrina and Raaviana—novices of the Sisterhood. They are not from the kingdom but from an isolated border village in the south called Razeb, where…some Zebulonians established a colony long ago. After spending the last three months training in Urbs Lucis, I thought it would be good for them to explore some of what Alvinoria has to offer, and I brought them here. And because I wanted them to experience the best food that Furan City has to offer, I brought them to your shop. I think they would enjoy a taste of your limpfish rolls."

"My Ladies, it will be my greatest pleasure to delight you." And with that, Master Brak went to prepare a few fresh cones for the group.

And the girls did indeed enjoy the rolls as well as bites of spiced conch meat. After a few more pleasantries from the fishmonger, and jovial questions directed at them about what they thought of the grandest capital of the world and of the most exotic delicacies of the place—which Raaviana was all too happy to answer as loquaciously as was her habit and Ooldrina responded to with half words and nods—the prince and Lux Baiula finally thanked the man, and the four left the market, walking toward the coach which waited on the south side.

Fifteen minutes later, they were at Domus Lucis. Elyana and the girls stepped off the coach. Raaviana wanted to thank the prince, and she motioned her friend to join her. After a very brief moment's hesitation, Ooldrina followed the red-haired girl's lead, and both bowed deeply to show their gratitude. Ooldrina could not help but feel a pang of guilt as she did so, and she turned to leave before she broke into tears.

The Ways of the Locari

The next day, in late afternoon with a clear sky overhead, Aithen and Elyana were on voranback, making their way to the Royal Bay where they had an appointment. And though the air was crisp, vests had already been removed for a rider soon overheated otherwise, both because of their mount and because of the rider's own work.

Aithen was petting Magnus's neck to thank him for the excellent, extended trot. With some irritation in her voice, perhaps because she was still struggling to completely slow down her own mount—an irritable voran in its female phase—Elyana said, "So, the Locara who's in you—"

Aithen interrupted the Lux Baiula at once and said, "She is not *in* me."

"Right, the Locara who placed a piece of herself in you," Elyana waited to watch the prince roll his eyes, "she has informed their leader? He is ready to meet with me to discuss some arrangement for us to learn the creation of these monitors?"

A crease appeared between Aithen's brows as he answered, "No, he has only confirmed that he will meet with you. Nothing else yet."

"Hmm, do you think he will discuss the monitors?"

Aithen turned to Elyana with an expression and gesture that said he wasn't sure but hoped Torrent would come to an agreement.

Elyana bobbed her head hopefully.

Clearing his throat, Aithen asked, "What do think was bothering our dark-haired Zebulonian so much? Does she resent the Order? Did she not want to come to Urbs Lucis when you brought her from Razeb?"

Elyana took a few frustrated breaths before blurting out, "I frankly don't know."

Aithen raised his right brow the way he often did when humorously questioning something. When Elyana seemed perplexed by his expression, he said, "You used a contraction."

Elyana froze a moment, appearing to be self-analyzing.

A sense of guilt took Aithen, and he returned to the topic, "Well, whatever it is, Ooldrina *is* struggling with something. If it is not leaving Razeb that troubled her, then it must be something she has experienced since being in Urbs Lucis."

"I know. She did not used to be this way. It started about two fourths ago. Both Clara—their instructor—and I have questioned her about it, but she would not say. We've also questioned Raaviana, but the girl doesn't know—or perhaps she does but thinks it will pass, whatever it is."

"That would not surprise me. Raaviana does not seem to worry about much, even though she should…worry about some things, such as their upcoming mission to Zebulonia."

"Indeed."

The prince and Lux Baiula continued riding in silence for a while, admiring the coastline's changing colors as winter approached. The trees' leaves were turning to yellows and greens, and the leaves of the everreds were thickening with a waxy layer that would protect them against the heavy snows of the winter. The thickening also came with an elongation and widening of the leaves that—when the autumn growth was complete—would create a shelter for the trees' trunks and the animals that would move in at the start of winter.

While observing a group of minor howlers who were undergoing their fourths-long gender alternation, and looking strangely comical during the peak of the transformation with proportions and colors all wrong, Elyana said, "Do you have any idea why this Torrent has remained in its male phase all these years? If you first met the Locarus ten years ago, you should have seen it switch multiple times already."

"No, I do not. Perhaps they do not alternate."

"Indeed." Presently, Elyana's voran jumped over a rock on the path. After she resettled herself in the saddle, she added, "Perhaps the leader retains one form or the other once they gain the species' leadership. Or perhaps the leader always retains the male form." Speaking to herself, she added, "I will need to ask one of the Yellow Sashes if there are cases of other species known to arrest the alternation of forms in leaders."

Aithen had half-listened to all that, not because of his disinterest in the question, but because Elyana's question had reminded him of another he had asked himself after learning

251

some incredible facts from Torrent. Now, he felt a strong urge to tell Elyana of the questions they raised in him.

Aithen slowed Magnus with a quick, gentle tug, and Elyana's voran—a tall brown and black animal with an unusually large trumpet—immediately slowed its own pace to match Magnus's.

Elyana asked, "Your mind seems to be elsewhere. Did you hear what I said?"

"I did…well…partly."

"What is on your mind, Aithen?"

"Have you ever wondered why Humanoids and a few other—unrelated—species are the only ones on K'Tara that do not alternate between sexes?"

"Hum, no. Not seriously. It *is* a teleological question, and the fact that we cannot understand how that might be, does not change anything."

The left corner of Aithen's lips went up, showing his surprise.

"The question most thinkers have asked and continue to ask is whether the non-alternation is what has allowed us to evolve our speech."

Aithen scrunched his face questioningly.

"They hypothesize that the constant alternation prevented the formation of stable thought and interpretive patterns required to generate speech. Of course, they do not seem to be bothered by the fact that the other non-alternating species have not developed the same speech capabilities."

Aithen shook his head and turned himself in the saddle to face Elyana. "It is *not* a teleological question. At least, not for me."

"Will you tell me what is on your mind, Aithen?"

With a sigh, Aithen began, "Some months ago, Torrent revealed something to me I was never taught; a history that completely upsets what we believe. He said that we are not from this orb, but that Aiala'Rhi *brought* us here and left someone

252

here to nurture us. In fact, the way he tells the story, it seems we are, well, we are descendants of the Foun–"

Elyana interrupted the prince, said, "What?! Aithen, I am not certain that the Founders are gods as we are taught. But I definitely would not believe in such a preposterous statement without great evidence."

"I know, I know. But if you tie the pieces together, logically, it all begins to make sense."

"How would Aiala'Rhi have brought us here? The mind traverses the Bind, and perhaps it can travel it across the entire universe if it is powerful enough. But the body does not. That is why our religion tells us to keep our bodies worthy, so that on the Day of Union, our Founders may come and join with us, finally embodying themselves into us, because they are spirits lacking form."

Aithen made a dismissive gesture. "I know you are not a believer, Elyana. And I still think what I'm saying makes sense. And the fact that *I* can't explain how the Originator might have brought us here does not mean it could not have happened."

Elyana kept quiet for a moment. She seemed to be wondering about him, about his beliefs. She had taught him many things, but mostly about politics and psychology, not about philosophy or science—Magister Setarcos had taken care of that.

Aithen continued watching her, as their vorans went up a short hill, and thought he saw a worry appear on her face. He said, "You are wondering why the Order's instructors never taught you these things—I mean what Torrent told me—if they are true?"

Elyana raised a brow. "So, you too can read minds now?"

"No, but I have learned to recognize your expressions, and I have asked myself the same question for a while."

"I do wonder about that, yes. But I also wonder how many more times you are going to surprise me with things you should not be the one to know."

Aithen gave her an indignant expression in response, then took his disk out of his pocket and noted the time as Five Ahs. The disk, a device only the wealthy could afford, functioned by means of the microbial colony on its face, and it needed to be reset daily at noon. When reset, the colony lit up the noon mark on the disk, and as time passed and the intensity of the microbes' emissions diminished, the marks of the subsequent hours lit up. The most expensive disks had metal faces sensitive enough to mark changes in emissions every fifteen minutes; the cheaper devices marked time only on the hour.

"We should probably speed up a bit if we wish to keep our appointment."

Elyana nodded, and the two spurred their vorans to a trot. Every so often, the two peeked at each other. Elyana wondered how many more secrets Aithen was holding from her. Perhaps he feared being judged strange or lunatic. Meanwhile, Aithen laughed at himself as he thought of what the Extraorbital Origins Theory opponents would do if they knew he was a believer of it. He wondered too what his father and brothers would think of his beliefs; his father might not find him so silly. Ori might find the theory interesting. Toras would probably snort at it.

Twenty minutes later, their vorans stepped onto the sandy beach of the Royal Bay. Their feet fell softly on the fine white sand. The cliff on the north side of the bay no longer glittered with the now brown-colored algae giving it a decidedly drab aspect. By this time of the year, most people ceased swimming outdoors because of the chilly breeze. But the water was still decently warm, and so long as one stayed *in* the water, it was still possible to enjoy the time.

Having promptly dismounted her cranky voran, Elyana asked, "Do we just leave them loose?"

"Sure, there is nowhere for them to go."

Prince and Lux Baiula took the saddles off their mounts then fished into their respective saddlebag to retrieve their bathing garments.

Aithen felt suddenly anxious. He looked toward Elyana, who shrugged her shoulders and turned around to change her clothes. Aithen decided he might as well get going with it since Elyana did not seem to be too bothered herself. As he undressed, he thought of Kil. The poor boy would surely faint now if he saw his master undress himself to his bare skin in front of the Lux Baiula, though he wasn't technically in front of her since they weren't looking at each other—or rather, since she wasn't looking at him. On the other hand, he could not keep himself from stealing glances at her between exaggerated grunts.

He saw her remove her riding robe, which had pant legs underneath the slit skirt. He watched her pull her arms out and then pull the robe down and off her legs. He swallowed involuntarily when her chest was bared to her strophium and her mid-section bared to her undergarment.

Aithen felt his pulse accelerate at the sight of her skin. And it was not for lack of experience that he reacted so because he *had* already been intimate with a few women. However, the unexpected uncovering of even the forearm, or neck, or shoulder, or foot of a woman one desired, could arrest a man, were he even in the middle of a battle. And Elyana, being a Sister of the Order of the Light, was ordinarily covered head to toe. So, when Aithen caught sight of—or rather spied—Elyana's taut and firm skin, which was the color of pale pink flowers, and of her hips which curved so pleasantly, his heart stopped and then sped at a gallop.

The prince became alarmed when his mind started imagining what he could *not* see, and he forced himself to stop. However, with his mind focused on the woman and on his reactions to her, he was no longer paying attention to what *he* was doing, and he tripped as his hands went to pull up the swimming trunks he had brought on this occasion. Elyana turned her head at the sound and caught him with his trunks half-way up. Aithen blushed furiously, then focused his thoughts and finished dressing, all the while silently cursing himself.

When he was done and had recovered some of his senses, and not knowing what to do but wishing fervently to forget what had just happened, he asked with unusual brusqueness and without looking at Elyana, "Are you done?"

"Almost...done."

For the first time in his still-young life, Aithen felt truly stupid, and he did not know how to react when Elyana turned around and faced him. But he wished to the Founders he could interpret her expression. Did she feel the way he did? Or did she think him a fool, too young and immature to be with a woman? The two of them had been intimate at the ball, that is, they had walked arm-in-arm and had danced with passion in their eyes which had been all the stronger for being hidden. And their hands, untouching, had burned with a desire made stronger by the distance. Surely, she must know that he was no young fool, that he could control his impulses as well as anyone else—or better, since it was said in certain circles that no man could resist a Lux Baiula who decided to woo him.

Would Elyana give herself to hi—

What am I thinking of? Now?! She couldn't, even if she wanted to! Not until I petition the Selection Council.

Elyana startled him out of his thoughts when she said, "Well, are you going to keep staring at me, or are we going to get into the water to meet the Locari?"

"Yes. No. I'm sorry, Elyana." Aithen swallowed. "You are beautiful."

If the prince had known what he would do with those three words, he might have chosen not to say them. But he hadn't known, and he had done it. Now he watched as Elyana stopped breathing, then began tapping her fingers nervously, closed her eyes, took a few calming breaths, and finally reopened her eyes and said without a hint of emotion on her visage, "The Locari?"

The sudden vanishing of the tension in Aithen's own body confused him, and he blinked a few times before saying, "Right, the Locari. Let us go then."

When Elyana responded with her typical business nod, Aithen thanked her silently for her ability to diffuse the worst of situations. But when he approached her to give her some final instructions before they entered the water, he did so with lesser assurance than he showed, and greater self-consciousness than he wished.

Few fish were visible in the bay's waters now; most had migrated to the greater—and warmer—depths around the islands between Aquinos and Mo'Tarkoth. The few species that remained were bottom-dwellers, and they would do their part—over the course of the fall and winter—in the recycling of matter by feasting on all the detritus left there by the myriad fish and lizards that occupied the bay in the warmer months.

Just now, Aithen turned toward Elyana, and was surprised to see how easily she swam. He touched her with a finger and pointed to the surface.

When Elyana appeared, had blown the water in her nose, and opened her eyes, he said, "This is where they will meet us. Take a few deep breaths, and then we will go back down. Remember, they will envelop you with a bubble of water within the water and within which you will be able to breathe."

"Water within the water. Strange expression."

"Well, that is how I think of it. I have no idea, really, what is inside the bubble, but it is not air. It is some kind of fluid, a breathable fluid."

"All right. I am ready."

"Are you sure you can last the five or ten minutes it might take for them to arrive?"

"I can. I will slow down my metabolism."

Aithen nodded, and the two took several deep breaths and returned underwater.

After perhaps seven minutes had passed with no one showing up yet to meet them, Aithen tapped Elyana's arm to ask how she was doing. The Lux Baiula laced her fingers together in a sign she was okay when the water suddenly pushed them back a meter or so, as if in the wake of a huge ship. Aithen watched as Elyana straightened herself—her hair spread around her like a stellar web—and her puffy face took on an expression of absolute wonder. Aithen thought: *Isn't this as wondrous as the Bind?*

Elyana turned toward him, her eyes a mix of fear and marvel. Just then, the Locari positioned themselves in a circle around the prince and Lux Baiula, and pockets of fluid lighter than water enveloped each of them. Elyana could not prevent a gasp, and panicked a moment, thinking she was going to drown from letting water into her lungs. But when the fluid entered her airways, she realized she could breathe!

Aithen saw her opening her mouth to ask a question, and he said with a distorted voice, "You can speak. But it's pointless. They will not hear it." Elyana did not catch all he said. He pointed to his forehead and then to the Locari and said, "Listen for their thoughts."

Elyana nodded and imitated Aithen, turning toward one of the creatures, the largest of them, which must be their leader, the one Aithen knew as Flowing Water, though its name was apparently Torrent. After a moment that seemed too long, she received a Sending, and her expression shifted from wonder to awe.

The Sending seemed to be a welcome, but it came in images accompanied by thoughts rather than words. The images were of fins touching, and of a young Human.

"Fins touch, Young of the Walking." The Locarus did not acknowledge Elyana yet.

While Elyana waited for Aithen's response, she berated herself for not suggesting that they connect so that she might know what he perceived and sent. But she did sense a set of vibrations coming from Aithen just then, and she focused, anxious to learn how this communication worked. The image she received was of Aithen prostrate in front of the Locarus who floated in the middle a gently moving stream. *Is he apologizing? Pleading for something?*

"Fins touch, Flowing Water."

A different Sending came to them now; it came as Human speech—not perfect, but still intelligible. And it had a different quality to it.

"Fins touch, Aithen."

Elyana followed Aithen's gaze, which landed on a Locar to Flowing Water's left. It seemed he was confused by its appearance. Aithen sent images of various Locari, one of them more focused, intense, and its vibration carried with it the feeling of a current and of a question. He repeated the sequence a few times before the Locar replied.

Was Aithen asking if the Locar was Current?

The reply took the shape of a fast-moving body of water within a sea, palpable and unchanging, except for its movement. Elyana supposed this was indeed Current, the Locara that was connected with Aithen.

Aithen's response came as Human language. He sent, *"Current! You are a male now."*

Elyana did not understand Current's next Sending. So, she waited for Aithen's reply.

It appeared Aithen did not know how to form the response because he frowned a while, and Elyana thought the frown looked funny in the bubble of water within the water with their skin distended.

In fact, Aithen was racking his brains for the proper imagery for "male." How could he send that? As the image of a male with genitalia showing? No. As the image of…genitalia? Certainly not. *Ah! Yes. As the image of a Locarus and a Locara, with the emphasis on the former.*

When Aithen nodded to himself and sent his thoughts, Elyana felt she understood them as well as she did Current's reply, which confirmed Aithen's statement. Elyana smiled with visible excitement. She sent to Aithen, *"I think I am starting to understand their Sendings."*

Aithen looked surprised and appeared to want to ask her a question when a thought came, which was directed to her.

259

The Sending's slightly edgy sensation marked it as Current's. *"The one who can link the Living and Nonliving."*

Elyana took a moment to process the images; she thought she understood them but did not know how to reply. Aithen replied in her stead. He sent a positive response, which was a replication of what Current had sent, but more intense, confirmatory.

Elyana wished to ask a question but found that sending was not as easy as understanding. So, she continued watching, becoming slightly frustrated at the thought that Aithen would have to translate her questions.

Meanwhile, Aithen felt a strong urge to question Current further about her transformation. Sure, most animals on K'Tara alternated between the sexes, but a speech-capable species? So, he sent another thought to the Locar regarding her metamorphosis, but he decided to continue using natural language and to follow that with images to help all of them learn Human speech, as well as to help Elyana learn theirs.

"This is the first moon where you have appeared to me as a male."

He followed this with the image of a Locara alternating with that of a Locarus, with several moon cycles passing and finally stopping on the form of a Locarus.

Current responded with thoughts that showed several moon cycles while in her present form before changing, which Elyana interpreted more or less as *"I will change again, in many moons."* Current continued with the images of a fish separating from its school and going off on its own, and the school chasing it to bring it back. Elyana did not understand this, and she asked for Aithen's interpretation of it. The logic of it amazed her, and she turned to gaze in wonderment at the Locari.

Aithen replied with Human language again, *"I am sorry for the digression,"* and he followed this with the images of him blushing against the sea's blueish background.

Elyana noticed a contraction of the Locarus's pectoral fins and then their relaxation.

Wishing to get to the point of the meeting, Aithen shifted his gaze toward the Locari's leader. He sent a thought to the creature, which he followed with the Human words, *"Flowing Water, my thanks to you again. My friend—the Linker—she is here to ask permission from you to learn the creation of monitors from Current."*

For a moment, Flowing Water watched Elyana, his skin shifting from his typical dark red to a dark blue hue as he weighed the newcomer. He seemed to be asking himself whether he had made a wise decision in revealing their existence to a Linker. After another tense moment, during which Elyana had watched him with continued, but hidden, fascination, he sent, *"Your friend's request, I will receive, Young of the Walking."*

As Elyana failed to respond—Aithen translated for her and reminded her of the imagery he had taught her so that she might thank the leader for his welcome. Elyana nodded and tried a Sending, *"I hope our fins will touch also, Great One."* Then she waited.

A moment later, Torrent sent, *"One who can unite, you are, Linker. Glad, I am."*

After Aithen explained the last part of Flowing Water's Sending, Elyana felt any remnant of her early apprehension vanish. The Locari's Leader had accepted her overture, had welcomed her. Aithen was not surprised; she was a Purple Sash, after all—one of the best.

Flowing Water—or Torrent, as Current referred to him—, Current himself, Elyana and Aithen spent some thirty minutes discussing the conditions under which the Locari would teach the Lux Baiula to create monitors, which included the wiping of a portion of Elyana's memory to remove anything indicative of the location of their meeting.

Elyana had almost refused the condition, but Torrent had assured her that it was not negotiable and that it would not harm her in any way. When Elyana agreed, Current placed a monitor in her. The procedure—if she could call it a procedure—took the space of a moment, during which Elyana had to fight against her desire to resist the invasion of her brain. Current spent a few minutes testing the monitor by sending thoughts to Elyana and waiting for her reply. The first two…connection requests—that's how she had decided to call the sensation she felt—caused her to hop in the bubble of water within the water, and she could not prevent her embarrassment from seeping through her expression.

So, this is what it feels like. I understand, now, why Aithen had become disconnected from things that one time during the Serpent's attack at Furan City, and then at the Royal Ball. I might need to work with Bilena to find ways to make this…implant less disruptive.

When all was done, and Current was satisfied with the proper integration of the signaling thought into Elyana's mind, he sent, *"Tomorrow, I will connect with you, when the Suns are high. Do you accept this?"* Elyana nodded. *"I will begin the teaching then…and…but…"*

Aithen interrupted Current and sent, *"Though?"*

Current acquiesced by bending his triangular face in that strange way and finished his sentence. *"Though try you can, to study the monitor."*

Elyana did not know how to send a nod in the Locari's language, but she tried sending one the way Lux Baiulae did, with the sound of snapping fingers—or the thought of it in any case. But the Locarus stared at her with a clearly confused expression.

Right. They do not have fingers, so that sound or thought will not mean anything to them. Aghr!

Elyana tipped her head, instead, hoping they had learned that from Aithen at some point. And it seemed they had because Current responded with the Human words 'All is agreed,' followed by what felt like the sound of something cupping water. Elyana sent the image of herself, prostrated in front of the Locarus, to thank him for the lesson. She then turned her head toward Flowing Water with a gloomy expression. Not knowing how to say what she wished to ask, she sent her question to Current.

Current considered the request a moment then relayed Elyana's question to Torrent.

The leader's color shifted to a somber black as he replied through Current, who continued to send thoughts in the way of his species and translating them into human language.

"There are traitors among your kind. I feel them in the way I feel the Hrackmol! Most of the foul vibrations I receive from your city are feeble, but one is very strong and another also. I am not able to...distinguish them, but perhaps I can share the sensation of the Hrackmol! with you."

The vibrations Elyana received from the Locarus were disquieting, and they felt oily, foul. She shivered, thinking that this was what she might sense from one or more of her Sisters. In fact, she hoped the Locarus was wrong. But he seemed so confident, certain in a way no Human ever felt. Perhaps it was his age; Aithen had told her he was over one thousand years old.

Elyana thanked Flowing Water, and the conference ended with the exchange of the customary Locarian parting expression directed to Aithen.

"Again, fins touch will touch when all the sea the moon lights." Elyana had to think on this a moment, as it had been sent by Flowing Water himself and his thoughts were in an unusual order.

The next moment, the Locari left, the bubble of water within the water disappeared, and Elyana coughed when salty water entered her throat. She rushed to the surface and coughed a long minute more. When she recovered, Aithen accompanied her back to the shore.

There, he grabbed the towels he had brought, gave one to Elyana, and started drying himself. But Elyana continued coughing, and now, a cool wind started blowing from the east, and she shivered. Aithen wondered why she couldn't warm herself up using the Bind. He asked, and Elyana replied she didn't know and continued shivering and drying herself.

Aithen took another towel from the saddlebag, approached her, and wrapped the towel around her shoulders and body. He held her. But she continued to shiver. So, he removed their towels, put his body against hers, and wrapped himself and Elyana together. He felt Elyana start to pull back, perhaps from a sense of prudishness, or from a sense of pride—he did not know. He let her pull back but looked at her with worried and pleading eyes. She let him take her, and they embraced suchwise for a long time.

They talked little, but every so often Elyana told Aithen of the wonder she had felt in the Locari's presence and how lucky he was to know such magnificent creatures. She also berated him for not telling her how to prepare herself for the bubble to disappear. Aithen apologized with the most honest regret, and Elyana pulled herself deeper into his embrace.

The Compromise

Krystiana paced in her office after having listened to Octavius's account of his uses of the Bind once more. The only part of it that comforted her was the fact that he had used it a surprisingly low number of times in his one hundred and forty-two years of life—if she could trust him. But she knew her Praefectae would want to know the extent of his skills, whether he had the power to affect another person's mind, and they would wish Octavius tested, inside and out, which he would refuse. In the end, the Praefectae would try to force something upon him to prevent him from ever using Mind Rape again. She rubbed her forehead and went to her desk, closed her eyes, and drew the Bound flames licking the marble spheres representing the Order—and K'Tara's twin suns—to her hand.

Octavius, sitting by the office's window, looking calm but determined to get out of this unscathed, said, "You *could* ask Elyana to verify my statements. I would not mind it. She would confirm that during the thirty-three years of her assignment to me, she has never caught me using any Bindings, and especially not to influence or harm anyone, not even in battle; it has always been my position that a ruler must be respected and loved—not feared, but if feared, then dreaded because of his natural skills and intellect."

The Magna Mater sighed. "Yes, Octavius. But that is just it: she has not *caught* you. How do we know you have not used your skills to affect persons when not in Elyana's presence?"

"Mater! How would my use of the Bind to influence others—if I ever used it for that purpose—be any less acceptable than yours?"

"The difference resides in the fact that those we meet are aware of our abilities, whereas no one knew of yours until now. And in any case, we do not use Bindings to affect the minds of others without their approval; it is prohibited. All we are permitted to do is sense their emotions to predict the likely direction of their thoughts and decisions."

"All right, so it comes back to you trusting me."

"To *us* trusting you. We are not your subjects, but the Sisterhood is so intertwined with your kingdom's political, economic, and social facets that it will not do you any good if anyone of us suspects you of using the Bind according to principles other than those we ourselves swear obedience to."

Octavius's initial reaction was a tensing of his body getting ready to fight. But he soon recognized the truth of the Magna Mater's words and, after a moment, nodded his understanding and agreed to swear obedience to the Order's law during a meeting of the Light's Assembly—Urbs Lucis's ruling council.

Krystiana turned her back to the king to take the blue sphere into her hand. She had always preferred it over the red one, perhaps because it gave her truth more than the red sphere. After a moment of consideration, she placed it back in its place over the red flames, which she stopped to feel. She then rubbed her fingers to her palm as if the flames' and the blue sphere's vibrations had revealed something to her. Tilting her head toward the king without immediately turning, she said with a hint of anxiety in her breath, "There remains, as you know, a much more serious matter to discuss, Sire; one which can only have a sour conclusion; one we should have resolved months ago after your return from…Spiritii."

Octavius made no reply for a long while during which the only sound audible to those with a sufficiently sensitive hearing was that of his nails skipping on each other. Then, he crossed his arms and put his chin in his hand. Finally, he gave a snort and asked, "Mater, do you agree that we are all fallible, regardless of our authority? That none of us can be certain to know the truth of *any* event, even when heard with our own ears or seen with our own eyes?"

Krystiana looked at Octavius with suspicious and resentful eyes but did not answer.

He said, "Do you think you might be tricked by my question into providing an answer you would prefer not to give? You are too clever to be tricked by anyone, which means that you do not wish to admit the possibility I am suggesting."

"What are you saying Octavius? That we erred—all of us— when we found Marcus Vrol guilty of the crime of violation?"

Octavius responded with a firm, assured tone. "Yes".

"And what leads you to believe we erred?"

Though Octavius had prepared for this meeting for a while now, he had not arrived at any acceptable answer. Should he tell her that he entered Marcus's mind? Octavius had proposed this answer to himself a hundred times, and a hundred times he had laughed at himself. With everything else now going on, it would do him no good to add this complication to the situation.

The king finally stood, took a few steps around Krystiana's office, pivoted toward her and said, "I know the truth of it, Mater, and 'how I know it' is a revelation for another day. As I explained to Elyana, I went to Marcus after he contacted me to tell me that my kingdom's safety depended on my meeting with him. Despite the crime you think he committed, Marcus was my most loyal subject and would have given his life to save mine— which he in fact did many times, and not so figuratively. I tried to obtain the information from him via courier, but he stated that it could only be shared by the holder of it, and the holder of it would not share it without something in return, which I could only give if I met with him, in Spiritii. So, I went. What I learned there from Master Lub Methor was confirmed by his conational Lusk Methrim, who is here in Urbs Lucis. True, I could have learned of Zebula's planned invasion from Master Methrim, but I did not know of him before I left for Spiritii, and Master Methor offers me something which Master Methrim does not: a means to prevent the invasion."

Krystiana raised an eyebrow and was about to ask, but Octavius preempted her and said, "In fact, I will require the Sisterhood's assistance in executing my plan."

"Octavius! You are here to be interrogated about your transgressions and to have your powers constrained. And, yet, you stand there and tell me you need to discuss diplomatic or military matters with me…to ask our support?!"

"Mater, we both know you cannot punish me for meeting with Marcus or limit my freedom for being a Binder. Yes, you could bring the Nethers on Marcus, but I would oppose you if you did because he is now vital to the kingdom's safety. And you could make things difficult for me, but there is this war which might very well swallow us all."

Krystiana fumed, and the muscles of her face were contracting furiously. How did the king reverse the direction of the arrow so easily? How was he now imposing *his* will on her? On the Sisterhood?

"Krystiana, you have known me for a long time, as have most of your Praefectae and Elyana. You *all* know me; you know the strength of my convictions and of my principles; you know the truth of my words because I have spoken them for over a hundred years. Yes, I have hidden things from many, and yet, you will find that I have not abused anyone. Does that not convince you that your trust in me was never misplaced, and that it is not now either?"

Krystiana gave a sidelong glance at the spheres on her desk; she eyed them as if resenting them. Can one truly learn from the past? Can it really provide useful insights into present events when myriad conditions may differ though the events themselves may look similar? She was beginning to doubt it.

"Very well, Sire. You say Marcus is now vital to your kingdom's safety. Why is that? Why should we not expel him or send him to the Observatory?"

Octavius frowned at the mention of the Observatory. That was where Urbs Lucis sent Soiled Women—Alterintrant women who were too dangerous to remain free and could not be healed—where they received daily washings with antimicrobials as well as concoctions of noxious suppressants. Krystiana had better not let her ruling council send Marcus there because he *would* retrieve him by force if he had to.

"Let me start from the beginning then." And the high king walked back to the couch by the study's balcony. He spent almost an hour explaining to the Magna Mater all that passed that led him to visit Marcus in his hidden villa, request his forgiveness after being convinced of his innocence, and finally meeting with one Lub Methor—a representative of the Organization for the Liberation of Zebulonian Males. He told Krystiana of the Organization's request for his support of their rebellion against Zebula, which would ensure that the violence remained in Zebulonia and that Zebula's invasion plans would be foiled—and of his subsequent agreement to provide that support.

Krystiana had listened patiently then asked, "And you decided to agree to Master Methor's request, even though you knew, then and there, that would require our involvement?" Octavius gave an embarrassed smile. Krystiana shook her head, amazed by Octavius's fortune. How could a man be so lucky as to so completely and utterly divert all flows from himself? But then, she remembered several instances where the king had avoided minor irritations as well as major catastrophes; it seemed the Founders must be with him, and if not all of them, one must be at the very least. She knew Elyana, herself, had often wondered at it over the years, and she remembered the king's sons debating his luck at various gatherings. Krystiana continued, "No matter. Elyana had already informed me of Zebula's intents before your returned to Furan City this summer; I was, therefore, ready for your request. In fact, I am preparing to send two…spies to Zebulonia."

"Spies? You have Sisters from the kingdom?"

With an awkward note to her tone, the Magna Mater replied, "They are novices; two Alterintrant girls from Razeb, a little village of expatriate Zebulonians on the northern edge of the Sagr."

"And you trust two untrained girls with such a vital mission?"

"We have no other choice, and your Frumentarii could do no better. All these girls will need to do is be in contact with one of us here to relay information. For the rest, they should have no trouble fitting in as they are of Zebulonian descent. Furthermore, Master Methrim assures us that their vocabulary, which he said was the vocabulary of twenty years ago, will now fool even the Court's instructors, and he has trained the girls in the usages and customs of Zebula's Court. They are readier than any of us could ever be."

The king said, "That is a bold plan. But we do need more information about our enemy. And I can see how using women as spies will help, given the status of men in the southern kingdom, even if the two you are sending are probably not used to what they will find in that Court."

Octavius wasn't sure if Krystiana's fingers had twitched nervously, but he noted it and continued, "When will they depart for their mission?"

"By month's end."

Octavius now took a moment to reconsider his situation and said, "Where do we stand, then, K—Magna Mater?"

He had been about to address her by her name, but Octavius stopped himself, not wanting to create the appearance that his transgressions and deeds were going unpunished as a result of their personal connection.

Krystiana understood the reason for the king's sudden correction, and put it in the back of her mind then said with great irritation, "We stand in a place now more comfortable for you but less so for me because it seems you have effectively passed your defense to me, and I will be the one needing to convince my Praefectae that we should continue to trust you and not impose any restrictions on either you or Marcus Vrol. All that on the basis of your word…and of whatever twisted logic about knowledge of the truth you trapped me with."

A guilty smile forced itself onto the king's face. "If you would speak for me, Mater, I would be most grateful. Though I *am* ready to address the Light's Assembly, myself. But because I would not speak with them as plainly as I spoke with you, I might not be able to convince them as I have you and that would surely lead to a confron—."

With an irritated and dismissive wave of her hand—a gesture only she could use with the high king—Krystiana said, "Yes…I know. It goes; I will speak in your favor."

Octavius nodded his thanks and was about to take his leave of the Magna Mater when she raised a finger.

"There *is* one concession you will need to make, Octavius."

The king took a deep breath and readied himself for whatever the Magna Mater had concocted to ensure the Sisterhood was not left totally empty-handed.

In contrast with the king's earlier smile, a shrewd one painted itself on Krystiana's face when she said, "It is for the good of appearances—as you are rightly concerned with—but also for your own good and for our peace of mind. We learned a few months back that you were looking for a privy attendant. We will recommend to you a candidate whom you will accept. That way, only those closest to you, and a few within Urbs Lucis, will know the truth of the manner of his assignment. To everyone else, it will appear as your own decision."

"You cannot be serious, Krystiana! I am *already* surrounded by your—"

Krystiana raised a hand. "The person whom we will assign to you is not a Lux Baiula. But he is one of us—a Junior."

Octavius's brow furrowed itself with surprise and confusion. "A male Alterintrant? Apprenticing here?"

"Yes, the only one. He is a bright young man, with a passion for the medical sciences as well as for administrative tasks, both of which will be useful to you in his capacity as Privy Attendant to your person. His only duties—aside from those you choose to assign him—will be to ensure that your use of the Bind does not affect you negatively, and to inform me, should he become concerned."

Octavius took a moment to reflect on the compromise which was being forced upon him. As he did, his expression slowly progressed from disbelieving, to pure anger, to considering alternative solutions he might offer Krystiana and rejecting them, and finally to acceptance. Once he reached this point, he signified his agreement and asked to receive the boy's curriculum vitae.

"Thank you, Sire. This will do much to appease the Light's Assembly. Now, there *is* another matter I wish to discuss with you."

The Magna Mater's tone, which seemed to indicate the matter would touch the king even more personally than the appointment of a personal attendant to him, caused all sorts alarm disks to ring in his mind. But he calmed himself, and, with a resigned sigh, he said, "What is it, Krystiana?"

"I assume you are aware of the high prince's interest in my Manu Dextra?"

Octavius was used to changing topics without preamble to unbalance someone, but this was not meant to take him off-guard. It was an honest concern both he and Krystiana had. He replied with crooked lips, "I am, Mater."

"And you will stop it? You know the Selection Council will oppose such a union, as I must, too."

Octavius was about to respond, but then slouched back. He snorted and sighed as he hesitated. He took a deep breath and said, "I will not, Mater. I did discuss the situation with my son, and I know he understands the risks. I left the decision to him."

Krystiana's jaw dropped, and she stared back wide-eyed. A moment later, her mind had calculated the king's motivations. "Though your decision is shocking, it does not surprise me, Octavius. You are…a unique ruler. This tells me you trust that whatever your son's decision may be, it will not harm your kingdom or our Order. But your calculations cannot enter mine, and as much as I love and respect Elyana, my mind tells me their union would only spell trouble. I will therefore oppose it if presented to the Selection Council, although with the war at our doorstep, I doubt very much that any such petition will be presented any time soon."

Octavius smiled a small, thankful smile. Krystiana would do as she had said, but she was also not prohibiting the courtship, believing that the war would take care of things, one way or another. He took leave of her and returned to his apartments on the top floor of the Residences.

When a Sister Fails

In the quiet of the thermals at Urbis Lucis, while the world teetered and tottered, while princes and leaders debated and others studied or created the growing chaos, Dana prepared to enter the Flogging bath. Lux Baiulae who came to the thermals typically did so to rejuvenate themselves by soaking in a soothing, relaxing bath and then laying on a reinvigorating microbial mat on the flats behind the building.

But Dana was not here to soothe her mind or body; she was here to—as they called it—flog herself. The tub was filled with noxious microbial species that killed a significant proportion of those already living on a Sister. This process caused a Sister excruciating pain, of course, but it also reset her energies and endowed her with a fresh, reinvigorating impulse given that the attendants would then rinse her with water containing beneficial microbes to replace the lost flora.

To begin, Tera Lux Baiula, the Keeper of Baths, and her assistant, Lotaria Lux Baiula, were going to create a mind-tie with Dana. This would allow them to monitor her vital signs and metabolism from within the Bind, given that they would have no direct access to her while she was submerged in the tub.

Tera, a tall, pale woman, motioned for Dana to approach them. Having formed a triangle, the Keeper of the Baths began the process. "Sorores, nostris mentibus nunc nos ligare!"

The women's hair snapped out toward each other while scarves of blue light stretched between them. Ethereal ribbons connected the women, zapping and crackling for two seemingly interminable minutes. When the three women gasped—their brains having connected and begun receiving thrice the sensory inputs—they opened their eyes, and Tera asked Dana to unclothe.

As she did, Dana cursed herself for what was to come. But what other choice did she have? The loss of three of her Sisters and her mismanagement of the crisis in the high king's bedchamber demanded that she take this punishment and start afresh. Having discarded her undergarments—she would be provided with new ones, exempt of all traces of her soon-to-be ex-microbial flora—she entered the rich yellow ardamantis tub with simple determination.

Tera Lux Baiula now nodded to her, and Dana closed her eyes. She then took several deep, hyperventilating breaths and immersed herself completely in the warm water. Once submerged, she slowed her pulse, doing her best not to grit her teeth with anticipation of the pain to come, and descended into a deep meditative state.

Satisfied, the Keeper of the Baths motioned her assistant to retrieve the large jar sitting on the windowsill—a pot filled with a dark red mixture of a dozen species of microbes—and pour it into the tub.

Dana repressed a desire to increase her skin's tension when she felt the microbial milk flow around her. The bath's water was now an opaque pink and the attending women could no longer see Dana, so they entered the Bind to monitor—and shield—her.

The rejuvenation by way of the Flogging bath was not a lengthy process, though the pain it caused sufficed for a lifetime.

When the toxic microbes had coated the Barrier's skin and penetrated every opening of her body, they began to replicate, and a growing searing sensation started to jolt Dana. As every square thumb of her body began to flare as if searing over top of a cook fire, Dana began repeating to herself: *I will do this. I will cleanse myself. I will reform my body and mind so that the next time there is danger, I will be ready and act to keep from harm and death those I am sworn to. I will do this; I will cleanse myself. I will do this; I will cleanse myself. I will do…*

The invading microbes were now forcing part of her native flora into frenzied autodestruction. The sudden release of vast amounts of cellular materials into Dana's body triggered an immediate and furious response from her immune system and from her liver, in a race for survival. Dana did not try to slow her metabolism; she needed the pain, the fresh start this would bring about.

Behind her closed lids, even her eyes were being scoured by the relentless microbes. The pain of it shot into Dana's brain with throbbing pulses, and she screamed in her mind, sending a horrible yell out into the Bind. And though she had skipped a few verses, she kept repeating: *I will do this; I will cleanse myself. I will do this; I will cleanse myself.*

Tera and the groak-like Lotaria, with her short, fat, wrinkled neck, watched and monitored their Sister. They had seen women put themselves through this procedure before, and not so infrequently. Indeed, every year, a dozen or so Sisters came to the thermals to *flog* themselves, though they did not actually whip themselves as did the members of the Order in its beginnings. Sisters subjected themselves to this procedure either as a punishment, or as part of a cleansing ritual, to rejuvenate their flora, and all of them suffered through it to a greater or lesser degree.

Dana's screams, yelled out in the Bind, were undoubtedly fierce, but Tera and Lotaria had heard women in such agony that they would have raised the dead if they had not been shielded by the Keeper of the Baths and her assistant.

Containing a Sister's screams was no easy task, and it often drained the two women to such a degree that they needed days to recover. However, monitoring the penitent's metabolism was even more difficult. For indeed, the procedure flooded the penitent's bloodstream with chemicals of all kinds, turning it into a real maelstrom. Tera had to sift through the myriad molecules and keep track of those that might pose a danger if they did not quickly become inactivated by the penitent's body. If she identified any such compound, she would immediately end the procedure. Tera was perhaps the most sensitive Sister of all, even more than Elia Lux Baiula. Because of her highly discriminant senses, she was often asked to participate in the investigation of mysterious deaths.

Now, Dana began experiencing spasms, and her movements caused water to splash on the attending Sisters. Tara sent a thoughtcall to Lotaria; it was time to reverse the procedure. The woman thus started to flush the bath with a flow of cool, soothing water containing beneficial microbes and a mixture of all those that gave Dana her skills. The pink, toxic soup slowly poured out and was replaced by the clean water flowing over and around Dana. The water penetrated her nostrils, eyes, and ears, as well as every other orifice of her body and rinsed them too.

As the toxic microbes were carried away to be reclaimed in the thermals' treatment vats, Dana's temperature slowly returned to twenty stones warm—just above normal—and she came out of the Bind to look upon the attending Sisters with pink eyes and raw skin. Because it would take her a day or two to recover fully and look presentable again, she would remain at the thermals, and spend her time chanting *'I have done this; I am ready to bear. I have done this; I am ready to act,'* on and on until all traces of the toxic substances that had flooded her body

275

were metabolized. She would then return to her post, ready to defend any put in her charge.

Lusk's Torment

After his meeting with Noctiferus, Lusk had spent two days hating him, but he had finally resigned himself to his fate and set to turning members of the Sisterhood in earnest.

He had already begun turning Moradien, a bright young woman who could have had an extraordinary future ahead of her if she had not been so rebellious—a trait he had obviously taken advantage of. She was now becoming as corrupt as he was, doing the Dark One's bidding even if she did not know it. It pained him, but what choice did he have? None that his brain would provide, or his reason allow him to act on.

Now, he needed to complete his work with Luvius, whom he had already started turning and sent on his first mission: befriending the high prince's squire at the Royal Ball, and through him, obtain a position in the high king's court. Once there, Luvius would have started befriending Court staff closer and closer to the king until he could either be assigned to the king's personal service or have influence on someone with direct access to the monarch. The process would have been a slow and long one. But luck had knocked at Lusk's door this fourth when he heard that the young Alterintrant, Koricki Dar'Muntake, had been assigned to the king to serve as his personal attendant. So, Lusk now had the perfect target for Luvius. As he thought about it, he felt a secret relief at not having to turn Koricki himself, as he had planned to do, because the young man was one of the most honest, good, and moral persons he had ever met. Better to leave the evil doing to someone else.

Luvius, on the other hand, had been an easy victim; he was handsome, lazy, and pretentious, and Lusk could more easily justify corrupting him, even if the doing continued to inflict wounds upon his own body and spirit.

Unable to bear either the sight or the thought of his deeds, Lusk spent the next hour looking out his window, staring numbly toward the south, with only one thought keeping his mind alive and away from alcohol: his mother, in that house the Founder showed him.

The Way of Discovery

Tania Lux Baiula paced in her office at Domus Lucis with a report in her hand, not because it spoke of trouble here or there, but because it contained the results of the testing that the laboratory at Urbs Lucis conducted earlier that fourth on the blood samples she and Elia had shipped there—the samples they had drawn from the bodies of their fallen Sisters.

"Elia, you are a geniusse! Your method for probing bodies, when we do not know what to probe for is an absolute revelation. You need to teach this to the Sisters of both our Sashes."

Elia, perhaps one of the humblest Sisters in all of Alvinoria, responded with a dismissive shrug.

Tania said, "Elia, dear. Stoppe being so modest. It is truly a great insight you had aboutte the way our minds work, learn, and do things, with the subconscious mind taking over when the conscious part might get overwhelmed. I can already imagine all the applications of this."

Elia resigned herself to the praise but quickly moved the conversation to more practical matters, saying, "Thank you, Tania. *Anyway*, what do we do now? The lab has isolated the foreign substance that killed our Sisters, but we still do not have a way to protect ourselves."

"That is our next task." Tania tapped her lips nervously. "We could try to generate the antidote then send it to the laboratory for them to manufacture vials of it for our Sisters across the continent." Tania paused, tapped her lips again, and said, "But that would not help a Sister fight the toxin's effect during an encounter with the assassins."

"No, it wouldn't."

"Perhaps we could try immunizing ourselves to it by having the lab replicate the substance so that we may ingest larger and larger quantities of it until we can all neutralize it."

Elia frowned at the idea. "That would be a very slow process. And we would need such great quantities of the toxin; I am not sure the lab could manage it."

"You are right. Founders! What *can* we do?!"

Tania started pacing again, pausing every so often to blurt out a "no" as various ideas crossed her mind, until her face shone with delight and excitement. The woman even skipped.

"What is it, Tania? You have an idea?"

"Yes. I've got itte! It has to do with your earlier discovery. I *said* we would find other applications for it. Well, listen to this. We have to use both our conscious and subconscious minds to train our Sisters to recognize the toxin and then neutralize it. We will schedule a grand training day—in the Bind—during which you and I will ingest the substance and open our minds—the conscious and subconscious parts of them—to our Sisters." At this, a crease of worry formed on Elia's face. "That is how we must do this, Elia. We will ingest small quantities of the substance as we open our minds to our Sisters, then trace the toxin and neutralize it. Our Sisters will observe with their conscious and subconscious minds, so the learning is complete."

Elia shook her head. "It would be better for the two of us to train ourselves to recognize and neutralize the toxin first, as that would allow us to teach our Sisters with only the use of our conscious minds."

"Are you afraid to share your subconscious thoughts? It would take too long to share our knowledge using our conscious minds only, and in the meantime, more Sisters will die. This is the faster route. This *must* be the route!"

Elia said, "I am scared, Tania, but not for what is in my mind. Still, you are right. But I have never heard of the Sisterhood holding such an event to train our Sisters,"

"That is because we have never needed to train all of us at once to protect against a new threat. But when faced with new challenges, we must find new solutions. This is the new solution!"

"All right, Tania. But first, you must convince me that this—the opening of our subconscious minds to every Roamer in the Bind—can be done safely because we will not be able to selectively connect with over six hundred Sisters."

Tania replied with the firm confidence of one who has developed a certain intuition after studying the complexities of the Human body and mind for a very long time.

The two women spent the next two hours discussing the idea, with the first part of it spent debating the dangers of their approach. When Elia was convinced that the certainty of death from the toxin outweighed the possibility that their minds might be raped during the short duration of the training session, she relented and began planning the event. This included everything from obtaining sufficient amounts of the toxin for the two of them to ingest at least four times before the grand training session, to planning for four test sessions during which they would also try to train two of their Furanite Sisters using the proposed method, and finally to informing the Magna Mater of their plans.

XIV OF EXCITEMENT AND TERROR

At the Fair

The capital was abuzz with a flurry of activities in anticipation of two great events planned for that eighth day of Undecimus: the launch of the Cross Alvinorian Race, and the official activation of the furanry, whose training had just been completed.

To the south of the capital's walls, large tents had been set up to house all the carriers. These would be taken to their point of departure at Yerlaya, four thousand five hundred kilometers from the capital, in cages carried by a team of six furans leased from the Royal Army by Lord Warbender, Lord of the Armory, who was the race's sponsor. The carriers would be released on the first day of the Second In-Between fourth, two fourths hence, when the Blue Sun would be hidden behind its Red twin, and all the hours of the days could be used by the racers for their long return trip. The carriers who did not die or quit along the way would return to their respective home pens, where their owners would welcome them with cheers—or not—remove the rings from their legs, stamp them with date and time using the Carrier Clocks, and finally take the clocks to the racing committee, which would determine the winners after comparing the time stamps on all the returned rings.

To the west of the capital's walls, there stood a Great Tent to receive the royal family and other nobles of the city as well as visiting patricians. In front of the tent, three thousand furanteams were assembled and waited, more or less patiently, for the ceremony to begin, flanked by companies of the voran-mounted regiment and of the infantry.

Food vendors were dispersed throughout both fields, and peddlers sold likenesses of the favored carriers and furans, while others sold golden brooches representing the furanry and golden quills representing the age-old tradition of the Cross-Alvinorian race. Others still, sold mementos of the Coriolan Crown, whose

281

members would all be in attendance today, except for Prince Toras, who was unfortunately detained in the west by a new gnarler attack.

The king, his wife, his heir, and his minder were presently being taken to the West Field by coach.

The king, who had come back to the capital the day before, had not yet had a chance to discuss with his son and wife what had passed in Urbs Lucis, and Aithen could not hide a certain anxiety as he sat on the seat across from the royal couple, while Mitsuko sat on a seat to their left.

Aithen glanced out the windows, every so often, to observe his father's augmented personal guard, trying to gauge their attitude: four new Red Sashes, who had come back with Dana Lux Baiula, complemented the five men of the Praetorian Guard. All sat proudly atop their furans, scanning the streets, the crowds, the shops, and homes for suspicious activity. The sight seemed to intimidate many a Furanite, which in turn appeared to frustrate Octavius.

The king said, "They are probably wondering whether Urbs Lucis has decided I need to be controlled."

Unable to contain his curiosity any longer, and with a suspicious edge to his voice, Aithen said, "It appears the answer is that it has not. After all, you are here in complete command of your movements, and you were in fairly good spirits up to a few moments ago when you saw the questioning gazes of some of your subjects. If I were to guess, I'd say that not only did they not put any restrictions on you, but that things went…well?! How did that happen, Father?"

Understanding that his son would not drop the question until he had the answer, Octavius sighed and said, "I suppose you have both waited long enough to find out."

Aithen gave a firm nod, and while Darya did wish to know what had passed in Urbs Lucis, her expression showed only annoyance at her son.

"The meeting with Krystiana was tense and at times frustrating—oftentimes more for her than for me. But she is a good leader, and she knows the way of things. Her only real dis—well, that is a matter for another time."

When Aithen and Darya looked questioningly, he made it obvious with a sign of the hand that he would not answer.

"As for my meeting with the Light's Assembly, it was not pleasant—far from it—even with Krystiana vouching for me. But in the end, they accepted to continue to trust me. They also agreed to not punish Marcus for my visiting him this summer. And because the Sisterhood values logic, the fact that they accepted my use of a…mind-penetrating Binding to defend my life forced them to accept Marcus's own action forty years ago—or rather, forty years late. They have therefore revoked his confinement, which means he is now a free man."

Aithen, rather than looking pleased, was furious. Darya tried to soothe him, knowing what was going through his mind, but he would not be silenced. Fortunately, he did not yell, perhaps because Mitsuko was there or perhaps to prevent anyone outside from hearing. But Darya did close the shutters to be certain no one would see her husband's or her son's hardening faces.

Aithen said, "You're saying that not only was there no consequence for your transgressions or for using the Bind without training, but you are also in a better position than you were before? How is that possible, Father?! How is it that you never suffer the consequences of your actions when everyone else does?"

Octavius's expression suddenly turned very dark, and Darya put a hand on his as he began to roar his son's name. She asked Aithen to simmer down, but he continued, heedlessly.

"I know you are the king, Father. But you are not above the law!"

At that, Octavius simply shook his head and sighed while Darya told her son to take a breath and use his reason for a moment before things got out of hand.

Mitsuko Lux Baiula frowned, not understanding why the prince always seemed so angry and wishing he would speak to the king more respectfully. And, remembering Elyana's revelation to her that morning, Mitsuko wondered whether the prince got this angry when he was in *her* company. Probably not, but then, why did he react this way with his father?

Having found his calm again and realizing what was angering Aithen and wishing to turn the table on him, Octavius said, "Aithen, your fortune could be better if you let it happen, if you invited it. But although you are like me in many ways, your outlook on life is definitely less positive, and that has kept you from seizing opportunities which would have made things better for you."

"In any case, if there comes a day when I do something wrong—something that harms those around me or my subjects—you can rest assured I will pay the price. But that won't make you feel better, Aithen. What will is opening yourself to what good life has to give and seizing it—or to be content otherwise. Which I am—content."

The prince remained silent for a while, brushing inexistent dust from the coach's velvet walls. When he spoke again, it was with a sense of resignation. "I know you are content, Father. And I am glad you are unburdened by any of the restrictions that the Sisterhood might have placed upon you or on Marcus—I really am. It's just that sometimes things seem quite unfair when I compare my luck to yours." Seeing that Octavius was going to object, Aithen added, "Yes, yes, I know. I need to seize opportunity when it comes. I suppose I just don't know how to do that."

Octavius considered his son's words, slowly rubbing his hands, and he finally spread them to say, "But today, you at least have something to be proud of, my son. The furanry may technically be a unit of my army, but it was your doing—yours and Harlion's. And when you add this to the success you had with the Locari yesterday, thanks to which the Sisterhood's capabilities will now be greatly increased, you must admit that this will have been a fantastic fourth for you."

"I am not sure I would put my fortune in the future tense, Father. Who knows what tomorrow—or even this evening—will bring? So, I prefer to enjoy the good things, such as they are, in the present."

This time, both Octavius and Darya sighed heavily and shook their heads at Aithen's persistent negativity, which he called realism.

"But I am…proud of what Harlion and I have done in such a short time. It was not easy. Especially not the part about capturing, bonding and then training the thousands of furans we needed. The Sisterhood was of great help with that, and I suppose I *was* also lucky."

Sensing that whatever dark cloud had rained on Aithen had now dissipated, Darya asked, "Speaking of the Sisterhood, where is Elyana? Will she meet us on the field?"

Aithen shrugged his shoulders, but Mitsuko Lux Baiula replied in his stead. "She should join us before the ceremony begins, Lady Darya."

"Thank you, Mitsuko. Will Irania accompany her?"

"No, I am sorry, my Lady. Irania has other urgent matters to attend to."

Darya leaned toward Octavius and said, "Shouldn't Irania be spending more time in court, Octavius?"

"Indeed, she should. I like and respect Irania, and her council *is* valuable. But I need an advisor I can turn to whenever I need her."

"You wish Elyana could be sent back here?"

Octavius nodded.

The exchange between king and queen-consort was not unheard by Aithen, who felt his pulse take-off like a hundred vorans; but he did not say anything. Nor was the exchange unheard by Mitsuko, who hoped the king would not get his way in this too; not that she resented him for walking away unscathed from Urbs Lucis. In fact, she had found new respect for this extraordinary man, a ruler unlike any other she had ever served. But she knew, too, that letting one have their way all the time could only spell trouble in the long run. So, she would continue watching him and hoping that it did not become necessary for her to take action.

It took some thirty minutes for the coach to arrive at destination and for the royal family and its retinue to take their places on the dais underneath the Great Tent. Once seated, the king, his wife, and his eldest acknowledged the multitude of welcomers and well-wishers.

Octavius then spent some time watching the soldiers, the furans, and the vorans arrayed in front of them like sunrays. It was a grand thing for the king to observe, especially knowing that a large number would be sent to Horn's Pass the next day to lend Toras a hand against the gnarlers, and he said as much to his wife. Darya commented with equal awe about the strength that the ensemble projected.

Aithen looked at the men and their mounts with an expressionless gaze. He turned an ear to his parents' chatter every so often but did not participate in the conversation. His mind was preoccupied with other things for the moment. Occasionally, he glanced at his father out of the corner of his eye.

All thoughts and musings ceased when the striking sounds of the tabellarii shook the air and rattled the spectators' chests. At the same moment, the proud-looking Harlion, the stern Kendor, bald and leathery-skinned Crassius, and wide-mustached Rinius walked onto the field. The high captain placed himself on a small dais, next to Elia Lux Baiula, who would enhance his voice, while the primi took position in front of their respective winged battalions.

Extending out and away from the winged regiment, the voran-mounted unit and the infantry waited quietly; this was not their day. But they were still proud in their ceremonial uniforms—the voranriders dressed in gold and red uniforms sitting astride beautiful beasts with gray, black or steel blue coats, and the infantrymen attired just as spectacularly in their red on black uniforms. No other nation in all the Terrae Regis had a professional army like that of Alvinoria. And, with or without the revived winged regiment, the army was still awe-inspiring, and both voranriders and infantrymen knew it and showed it in their posture.

The spectators shifted in their seats with animated eagerness. The king exchanged a nod with the high captain, and the man motioned to the Tabellarius, who hit the drum with a quick sequence intended to quiet the audience. An anticipatory silence fell at once on the entire field. The civilians looked at their neighbors wide-eyed and jittery.

Elyana arrived just then and sat herself behind Aithen, next to Mitsuko. She gave the king and queen-consort quick, respectful nods, but gave the prince a lingering one, which the prince returned with a half-smile. Elyana raised a brow questioningly, but the prince shrugged his shoulders and indicated with another gesture that he would explain later.

Elyana sighed then turned to acknowledge her Sister, who welcomed her with the stony face typical of Lux Baiulae. However, Elyana could tell from the woman's motions and expression that she wondered about her decision to court the high prince. Elyana responded with a look which meant there was no need for concern, when her attention was caught by Harlion's reverberating voice, and she pivoted to look toward the field along with everyone else.

"My King, my Queen. My Prince. Lords and ladies. Today is a grand day. It marks the start of a new chapter, the reactivation of the furanry, which—if it is not the Coriolan Ten Thousand of our forefathers—is still the mightiest force in all of Terrae Regis."

Spears and boots rapped the ground in agreement, and the reverberations spread as an earthquake to the seats and benches under the Great Tent to shake the bones of the audience.

Someone arrived panting, just then, and sat himself to the queen consort's left, with apologies but with evident excitement

287

too. "Father, Mother, I ran as fast as I could. I did not want to miss this."

Darya arched a brow and said, "And what about Master Rackeli?"

Still huffing, Ori replied, "He's coming."

The king gave a quiet chuckle and returned his gaze to the spectacle. Darya welcomed her son with an amused but warm smile, which the boy returned with bright, shiny eyes and nervous anticipation. Soon after turning her gaze away, Darya glanced at Ori again, wondering at the shine of his skin. Something seemed different, but she couldn't quite put her finger on it. Perhaps it was the heat. She set the question aside and returned her attention to the field.

Aithen, sensing his brother's excitement, let go of any lingering irritations he still felt in the face of his father's unnatural good fortune and said, "You wish you could be on one of the furans, littl' brother?"

This time, Ori's smile stretched from ear-tip to ear-tip.

Harlion's voice boomed again and refocused everyone's attention.

"These three thousand furanteams are ready to serve, Sire; ready to live, fight and die to protect our great kingdom. Two-thirds of them have traveled far to attend this ceremony, Sire, and the fact that they are looking as resplendent as the others is a testimony to their readiness." At that moment, a most wonderful song arose from the vorans, which was immediately accompanied by the deep throat song of the voranriders and infantrymen. It was an overwhelming experience, and many a tear flowed among the spectators. Ori watched and listened, utterly enthralled.

Harlion signaled the Tabellarius, who called every soldier and animal to attention with three beats of his drum.

Harlion continued, "Sire, Primus Rinius, Leader of the winged spear battalion!"

Hands clapped on legs.

"Primus Crassius, Leader of the winged archer battalion!"

More claps and hurrahs.

"And finally, Primus Kendor, formerly of the Black Guard and now officer of the Royal Guard, Leader of the winged assault battalion!"

Hands clapped on legs furiously, welcoming the man who was well-known for his courage and character.

Harlion signaled the Tabellarius again, and the young man initiated a new drumming sequence, which was picked up by the other four tabellari encircling the force. Having received the order to mount, the three thousand furanriders climbed atop their steeds, as did the captains. When all were ready, the high captain about-faced and invited the king to order the take-off.

Octavius looked at Aithen, with an acknowledging smile, as he stood up with excited motions. Behind him, a young Yellow Sash, who had just arrived, prepared to enhance his voice. When the king looked back and the woman confirmed her readiness, he began.

"Guardians! This is a grand day indeed because the sight brings hope, a hope underpinned by the *knowledge* that you are master furanriders, trained and formed by the best—your commanders, High Captain Harlion and High Lord Commander Aithen." Octavius looked toward his son to invite him to give the authorization to depart, a proud smile lighting his face.

As the prince stood up, he could not hide his emotions, and he tightened his lips reflexively. He acknowledged his father's invitation, looked back toward Elyana and—with the excitement in his voice made unmistakable by the Yellow Sash's enhancement—gave the high captain permission to send-off the furanry. He then stood rigidly for a moment, as if surprised and perhaps embarrassed by his words' intensity.

The sound of the tabellari transmitting the order, followed by that of the three thousand and three furans taking to the air with beating wings and shrieks, drowned the prince's self-conscious throat scratches. The roar reverberated throughout the capital and startled every living thing as far as the eye could see. Furanites not on the field to watch the furanry's departure jumped out of their skins while those in attendance either stood mute or cheered as they never had before, especially the children who screamed and squealed.

Octavius turned to look at his eldest, his pride evident on his grizzled face.

Aithen's eyes, too, gleamed with pride.

But underneath the pleasure the king felt, caution demanded its space as well, and he let it surface.

The prince knew what his father was thinking, and he let it show with a nod and a lip slightly pulled to the right: would all this strength suffice to repel the Serpent, the gnarlers and Zebula? That was the question, and hope could not enter the calculation.

Just then, Elyana coughed and leaned forward, toward Aithen. Her voice straining to overcome the sound of the furans' screams, she said, "I am glad you are not out there with Xyre, or the dust would have been rightly unbearable."

It took Aithen a moment to realize Elyana had spoken to him, and he mumbled a 'hm?' as he leaned his head back.

"I said 'I am glad you are not out there with Xyre, or the dust would have been rightly unbearable.'"

Aithen tilted his head back further and gave Elyana a playful scowl. When his eyes accidentally crossed Mitsuko's, he thought: *I wonder why she keeps looking at me that way. Does she disagree with our relationship, or is she merely surprised by it? I hope Elyana teaches me to read their faces better.*

Another bout of simultaneous screeches drew all eyes back toward the spectacle now unfolding in the sky, a spectacle unseen in ages. Continuing to use the tabellari to transmit his orders, High Captain Harlion orchestrated a complex choreography of the three companies who arranged themselves to draw the emblem of House Coriolis, with the Spear battalion tracing the left wings and legs, the Archers the right appendages, and the Assault battalion composing the two-headed furan's body. The furans, mounted by their riders, created strange interconnected shadows on the ground.

Responding to an unseen and unheard command, alternating members of each wing battalion broke formation and descended to cross each other and take up position in the opposite formation with perfect and synchronous movements. Next, the wing companies dissolved and positioned themselves behind and above the central battalion. That done, the entire furan-mounted brigade spun in the air and came back down as a bolt with one final deafening screech, landing in a spear-shaped formation in front of the Great Tent.

Hands clapped loudly on legs for a long minute and the crowd quieted only when king and queen-consort—followed by the princes—rose and walked down to congratulate the officers.

A quarter of an hour later, the inauguration over, soldiers and animals returned to the base, and the royal cortege made its way to the southside fields.

As they walked, the Red Sun reappeared from behind a mass of clouds and brought smiles to all their faces, except to Mitsuko's.

Indeed, the woman's lips kept alternating between interest and concern in the restrained manner of Lux Baiulae as she watched the high prince and the Manu Dextra. The two were strolling in front of her, arm-in-arm, and the electricity that flowed between them could be sensed by even a novice of the Order.

Presently, something Elyana said snatched a loud and amused '*Ha!*' from Aithen, which caused Darya to glance backward.

The queen-consort whispered to her husband, "It appears our son has decided to pursue his relationship with Elyana."

Without turning his head, Octavius replied quietly, "Indeed. He came to inform me this morning."

Darya made a small nod but could not prevent her arm hand from squeezing Octavius's. Octavius sent Darya a thought, *"It will be fine, my Love."*

Darya started, surprised by a thoughtcall she had not expected and had not fully perceived. Octavius sent it again, and Darya's jaw dropped as she turned toward her husband. She was going to whisper a question but decided to send it instead, *"You haven't used the Bind to communicate in years, even when it would have helped a negotiation. Why now?"*

"Perhaps, in my old age, I am finally finding the strength to free myself of my fears."

Darya sent a playfully mocking reply. She knew what had caused her husband to reveal his abilities, and it was not old age. Still, she had to admit to herself that she quite enjoyed Octavius's Sendings; they were so much more intimate than sound. She squeezed his hand, then snorted quietly when she realized that this was the first time in a long time that she had enjoyed using the Bind for *any* purpose, and she smiled.

Octavius stretched his thin lips in return, then let the sights and sounds of the fairgrounds absorb him. The king loved this time of year, between Octavus and Dodecimus, when there were events bringing people together almost fourthly and the majority of the population enjoyed fourth-long holidays each month to revel with family, friends, or colleagues, for one reason or another.

Walking behind his parents, Ori watched them interact quietly, wondering what they might be saying to each other. Master Rackeli, who marched next to him, leaned his head in and said with a voice unused to speaking—being the taciturn man he was, "The king and queen-consort have always loved each other, young prince, and her absence was never a sign of a lack of affection. But your mother seems to have made a decision of late, and it is painting smiles on their faces, which I have not seen in a long time."

Ori continued watching his parents with hope lighting up his face.

Leaning her head in Aithen's direction, Elyana said, "So, will you tell me why you looked so cross earlier?"

Aithen threw a few cautious glances around before whispering, "Well, it's just...my father told us how...he left Urbs Lucis not only unconstrained, but somehow in a better position than before he went."

"Ah."

"Ah?"

"Yes. Knowing you, you probably did not hold back your indignation."

Aithen did not reply, except with a sequence of head shakes and grunts.

"Well, it looks like he did not mind your eruption too much if I am not mistaken about his joyful demeanor."

"No, he didn't. He said I should...be more welcoming of fortune."

Elyana properly chuckled just then, which caused the prince to stiffen momentarily.

Elyana said, "You know he does have a point, right?"

"I suppose he does."

Prince and Lux Baiula continued walking and observing quietly for a while, until the prince had understood the truths in his father's statements. When that happened, he sighed and snorted silently, feeling...content.

But the sentiment faded when he noticed Senator Sisipe, one of Lord Arotek's supporters in the capital, look at him with his head tilted toward his wife, obviously whispering something about him to her. When the man caught the prince's stare, he hurried to smiled and nod in his and Elyana's direction. That did not, however, fool the prince. He knew, of course, that gossipers would find a way to talk about the 'scandalous relationship between the high prince and the Lux Baiula.'

People. How I wish I could find all those Serpent's Tongues that have kept spreading rumors ever since the ball. I am certain Aroteka is one of them and that she told the wife of that bleater of a Sisipe about my dancing with Elyana. And the senator is definitely a Fifth Columnist who's waiting only for a reason to attack me. When I find the proof, I will make Aroteka regret every vile word she's been spitting.

At least Father has kept his word and accepted my decision. A contradictory voice irrupted just then, in Aithen's mind, and said: *I hope you don't make him regret it.*

Aithen felt a tug on his hand.

"I can sense your shifting moods. They keep switching between irate and content and back to irate. What are you thinking of, Aithen?"

Obviously having no desire to tell the truth in the present situation, Aithen rushed to say, "Have you found anything regarding…those that the Locari warned us about?"

Elyana cocked a brow in a suspicious manner, but she did not pry. "No. Not yet. I opened myself to the Bind this morning, while keeping the sensations that Flowing Water shared with me as vivid as I could make them in my conscious mind, but I did not feel anything resembling them, here or anywhere else; I suppose that is a good thing. Though I have to admit that I do not enjoy having to probe my colleagues without their knowing—not at all."

Aithen gave Elyana an empathetic glance along with some words of encouragement he suspected she did not need. He gently squeezed the hand she had on his arm, putting aside his own concerns, and the two returned to watching the performers of all sorts, who were spread along the paths, as well as to breathing in the mouthwatering smells that began to drift their way from up ahead, where the food vendors were located.

The cortege now approached the southside field, where the carriers' squawks—some nervous from the anticipation of the race and others irritated by the proximity of so many other unfamiliar carriers—began to fill the air. Their clacks excited a few members of the king's retinue while they made some others—who found the flyers repulsive—roll their eyes.

First Senator Leo, who followed at the end of the cortege with Eldest Paula and Senator Luma Kraelion, was one of the latter types. He grimaced and complained to the two women. He grumbled when Senator Kraelion responded that she quite liked carriers because they were beautiful and smart animals.

Leo said, "Well, as for me, I hope the Sisterhood succeeds in their attempt to develop a means for Sisters to be in constant, instant communication. That way, we can quickly eliminate all the carrier coops and be done with the noise and the smell."

The First Senator growled again when both women shook their heads in response to his comment.

Eldest Paula said, "Fortunately for you, Leo, I believe the king will let us go our own way now, so—"

Presently, High Captain Harlion arrived and interrupted the senators' conversation. He said to Paula, "I am sorry, Eldest." Then, turning to Leo, he said, "First Senator, the high king would welcome your company as he tours the racers' tents."

The senator's expression could not have been worse if he had just suffered the most complete oratory defeat. When the high captain's brow began to furrow, Senator Leo put on the expected smile, accepted the invitation, and told the officer that he would be there at once. After Harlion had gone, Leo turned to Paula and said with plain sarcasm, "What was it you were saying, Paula?"

The woman raised her hands defensively, "This is a good sign, Leo. The king's invitation means he still believes the Senate matters. This should help you tolerate the *smelly* flyers."

"I suppose. Until later then."

When Leo arrived at the front of the cortege, the king received him with a cheerful welcome, which only made Leo wonder what it was the king wanted to discuss with him. Still, he replied with as much merriment as he could muster and followed.

The ten men and women guarding the royal couple soon unnerved the First Senator, however. He had heard about the attempt on the king's life earlier that fourth, and about the death of three of the four Lux Baiulae who had been assigned to his protection. If the assassins tried again, would *he* be safe or would he be a collateral casualty? But no one would try to get to the king in such a public venue, would they?

Leo was pulled out of his frightening thoughts by Octavius, who said, "First Senator! I have been wanting to hear your report on the settlement of the Horn's Passers who decided to stay rather than return to Horn's Pass for a while now. How *are* they settling?"

"Ah! The Horn's Passers. Yes. Twenty families decided to remain here—that's a little over a hundred individuals. There is a group of citizens who still fear that the foreigners' children will have a bad influence on theirs." Seeing the sudden and dangerous change in the king's disposition, Leo hurried to add, "*But*, the rest of our good Furanites have accepted the westerners and have welcomed them as proper members of our city, as the high prince had rightly predicted would happen."

Leo watched Octavius's lips curl in a frown on the left; it appeared that the good citizens' welcome did not make the others' behavior any more acceptable.

The king said, "I am glad the majority approve, First Senator." He continued with an icy edge, "But what of these complainers? *What* do they fear the Horn's Passers' children will do to theirs?"

The First Senator pulled at his collar as if the loose garments were suddenly quite uncomfortable. He replied, "They are...simply concerned that the Horn's Passers' children will contaminate the language of theirs and...that they will be a bad influence on them."

Octavius replied with a simple, terse, "I hear," and did not say anything else as the group finally walked into a large tent filled with cages containing squawking and grunting carriers. Octavius remained worrisomely quiet while the others around him reacted with audible surprise or excitement or revulsion at the sight and sound and smell; his thoughts were consumed with the weighing of the response he might give to the bigots among his people. Finally coming to a conclusion, Octavius smiled and said loud enough for his entire entourage to hear, "It seems some

Furanites might benefit from a temporary exchange, First Senator, and although the kingdom is not as safe as it was, it might still be worthwhile sending them and their children to Horn's Pass for a few months."

Everyone froze, if only for the briefest moment, before continuing as they had been doing, pretending not to have heard or understood what the king said.

Old Leo almost missed a step, and he looked around himself before averting everyone's gaze, turning to the king, and saying, "I...I must have misheard, Sire. Did you say—"

"I did, First Senator. And I am perfectly serious. If you remember, it was a common practice under my father's reign. It helped build trust between the various peoples of the kingdom."

"But with the war—"

"There is no war yet. Although I wish I knew how to call this...insecurity. They will be as safe in Horn's Pass as they will be here."

Leo tried to catch the queen-consort's or the minder's eyes hoping for one or the other's support against the king's unreasonable plans, but they did not look his way, and he continued on his own. "But Sire, I am certain that your father never sent families away during unsafe times."

"As a matter of fact, Leo, he did. It makes sense when the danger is just approaching and showing its fangs. Imagine how it will be if more so-called outsiders come into the capital during a time of strife and Furanites are still ignorant of them. No. There is still time to remedy our people's obliviousness to each other and build a minimum sense of trust between them before the enemy's true assault. We will do it so that if the time comes when the capital will become a place of refuge—or if we should need to abandon the *capital* for some other town—people will be more accepting and welcoming of each other."

Leo swallowed hard, and Octavius's penetrating stare caused him to swallow once more before finding the strength to form a smile and speak. "My King, I must say that you have always had unusual views about how the world should work, and

I am...not certain I understand them fully. But Your Majesty knows best, and I will support your decisions."

"Good. Good, First Senator. Now, let us forget about politics for a while and enjoy the festivities."

With that, the group separated. Aithen, Elyana and Harlion went toward the fancy flyers' section, whereas the king, his wife, and the rest ambled toward the racers' section, visiting one carrier master after another. Octavius inquired about the masters' origins, about their flyers, and about the animals' winning odds. Leo frowned every so often, while Darya—a decent Beast Reader, as were most Kynarian clerics—provided encouraging opinions about the racers' health and mental condition. As for Mitsuko, she watched the king handle one carrier after another with the greatest interest, and one who could read her faint twitches and lip movements would be able to tell that she was frankly surprised by the man.

Just now, Octavius stopped in front of a finely worked cage, which contained the most beautiful carrier he had seen yet. He was about to ask who the owner was when a young, hesitant voice came from behind.

It was a young man of about fifteen or sixteen. He was clad in roughly woven, but clean and whole, trousers and shirt. The boy stood with an honest, nervous smile on his face, a face that was beginning to show reddish facial hair.

Octavius said, "This is a fantastic flyer, young man. Master...?"

With a nervous stutter, the boy answered, "Albo, Sire."

"Master Albo. How did you come by such a beautiful specimen?"

The young man suddenly lost his smile and became alarmed.

Octavius realized what had frightened the boy and said, "I have no doubt it belongs to you. I only asked because a flyer of this type is rarely seen in these parts. You must have traveled here from afar."

The young man did not seem convinced by the king's reassuring words, but he happened to catch Ori's honest grin and nod, and he relaxed, though he was utterly mystified that the young prince would deign smile at him. Indeed, all the other lordlings he knew only ever sneered at him. But the prince looked genuine.

Albo licked his lips and said, "Yes, Sire. I'm originally from Horn's Pass. My parents let me bring my flyers when we relocated here, four months ago, and I was able to find a coop to keep 'em in and continue training them. This is a Western Red carrier. They're native to Upper Alvinor, but my *pa* travels there once in a while, and he brought this one back two years 'go. He's my best racer, and I'm sure he could beat one of the Sisterhood's carriers too. He's a strong flyer, and really agile too so he can evade predatory flyers quite easily, though he does better at dodging predators when he's in his female form. I've watched him do it several times."

Octavius chuckled and asked, "Do you always talk that long when someone asks you a question, Master Albo?"

"'M sorry, Majesty. At first, I thought you thought, well, an'way, but you didn't, and my family and me—all the people from Horn's Pass actually—we all have a lot of respect for you and the high prince, and—"

The boy stopped himself before he went on for another eternity and looked down.

The king said, "There is no need to be embarrassed young man."

The injunction caused the boy to blush. While thinking of a way to move the conversation, an idea sprouted in the king's mind, and he raised his voice a little to be certain the First Senator heard him. "I am glad to know you and your family feel welcome in Furan City. As I have told ministers and senators and soldiers alike, Horns' Passers are Alvinorians too and you deserve to be treated as such. Now, tell me about your flyer. What makes it such a strong racer?"

While the boy explained the adaptations that allowed his carrier to fly at speeds greater than other racers and for longer periods, another carrier master—who had watched with pondering eyes the prince and his Lucian companion chat laughingly a few isles to the left—approached and listened to the conversation between king and boy from behind the Guard.

Albo had impressed the king with his deep knowledge of the carrier's lineage and physical adaptations, but when he tried to explain the creatics which gave his flyer those winning adaptations, he hesitated and blushed. He was going to apologize for his ignorance when the listener interrupted him and said, "Sire, I believe the boy is thinking of the carrier's *heterozygosity*. It is a biological principle which allows the progeny of dissimilar parents to be better adapted to environmental conditions than the progeny of like parents."

The king looked toward the woman questioningly. But when he saw her robe, he welcomed her.

"I am sorry for the interruption, Sire. I am Emissa, Urbs Lucis's carrier master."

"Lux Baiula, I believe you are the winner of last year's Cross Alvinorian Race."

"I am, Sire."

"You are welcome to join our conversation."

The woman nodded her thanks, and the king's guardians let her through.

Octavius continued, "You say, then, that the offspring of unlike parents are often better than those of more similar parents?" The woman nodded. "Is that what you were trying to say, Master Albo?"

"Yes, your Majesty. I just couldn't remember the word."

"You would be surprised to know there are words I, myself, do not remember, Master Albo. But you have a very bright mind, and it *would* be nice to see you expand it further."

Turning to his wife, who had been listening quietly all this time, he said, "What do you say we offer young Master Albo a seat in Magister Setarcos's class, my love?"

The queen-consort responded with the warmest smile the young man had ever seen, aside from that of his own father.

Albo stood mute for an inordinately long time, and he then thanked the king and queen-consort repeatedly and effusively with his words, and everyone else with his gaze.

When the boy became exhausted and stood silently and in shock again, the king instructed him to come find Master Rackeli at the palace, who would give him a permission for Magister Setarcos's class. He then wished him good luck for the race and left with his retinue, except for Ori and Master Rackeli, who stayed behind a moment.

Albo looked at the stern man, thinking he might speak, but he did not and simply nodded his head. The boy cautiously shifted his gaze toward the young prince, thinking he might be displeased that the king had rewarded a peasant with such honor. But the prince's genuine smile erased all fear in Albo, though incredulity remained painted on his face.

Ori said, "Perhaps I will see you in Magister Setarcos's class; I attend some of his lessons with the other students."

Albo remained motionless, too dumbstruck to reply or do anything as prince and majordomo left to rejoin the royal cortege.

As they walked out of the tent, Octavius felt joyous. They were such simple things, those that could make a person smile and momentarily forget about their troubles. Octavius took his wife's arm again and pulled her closer when a dart stuck him in the neck, and darkness enveloped him. The king wobbled and fell to the ground before anyone could react. Darya screamed, and chaos erupted.

Primus Julian yelled and kneeled next to the king, while Dana and her Sisters immediately dispersed the crowd and formed a cordon around the royal family.

Julian shook the king, calling his name, but to no avail. He put an ear to the king's chest and sighed when he heard the heart still beating. "The king lives, but his breath is shallow. Mitsuko, call Tania, now!" Julian then turned around with deadly eyes, scanning the crowd for the attacker. Not seeing anyone rushing away, he yelled again, "Emil! Find the prince or the high captain; they need to have all passes out of the region blockaded. Run!"

The newest member of the Praetorian Guard left like a blur, dodging and jumping, in search of Aithen or Harlion.

While Jashan held the queen-consort and young prince back, Mitsuko probed the king and placed a thoughtcall to Tania Lux Baiula, and Primus Julian continued to scan the fairgrounds.

"Where is he? Where is he? Where...there!"

Pointing to a figure some two hundred meters away that seemed to be running toward the edge of the field where the visitors' mounts, carts, and carriages were tied, Julian ordered the chase.

Without a moment's delay, three praetorians and three Lux Baiulae started running. But panic had struck the crowd by now, and this made a swift pursuit difficult, if not impossible.

Merr paused, hoping to stop the escapee with an arrow. But he spat and scratched the idea when he realized he was more likely to hit a civilian than the assassin.

The Lux Baiulae were no more successful in their own attempts at launching Bound projectiles toward the man.

So, guardians and Sisters resumed their chase. And Primus Julian—though he was not the fastest runner in the company— moved like a battle voran, deciding to plow through anyone who stood in his way. His singular focus, combined with the hatred he still felt for the Dark One and all his minions after the Serpent killed his sister, dowsed the pain developing in his bones and muscles. His legs burned the ground, and his body avoided, sidestepped, jumped, leapt, and toppled.

From the right finally came the high captain and the prince. Harlion ran on legs strengthened by decades of martial exercises. Watching him go, one would not know he was now in his sixties, except for the flushing of his face and more labored breathing.

The pursuers still had a hundred meters or more to cover before any of them could put their hands on the assassin, when

Dana saw another dart launch forth from the assassin's blowgun. With her Bind-enhanced eyesight, she saw the dart fly directly toward Julian, who was the furthest ahead. Dana hesitated a moment—a fraction of a moment—to decide whether to keep running after the man or try to help Julian. Her decision made, she slowed her pulse and from her mouth blew forth a sonactic Binding which tripped the officer after two attempts, just in time for the dart to miss him.

However, that did not stop the assassin, who was now looking for an opening to launch his poisonous projectiles at—Harlion and Aithen!

Dana tried to trip the two men as she had done with Julian, but there were still too many people in the way, so she screamed to warn them, but alas. She searched for another solution. Her only—clearer—line of sight was toward the assassin and she decided to launch a Bound arrow toward the man despite the risk to the civilians. However, a commanding hand on her arm stopped her before she could generate her Binding.

It was Elyana. Without any word and with a murderous look in her eyes, the former Red Sash—one of the few holders of a forbidden power—entered the Bind while watching the assassin aim his weapon at the captain and the prince—the prince who was now also her...her lover. Just then, Harlion stopped and fell; the prince slowed, turning toward his captain. The assassin had his opening. Without another moment's delay and with the eyes of one whose family had just been threatened, killing eyes set in a stone hard face, Elyana reached for the man's mind, penetrated it, and blasted it with such a powerful vibrational discharge that the air around him crackled.

Not only did her Binding bring the man down, but his agony and the zapping of the air terrorized whatever remained of people running away from the chaos, and they ran faster for it.

Dana Lux Baiula turned to her colleague with a shocked expression on her face, and with a constricted voice, she said, "Elyana, what did you do?"

Elyana locked her jaw in response then ordered the woman to secure the assassin while she, herself, ran to the captain and the prince.

Dana went, but she did so with an apprehension she had rarely felt, a feeling that clenched her gut while tens of suppositions fought each other in her mind.

Dropping to her knees next to Harlion, Elyana looked at Aithen, who had his ear on the captain's chest.

Aithen sat up. With desperate eyes and a trembling voice, he said, "I can't see any dart on him. I don't know what happened, but he just fell over clenching his chest."

Elyana started to probe the captain. Her expression was easily readable now, and it was creased with worry and concern.

While she probed Harlion, Aithen asked about the king and was relieved to hear that Tania, who had arrived before Elyana too started chasing after the assassin, said that he would live.

"What about Harlion?"

Elyana shook her head. She was no medic, but her probing picked up worrisome signals from his heart and brain. Aithen felt everything within him clench and shake miserably. The next moment, his face darkened, and he ran with murder in his eyes toward the fallen killer, who lay groaning and crying.

In Solinor

With a tone of utmost joy and bewilderment, Aria said to her friend, "Cari, it was just—how can I describe it—amazing! But it was also weird."

The friends were in Aria's bedchamber.

"What do you mean?"

"I mean, the things Ylana showed me were just out of this orb. I never knew a priestess could do the things she showed me. None of our teachers have ever shown us, and our textbooks don't speak of it. But it was weird too, because I couldn't understand why she would want to show me those Bindings. Why me?"

"Aria, what are you talking about? What did she show you?"

"She showed me how a true priestess can control all creatures."

"That's it? We are already taught how to read animals' minds and influence them."

"That's not what I'm talking about. Influence is nothing compared to what the Supreme Priestess showed me. She is truly a master, and now I know what I want to be."

Carasina pinched her brow, still not understanding what Aria was talking about.

"Cari, Ylana can control—actually *control*—ten, twenty, a hundred animals, all at once. And she does it effortlessly, as if she were conducting the Voces Creatoris."

"Voces Creatoris?"

"*Ughr*! The royal choir in Alvinoria. She does it as easily as conducting a choir. She had all the flyers—all of them! —in the woods behind her residence sing at once. Flyers of different species, all responding to each other's songs in perfect harmony. And then," Aria stretched her head back and moaned, "then she had them all fly off and perform for us in some magical choreography."

"That seems incredible. If she can do all that, why haven't we ever heard of it?"

"Don't you think I asked her? Ylana said she's like my uncle in that way; she doesn't like to use her powers to show-off, especially because not many people can do what she does."

"Aria, I think you're taking me on a ride. Kynarians are not Binders; we're some of the best Sensors, yes, but not really Binders."

"Cari, I'm not taking you on any ride. She said that some of our people *can* Bind, and she said that I have the potential too."

Cari blinked, and Aria added, "I didn't want to believe I could, Cari, but she was so convincing that I let myself believe her, and I tried it. I spent the next three days learning her Sensings and Bindings, and—"

"And what?"

"She's right. I can do it. I did it. Not like she did, but I had a dozen flyers sing together. With practice, I can become a master beast speaker, myself."

"You mean a master beast reader."

"Beast speaker."

"I've never heard of a *beast speaker*. And this is still unbelievable. But given that you were able to develop a way to communicate with wild lincots instead of the trained ones we use, I guess maybe you *do* have an unusual talent; you're not a full Kynarian after all."

Aria's face darkened with pain at that.

"I'm sorry Aria, I didn't mean to say you're…you're not one of us. Of course, you are. But there might be reasons for your unusual capabilities."

"So, are you saying that perhaps the Supreme Priestess is not a full Kynarian?"

"What? No. Of course not. Ohh, I'm sorry, Aria. It was completely uncalled for and illogical on top of it."

"It's all right."

"So, you want to become a…beast speaker?"

Aria nodded. "The Supreme said something that really stuck with me when I got discouraged at one point. She said that our Order represents society not because of its political power but because it binds us to our existence and to every living creature on this orb. She said that we are the glue of our people, that our ability to influence creatures helps keep us safe, as can the ability to control them."

"But we are not taught control, because it can cause harm."

"That's right, but in the end, she told me she's teaching me because I may need it to help us in what is coming.'"

Cari plumped herself down on a chair and did not respond. Confusion and fear, and even a hint of jealousy, took hold of her thoughts and muddled them then.

Taking Risks or Hubris

With a voice croakier than usual, the old Praefecta said, "Master Methrim, please sit."

When the Zebulonian had sat himself, Saara continued, "Bilena Lux Baiula has kept us informed of your progress instructing the girls for their mission to Zebulonia. It appears they are improving their language skills, but Ooldrina has become quite defiant and withdrawn. Because you spend so much time with her, I would like to hear from you what you think might be happening before I have her brought in for evaluation, given that this attitude of hers would not bode well for the mission if it should persist."

Lusk had come prepared this evening to begin working the head of the White Sashate too. He had only had an hour's warning, but he had spent it rehearsing his methods and honing his skills on a culture of human brain cells he kept in Urbs Lucis's Medical laboratory—to which he had access given that he was a Healer—watching for the tell-tell changes in color that indicated his vibrations were having the intended effect. Presently, he modulated his voice to initiate a neurochemical cascade, which should open the old woman's mind to him. He said, "Thank you, Praefecta," and very gently probed her reaction.

Saara took an unexpected pause, surprising herself, and she pretended to shuffle through some documents on her desk while she processed her reaction.

Why did he thank me? And why did I pause?

Finding no answer to either question, she set her gaze back on Lusk. As she did, she was beset by an unexplained desire for the man. His face, his body, his bulge while he sat there in front of her, it was all suddenly overwhelming. She felt her blood rush through her veins in a way she had not experienced in a very long time. She closed her eyes for the briefest moment to regain control of herself. Finding that she was able to return her pulse to its placid but alert tempo, she breathed a silent sigh of relief.

"Please tell me what you think is troubling the girl."

Modulating his vocal vibrations with the perfection of a surgeon, Lusk gave the Praefecta the explanation he had devised for anyone who wondered about the girl's state of mind. He expected to convince her as easily as he had all the others, including Clara Lux Baiula, the girl's instructor.

However, Saara Rucius, Leader of the White Sash Assembly and the oldest Lux Baiula alive, was not responding as he had expected, and the situation was beginning to unnerve him. Indeed, every so often, the woman asked a question that seemed to originate from some unconscious suspicion she had, regardless of the dulling vibrations he sent to stimulate her endorphin production.

Lusk decided to change tactic and simply focus on tempting the woman instead. That is what he had prepared himself to do, in any case, using those cell cultures to activate hormonal responses and then quickly letting them return to baseline. He was capable of tempting most women without raising their suspicions, but the Praefecta medicas was not 'most women.'

After the Lux Baiula nodded pensively in response to his last statement, Lusk modulated his voice again, accompanying it with vibrations meant to cause a very brief surge in the woman's sexual hormones, to say: "Praefecta, perhaps Ooldrina will benefit from a day off, perhaps visiting the region with me, Clara Lux Baiula and Raaviana. If you enjoy the countryside, yourself, you could join us to observe the girl."

Saara felt her pulse accelerate again at the idea of being in the young man's company on such a stroll through the country. She brushed-off dust from her desk with the excuse of considering the suggestion. *This should not be happening to me.* Another part of herself replied: *Why not? You told Bilena not so long ago that Lux Baiulae should not be castrates.* Saara's first part acknowledged the statement's truth, but there was still something troubling about her present reactions.

Looking up, she said, "Thank you for your suggestion and invitation, Master Methrim. I will consider it further."

Lusk nodded.

Having come to a decision, Saara took a deep, quiet breath and said, "Now, if I may ask for your assistance. I would like you to probe me; I have been having these strange sensations for the past few minutes, which I cannot explain. Would you mind probing me?"

Lusk did his best to hide his uncertainty. "Are you sure, Praefecta? It might be better to have Sarrinia Lux Baiula do it."

"I know. But Sarrinia's procedures are too tedious, and I have no time for them. And, given that you were a queen's healer, you *are* qualified to probe me as well."

The Praefecta's explanations were perfectly sensible; the Healer of Bearers was definitely very slow in her evaluations. So, retaking possession of himself, Lusk said, "You are right, Praefecta, my apologies. I will be happy to examine you."

Saara closed her eyes to enter the Bind and readied herself for the examination, an examination during which she would secretly probe her prober. She did not truly want to let Master Methrim into her mind, but she needed a way to get into *his* mind unawares, with his guard down.

One of her Transferred Memories surfaced just then, the memories of Liboria Lux Baiula, a woman who had been a powerful but reckless Barrier during the Trionian War, nearly five hundred years earlier. The woman's memories said: *Shield your mind with an intermittent pulse. He will be able to get through, but you will be able to cut-off his vibrations if he should prove to be ill-intentioned.*

Acutely aware of Lusk Methrim's approaching presence in the Bind, Saara objected: *I do not know this shielding technique.*

Liboria Lux Baiula's memories replied: *It is done this way.* Saara accepted the instructions, executed them promptly, then let Master Methrim in.

Completing the Turning

The Leate had just laid herself on her bed and entered the Bind to connect to Marcus Vrol's mind. She did not immediately reach for him, though; the day before, an error had been made in the dosing of his suppressive medication, and when she entered his mind, he almost locked her in. She had given Kina quite a beating, and the woman promised not to make any more errors.

However, the man's strength in the Bind was not her only challenge. Marcus Vrol was also proving to be a lot more difficult to turn than she had expected. Indeed, although she had spent days studying him and prodding him to uncover his weaknesses and secret desires, all she had discovered was that he longed for feminine company—not to appease sexual urges, but to fill his emotional needs—and emotional attachment was the slowest and most difficult method to turn a person. Satisfying his sexual wants, appetite for power, or need for escape would have been much easier to accomplish, even without the Bind.

And this was an old man—though he looked only sixty or seventy years old—so he probably had very unique and unyielding emotional sensibilities which developed over his decades of secluded life. The Leate knew that unless she could act on him with a Binding, she had no chance of turning him in time for his mission. So, she decided to try and learn the required Binding through her contact in Urbs Lucis, a Binding which she had then tested on her people with annoying consequences. But it had worked, and she *needed* it to work on him, now. After all, he was an Alterintrant, and if she succeeded, she could turn him into a powerful Temptator, perhaps even more formidable than Lusk Methrim. *It has to work. I just need to release enough of the right neurotransmitters to ease my way into him; once in, I will do the rest my own way.*

Having convinced herself of the soundness of her plan and having probed her captive to verify that his powers were properly blocked, she reached for him in the Bind.

She found him quickly amid the myriad other vibrations. After probing his mind once more to confirm that he was fully unconscious, she approached his form. It was constantly changing shape and location, the way an unconscious mind did. *I need to hook him to this place, otherwise staying with him will be like trying to keep up with a finger flyer, and I have no desire for it.*

The Leate formed the image of a woman she had seen in the man's mind a few nights before. She wasn't very good at conjuring visual memories, but she could invoke voices quite well. So, after checking her form in a mirror she created, and finding it acceptable—if not perfect—she imagined a grassy field, then concentrated on the voice. A smile appeared on her form's face when she was satisfied with the voice's rendering.

Just as the man was about to disappear again, she focused and whispered to him, *"Marcus, dear."*

The man's form responded with a woosh that shook everything, but it began to dissolve in the next moment.

The Leate wasted no time and said, *"Marcus, the redmelon plant; it's starting to grow."*

She had learned during the same unfortunate foray in his mind the day before that redmelons had always had a special significance to him, and that his first memories of them were in the company of the woman whose voice she was using.

Marcus's form *wooshed* again then stilled itself longer. It looked down at the redmelon the Leate had placed in front of herself, and then looked up at her.

The Leate put all her will and passion in the woman's form and prepared to meet the man's gaze with a soft, warm, and tender loving smile.

Marcus locked eyes with the Leate. It was working…until his eyes widened in alarm, and he disappeared.

On the verge of exasperation, the Leate tried again—twice more, in fact. On the last attempt, she succeeded in stilling Marcus's mind, placing herself—or the image of the woman he had loved—within a representation of his villa, which she had

had drawn in great detail so that she might use it just for such a purpose. It seemed that the memory of it relaxed him, though it had been a prison for him for nearly forty years. Then, she walked with him, but did not take his hand, for fear that she might not properly render his tactile memories of the woman.

They sat under the porch and began to converse, while she cut the redmelon for him. When she gave him a slice, his hand touched hers and, after a split moment's hesitation, she let her apprehension turn into passion. Marcus Vrol's form stood and grabbed her arms. Feeling success at hand, she sent gentle vibrations into his brain to release neurotransmitters of attachment.

She waited, watching his reaction. When he pulled her form to his, she breathed a relieved sigh and entered his mind again.

XV WORRIES AND PAINS

Following the Second Attempt

It was now late morning. The king had awoken from a restless and groan-filled sleep. But despite his weakness, he had called his family, the officers of his Personal Guard, as well as Elyana and Mitsuko Lux Baiulae to discuss the latest attempt on his life; the mood was troubled and heavy.

The king had survived and was expected to make a full recovery. On the other hand, Kiron and Sikka Lux Baiula, who had been struck with poisoned darts, and Harlion, who had suffered a heart attack, were all fighting for their lives on the medical floor at Domus Lucis.

Adamant that he would not be seen lying in bed and frail, the king had had his personal attendant—young Koricki Dar'Muntake—place a Lacora Leaf chair behind his desk so that he might receive his guests from a more dignified position. But one could tell, from his flushed skin and slightly stooped posture, that Octavius still suffered from the toxin's effects. Darya watched him, praying that his foolishness would not cost him.

Octavius addressed his eldest and the captain of his Guard, who were both intent on bearing the blame for the attack. Meanwhile, Ori listened without looking, shaping and reshaping the Lacora Leaf chair upon which he sat at the other end of the room. His face looked troubled and his eyes shifted about as he processed his father's words with all the understanding of his young mind.

With a voice still weak but becoming firmer because of his desire to be heard by his youngest, Octavius said, "The two of you will stop this nonsense now. I should not have walked so freely in public under the circumstances. But I did it because we all misjudged the enemy. I am certain none of us will make that mistake again. Therefore, we will discuss only of our response to this second attempt on my life. Know this, though: I will *not* tolerate any questioning of Elyana Lux Baiula's actions in my Court. I cannot prohibit nor prevent Urbs Lucis's inquiry into the matter—that is their right—however, while she is here, Elyana will be free to continue as she has always done, unconstrained and unharmed."

All tipped or bobbed their heads, except for Dana.

After wiping his forehead, Octavius added, "I know what you are thinking, Dana: First the king, and now the Manu Dextra. How many more people will be found to have powers they shouldn't have? As far as I know, you should not find anyone else with the power to…violate another's mind, as your Order calls it. Though that is truly not the question to ask. Rather, you should ask: Have those who have used it done so other than to defend their own or another's life."

Octavius gave Elyana a quick, nervous glance, which he hoped Dana would interpret only as him being worried about referring, once more, to what he himself had done a fourth ago. Elyana, of course, knew why the king had looked at her with that nervous look. He was not being completely sincere.

Dana did not make any reply; she had learned her lesson and would let Irania, as Urbs Lucis's representative in Furan City, handle the situation with Elyana' breach of the laws. But would the Purple Sash do it given that Elyana was now the Manu Dextra? Would she really go to Krystiana with such news to force an action that might be against the Sisterhood's current best interest? Perhaps Irania would only tell Ramela, who—as Head of the Purple Sashate—was responsible for her acolytes' actions, so as to let the woman deal with the matter herself, quietly. Of course, Dana knew that Elyana's actions had saved the prince and the captain. But could anything, then, be excused? Her face as blank as a stone, and her shifting eyes alone showing her conflicted thoughts, Dana nodded in agreement.

That being done, Octavius asked, "How is Harlion?"

Elyana replied plainly and factually, despite the sentiments which she knew motivated the king's question. "Tania has refused to make any prognosis on the matter, Sire."

Octavius repressed a swell of anger, but his voice still cut when he said, "*Will* he live?"

Elyana continued with her stoic façade. "All she would say is that he is in critical care, now, Sire. I am sorry."

Realizing that it was unreasonable to expect such an answer simply because he was the king, Octavius aghred and said, "No need to apologize, Elyana. I suppose we will know when we will know."

Snorts and grunts and soft curses echoed each other across the king's office. Anguished looks passed from Octavius to Aithen and from Aithen to Elyana. Darya observed the exchange and realized that though she and Octavius had never grown apart, she was not yet a member of that intimate inner circle, and it saddened her until the king looked at her too, and she realized she was being a fool.

The king wiped his damp forehead again while a shadow passed over his age-old visage, and he considered his own vulnerability in the face of his long-serving officer's sudden decline. A certain bitterness pinched his lips just then. "Assuming that he will recover, what do you think we can do for him, Aithen? Could we reduce his charge without insulting him?"

Aithen hesitated a moment, feeling especially uncomfortable under the saddened and anxious looks of everyone in the room, who knew and cared for the sexagenarian captain.

"Perhaps we can split his charge, Father; have him continue as head of your Secret Police, but...*and* appoint Primus Kendor as captain of the Guard; Harlion respects him and would probably not mind seeing him take his place as high captain—if someone has to."

As groggy as his mind felt, Octavius did notice his son's self-correction and he smiled proudly. "You will make a fine king someday, my son."

Everyone indicated their agreement with the king's statement, including Darya, who looked at Elyana with a quiet smile.

Elyana forced a rush of emotion down as she wondered if the queen-consort had accepted her relationship with Aithen.

Seeing his son's discomfort in his uneasy motions—Aithen had always disliked being the center of attention unless it was while he debated the truth of a matter or explained the nature of a thing—Octavius said, "Let it be so, then. When Harlion has recovered, we will announce the change as part of another ceremony to thank him for his long—" The king's last word was cut-off when he was overtaken by painful jolts that shot through his body.

Darya rushed to ask if he was okay and whether they should let him rest. When she turned to call Koricki over, the king stopped both with a growl, "I am *not* alright, Darya; but I know my limits, and I haven't reached them yet. Just have Tania attend to me after we are done here."

"Would it not be better to postpone this audience until you are fully recovered?"

With an annoyed but insistent voice, Octavius replied, "No. I know my body, Darya. I will be fine."

The queen-consort nodded, and the king surprised everyone with his next question, though they were not surprised by the sudden change of topic, which he was wont to do. He said, "By the way, what happened with the Carrier Race?"

"The Master of Ceremonies came to find me to ask whether he should cancel the event. I told him to proceed with it, given that the carriers could not easily be readied again for such an event if it were to be postponed. But all the music and performances *were* cancelled."

"And how did the public react—if it even returned?"

"With the expected somberness."

"Good. I am glad our people understand that not all things can always go on as they were. Thank you, my Love."

Presently, Octavius's eyes shifted searchingly as he tried to recall something. He fixed them on his wife when the memory returned, "Darya, can you make certain the young Carrier boy...Master Albo, receives his admission to Magister Setarcos's class today or tomorrow? I do not wish him to have to wonder about my promise following what happened."

Darya responded with a snort, a sigh, and a smile.

The king now moved the conversation to the investigation being conducted to identify his attacker, and to the progress being made on a serum against the toxin. Octavius first heard Aithen and Julian tell him that the latest would-be assassin was probably a member of the same group that attacked him last fourth, though their prisoner would not confirm it. The king turned to Elyana to ask if the Sisterhood had tried to obtain information from the man, to which Elyana replied that they had but that the man was in a critical state and quite confused, and—because they could not force themselves into his mind, which statement painted a cynical frown on Dana's face—they were just as empty-handed as the king's questioners. Octavius was about to suggest that they should do just that but thought better and cursed instead.

After a new surge of pain subsided, Octavius said, "Then bring the prisoner to the Frumentariat and have *them* question him. They will get the answers."

Though their failure at getting their prisoner to talk frustrated them, both Aithen and Julian were relieved by the thought of getting the Frumentariat involved for, indeed, they were known to have more...productive techniques, though no one really knew what those were. The few times Aithen had asked Harlion about it, the man had refused to give any straightforward answer and had recommended that the prince stay out of what went on at the Frumentariat. The prince had found the statement troubling but had nevertheless followed the high captain's advice. This time, though, given the situation, he might just be able to find out what the Secret Service did. But did he truly wish to know?

317

Octavius dragged Aithen out of his cogitations when he dismissed everyone, except for his wife, after receiving Elyana's report on the antidote.

Feeling a little lost, the high prince was glad when his little brother stepped up to him and started explaining what he had missed. Every so often, Aithen eyed Elyana—who walked to his right— to be sure Ori had heard correctly.

Once the others had gone, Octavius began to rub and squeeze the back of his neck, grimacing every so often. He watched Darya take a chair from the front of the desk and move it next to him.

Darya sat herself, took her husband's hands, squeezed them nervously, then said, "I need to return to Kynaria." The queen-consort watched as her husband stopped breathing for a second, but he did not say anything, and she continued, "I am truly sorry, Octavius. I wish I could stay until you have fully recovered, but Ylana has called me back."

As weak as he felt, Octavius leaned forward and pulled his wife into him. "I will be fine, Darya. Though I have become accustomed to your presence, and it will be hard to not have you by my side."

Darya took a deep, guilty breath.

"When do you leave?"

"In two days."

Octavius nodded and sat back a little.

"Are you going by ship or furan?"

With a chiding smile, Darya said, "You know I will never get on a furan. I will leave with Master Brak's passenger ship. It will be faster and more comfortable."

With a wince that sent shivers through Darya's spine, the king said, "Master Brak. *There* is a useful, trustworthy, and quiet man. I wish I could go with you. But I can no more come there than you can stay here. Still, it would be nice to stroll the Bay of Lardos together again. Someday, perhaps, if fortune will let us."

A pang of guilt seized Darya. "Octavius, I *will* be back soon; I promise you." She paused, watching for her husband's reaction. When she saw in his eyes that the prospect of having her back soon reassured him, she continued. "In fact, I have already discussed my desire to spend more time here with Ylana, and she has agreed to talk about it upon my return."

Octavius squeezed his wife's hand with a pained and cautious smile on his face. She squeezed back to affirm her promise to him.

With the silence of trust enveloping them, Octavius mulled a thought that had just come to him, turning his head away and back toward his wife a few times as if uncertain how she would receive it.

"What is it, Octavius?"

Responding to his wife's invitation, the king said, "I would like you to take Ori with you."

Tears did not need to flow to show the intensity of Darya's emotions as she debated silently whether she had really heard Octavius suggest that she take their youngest with her.

"War is coming, Darya. And it may reach the capital itself, though we are far from the border with Zebulonia. I would prefer Ori be in a safer location even if—"

Darya looked at Octavius inquiringly.

"Even if the war will eventually reach Kynaria's shores too. But we have no other ally to turn to, for now. Hopefully, others will present themselves sooner or later."

"You are thinking of the Unumians."

Octavius nodded.

"Did they refuse your delegation?"

"They did. Their continent has not seen any trouble, and they did not wish to be dragged into ours."

"Will you try again?"

"I will. After all, I am not asking for their support; only for their welcome in case there is no other recourse and I need to send some of our people there."

When a moment had passed, Octavius said, "Anyway, what about Ori?"

An unexpected vibrato carried Darya's response. "I will take him. But you know he will not be happy. He loves you very much and barely knows me, even if we *have* grown closer."

"Then this will be the perfect opportunity for the two of you to complete your bond. And I will have a new role for him; an important one, which he can only fulfill from your homeland."

Darya raised curious eyebrows.

"You will hear it when he does too."

Darya did not insist. She knew her husband. Secrets were secrets, no matter how big or small, and he liked to surprise people with them.

"You always find a way to make my departures bittersweet."

Octavius smiled with a wince. Darya leaned over, kissed him, and went to fetch Tania Lux Baiula.

Forced to Rest

When the Red sun had reached its apex—its Blue twin hiding behind it in this First In-Between-Fourth—a reproachful Yerlayan voice, which clashed with the Red Sun's soft yellow light, said to Octavius, "I do notte thinkke you shouldde be about and active, Sire, not until the toxin is completely cleared from your system. That will only exacerbate your body's condition."

Octavius was about to object, and Tania quickly added, "But I am confident that you will be able to resume your normal activities by tomorrow, assuming you give your body this day to finish neutralizing the toxin and repairing the damage it has done." When Octavius appeared to want to object again, Tania said, "Sire, I am saying this as a medic experienced not only with health in general but also with your majesty's health in particular."

Octavius groaned, irritated by the Lux Baiula's insistence. "*Aghhr*. Very well."

Tania bobbed her head satisfactorily and turned toward Darya and Koricki. The two promised, one with a word and the other with a nod, that they would ensure the king did as he promised.

Octavius noticed the exchange and cleared his throat to interrupt it. "Darya dear, there is no need to make secret agreements with Tania Lux Baiula. I will rest until tomorrow, and if I should be tempted to do more than lay in my bed all night, I am certain young Koricki, *here*, will alert the household to lay me back down."

The junior apprentice of the Light shifted uneasily under the king's sarcastic stare, but Octavius soon took his eyes off him and said, "Now that we are agreed upon my treatment, *Head Medica* Tania, there is something else I would very much like to know."

Tania and Darya sighed as one, having intuited at once—from the softened look on the king's face—what he wished to know.

"I am sorry, Sire, High Captain Harlion had notte regained consciousness when I left Domus Lucis to come here. His brain was without oxygen for quite a while, and even with the Bind, we cannotte easily undo the damage done."

It was with a perturbed look that Octavius said, "But will he live?"

"I do notte know, Sire. It is possible. He should. He was otherwise a healthy man, never given to excesses of any kind; yes, he should recover. He might regain consciousness in an hour or in a day; we cannot know before certain regions of his brain become activated again. All we can do for now is to care for him and watch."

Shaking his head in resignation, the king said, "All right. Thank you, Tania." The king paused a moment, then added, "Please leave me, now, but keep me informed of any changes in the high captain's condition."

The Head Medica tipped her head respectfully, gave Koricki Dar'Muntake silent instructions, and left. Darya followed soon after, to let her husband rest. As she passed the young Dar'Muntake, she gave her husband's privy attendant her own silent instructions about ensuring the king's comfort and making certain that Octavius did as he had promised.

A few hours later, just as the king finished the broth Koricki had ordered for him, someone arrived who would not be refused an audience.

When the king saw Master Rackeli, he asked what was so urgent that he needed to be disturbed.

"I apologize, my King, but I have an urgent missive."

"An urgent missive? From whom? And what about?"

Master Rackeli presented the front of the letter so that the king might recognize the seal. The king snorted and scrunched his face confusedly.

"Well, read on, Alturo."

Master Rackeli cleared his throat a few times, obviously uncomfortable with his task, and began. *"Sire, I send this because I cannot make my case to you personally. Notwithstanding, I urge you to consider it as valid as if I had presented it to you in person."* Alturo Rackeli raised his head to verify the king's mood. When he saw his impatient stare, the majordomo cleared his throat once more and finished reading the short letter.

"I have heard that the queen-consort is returning to Kynaria and that you are sending Ori with her."

Octavius's features became very tense upon hearing those words, but he let Rackeli continue without interruption.

"If I may, I would advise that you keep them here, Sire. I know you believe the risk to be greater in Alvinoria, but as remote as the western continent is from all this chaos, danger is bound to visit them too, sooner or later. This, I know to be a fact. Should you believe my concerns to be misguided, I would urge to, at least, send a guard of Royals with them. Your servant, as always."

322

Fury twisted the king's face. As open as he was to everyone's ideas, he hated going back on his decisions. His agitation was evident in his jerky movements as well as in his repeated puffs and head shakes.

"Sire, do you wish to send a reply?"

After one more snort and a brief hesitation, he said, "No. Not now; I appreciate his concern, but I disagree with his assessment. And how can—? *Aghr*! No matter. Please leave me now, Alturo, and I will let you know when I have a response. And if there are any more urgent matters, please refer them to the high prince. I do need to rest now."

Master Rackeli bowed respectfully and left his king, eyeing Dar'Muntake as he did so.

When the door closed, the king barked a question to Koricki. "Why does everyone keep looking at you as if either distrusting you or expecting something from you, Apprentice Koricki?"

Replying with less-practiced deflecting prowess though with nearly as much composure as a Lux Baiula—a swallow alone betraying his own perplexity—Koricki said, "They all have different reasons, I suppose, Sire. But—"

Still incensed by the letter Master Rackeli had just read, the king cut-off the Kynarian with a harsher tone than he had meant to use. "You started off well, Apprentice. Do *not* ruin it with a '*but*.'"

The young man swallowed despite himself and continued, "Thank you, Sire. I am sorry. They all simply wished to urge me to ensure you do as instructed…I will retire now and let you rest, too. I will be sleeping in the antechamber in case you need me. Good night, Sire."

The king grunted his response then watched the young Alterintrant go, this boy who had been forced upon him by the Sisterhood. *At least, he's unintrusive…and he* is *attentive and useful.* The king sighed a long, slow, frustrated sigh as a hundred battling thoughts invaded his mind, pausing only to let him wince as a sudden access of pain shot through his body. There was not going to be any sleep for him that night despite everyone's injunctions.

Suspicions

Sitting at his desk digging through papers, and his mind only partly attentive to his squire, the high prince said, "Who did you say this Luvius is, Kil?"

With some unease in his voice, which the prince mistook for his typical timidity, Kildare replied, "My Prince, Luvius Arco is a friend of my cousin, Rovere. My cousin introduced us at the Ball. Master Arco would like to receive an appointment in the stables, to apprentice with Master Vorak."

"Hmm, and *why* would I or Master Vorak receive him as an apprentice in the stables?"

Kildare shifted uneasily, said, "He is a bright young man, and of a good family in Antar, my Prince. And he…it is hard to…well…he is just very persuasive. But…but you and the king have always said how important it is to 'build bridges' across the land," Kil raised his shoulder and added, "and there currently is no one in the court from Antar."

"And you thought I would therefore welcome the suggestion?"

Kildare began rubbing his hands nervously. His master was obviously preoccupied with something else and very displeased by this unimportant interruption. "I am sorry, my Prince. This is the wrong time to bring such a matter to you. I will tell Master Arco that I may make another petition for him when you are not so busy."

Reacting to his squire's apology, Aithen dropped the papers then looked up. "No, no. It is fine, Kil. The king and I *do* find it important to build these connections with the minor nobles, and I assume that in a time of uncertainty like this, it is even more important. Are the stables his only office of interest?"

"I believe so, my Prince."

"Hmm, the Magister Furanum[20] has rarely accepted anyone into that position that has not first cleaned the stalls and taken care of the animals. But if Master Luvius has the credentials and Master Vorak accepts him, I will not be opposed to it."

"Thank you, my Prince. I will go see Master Vorak and provide him with Luvius's letter of introduction." Kildare bowed and made to turn toward the door. Recalling something, he stopped and asked the prince what he had been searching for earlier.

"What was I looking for? For this morning's financial report. I must have misplaced it. Before you go to see the Magister Furanum, please find Neaj and send him here."

"Yes, my Prince."

Neaj Trebloc arrived promptly and stood himself at attention to receive the prince's orders. Aithen was returning to his desk with a frustrated step.

"Master Trebloc! Did you perhaps come to take back this morning's report? I cannot find it anymore."

Before replying, the young Neaj gazed at the prince's desk. After a few short seconds of scrutinizing the piles of documents, he said, "I did not my Prince, but I think I see it."

Aithen gave him an incredulous look and turned his head toward his desk. All the documents looked the same: sheets of cream-colored paper stacked atop each other. "You can see it from where you stand?"

"I can, my Prince. I see a stack between the others whose sheets are all perfectly aligned, except for one, and the stack's thickness also seems to be right."

"In that case, I would be grateful if you retrieved it for me."

Neaj Trebloc walked to the desk with his precise, diligent movements and found the report exactly where he thought he had seen it. He handed it to the prince with some pride bleeding through his straight, small lips.

---

[20] Master of the Furans.

"Master Trebloc! you are an amazing fellow. I swear I searched through that precise pile several times without finding your report.

After a moment of silence while he considered some things, Aithen said, "I have a special assignment for you."

Neaj's pupils widened with excitement and quickly returned to their small, piercing state. "I am at your service, my Prince."

"A friend of Kildare's cousin is interested in apprenticing in our stables. Normally, I would leave the investigation and decision to Master of the Furans Vorak, but something about Kil's behavior makes me uncomfortable, and I want to know what is happening—if anything is happening."

"Do you believe Kil put his name forward against his better judgment, my Prince?"

"No. Not at all. It is just that with talks of Temptatori infiltrating the kingdom, my mind is conjuring possibilities I would not have thought of before. Understand that I do not suspect Kil in any way, but I *would* like you to quietly investigate his acquaintance's doings, as well as this young man's and his family's finances and report to me in two days. Can you do it?"

Neaj blinked and asked, "My Prince, you know I am an accountant, and I find it easy to comb through financial records, but I am not a frumentarius."

"I know. And yet, if you think of it Master Trebloc, this skill you have is really about seeing patterns. I think you can apply it to investigating people's habits as well as their finances. And with High Captain Harlion currently indisposed, and me not being so familiar with his underofficers in the Secret Police, I thought of giving *you* the assignment."

Neaj Trebloc accepted the task with a firm nod, and after receiving the name of the person to be investigated, he left with a promise to return with the results within two days.

I am glad my father gave him to me. And it feels good to know that there are *dependable people around me; it helps counterweight my continuing worry about the lessening quality of the recruits.*

This last thought reminded Aithen of his captain, and a worried frown appeared on his forehead. *I wish Harlion was able to continue serving as leader of the army. I know Kendor will do an excellent job, but I also know that this is not how Harlion had imagined his final years of service. Founders!*

A Feeling

As another long day neared its end, and with dessert sitting untouched on the table between them, Aithen asked Elyana, "Are you going back to Urbs Lucis tomorrow?"

"I am. I need to discuss what I did yesterday with Krystiana and Ramela." Elyana paused and let Aithen see her hesitation through the softening of her features.

Aithen shook his head. "This should be an exciting moment for you, Elyana—going back with Locari's skill, a new skill the Order desperately needs. Instead, you are going back with undeserved apprehension."

"It is the way of things, Aithen." Elyana picked up her spoon and started tapping it on the cloth beneath her plate, which dampened the sound.

Aithen asked nervously, "What do you think Krystiana and the Light's Assembly will say or do?"

Again, Elyana hesitated before answering. "This will most certainly have bad consequences because the Praefectae will connect the dots and figure out how Krystiana and I uncovered what we did when we searched for the Serpent in the Bind this summer. They will know Krystiana lied to them about it. And they could start questioning her leadership if they conclude that our actions turned the Serpent's and Noctiferus's eyes onto the Sisterhood."

Aithen wondered how much fear and angst Elyana was hiding behind her mask. Though it was softening and hardening, it was a mere projection of her will. As for himself, the possibility that Elyana might be punished by the Order knotted his guts.

An uncertain smile appeared on Aithen's face, drawn there by the uneasy hope he felt combined with the ardent desire to give courage to this woman he was undeniably beginning to love. He said, "Perhaps they will just accept your ability, and Krystiana's, as they accepted my father's."

"I do not know Aithen. What the king did, he did in the 'privacy' of his chambers with only you and his Guard to witness his actions, though with the complication that one of witnesses was a Lux Baiula. What I did...for all to see...especially as a Purple Sash...was unacceptable; we are not supposed to be killers. A lot of people already distrust us as it is. If voices spread that a *Purple Sash* killed someone with the Bind, our position will be severely undermined."

Elyana's reply baffled Aithen. He stabbed the dessert which he had begun to poke at with his spoon. "But Elyana, this is insane! You *saved* someone and stopped an assassin. And yes! he has now died, but he was not some innocent *wretch*."

When Elyana did not respond except with her typical blank face, Aithen continued, "And you always tell me how the Sisterhood reveres logic. Well, the Praefectae have accepted that ability not only in my father but also in Marcus. They *must* extend the logic and do the same for you and Krystiana!"

Elyana regarded the prince for a moment. He was a remarkable, intelligent, and cultured man, but he still held idealistic views, views which colored his understanding and inspired his responses.

Isn't that why you fell for him?

But she was not him.

"Perhaps," she said.

Aithen grimaced and purposefully set his utensil on the wood of the table with a clang. "They must Elyana. I am certain they will!"

Elyana sighed and smiled, a smile that did not indicate hope but resignation. "It's—it is just a feeling I am getting from seeing everything we knew become unraveled."

Hearing Elyana make that statement with such detachment disconcerted Aithen. He decided to try and lighten the mood by changing topics, the way Elyana liked to do. "Elyana, I noticed the contraction you were about to use. It tells me more than anything else that you *are* truly concerned. But, as you are so fond of telling me, worrying does not help anything. In fact, it—"

"In fact, it only makes things worse, yes." Elyana let herself take a deep breath in response then thanked the prince.

Aithen extended his hand to take Elyana's, which had let go of the spoon she had been tapping on the table. His touch warmed her. "Would you like to take a walk?"

Elyana turned toward the balcony, saw the sky was still clear. She turned her head back toward Aithen and nodded with an indescribable—no—an almost pleading softness on her face.

Aithen stood from the table and Elyana—her hand still in his—followed him into the gardens without the slightest resistance.

On the Way to Zeblinia

Sitting behind a burly, quiet guardian atop a nervous furan, Ooldrina turned to look at her friend riding with another soldier. They had left that morning to make their way to Wakideb, a remote village in the Sagr Mountains from where they would then be smuggled into Zebulonia.

Raaviana seemed nervous; oh, she had learned to master proper Zebulonian, as she had also mastered the spy speech Molara Lux Baiula, their handler, taught them to ensure they could communicate their findings and receive instructions without blowing their cover while in Zebulonia. But she was still nervous, nervous about going to a nation that had, for some reason, rejected their ancestors and forced them to live as refugees on the border between the two kingdoms.

Ooldrina did not feel the same nervousness. In fact, she was glad to be leaving and to get as far away from Urbs Lucis as possible, even if it meant going to this place her birth mother did not speak of. She wished she could tell Raaviana, but how could she do that without then being forced to explain why? She realized that she could not speak of the horrible things that had been done to her when she tried to do so twice before and panicked each time. No, it was better to forget it all, which meant to be as far away as possible from her violator.

One thing worried her: telling her friend, when the time came, that she was not going back. She looked briefly at Raaviana with a great sense of guilt, then turned away and kept her eyes down on the passing prairies and forests without seeing them.

Troubled Feelings

The Praefecta medicas was sitting on her balcony, letting the cool air and the sweet smells of another autumn rain soothe her mind.

Lying by the terrace's edge was Kinu, her green furan. The Praefecta had acquired the animal the year she realized that her advanced age was beginning to leave its marks on her body. Someday, she would pass, and she did not wish to be alone when that happened, though her memories would likely be transferred to someone else—assuming they found her before all activity ceased in her brain.

Two decades had passed since that year, and she was still alive and in good health. Soon, she would be marking her one hundred and seventy-sixth year of life, and it had been a good life as a member of the Order, which she had joined when she had still been innocent. She had had a successful career, to be sure, participating in the development of numerous medical techniques and enabling the White Sashate to gain great honor and influence by placing respected Administrators of the Assembly in many cities across the kingdom.

But personally, well, that was another matter. She certainly hadn't been as liberal as Bilena believed her to be. Of course, she had known men through the decades, but her duties had always taken precedence and had thus limited her experiences to short-lived trysts, which she had accepted and was content with.

When Lusk Methrim probed her mind, however, something happened, something she had neither expected nor been able to comprehend. And now, she desired only to experience that connection again. The feeling had interfered with her tasks all day long.

"What is happening to me, Kinu? Do you know? Do *you* sense it?"

Kinu stood and approached her owner with a soft, empathetic purr. The middle-aged furan was in her female phase now, and she was able to sense Saara's emotions particularly well. When Saara caressed her head, Kinu shook her wings, sending droplets of water flying. These created a reflective yellowish spray as the microbes, which the rainwater carried from Kinu's body, luminesced. Saara had not expected to see that and exclaimed, "Ha! Approaching your fertile phase again, Kinu?" She then noticed the luminescent droplets on her robe and added, "Or are you trying to tell me that somehow, something...or *someone*, such as Lusk Methrim, put me back in my blazing phase?"

The green furan did not reply; she had no answers to her master's questions. "Oooh, Kinu. How is it that one can live decades and centuries and still not learn anything, still commit foolish mistakes, and still be unable to protect oneself?!"

Saara's raspy voice made her outburst doubly jarring, and Kinu pulled back suddenly, worry visible on her green face.

When the old Praefecta noticed her furan's reaction, she groaned, apologized, and sat back. She then called Kinu to her side and spent the next hour trying to make sense of own her condition, probing herself every so often, and promising her furan to go see the Healer of Bearers on the morrow—or to submit to a cleansing flogging at the thermals if she did not find a way to quash those foolish urges. And, despite a part of her mind telling her otherwise, she rejected the notion that her present condition had been intentionally caused by the foreigner.

PERMANERÉ USQUE AD FINEM

334

XVI COMINGS AND GOINGS

A Mission

On a summit overlooking what appeared to be Kartak, the Umbra sent to the Serpent, *"Dominus noster nos in inceptum mittit, Alis Domini."* [21]

The Serpent responded with excited anticipation though with some frustration because of the difficulty he had with the Ancient Tongue, *"Inceptum, dicis? ad Kynariam, ut spero. Tempus est hostes nostros opprimere."* [22]

"Minime, non iam, sed proximum. Ille in conventu nostro mihi duabus abhinc quartis dixit se velle ut nos Yeltchek adiremus." [23]

"Why? And please, Umbra, none of that Ancient Tongue."

"To see whether its inhabitants pose any threat to his plans; whether they should be left alone or used in some way."

"Isn't it a little late to worry about yet another group?"

"It is not a group, as you say, but a proper nation with possibly even more advanced capabilities than Humans, Kynarians or Zebulonians."

"If that is so, why didn't you think of investigating them yourself?"

Umbra's form zapped and distorted itself with dangerous but contained anger. When he had recovered his calm, he said with an icy edge to his Sendings, *"Remember who you are, Alis Domini. Despite your name, you are not our Lord's commander here, but only a creature for him—and me—to use as the needs of our Great Mission dic—dictate."*

The Serpent's form writhed with indignation and hatred.

---

[21] Our Master is sending us on a mission, Alis Domini.

[22] A mission? To Kynaria, I hope. It is time we begin crushing our enemies.

[23] No, not yet. But it will be next. He informed me during our encounter, two fourths ago, that he wishes us to go to the Yeltchek.

Meanwhile, the Umbra cursed at himself for his stammer. Outwardly, however, he simply watched the lizard, unconcerned, and waited until it quieted itself to continue.

"Now, are you ready to discuss our mission?"

Getting no response from the Serpent, the Umbra said, *"That is better. You will meet me in the Mountains of the Sagr three days hence, near a village called Razeb. Bring a team of your linked rokons for additional protection. From there, we will fly to the mountains near a coastal village to the south west of Yeltchika. There is a man there who can secure an audience for me with someone who will have the information I need as well as provide resources I require. As for you, you will stay with your brothers and out of sight to wait for me."*

The Serpent's misty shape twisted itself with even greater indignation, this time. *"They are* not *my brothers; they are nothing like me."*

"No, you are more, in all the senses of the word, and I cannot take the risk that the Yeltcheki will suspect me if they should see me with you."

The Serpent sent an accepting growl then asked, *"May I ask how you plan to find out whatever information you seek? You do not know their language, nor their ways, nor do you look like them."*

"As a matter of fact, I do know their language and have a decent idea of their ways. But this man, who will facilitate my introduction, will tell me whatever else I need to know to be welcomed in the capital. He is one I know from his illegal dealings in Zebulonia. And as to my appearance, do not concern yourself with it."

"Of course, Umbra. Three days hence, then."

"Near Razeb."

With that, the Serpent disappeared. But the Umbra did not return to his body yet. He lingered there, grinding his teeth as he thought of the Serpent's question: Why hadn't he thought of reconnoitering Mo'Tarkoth? He did not know, and it troubled him. He shook his head and looked down toward the form of Kartak and nodded. He then moved himself to a tall hill near Urbs Lucis and sent a whorl of yellow fire toward the imagined city as his hatred for the women filled him. Finally, he took his mind to Solinor, Kynaria's capital, and his grimace was replaced by a vicious smile. *Hic incipit.*[24]

Moradien and her Group

Moradien paced in her room while she waited for her accomplices to arrive with the girls they had apparently convinced to join their cause.

Speaking to herself, she said, "I hope they not only convinced them but persuaded them too. This is too important for anyone to join half-heatedly. With a new Dark Battle coming, everyone must be committed."

Before Moradien could think her next thought, a knock sounded on the door.

"Who is it?"

"It's us, Lis and Morla…with company."

Finally, "Come in."

Lisandeka came through the door first, with a suspicious look on her face. Carrain and Lopenia followed with six other girls; Morla came last. Moradien looked pleased but did not immediately welcome Carrain or Lopenia. Instead, she looked at them suspiciously and said, "I'm glad to see you. But I did not doubt you would come. This is a good cause, and it's a growing cause."

After some introductions and welcoming words for the new girls, Moradien invited them all to sit on the floor, around two large bowls of finger foods.

Moradien asked, "Do you know why you're here?"

---

[24] This is where it starts.

The girls looked at each other nervously, hoping someone would take the lead and answer. Moradien's face darkened a little when neither the short, dark-haired Carrain nor the brown-haired Lopenia answered; it seemed they were still uncommitted.

A skinny dark girl spoke up, and Moradien's face softened, if only a little, "To change things. To help get us ready for the next Dark Battle."

Directing her eyes toward the two defectors first, Moradien said, "Exactly! Nakira, right?"

The girl blushed as she nodded.

Moradien said, "The Sisterhood is not what it used to be, and if we don't do something about it, none of us will survive when the war comes."

The skinny girl asked, "Because they are letting undeserving girls join?"

"That, and because they are not teaching us the things we need to know to protect ourselves."

Another girl, taller and fuller, said, "I agree. I know I can steal thoughts, but the Sisterhood's stupid rules prevent me from developing my skill. I could really help by spying on subversives and traitors, but they won't let me. So, what do they have me do instead? Learn to make stupid fireballs that can't even singe that stupid Serpent."

Moradien became excited. "Exactly! They know our world is teetering on the verge of annihilation, and they're stuck in blind obedience to rules they defined for ancient times. Well, these are new times."

Nakira clapped her hands to speak. She looked around, unsure how the others would react. "I heard First Cleric Galadrin give a speech recently. He said the Originator released Noctiferus to punish the wrongdoers and the unbelievers before the Day of Union and that the believers must...reveal themselves through their actions."

The girl paused to assess the others' reactions. Seeing that most of the girls, including Moradien, were listening with keen interest, she added, "I believe he's right and that the only way we're going to be able to find and stop the wrongdoers is by being taught to use all our powers."

Outrage gave Lopenia a shrill voice as she asked, "Why do you say that? I mean, I agree things aren't exactly right in the world, but it is not full of *deviants*."

Unable to contain her disappointment with the defectors anymore, Moradien cut in and said, "No? What about the Sisters who sell their services to filthy men to give them sexual pleasures through the Bind?"

Lopenia objected, "Mora, you know that's not true!"

"It's not? I overheard Elyana Lux Baiula discuss it with our *oh so great* Magna Mater recently. Apparently, they allow it because it helps keep soldiers in line. It *is* true, Lopenia."

A pitiful look of confusion and horror marred the brown-haired girl's face and she fell silent again.

Encouraged by their leader, Nakira added, "And we all know about the royal family's atheism. It seems that's also angering the gods."

Another girl asked, "So, how are we supposed to help change all that?"

Moradien's eyes and voice hardened. "By demanding that the Sisterhood update its rules and remove its interdictions, or else."

Several girls echoed Moradien's words, but Carrain asked fearfully, "Or else what?"

"Or else we turn our ears from them and listen to new voices, voices that will make the needed changes. And we continue recruiting people to our side until we have enough to either force the changes we need or create a new Sisterhood."

Murmurs spread like fire at that moment. Some of the girls looked at each other excitedly while others did so anxiously.

Someone asked, "But how should we go about doing all that, Moradien?"

"By whatever means possible."

Carrain stepped back and asked what she meant.

Moradien embraced all the girls with her wild gaze before stopping on the short, dark-haired girl. "Carrain, '*by whatever means possible*' means precisely that. Because no one will care, or be here to care, if we lose but keep to the Order's strait-laced ways. Would you want us dead—or worse, enslaved—just so long as we hold to the Order's ways?"

All the girls shook their heads, except for Lopenia and Carrain.

Her tone seething with incredulity, Moradien said, "*You* two would rather be enslaved?"

Carrain stiffened and replied, "I am willing to do certain things, yes, to save us, but—"

"But what?"

"But I will not act *wrongly* for it. The proof of a person's goodness doesn't come from staying true to our faith or principles or morals when it's easy to do, but from staying true to them when it's hard."

Moradien snorted, "You are so misguided." Then, looking at the others, she added, "Carrain must have read a book I have not to believe that using our powers to stop wrongdoers or the enemy might be immoral...or go against our faith."

Clenching and unclenching her fists, and with a shaky voice, Carrain said, "I will not join your...whatever it is you are trying to start here."

Ignoring Carrain's remark, Moradien turned to stare the girl's friend down. She said, "What about you Lopenia? Are you with us?"

Lopenia did not reply right away and instead gave her friend an anxious look.

Carrain said with a croak, "I am sorry, Lopenia. I can't go along with this."

Having had enough and wishing to move the discussion to other matters, Moradien said, "It goes! You may stand back, Carrain, but please do not leave." Putting a finger on her red lip and softening her tone, she added, "In fact, would you wait for me in my bedchamber? I wish to speak with you in private before you go."

Carrain started to do as requested but stopped. She looked confused and scared.

"What is it, Carrain?"

"I…I…why would I wait for you? I'm leaving."

The other girls—except for Lopenia whose face turned white with fear for her friend—watched with fascination and eager faces.

Using a surprisingly soft and tempting voice this time, Moradien replied, "Because I asked you to, Carrain."

Carrain glanced at her friend as she battled something, which she could not see though she could feel it deep inside her. Lopenia put pleading hands together.

After a long, tense moment, Carrain relented. The lines on her face showed fear and confusion as she turned and walked to Moradien's bedchamber. After closing the door, she dropped to the floor and let out silent sobs as she wondered whether she could reach a Sister through the Bind to ask for help.

Entangled

With the cover of darkness, and the tavern having closed for the night, Ksarina Lux Baiula, a Red Sash, made her way into the Kartak hostel she had selected to spy on, following a reconnaissance trip she had taken into the city earlier in the month. Gina Lux Baiula, a Yellow Sash, walked in gingerly behind her.

After sending careful probing vibrations through the building to ensure that the owners were sleeping, Ksarina established a Sound Shield and took Gina to the back of the tavern where a small, private alcove was located.

341

The tavern was regularly frequented by the types Ksarina believed to be involved with the attacks on the high king and with the Temptatori cell the Order had been tracking for a couple of months. This was a slightly cleaner and more reputable tavern than the others to be found around Kartak owing to the fearsome disposition of the owner, whom even the rabble that patronized the place did not dare challenge or vex. But as clean as it was, the smell of smoke and brew still pervaded the place.

Just now, Ksarina Lux Baiula pointed to the right of the alcove, indicating the area where the device should be set, close to the table.

Gina stepped carefully to the wall, despite the sound shield, making sure she did not bump into any chair. Even more carefully, she moved the chair next to the wall and finally inspected the surface, passing her hand over it a few times, back and forth, whispering "No, not this one. Maybe this one, no. Not this one either. No. No." and so on.

When she finally perceived what she was sensing for, she blurted a 'This one,' drawing a soft growl from Ksarina.

The Red Sash had expected the mission would be a quick and easy one, so long as Gina did not mess it up, but the woman's chattiness might do just that. How tired she was of putting her life at risk for Whites and Yellows and Purples. In fact, Ksarina could not understand why the Red Sashate was not in charge of all Sisterhood activities. Sure, Larca had been named General Supreme of the war effort by the Magna Mater a few months back, but she and her Sisters still served those of the other Sashates.

Gina now focused her mind on the brick and started sending vibrations, which appeared as blue ribbons of light, into the mortar joints.

Ksarina's eyes shifted this way and that as she sent probing vibrations across the tavern for anyone that might be coming. Indeed, the owners had their living apartments on the second floor of the building.

The mortar slowly disappeared, speck by speck, and as it did, the brick loosened. Gina sent a proculactic vibration with her left hand to prevent the brick from falling. A tense minute later, the brick came out, and Gina turned a satisfied smile toward Ksarina, who just grunted and looked anxiously toward the steps leading to the owners' chambers.

When Gina placed the old brick in her bag, the Red Sash whispered, "Couldn't you have simply disappeared the entire brick?"

"We don't have the time, you said."

Ksarina exhaled impatiently and said, "Fine, hurry."

Gina now removed the device from her bag—an entangled brick that had a twin in Urbs Lucis. She took a short moment to admire it, her mouth gaping with awe, and she hoped, prayed, that it would work.

Ksarina raised impatient hands and whispered a harsh, "Hurry! We do not know if the owners are sound sleepers, and I do not wish to find out. As bad as everyone here is, I would rather not have to harm the man or his wife—or give the alert to the entire town."

Gina made an ugly frown and said, "I just need a few more minutes."

Just as the Yellow Sash put the finishing touches to the brick, calling the Bind to fashion its surface so that it resembled its neighbors, Ksarina heard a noise upstairs. She turned to Gina and whispered more urgently still, for her to hurry.

While Gina finished securing her knapsack, another noise—louder this time—came from upstairs. It sounded like a heavy person from the creaking of the floorboards. Ksarina's body and face stiffened while Gina gasped.

A female voice asked what was happening. A male voice replied, "Don't know. I just heard some' strange downstairs."

Gina risked a whisper and said, "Didn't you soundproof the room?"

Ksarina replied with a hiss and a scowl.

As the man descended the steps, he wondered what it was that caused his skin to tingle. He moved his lamp to try and light the tavern. The light did not reach far, but it sufficed for him to see two dark figures moving toward the front door. He bellowed, "Who's there?"

When the door opened, the man saw the same two shadows exiting and closing the door, but he did not hear anything, except for a strange crackling noise and then nothing else but the typical quiet of the room at this hour of the night. The tavern keeper did not give chase, though he did go down to inspect the storeroom and his safe.

While running, Gina asked her companion how the man could have heard anything. The Red Sash replied with obvious frustration that she had no idea how, but that she hoped the brick was properly set and would do what it was supposed to do because she did not wish to return for a second attempt.

The two women fetched their vorans from under a copse of trees, which Ksarina had covered with an illusion to hide the animals. And, given the late hour and dressed as they were in the local garb, they got out of town safely and without raising any alarm.

As they rode, Gina entered the Bind and initiated a thoughtcall to her colleague in Urbs Lucis. It did not take very long for the connection to be established and for Gina to hear the chime generated by it, given that her colleague was awaiting the contact. Gina's thoughts were filled with anxious excitement: *"Kelysia, was the test successful? Did you hear me?"*

"I did, though the sound was screechy and intermittent. But I did hear the challenge of a male. Were you discovered?"

"We were, but we avoided being caught. And the Founders burn me if I know how the owner could have heard anything with the Sound Shield up."

Kelysia sent, *"Well, as you know, we are all different, and some people—though they be Unsensing—do have more acute*

*senses, and it is possible the owner felt the distortion caused by
the shield."*

"*I suppose. So, now we wait?*"

"*Now, we wait.*"

A Welcoming

In brown stable-stained trousers and a tan vest, a middle-aged man handed a letter of admission to an applicant he was sure would cause trouble with the girls. But given the recommendation the affable fellow came with and his clean background verification report, he had decided to hire the young man. With a strong Kirgadi chopping accent and another scrutinizing gaze, Magister Furanum Vorak said, "You can 'gin straight yet. Just go to Master Rackeli who'll assign you a room and proper 'ttire. Lunch be served soon; you can eat with the palace staff to get 'quainted. Be here 'fter lunch; I'll show you 'round then so you know what'you get."

The red-haired pretty boy made sure he understood his instructions then smiled and left. He had not been hired as a stables manager, but he was not going to muck the stalls either. He was going to start by cleaning up the records of the more than ten thousand furans now owned by the Crown, furans which were spread out across the kingdom and in Kynaria.

After finding Master Rackeli, who handed him his uniform and room assignment with raised brows and a grunt, and after donning his royal service garb, Luvius walked to the commons, located on the ground floor of the northeastern corner of the palace. There, he searched for a young Kynarian with a hunter's gaze and found the boy sitting alone toward the far end of the refectory.

Luvius smiled to himself and made his way toward the back. As he did, he looked around for someone else—the prince's squire—and was happy to see him sitting with a mixed group of young men and women. He waved at him.

345

Kildare gave a hesitant smile back and quickly returned to his conversation, as if afraid to linger too long on Luvius.

Master Arco shrugged his shoulders and continued toward Koricki.

"Ahem!"

The king's personal attendant looked up with a most uninviting look, which, however, did not deter Luvius, who asked, "May I sit with you?"

Koricki waited a longish moment before gesturing with a finger.

The merchant's son sat himself across from the Kynarian, offered his hand and said, "My name is Luvius. I have just been hired on the Stables staff, and don't know anyone else, except for Kildare Kildari. But there isn't any space over there, and you seem like you would welcome company."

Koricki did not respond to that, nor did he take the stranger's hand. Instead, he bit a lip and returned to his meal.

Unbothered by the cold reception, Luvius continued, "I think I've seen you in Urbs Lucis, a few months ago. You were shopping in the Lower City's main market. I thought 'There's a confident fellow, the kind I'd like to befriend.' Unfortunately, I never got the chance. And now, here we are!"

This time, Koricki lifted his head with a somewhat more curious expression than the one he had given earlier and said, in his faint Kynarian accent, "You talk a lot."

"Only when I want something or meet someone I like or think I might like."

The brown-skinned, coiled-haired medic apprentice of the Sisterhood bit his lip again, made to look up but returned his attention to the reds on his plate and formed a frown when he realized he did not have enough bread left to dip into the sauce.

"That smells good, on your plate."

"It's spiced reds. If you go to the kitchen now, they might still serve you some."

"I think I will. I'll be right back."

When Luvius returned, he sat without a word then gave Koricki a piece of bread. The young Alterintrant regarded him diffidently.

Luvius said, "I noticed you were annoyed at finding you had no more. When I smelled the fresh bread at the kitchens, I thought I'd bring you some."

Koricki said, "Whatever you are trying to do, it will not work on me. But as I do not have any other company, you are welcome to keep that seat."

Luvius did not look offended by Koricki's words; on the contrary, he looked piqued by the other young man's diffidence, and he considered his response for a while. The changing expressions on his face showed the progression of his thoughts. Finally, he said, "Well, I take this as a good omen. May I know your name?"

"Koricki."

"Just Koricki?

"Dar'Muntake."

Luvius's expressive reaction at being in the presence of a relative of the Supreme Priestess of Kynaria drew a frustrated and irritated breath from Koricki, and the merchant's son decided that it was time to stop talking and try some of the food instead. So, he dipped his dark bread in the sauce, as he had seen Koricki do it, then grabbed some of the reds with it. When he put it in his mouth, his face lit up, and a moan of pure pleasure escaped him. When he noticed—out of the corner of his eyes— that Koricki was eyeing him, he raised his head and locked eyes with the king's attendant. The Kynarian looked away, flustered, and Luvius nodded to himself as a hidden smiled tensed his lips.

Questions while Drinking

Inside a busy tavern of the lower city, a nutmilk-skinned man discussed quietly with his narrow-faced, straight-backed, red-sashed companion despite the noise.

Urbs Lucis's population had become used to seeing the foreigner—former citizen of an enemy nation—about the city, though there were still those who regarded him hesitantly and sometimes challenged him when he was alone, ignorant—as they were—of the consequences to themselves of challenging a man with Lusk's skills. But tonight, he was accompanied by a Sister, and even the most rebellious Lucians let him be.

After taking another swallow of his tallbrew, Lusk said, "I heard you completed your mission in Kartak successfully."

Ksarina replied with a sneer, "Despite everything."

Lusk nodded knowingly. "As they say in my country, 'True beauty and perfection can only arise from chaos.'"

Ksarina raised a suspicious brow.

"Think of our suns. They *are* chaos. But it is that chaos that breathes life and beauty into everything we know. Our civilization is a product of that chaos. In its youth, civilization opposes chaos to create order. But that order is not a static thing, and civilization continues to evolve. When a society grows too heavy and too old—as it has now become—it can no longer adapt, and it returns to the chaos that had given it birth."

"I don't understand what this analogy has to do with the Kartak mission."

"Simply that your actions are the result of the growing disorder. They may also add to it, in fact, but it is how things must be."

Ksarina had been about to take another sip of her drink when understanding began to bloom, and she paused to wait for Lusk's conclusion.

"In order to regenerate the original beauty and freedom birthed by chaos, this *must* come undone."

After a moment during which Ksarina's facial expressions moved from stony to aroused, she bobbed her head excitedly and said, "My father—may his body still be worthy—used to say that 'A good war is needed every so often to restart things.' I did not understand it then, but I do now."

"He was right."

Lusk took a last gulp of his tallbrew then said, "Have you ever visited Domus Medici?"

"Only as an apprentice, very long ago now. I sometimes wonder what they do in there these days."

"Perhaps you can accompany me to it. There is something I wish to show you there, something that will perfectly illustrate what I am talking about."

Ksarina smiled a complicit smile, finished her drink, and left with Lusk Methrim to return to the Inner Sanctum.

A Leaving

Sitting in the royal coach, Ori listened to his father with quivering cheeks and conflicted emotions, though he withheld the tears which wished to breach through. He did not know what to make of his father's request that he go with his mother. Not that he disliked her—on the contrary—, but he did not know her much either. The few times each year she visited Furan City had not been enough to build any strong relationship between them. His friends might retort that he had been able to develop a fierce love for his uncle Claudius, even though he saw the man only once or twice a year, but his time with his uncle had always been dedicated to one thing alone: enjoyment. Whereas his mother had dedicated her visits to 'catching up' with him, or—rather—questioning him about all the things she had missed; there had therefore been little chance for them to develop any complicity. Until this year.

Somehow, things had been different. In fact, Darya had spent a lot of time with him, really getting to know him, and he had enjoyed it. It seemed to him she did love him after all. Furthermore, it had truly looked like Darya had decided to remain there with them, to be a mother to him and a wife to his father. And yet, now she needed to go, and Octavius was sending him with her. Ori was torn between his desire to remain with his father to continue to learn from him, and his developing love for his mother and the desire to not lose it again.

Octavius now said, "Ori, I do not send you away to an uncultured place; Kynaria is a land of great beauty and even greater knowledge. You will be able to learn things over there which you might not even come across here."

"But I don't want to learn about philosophy or…or about *beauty*. I want to learn what it is to lead people, and I want to learn it by watching *you*."

That warmed Octavius's heart unexpectedly. He gave his wife a quick guilty glance, then said, "Ori, in any other situation, I would have let you stay by my side. But the enemy we are facing this time is…pure evil. I do not know that I can guarantee your safety if you remain here." Ori was about to object again. Octavius raised a hand and said, "But, I have a mission for you, a very important one, which can only be carried out in Kynaria by you."

Ori now knit his brows suspiciously. Was his father trying to trick him into leaving? His mother turned to Octavius, expectant, wondering what Octavius had devised to make his son's departure more palatable.

"While in Kynaria, I wish you to record all public actions and events, whether initiated by the government or the people, and record the responses. I am asking this of you because, as young as you are, you are one of the most objective persons I know. You can help me understand how the country's plebe and patriciate are reacting to the Supreme Priestess's position on the events affecting Alvinoria."

Ori's face had lit up with cautious excitement, and Octavius continued, "Moreover, you are never without a hollow and paper, which means you are always ready to record what you hear and see."

"You taught me that."

"*You* learned it."

Ori raised his chest with pride.

"I will have Octavian send you what he records of the events here." Ori was about to object again, and again Octavius put his hand up. "I know the project is his. But his focus is not political. You will be focused on gathering this information from the perspective of a ruler. Octavian will incorporate your observations into his research. Once this is all over, it will be good to understand how it happened, how our governments acted and reacted to the events, and how the people did."

"Are you asking me to spy?"

"No! That is why I said to record *public* actions and events. I am sending you away to be safer; I would not endanger you by making you a spy."

Ori considered the 'mission'. He regarded his father with scrutinizing eyes for a long moment, snorting and shaking his head every so often. He looked at both his parents with his weighing gaze.

Darya watched Octavius and Ori, moving her eyes from one to the other. How she wished her life had been different. How she wished she had been more present in Ori's life. *Will we be able to grow closer now? At least Aria will be happy to have her cousin there.*

"Why can't Mother do this?"

Octavius should have expected this question, but he had not. Darya came to his aid and said, "Unfortunately, constrained as I am by my official duties, I only hear what other officials say. You, on the other hand, will have no such constraints imposed on you. Your circle will be more diverse and less guarded."

Ori took a moment to reflect on his mother's comment then looked up at his father with the determination and self-assurance which had always marked him, and he said, "I accept the *mission.*"

"Hum, your tone suggests you believe it is not what I made it out to be. But you still accept it?"

"I do. I will make it be a real mission. I assume the Kynarians will speak about your decisions and take action or not

351

based on them or based on what they understand your reasons to be. I will learn how you lead through the eyes of those affected by your decisions."

Octavius and Darya looked bewildered by the sudden change and by the…accusations? "You think my actions will affect *them*?"

"They already are. I saw the Supreme Priestess's look when you all left the gardens after your meeting at the ball. I think you were asking something of her or of Kynaria, which she disagreed with."

Darya and Octavius stared at their son wide-eyed for a moment, then looked at each other with a sign of agreement.

The king said, "All right. I think it is time for the two of you to embark, if Master Brak's shouts are any indication. Ready?"

Ori tried for a courageous grin while Darya responded with a bitter-sweet sigh.

The ship departing for Kynaria was a bolter—a fast, medium-sized passenger vessel carrying plebeians and nobles between the two countries, twice-monthly. The reserved sections were warded and protected by a guard of Red Sashes hired by the Brak Shipping Company.

Surrounded by the Praetorian, the royal family met with Master Brak himself by the gangway. Behind him were three fierce-looking Lux Baiulae who exchanged stiff, defiant nods with their counterparts in the king's guard. No other passengers were present on deck; they had already gotten in and had been sent to their assigned quarters in anticipation of the arrival of the royal guests.

The wonderful scents of the sea and the songs of the seaflyers accompanied Master Brak's wide-open arms, and disarming greeting, "My King, my Lady! And young prince Ori; it's the greatest pleasure to have such a fine young man on my ship this day. If you make me the honor of assisting me, as I know how interested you are in all things of science—and guiding a ship *is* a thing of science, especially through the reefs littering the coast here—I promise you a most enjoyable and memorable experience, my Prince."

Ori, as everyone expected, did not hesitate to accept the merchant's offer, after which the king embraced his wife as tenderly as he could manage it in front of the merchant, then took his son by the shoulders, putting all the love he felt into the action while repressing a sudden rush of emotion before it discombobulated him, and finally let him go.

As Darya and Ori boarded the ship, Octavius let out a quiet sigh then watched the ship undock and leave the port.

On deck, Ori was listening to Master Brak's skipper instruct his crew while also observing his mother wave goodbye to his father when a horrifying vision of Darya suddenly seized him and put him in a terrible, catatonic state. Confused and unable to shake the vison, he screamed. The others turned to him, alarmed. That broke the spell. Embarrassed, but still confused and frightened, he ran into the reserved quarters, ignoring his mother's calls.

EPILOGUE

"**M**y Queen, given that the Alvinorian court has refused our offer of peace in exchange for their males, it is time to activate our troops."

Zebula sighed resignedly as she watched her lover playing a game of strings in the interior courtyard. His motions—as he positioned himself to catch the ball and then throw it back to his opponent—were as enthralling as they had been that first time, when she had discovered him in that Shutsha Contest.

"I assume you have completed your analysis of the political and military situation in Alvinoria?"

Nihildrina nodded.

"What about you, general? Do you agree with the Eternal Advisor? Can you guarantee me a successful campaign?"

The general squinted distrustfully at the queen's advisor before answering. "If I am authorized to fill the infantry's ranks with the two-hundred thousand males I requested, yes."

The queen looked at her advisor for confirmation that the general's request was acceptable.

"According to my calculations, their removal should be no more than a temporary inconvenience for our society—so long as the general brings back a sufficient number of quality prisoners to rejuvenate our creatics and another equally sufficient number of prisoners to take the place of any Zebulonian males that may be lost in the war to ensure the continued functioning of the kingdom's economy."

Zebula turned a doleful gaze at her lover.

When the queen's expression began to harden, Nihildrina said, "My Queen, I understand your hesitation, but you know it is important that you, too, strengthen your creatic line by inserting new blood into it."

"Foreign blood."

Nihildrina did not reply but glared in General Marikai's direction to ensure the woman would make no comment to discourage the queen from what needed to be done.

"Very well. So be it."

APPENDIX I – MAPS

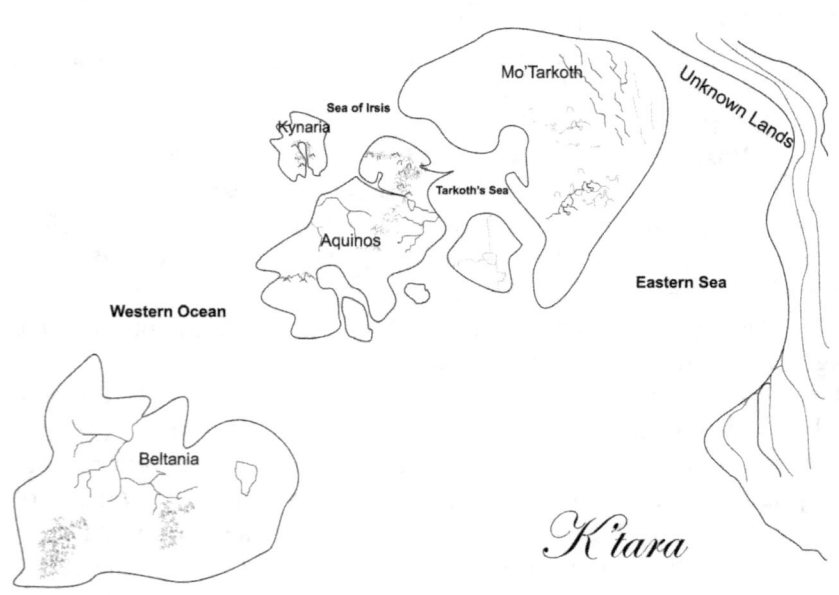

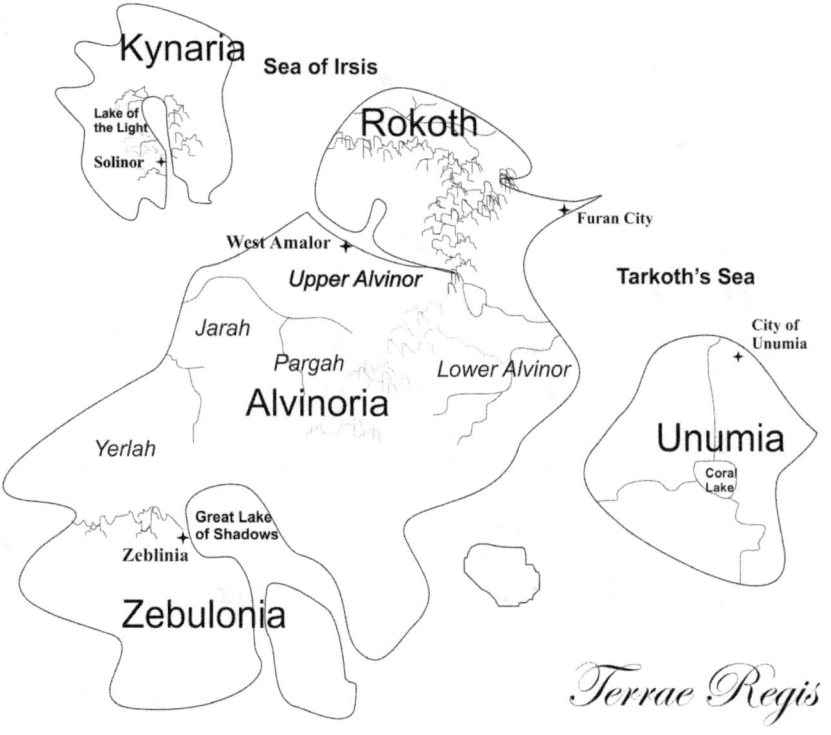

Kynaria

Sea of Irsis

Lake of the Light

Solinor

Rokoth

West Amalor

Upper Alvinor

Furan City

Tarkoth's Sea

Jarah

Pargah

Lower Alvinor

City of Unumia

Alvinoria

Unumia

Yerlah

Coral Lake

Great Lake of Shadows

Zeblinia

Zebulonia

Terrae Regis

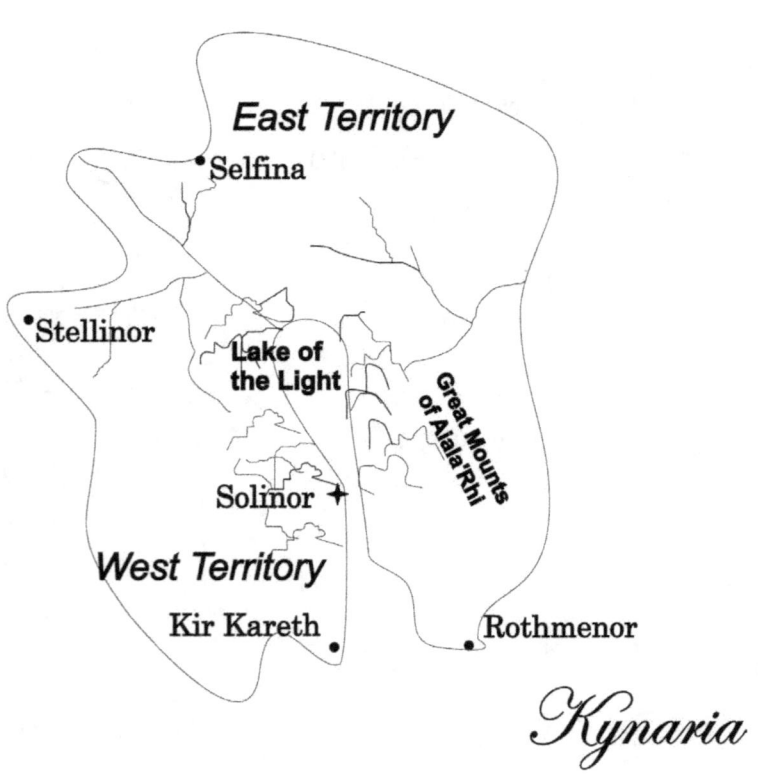

East Territory

• Selfina

• Stellinor

Lake of the Light

Great Mounts of Alala'Rhi

Solinor +

West Territory

Kir Kareth •

• Rothmenor

Kynaria

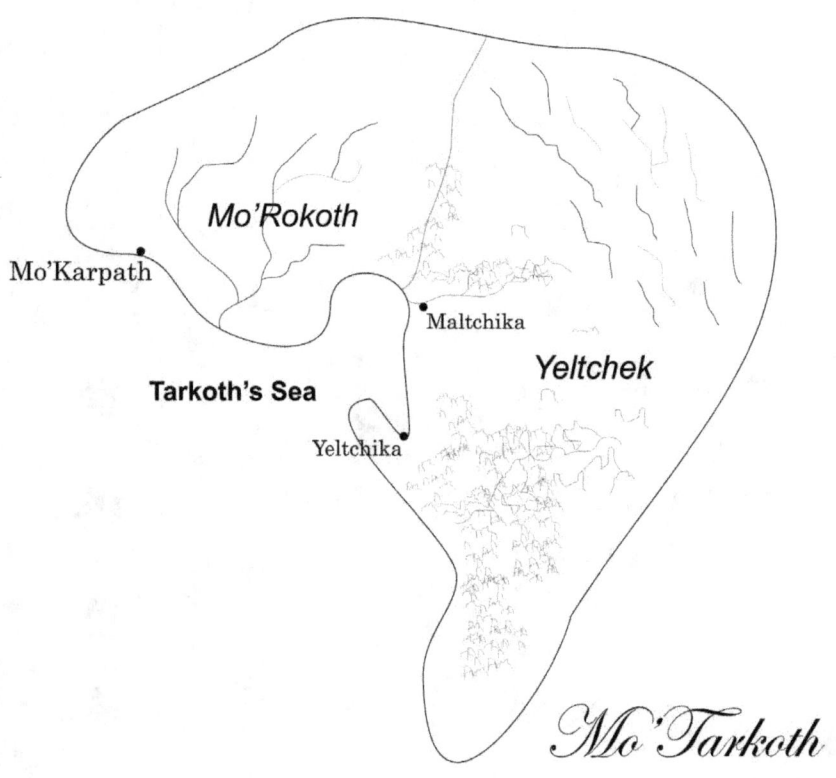

Mo'Rokoth

Mo'Karpath

Maltchika

Tarkoth's Sea

Yeltchek

Yeltchika

Mo'Tarkoth

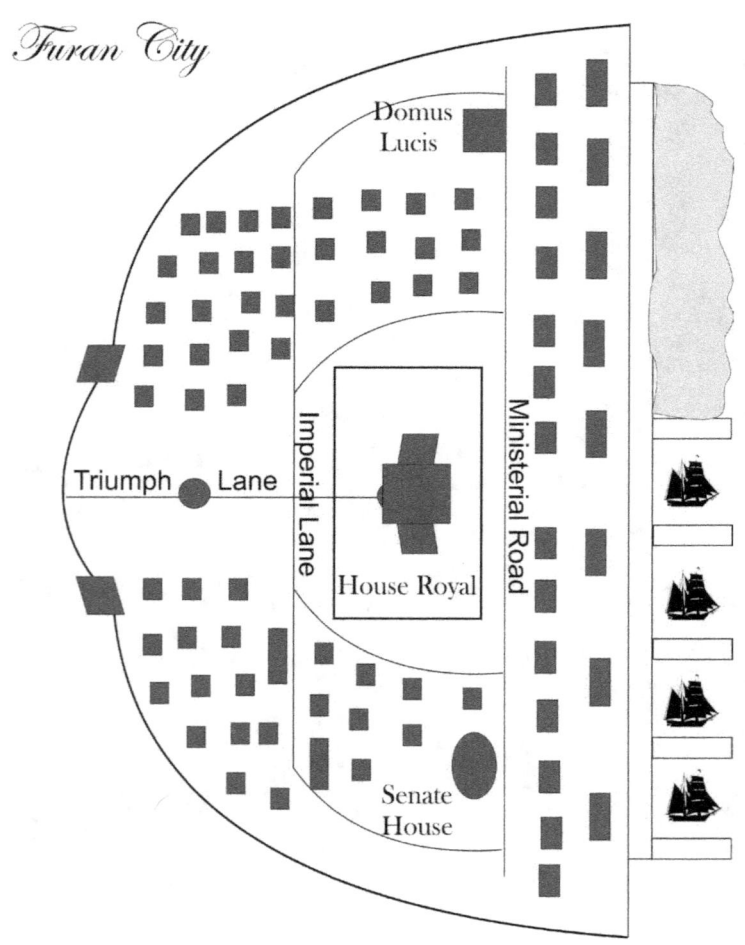

Furan City

Domus
Lucis

Imperial Lane

Ministerial Road

Triumph Lane

House Royal

Senate
House

High Prince's Apartments

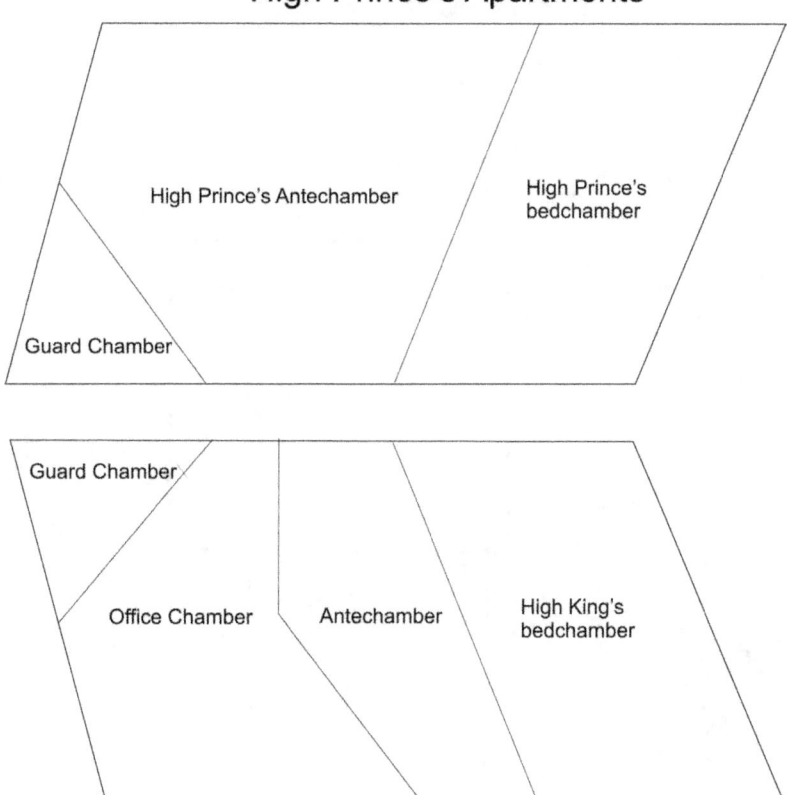

High Prince's Antechamber

High Prince's bedchamber

Guard Chamber

Guard Chamber

Office Chamber

Antechamber

High King's bedchamber

High King's Apartments

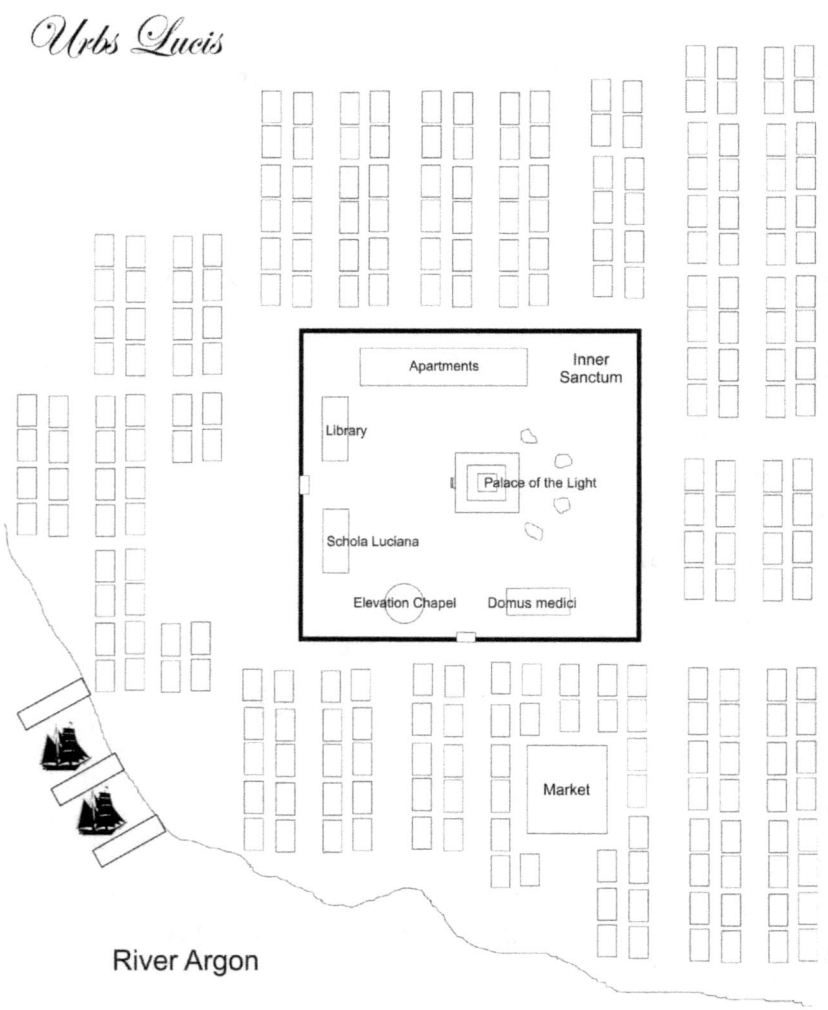

Urbs Lucis

Apartments

Inner Sanctum

Library

Palace of the Light

Schola Luciana

Elevation Chapel   Domus medici

Market

River Argon

APPENDIX II – NEW CHARACTERS OR CHARACTERS WHOSE ROLES HAVE CHANGED SINCE FOREBODINGS

Black Guard
1. **Bartus:** A young soldier.
2. **Corian**: Dies in the caves.
3. **Domar**: Dies in the caves.
4. **Francis**: Dies in the caves.
5. **Larus:** A member of the mission against the gnarlers in the caves.
6. **Mirko**: A member of the mission against the gnarlers in the caves.
7. **Ruvius**: A member of the mission against the gnarlers in the caves.
8. **Yaris:** A small-statured middle-aged fellow; easily upset.
9. **Yuuto:** Secundus; a Pargahni; deeply religious.
10. **Zeb**: Dies in the caves.

Royal Guard
11. **Boros**: Guardian who helped during the first assassination attempt on the king.
12. **Crassius**: Primus; leader of winged archer battalion; bald, dark, and leathery skinned.
13. **Emil**: Newest member of the high king's personal guard, to replace Almiar.
14. **Kendor**: Formerly primus in the Black Guard, now Leader of the Winged Assault Battalion in the Royal Guard.
15. **Rinius**: Primus; leader of the winged spear battalion; wide-mustached and square-shouldered.

Others

16. **Elnon**: A veteran Frumentarius, commander of the Frumentarii he stood perfectly calm and blank-faced, except for the irritation revealed by the barely perceptible periodic twitching of his mouth.

Civilians

17. **Albo**: A young carrier keeper.
18. **Eenosh**: A man working for the Leate.
19. **Kina**: A woman working for the Leate.
20. **Leate, The**: Leader of the Assassins and Temptatori.
21. **Luvius Arco**: A red-haired, pale-skinned, tall, pretty boy, son of a rich merchant,lazy, and pretentious.
22. **Moradina Solis**: Lady of Antar, the city where High King Octavius has his secondary residence.
23. **Neros**: Master carpenter at Horn's Pass.
24. **Octavian**: The son of High Captain Harlion; received his name from Octavius; seventeen years old.
25. **Rakel**: An assassin.
26. **Rovere**: A cousin to Kil.
27. **Vorak:** Master of the Furans

Sisterhood

28. **Clara Lux Baiula**: A Yellow Sash; responsible for training Ooldrina and Raaviana; she had auburn curly hair, a straight nose, deep gaze, and unwrinkled face.
29. **Dana Lux Baiula**: A Red Sash and Second Barrier; assigned to High King Octavius's enhanced guard.
30. **Elyana Lux Baiula**: A Purple Sash and former Red Sash; formerly advisor to High King Octavius and now Manu Dextra to the Magna Mater.

31. **Emissa Lux Baiula**: A Yellow, carrier trainer; speaks with a street dialect.
32. **Gina Lux Baiula**: A Yellow Sash; a member of the Order's spy team.
33. **Ksarina Lux Baiula**: A Red Sash; helped Gina Lux Baiula place the entangled brick in Kartak.
34. **Laiella Lux Baiula**: First Barrier and now Toras's First Officer; she was a tall, stern warrior with deadly skills; a native of Bremin Island, she had a pale green complexion, and red hair.
35. **Larca Lux Baiula**: Praefecta milites, Head of the Red Sashate, and now General Supreme.
36. **Lina Lux Baiula**: A Yellow Sash at Horn's Pass; a member of the Beacon team.
37. **Lira Lux Baiula**: A Red Sash; helped during the attack on the gnarlers.
38. **Lorina Lux Baiula**: A White Sash in Lady Moradina's service.
39. **Lotaria Lux Baiula**: A White Sash; assistant to Keeper of the Baths; she was a funny-looking woman with her glort-like short, fat and wrinkled neck.
40. **Mitsuko Lux Baiula**: A Purple Sash; Minder to High King Octavius; an immigrant from Beltania, she slurred her "r"s.
41. **Na'Riina Lux Baiula**: A Red Sash and Second Barrier.
42. **Ooldrina**: A refugee from Razeb; an Alterintrant; nut-milk skin color, wide-faced as all Zebulonian females, long dark hair, dark eyes; a Novice in the Sisterhood.
43. **Raaviana**: A refugee from Razeb; an Alterintrant; wide-faced, long reddish hair, green eyes; a Novice in the Sisterhood.

44. **Sasha Lux Baiula**: A Red Sash and Second Barrier; square woman with shoulders as broad, and arms as muscled as those of a fisher.
45. **Silla Lux Baiula**: A Purple in Lady Moradina's service.
46. **Sikka Lux Baiula**: A Red Sash; member of the king's enhanced personal guard.
47. **Tania Lux Baiula**: A White Sash and Head Medic in Furan City; she was 95 y.o.
48. **Tera Lux Baiula**: A White Sash; Keeper of the Baths at the Thermals.

Kynarians
49. **Koricki Dar'Muntake**: Distant cousin of Ylana Dar'Muntake; average height, brown-skinned, small mouth, coil-haired; honest and humble, slightly insecure despite being an apprentice in the Sisterhood.
50. **Yuri**: Priest Geologist.

Furans
51. **Bold**: Yuuto's furan; killed by a gnarler.
52. **Cray**: Elmanon's furan.
53. **Kaless**: Furan descended from Lumos, Octavius's first furan; ridden by Octavius on his way to Urbs Lucis.
54. **Root**: Laiella's furan; maroon hair amidst his black fur, with a short, squat beak.
55. **Runner**: Secundus Sheffar's furan.